THE ENGLISH IN ENGLAND

RUDYARD KIPLING was born in Bombay, India, in 1865 and was educated at the United Services College in England. He returned to India after his education was completed to edit a Lahore paper and, later, to write for the Allahabad *Pioneer*. His first short stories of Anglo-Indian life appeared in 1888, *Plain Tales from the Hills* and *Soldiers Three,* and in 1889 he returned to England where *The Light that Failed* was published in 1890. He then wrote many of his most famous books, among them *Kim* (1901). In later life he lived in Sussex, the setting for *Puck of Pook's Hill* (1906), and in 1907 he became the first Englishman to win the Nobel Prize for Literature. He died in 1936 and was buried in Westminster Abbey.

RANDALL JARRELL, whose book of poems *The Woman at the Washington Zoo* received the 1961 National Book Award for Poetry, is Professor of English at the Woman's College of the University of North Carolina. Mr. Jarrell has also taught at Sarah Lawrence and Kenyon colleges, the universities of Texas, Illinois, Indiana, and Cincinnati, and at Princeton University.

He has published five other volumes of poetry; a novel, *Pictures from an Institution,* and two books of essays, *A Sad Heart at the Supermarket* and *Poetry and the Age.* Mr. Jarrell has also edited *The Anchor Book of Stories* (A145) and *Six Russian Short Novels* (A348).

From 1956 to 1958 Mr. Jarrell was Consultant in Poetry at the Library of Congress. He is a member of the National Institute of Arts and Letters and a chancellor of The Academy of American Poets and has been poetry critic of the *Nation, Partisan Review,* and *The Yale Review.*

The English in England

SHORT STORIES BY RUDYARD KIPLING

*Selected and with an Introduction
by Randall Jarrell*

Anchor Books
Doubleday & Company, Inc.
Garden City, New York
1963

The Anchor Books edition
is the first publication of
The English in England.

Anchor Books Edition: 1963

INTRODUCTION

To most of us Kipling means India. Kipling's masterpiece, *Kim*, is an Indian story; so are the *Jungle Books;* so are the stories that made Kipling, in his thirties, the best-known writer in the world. It was this Indian Kipling whom Henry James called "the most complete man of genius (as distinct from fine intelligence) that I have ever known." Yet many, even most, of Kipling's best stories are stories of the English in England; the stories of Kipling's old age or late middle age—work that shows the easy and decisive mastery that was the result of a lifetime of imaginative realization —are with a few exceptions stories about England.

Here are fourteen such stories. Ten or eleven of them, perhaps, are among the best stories Kipling ever wrote, and the others have a particular interest of one kind or another. *Baa Baa, Black Sheep* is the one purely autobiographical story of a reticent and private-spirited author (his story of the future, *As Easy as A.B.C.,* makes "invasion of privacy" the sin upon which his new society is based); and since *Baa Baa, Black Sheep* is the only early story in this volume, it gives the reader a chance to compare some good and some excellent examples of his later style with an example of the live and effective, but relatively crude, style of the earlier stories. *The Vortex* is one of the funnier examples of a compulsive form, Kipling's practical-joke story; the reader may feel, as I do, that he enjoys Kipling's farce for its charm and landscape, and is indifferent to its point. As for *"In the Interests of the Brethren,"* it is pure charm—who would have supposed that you could make, of the meeting of an imaginary Masonic lodge, one of the most winning of sketches? I imagine that, except for *The Magic Flute*, it is the most attractive work of art Masonry has produced.

But at this point the reader may feel like remarking: "Autobiography, compulsive practical jokes, Masonry—do the subjects of the stories keep on like this?" Well, yes. But let me sum up the subjects in a sentence, and you can judge for yourself. In these fourteen stories a drugged, lovesick, and consumptive pharmacist, on an icy winter night, writes part of *The Eve of St. Agnes;* an elderly cook tells an elderly countrywoman, her friend, the story of how she took upon herself her lover's cancer; an urban intellectual, after inheriting a place in the country, gradually falls in love with country and county ways; a man visits the house of a blind woman, a house haunted by children; the boys of a Latin class translate an ode of Horace's and apply it to their everyday affairs; two countrymen eat their midday meal beside a flooded brook, and discuss a providential murder the brook has committed; a child from India undergoes five years of bullying and torture in a lower-middle-class English household; the railway station and crossroads of an English village are immobilized by four cartons of bees; a rich and nervous American and his wife are converted to the tranquil country ways of their English forebears; some motorists of varied distinction, fined and insulted in a village road-trap, avenge themselves by a geometrical progression of practical jokes that leaves the village the laughingstock of several continents; a shell-shocked artilleryman encounters at the front a little group of admirers of Jane Austen; a middle-aged woman, while burning the effects of a dead R.F.C. pilot, her employer's nephew, finds a wounded German pilot in the underbrush and watches him die there; a man gives up, out of ordinary human feeling, his long-prepared revenge upon a petty and despicable scholar.

Revenge, love, disease and death, the supernatural, extreme situations, practical jokes, country ways, literature:

these are some of the things that keep recurring in the stories. Yet the list of subjects seems to me, as I imagine it seems to the reader, a surprisingly varied and unusual one. Kipling is one of the most effectively realistic of writers—his stories are dazzling in their verisimilitude, their extraordinarily broad and detailed knowledge of special ways of speech and life, of a hundred varieties of local color; yet they are never mere slices of life, and are even more notable for their imagination than for their realism. If the reality principle has pruned and clipped them into plausibility, it is the pleasure principle out of which they first rankly and satisfyingly flowered. Kipling is far closer to Gogol than to a normal realist or naturalist: in Kipling the pressure of the imagination has forced facts over into the supernatural, into personally satisfying jokes or revenges, into personally compulsive fantasies or neuroses. Then too, like Gogol, Kipling is one of the great stylists of his language, one of those writers who can make a list more interesting than an ordinary writer's murder. For instance: "Everything his eyes opened upon was his very own to keep for ever. The carved four-post Chippendale bed, obviously worth hundreds; the wavy walnut William and Mary chairs—he had seen worse ones labelled twenty guineas apiece; the oval medallion mirror; the delicate eighteenth-century wire fireguard; the heavy brocaded curtains were his—all his. So, too, a great garden full of birds that faced him when he shaved; a mulberry tree, a sun-dial, and a dull, steel-coloured brook that murmured level with the edge of a lawn a hundred yards away. Peculiarly and privately his own was the smell of sausages and coffee that he sniffed at the head of the wide square landing, all set round with mysterious doors and Bartolozzi prints. He spent two hours after breakfast in exploring his new possessions. His heart leaped up at such things as sewing-machines, a rubber-tyred bath-chair in a tiled passage, a malachite-headed Malacca cane, boxes and boxes of unopened stationery, seal-rings, bunches of keys, and at the bottom of a steel-net reticule a little leather purse with seven pounds ten shillings in gold and eleven shillings in silver."

All the things of the list—beginning and ending with that great thing, money—are alive, and either move us specifically or hold out to us the general possibility of motion. The man who can fill two sentences with those semicolons, and then not use another in the paragraph; who can begin two sentences *So, too, a great garden . . .* and *Peculiarly and privately his own . . .* and give every other sentence a perfectly ordinary beginning; who can invent the passage-work that, from *a rubber-tired bath-chair in a tiled passage,* makes its way, through an elderly invalid's possessions, into the culminating *little leather purse with seven pounds ten shillings in gold and eleven shillings in silver—* the man who can do this, and still not have a word obvious or a rhythm obtrusive, really knows how to write. As Chekhov said, and as everybody remembers, you must never hang a pistol on the wall in the first act unless someone is going to shoot himself with it in the last; here the dull, steel-colored brook murmurs level with the edge of a lawn a hundred yards away only because, twenty pages later, that brook is to flood the whole story.

Yet the story from which I am quoting, *"My Son's Wife,"* is a live thing with one leg missing. If Kipling had read it and not written it, he could not have helped seeing that the country is created in beautiful detail, favorable and unfavorable, but that the city intellectuals are set up and knocked down with blankly abstract, pharisaical irony; they are just Bandar-log, after all, and the few details Kipling is willing to waste on them are not observed but invented. We more or less gather that Midmore spent his London hours lying on pillows with women, at teatime, but we neither see the women nor feel the pillows. When we finish the story we are as sure that the country Midmore read Surtees (down to that last haunting sentence: "When at length they rose to go to bed it struck each man as he followed his neighbour upstairs, that the man before him walked very crookedly") as that the idiot wailed, " 'Fraid o' the

water! 'Fraid o' the water!" But what did the unconverted
Midmore read in London? The Webbs? Wells? Frazer?
We respond: "Since you say so," to Midmore's previous
condition of servitude, but it is about as real to us as is the
earlier career of one of those people in Mark Twain who
used to be pirates but have taken to making testimonial
speeches for temperance societies, now. Yet, ordinarily, no
writer of fiction is better at making literature alive to us as
social fact. Literature, in Kipling's stories, is something
that makes behavior, is as much an effective part of life
as religion or politics. We see this in exaggerated form in
The Janeites: part of the reader's pleasure in the story—
as in so many of Kipling's stories—is that it couldn't possibly really have happened so, and yet it is happening before our eyes. But Kipling's treatment of literature and
education in *Regulus* seems exactly truthful in both essence
and detail—*is* there a better treatment of a class in fiction?

If Kipling had written: "What do they know of England
who only England know?" a few years earlier than he did,
his readers might have replied: "What does he know of
England who has spent most of his life in India and Ver-
mont?" But in 1896, after the public difficulties with his
wife's brother that led him to remark: "There are only
two places in the world where I want to live—Bombay and
Brattleboro. And I can't live at either," Kipling and his
American wife went to live in the English countryside, in a
house so hauntingly unpleasant to them that Kipling wrote
a kind of psychiatric ghost story about it (*The House Surgeon*); they did not find "Bateman's," the Sussex house
where they spent the rest of their lives, until 1902. *An
Habitation Enforced* is, I think, a fantasy about the way it
would have been if the Kiplings had returned to a house
and country at once magically their own: the American
millionaire and his wife are blank sticks on which a wish is
hung. And, too, there is the same family romance behind the story that is behind *Kim* and the *Jungle Books;*
it is not until they leave their ostensible ones that the Ameri-
cans discover their true home and family. (*Baa Baa,*

Black Sheep and the chapter on the same subject in *Something of Myself* show us why Kipling, the most devoted of sons, had his lifelong compulsive belief in this fantasy.) *Friendly Brook* and *The Wish House* are two of the stories that demonstrate the microscopic, loving knowledge of Sussex and its inhabitants that Kipling eventually came to have. A farm laborer whom Kipling knew particularly well said to someone, after Kipling's death, that the old fool did nothing but ask you questions; stories like these are the result of many asked and many unasked questions. The primary pleasure of a story like *Friendly Brook* is the atmosphere ("so choked with fog that one could scarcely see a cow's length across a field") through which it comes to us; grim, plain, warped through work and workaday speech, the happenings have the harshly satisfactory reality that they have in one of Frost's country stories: " 'Dada' he says, an' 'Mumma' he says, with his great rollin' head-piece all hurdled up in that iron collar. *He* won't live long—his backbone's rotten, like. . . . No! 'Twadn't no stroke. It stifled the old lady in the throat here. First she couldn't shape her words no shape; then she clucked, like, an' lastly she couldn't more than suck down spoon-meat an' hold her peace. Jim took her to Doctor Harding, an' Harding he bundled her off to Brighton Hospital on a ticket, but they couldn't make no stay to her afflictions there; and she was bundled off to Lunnon, an' they lit a great old lamp inside her, and Jim told me they couldn't make out nothing in no sort there; and, along o' one thing an' another, an' all their spyin's and pryin's, she come back a hem sight worse than when she started. Jim said he'd have no more hospitalizin', so he give her a slate, which she tied to her waist-string, and what she was minded to say she writ on it." The happenings of *The Wish House* are given something of the same atmosphere and the same reality, but the happenings themselves are the strange mixture of love, disease, and the supernatural that had an almost obsessive attraction for Kipling. The love affairs of most stories, compared to those of Kipling's later stories, seem attractive preoccupations of the young; in his the poor and ugly and sick and middle-aged are overwhelmed by something drab, raw, but ultimate.

There are few stories that seem, first of all and last of all, beautiful; *"They"* is one. It is almost as if the story's extraordinary beauty of picturing, and of the style which pictures, came out of Kipling's desire to have the story a memorial to his own dead daughter. It is a memorial in three tapestries, an early-summer, a late-summer, and an autumn day; the days themselves are hardly more beautiful than the story's movement through the days, the gradual change from loving ignorance into knowledge, the change from the first glimpses of the children, out of the corner of the eye, into the last "little brushing kiss" that "fell in the centre of my palm—as a gift on which the fingers were, once, expected to close: as the all-faithful half-reproachful signal of a waiting child not used to neglect even when grown-ups were busiest—a fragment of the mute code devised very long ago. Then I knew." The treatment of the children is so delicately and hauntingly convincing that it is no wonder *Burnt Norton* should have been influenced by it; yet the tallies with which the blind woman runs her farms, the colored Egg of the soul which the blind woman sees, the blind woman's last piteous, "Oh, you *must* bear or lose. There is no other way"—all this and much more than this are as convincing.

It is interesting to compare the naturally beautiful *"They"* with the harshly and uncannily colorful *"Wireless,"* a story that leaves a sort of stained-glass deposit in the memory. It is seen and felt and heard as few stories are: if genius is the ability to perceive (and to make us perceive) likenesses never before seen, in concise hallucinatory form, then *"Wireless"* is a work of genius. It is certainly a work of astonishing originality, of the most extraordinary professional skill. Here, for instance, is Kipling's description of a drugstore on a cold night: "Across the street blank shutters flung back the gaslight in cold smears; the dried pavement seemed to rough up in goose-flesh under the scouring of the savage wind, and we could hear, long ere he passed, the policeman flapping his arms to keep himself warm. Within, the flavours of cardamoms and chloric-ether disputed those of the pastilles and a score of drugs and perfume and soap scents. Our electric lights, set low down in the windows before the tun-bellied Rosamond jars, flung inward three monstrous daubs of red, blue, and green, that broke into kaleidoscopic lights on the faceted knobs of the drug-drawers, the cut-glass scent flagons, and the bulbs of the sparklet bottles. They flushed the white-tiled floor in gorgeous patches; splashed along the nickel-silver counter-rails, and turned the polished mahogany counter-panels to the likeness of intricate grained marbles—slabs of porphyry and malachite. Mr. Shaynor unlocked a drawer, and ere he began to write, took out a meagre bundle of letters. From my place by the stove, I could see the scalloped edges of the paper with a flaring monogram in the corner and could even smell the reek of chypre. At each page he turned toward the toilet-water lady of the advertisement and devoured her with over-luminous eyes. He had drawn the Austrian blanket over his shoulders, and among those warring lights he looked more than ever the incarnation of a drugged moth—a tiger-moth as I thought." One feels after reading this: well, no one ever again will have to describe a drugstore; many of Kipling's descriptive sentences have this feeling of finality.

As he got older, Kipling found it necessary to write more and more elaborately farcical practical-joke stories —stories of revenge, often; the confirmed reader will immediately think of pieces like *"Brugglesmith," My Sunday at Home, The Puzzler, The Vortex, The Village that Voted the Earth was Flat, The Bonds of Discipline, Steam Tactics, "Their Lawful Occasions," Aunt Ellen, The Miracle of St. Jubanus, Beauty Spots.* I myself can read these stories with pleasure. (But if Kipling had written instructions on how to make a bed with hospital corners, or how to can gooseberries, I could read them with pleasure: as one of his characters exclaims, "It was the tone, man, the tone!") Most of these farces are stories for the confirmed reader only, since they have been written by the writer for the writer: in them, often, the writer tells us how he laughs so hard that he cannot speak or see or stand up, and how that luckiest of all winds, the dawn wind, comes and whispers to him that the next day everything is going to be even better. *The Village that Voted the Earth was Flat* quite overcomes these humble, compulsive beginnings: a little of it is a little too good to be true, but what a knowing ingenuity of invention it has, how extraordinarily it is imagined! When the true flat-earthers strike up their hymn,

> "Hear ther truth our tongues are telling,
> Spread ther light from shore to shore,
> God hath given man a dwelling
> Flat and flat for evermore.
>
> "When ther Primal Dark retreated,
> When ther deeps were undesigned,
> He with rule and level meted
> Habitation for mankind!"

you feel like muttering with the envious music hall impresario: "Curse Nature, she gets ahead of you every time," till you remember that it is Kipling himself, here, who is both Nature and Art.

I had always supposed that Kipling wrote *Mary Postgate* a few months after his son was killed in the first World War, and it had seemed to me an awful but in some sense normal thing. When you learn that the story was written several months before his son's death, you are troubled just as you are when you learn that Mahler's *Kindertotenlieder* was written before and not after the death of his child. This truthfully cruel, human-all-too-human wish-fantasy is as satisfying to one part of our nature as it is terrible to another. What happens is implausible but intensely actual: the German pilot isn't really there, of course, except in our desire, but his psychological reality is absolute, down to the last groan of the head that "moved cease-

lessly from side to side . . . as pale as a baby's, and so
closely cropped that she could see the disgusting pinky
skin beneath"; we are forced to believe in him just as
Freud was forced to believe in his first patients' fantasies
of seduction. *Dayspring Mishandled,* one of the most mor-
ally appealing of Kipling's stories, is very human in the
opposite sense of the word. When, dying under the expectant scrutiny of his knowing and faithless wife, the
knighted and successful Castorley, in puzzled misery, in all
the agony of disease and doubt, begs for the reassurance
of the man who for twenty years has worked out the ruin
he can accomplish with a word, and who now interrupts
unsteadily: "I can confirm every word you've said. You've
nothing to worry about. It's *your* find—*your* credit—*your*
glory and—all the rest of it"—when he gets to this point,
Kipling has made his way to something past revenge, past
any human division: the sentences are as beautiful in their
inclusiveness as the last sentence of the story is beautiful
in its precise exclusion: "As, on the appointed words, the
coffin crawled sideways through the noiselessly-closing
door-flaps, I saw Lady Castorley's eyes turn towards
Gleeag."

If you compare one of the best of Kipling's early stories
(*Without Benefit of Clergy,* say) with some of the best of
his late stories, you realize that the late stories are specialized in their moral and human attitudes—in their subject matter, even—in a way in which the early story is not.
The early story's subject is a general subject that will repay
any amount of general skill or general talent: you can
imagine a greater writer's rewriting *Without Benefit of
Clergy* and making a much better story out of it. But this
is precisely what you cannot imagine with Kipling's later
stories: Chekhov and Tolstoy and Turgenev together
couldn't improve *"They"* or *"Wireless,"* since in each a
highly specialized subject has received an exactly appropriate, extraordinarily skilled and talented treatment. These
later stories of Kipling's don't compete, really, with *Gusev*
and *The Death of Ivan Ilych* and *A Sportsman's Sketches,*

but have set up a kingdom of their own, a little off to the side of things, in which they are incomparable: their reader feels, "You can write better stories than Kipling's, but not better Kipling stories." This kingdom of theirs is a strange, disquieting, but quite wonderful place, as if some of the Douanier Rousseau's subjects had been repainted by Degas. If we cannot make the very greatest claims for the stories, it would be absurd not to make great ones: as long as readers enjoy style and skill, originality and imagination —in a word, genius—they will take delight in Kipling's stories.

Randall Jarrell

CONTENTS

THE ENGLISH IN ENGLAND

'WIRELESS'

'It's a funny thing, this Marconi business, isn't it?' said Mr. Shaynor, coughing heavily. 'Nothing seems to make any difference, by what they tell me—storms, hills, or anything; but if that's true we shall know before morning.'

'Of course it's true,' I answered, stepping behind the counter. 'Where's old Mr. Cashell?'

'He's had to go to bed on account of his influenza. He said you'd very likely drop in.'

'Where's his nephew?'

'Inside, getting the things ready. He told me that the last time they experimented they put the pole on the roof of one of the big hotels here, and the batteries electrified all the water-supply, and'—he giggled—'the ladies got shocks when they took their baths.'

'I never heard of that.'

'The hotel wouldn't exactly advertise it, would it? Just now, by what Mr. Cashell tells me, they're trying to signal from here to Poole, and they're using stronger batteries than ever. But, you see, he being the guvnor's nephew and all that (and it will be in the papers too), it doesn't matter how they electrify things in this house. Are you going to watch?'

'Very much. I've never seen this game. Aren't you going to bed?'

'We don't close till ten on Saturdays. There's a good deal of influenza in town, too, and there'll be a dozen prescriptions coming in before morning. I generally sleep in the chair here. It's warmer than jumping out of bed every time. Bitter cold, isn't it?'

'Freezing hard. I'm sorry your cough's worse.'

'Thank you. I don't mind cold so much. It's this wind that fair cuts me to pieces.' He coughed again hard and hackingly, as an old lady came in for ammoniated quinine. 'We've just run out of it in bottles, madam,' said Mr. Shaynor, returning to the professional tone, 'but if you will wait two minutes, I'll make it up for you, madam.'

I had used the shop for some time, and my acquaintance with the proprietor had ripened into friendship. It was Mr. Cashell who revealed to me the purpose and power of Apothecaries' Hall what time a fellow-chemist had made an error in a prescription of mine, had lied to cover his sloth, and when error and lie were brought home to him had written vain letters.

'A disgrace to our profession,' said the thin, mild-eyed man, hotly, after studying the evidence. 'You couldn't do a better service to the profession than report him to Apothecaries' Hall.'

I did so, not knowing what djinns I should evoke; and the result was such an apology as one might make who had spent a night on the rack. I conceived great respect for Apothecaries' Hall, and esteem for Mr. Cashell, a zealous craftsman who magnified his calling. Until Mr. Shaynor came down from the North his assistants had by no means agreed with Mr. Cashell. 'They forget,' said he, 'that, first and foremost, the compounder is a medicine-man. On him depends the physician's reputation. He holds it literally in the hollow of his hand, sir.'

Mr. Shaynor's manners had not, perhaps, the polish of the grocery and Italian warehouse next door, but he knew and loved his dispensary work in every detail. For relaxation he seemed to go no farther afield than the romance of drugs—their discovery, preparation, packing, and export—but it led him to the ends of the earth, and on this subject, and the Pharmaceutical Formulary, and Nicholas Culpepper, most confident of physicians, we met.

Little by little I grew to know something of his beginnings and his hopes—of his mother, who had been a school-teacher in one of the northern counties, and of his red-headed father, a small jobmaster at Kirby Moors, who died when he was a child; of the examinations he had passed and of their exceeding and increasing difficulty; of his dreams of a shop in London; of his hate for the price-cutting Co-operative stores; and, most interesting, of his mental attitude towards customers.

'There's a way you get into,' he told me, 'of serving them carefully, and I hope, politely, without stopping your own thinking. I've been reading Christy's *New Commercial Plants* all this autumn, and that needs keeping your mind on it, I can tell you. So long as it isn't a prescription, of course, I can carry as much as half a page of Christy in my head, and at the same time I could sell out all that window twice over, and not a penny wrong at the end. As to prescriptions, I think I could make up the general run of 'em in my sleep, almost.'

For reasons of my own, I was deeply interested in Marconi experiments at their outset in England; and it was of a piece with Mr. Cashell's unvarying thoughtfulness that, when his nephew the electrician appropriated the house for a long-range installation, he should, as I have said, invite me to see the result.

The old lady went away with her medicine, and Mr. Shaynor and I stamped on the tiled floor behind the counter to keep ourselves warm. The shop, by the light of the many electrics, looked like a Paris-diamond mine, for Mr. Cashell believed in all the ritual of his craft. Three superb glass jars—red, green, and blue—of the sort that led Rosamond to parting with her shoes—blazed in the broad plate-glass windows, and there was a confused smell of orris, Kodak films, vulcanite, tooth-powder, sachets, and almond-cream in the air. Mr. Shaynor fed the dispensary stove, and we sucked cayenne-pepper jujubes and menthol lozenges. The brutal east wind had cleared the streets, and the few passers-by were muffled to their puckered eyes. In the Italian warehouse next door some gay feathered birds and game, hung upon hooks, sagged to the wind across the left edge of our window-frame.

'They ought to take these poultry in—all knocked about like that,' said Mr. Shaynor. 'Doesn't it make you feel fair perishing? See that old hare! The wind's nearly blowing the fur off him.'

I saw the belly-fur of the dead beast blown apart in ridges and streaks as the wind caught it, showing bluish skin underneath. 'Bitter cold,' said Mr. Shaynor, shuddering. 'Fancy going out on a night like this! Oh, here's young Mr. Cashell.'

The door of the inner office behind the dispensary opened, and an energetic, spade-bearded man stepped forth, rubbing his hands.

'I want a bit of tin-foil, Shaynor,' he said. 'Good-evening. My uncle told me you might be coming.' This to me, as I began the first of a hundred questions.

'I've everything in order,' he replied. 'We're only waiting until Poole calls us up. Excuse me a minute. You can come in whenever you like—but I'd better be with the instruments. Give me that tin-foil. Thanks.'

While we were talking, a girl—evidently no customer—had come into the shop, and the face and bearing of Mr. Shaynor changed. She leaned confidently across the counter.

'But I can't,' I heard him whisper uneasily—the flush on his cheek was dull red, and his eyes shone like a drugged moth's. 'I can't. I tell you I'm alone in the place.'

'No, you aren't. Who's *that*? Let him look after it for half an hour. A brisk walk will do you good. Ah, come now, John.'

'But he isn't——'

'I don't care. I want you to; we'll only go round by St. Agnes'. If you don't——'

He crossed to where I stood in the shadow of the dispensary counter, and began some sort of broken apology about a ladyfriend.

'Yes,' she interrupted. 'You take the shop for half an hour—to oblige *me*, won't you?'

She had a singularly rich and promising voice that well matched her outline.

'All right,' I said. 'I'll do it—but you'd better wrap yourself up, Mr. Shaynor.'

'Oh, a brisk walk ought to help me. We're only going round by the church.' I heard him cough grievously as they went out together.

I refilled the stove, and, after reckless expenditure of Mr. Cashell's coal, drove some warmth into the shop. I explored many of the glass-knobbed drawers that lined the walls, tasted some disconcerting drugs, and, by the aid of a few cardamoms, ground ginger, chloric-ether, and dilute alcohol, manufactured a new and wildish drink, of which I bore a glassful to young Mr. Cashell, busy in the back office. He laughed shortly when I told him that Mr. Shaynor had stepped out—but a frail coil of wire held all his attention, and he had no word for me bewildered among the batteries and rods. The noise of the sea on the beach began to make itself heard as the traffic in the street ceased. Then briefly, but very lucidly, he gave me the names and uses of the mechanism that crowded the tables and the floor.

'When do you expect to get the message from Poole?' I demanded, sipping my liquor out of a graduated glass.

'About midnight, if everything is in order. We've got our installation-pole fixed to the roof of the house. I shouldn't advise you to turn on a tap or anything to-night. We've connected up with the plumbing, and all the water will be electrified.' He repeated to me the history of the agitated ladies at the hotel at the time of the first installation.

'But what *is* it?' I asked. 'Electricity is out of my beat altogether.'

'Ah, if you knew *that* you'd know something nobody knows. It's just It—what we call Electricity, but the magic—the manifestations—the Hertzian waves—are all revealed by *this*. The coherer, we call it.'

He picked up a glass tube not much thicker than a thermometer, in which, almost touching, were two tiny silver plugs, and between them an infinitesimal pinch of metallic dust. 'That's all,' he said, proudly, as though himself responsible for the wonder. 'That is the thing that will reveal to us the Powers—whatever the Powers may be—at work—through space—a long distance away.'

Just then Mr. Shaynor returned alone and stood coughing his heart out on the mat.

'Serves you right for being such a fool,' said young Mr. Cashell, as annoyed as myself at the interruption. 'Never mind—we've all the night before us to see wonders.'

Shaynor clutched the counter, his handkerchief to his lips. When he brought it away I saw two bright red stains.

'I—I've got a bit of a rasped throat from smoking cigarettes,' he panted. 'I think I'll try a cubeb.'

'Better take some of this. I've been compounding while you've been away.' I handed him the brew.

' 'Twon't make me drunk, will it? I'm almost a teetotaller. My word! That's grateful and comforting.'

He set down the empty glass to cough afresh.

'Brr! But it was cold out there! I shouldn't care to be lying in my grave a night like this. Don't *you* ever have a sore throat from smoking?' He pocketed the handkerchief after a furtive peep.

'Oh, yes, sometimes,' I replied, wondering, while I spoke, into what agonies of terror I should fall if ever I saw those bright-red danger-signals under my nose. Young Mr. Cashell among the batteries coughed slightly to show that he was quite ready to continue his scientific explanations, but I was thinking still of the girl with the rich voice and the significantly cut mouth, at whose command I had taken charge of the shop. It flashed across me that she distantly resembled the seductive shape on a gold-framed toilet-water advertisement whose charms were unholily heightened by the glare from the red bottle in the window. Turning to make sure, I saw Mr. Shaynor's eyes bent in the same direction, and by instinct recognised that the flamboyant thing was to him a shrine. 'What do you take for your—cough?' I asked.

'Well, I'm the wrong side of the counter to believe much in patent medicines. But there are asthma cigarettes and there are pastilles. To tell you the truth, if you don't object to the smell, which is very like incense, I believe, though I'm not a Roman Catholic, Blaudett's Cathedral Pastilles relieve me as much as anything.'

'Let's try.' I had never raided a chemist's shop before, so I was thorough. We unearthed the pastilles—brown, gummy cones of benzoin—and set them alight under the toilet-water advertisement, where they fumed in thin blue spirals.

'Of course,' said Mr. Shaynor, to my question, 'what one uses in the shop for one's self comes out of one's pocket. Why, stock-taking in our business is nearly the same as with jewellers—and I can't say more than that. But one gets them'—he pointed to the pastille-box—'at trade prices.' Evidently the censing of the gay, seven-tinted wench with the teeth was an established ritual which cost something.

'And when do we shut up shop?'

'We stay like this all night. The guv—old Mr. Cashell—doesn't believe in locks and shutters as compared with electric light. Besides, it brings trade. I'll just sit here in the chair by the stove and write a letter, if you don't mind. Electricity isn't my prescription.'

The energetic young Mr. Cashell snorted within, and Shaynor settled himself up in his chair over which he had thrown a staring red, black, and yellow Austrian jute blanket, rather like a tablecover. I cast about, amid patent-medicine pamphlets, for something to read, but finding little, returned to the manufacture of the new drink. The Italian warehouse took down its game and went to bed. Across the street blank shutters flung back the gaslight in cold smears; the dried pavement seemed to rough up in gooseflesh under the scourling of the savage wind, and we could hear, long ere he passed, the policeman flapping his arms to keep himself warm. Within, the flavours of carda-moms and chloric-ether disputed those of the pastilles and a score of drugs and perfume and soap scents. Our electric lights, set low down in the windows before the tun-bellied

Rosamond jars, flung inward three monstrous daubs of red, blue, and green, that broke into kaleidoscopic lights on the faceted knobs of the drug-drawers, the cut-glass scent flagons, and the bulbs of the sparklet bottles. They flushed the white-tiled floor in gorgeous patches; splashed along the nickel-silver counter-rails, and turned the polished mahogany counter-panels to the likeness of intricate grained marbles—slabs of porphyry and malachite. Mr. Shaynor unlocked a drawer, and ere he began to write, took out a meagre bundle of letters. From my place by the stove, I could see the scalloped edges of the paper with a flaring monogram in the corner and could even smell the reek of chypre. At each page he turned toward the toilet-water lady of the advertisement and devoured her with over-luminous eyes. He had drawn the Austrian blanket over his shoulders, and among those warring lights he looked more than ever the incarnation of a drugged moth—a tiger-moth as I thought.

He put his letter into an envelope, stamped it with stiff mechanical movements, and dropped it in the drawer. Then I became aware of the silence of a great city asleep—the silence that underlay the even voice of the breakers along the sea-front—a thick, tingling quiet of warm life stilled down for its appointed time, and unconsciously I moved about the glittering shop as one moves in a sick-room. Young Mr. Cashell was adjusting some wire that crackled from time to time with the tense, knuckle-stretching sound of the electric spark. Upstairs, where a door shut and opened swiftly, I could hear his uncle coughing abed.

'Here,' I said, when the drink was properly warmed, 'take some of this, Mr. Shaynor.'

He jerked in his chair with a start and a wrench, and held out his hand for the glass. The mixture, of a rich port-wine colour, frothed at the top.

'It looks,' he said, suddenly, 'it looks—those bubbles—like a string of pearls winking at you—rather like the pearls round that young lady's neck.' He turned again to the advertisement where the female in the dove-coloured corset had seen fit to put on all her pearls before she cleaned her teeth.

'Not bad, is it?' I said.

'Eh?'

He rolled his eyes heavily full on me, and, as I stared, I beheld all meaning and consciousness die out of the swiftly dilating pupils. His figure lost its stark rigidity, softened into the chair, and, chin on chest, hands dropped before him, he rested open-eyed, absolutely still.

'I'm afraid I've rather cooked Shaynor's goose,' I said, bearing the fresh drink to young Mr. Cashell. 'Perhaps it was the chloric-ether.'

'Oh, he's all right.' The spade-bearded man glanced at him pityingly. 'Consumptives go off in those sort of dozes very often. It's exhaustion . . . I don't wonder. I daresay the liquor will do him good. It's grand stuff.' He finished his share appreciatively. 'Well, as I was saying—before he interrupted—about this little coherer. The pinch of dust, you see, is nickel-filings. The Hertzian waves, you see, come out of space from the station that despatches 'em, and all these little particles are attracted together—cohere, we call it—for just so long as the current passes through them. Now, it's important to remember that the current is an induced current. There are a good many kinds of induction——'

'Yes, but what *is* induction?'

'That's rather hard to explain untechnically. But the long and the short of it is that when a current of electricity passes through a wire there's a lot of magnetism present round that wire; and if you put another wire parallel to, and within what we call its magnetic field—why, then the second wire will also become charged with electricity.'

'On its own account?'

'On its own account.'

'Then let's see if I've got it correctly. Miles off, at Poole, or wherever it is——'

'It will be anywhere in ten years.'

'You've got a charged wire——'

'Charged with Hertzian waves which vibrate, say, two hundred and thirty million times a second.' Mr. Cashell snaked his forefinger rapidly through the air.

'All right—a charged wire at Poole, giving out these waves into space. Then this wire of yours sticking out into space—on the roof of the house—in some mysterious way gets charged with those waves from Poole——'

'Or anywhere—it only happens to be Poole tonight.'

'And those waves set the coherer at work, just like an ordinary telegraph-office ticker?'

'No! That's where so many people make the mistake. The Hertzian waves wouldn't be strong enough to work a great heavy Morse instrument like ours. They can only just make that dust cohere, and while it coheres (a little while for a dot and a longer while for a dash) the current from this battery—the home battery'—he laid his hand on the thing—'can get through to the Morse printing-machine to record the dot or dash. Let me make it clearer. Do you know anything about steam?'

'Very little. But go on.'

'Well, the coherer is like a steam-valve. Any child can open a valve and start a steamer's engines, because a turn of the hand lets in the main steam, doesn't it? Now, this home battery here ready to print is the main steam. The coherer is the valve, always ready to be turned on. The Hertzian wave is the child's hand that turns it.'

'I see. That's marvellous.'

'Marvellous, isn't it? And, remember, we're only at the beginning. There's nothing we shan't be able to do in ten years. I want to live—my God, how I want to live, and see it develop!' He looked through the door at Shaynor breathing lightly in his chair. 'Poor beast! And he wants to keep company with Fanny Brand.'

'Fanny *who?*' I said, for the name struck an obscurely familiar chord in my brain—something connected with a stained handkerchief, and the word 'arterial.'

'Fanny Brand—the girl you kept shop for.' He laughed.

'That's all I know about her, and for the life of me I can't
see what Shaynor sees in her, or she in him.'

'*Can't* you see what he sees in her?' I insisted.

'Oh, yes, if *that's* what you mean. She's a great, big, fat
lump of a girl, and so on. I suppose that's why he's so crazy
after her. She isn't his sort. Well, it doesn't matter. My
uncle says he's bound to die before the year's out. Your
drink's given him a good sleep, at any rate.' Young Mr.
Cashell could not catch Mr. Shaynor's face, which was half
turned to the advertisement.

I stoked the stove anew, for the room was growing cold,
and lighted another pastille. Mr. Shaynor in his chair, never
moving, looked through and over me with eyes as wide and
lustreless as those of a dead hare.

'Poole's late,' said young Mr. Cashell, when I stepped
back. 'I'll just send them a call.'

He pressed a key in the semi-darkness, and with a rending crackle there leaped between two brass knobs a spark,
streams of sparks, and sparks again.

'Grand, isn't it? *That's* the Power—our unknown Power—
kicking and fighting to be let loose,' said young Mr. Cashell.
'There she goes—kick—kick—kick into space. I never get
over the strangeness of it when I work a sending-machine
—waves going into space, you know. T.R. is our call. Poole
ought to answer with L.L.L.'

We waited two, three, five minutes. In that silence, of
which the boom of the tide was an orderly part, I caught
the clear '*kiss—kiss—kiss*' of the halliards on the roof, as
they were blown against the installation-pole.

'Poole is not ready. I'll stay here and call you when he is.'

I returned to the shop, and set down my glass on a marble slab with a careless clink. As I did so, Shaynor rose to
his feet, his eyes fixed once more on the advertisement,
where the young woman bathed in the light from the red
jar simpered pinkly over her pearls. His lips moved without
cessation. I stepped nearer to listen. 'And threw—and threw
—and threw,' he repeated, his face all sharp with some in-
explicable agony.

I moved forward astonished. But it was then he found words—delivered roundly and clearly. These:—

'And threw warm gules on Madeleine's young breast.'

The trouble passed off his countenance, and he returned lightly to his place, rubbing his hands.

It had never occurred to me, though we had many times discussed reading and prize-competitions as a diversion, that Mr. Shaynor ever read Keats, or could quote him at all appositely. There was, after all, a certain stained-glass effect of light on the high bosom of the highly-polished picture which might, by stretch of fancy, suggest, as a vile chromo recalls some incomparable canvas, the line he had spoken. Night, my drink, and solitude were evidently turning Mr. Shaynor into a poet. He sat down again and wrote swiftly on his villainous notepaper, his lips quivering.

I shut the door into the inner office and moved up behind him. He made no sign that he saw or heard. I looked over his shoulder, and read, amid half-formed words, sentences, and wild scratches:—

> —— Very cold it was. Very cold
> The hare—the hare—the hare—
> The birds——

He raised his head sharply, and frowned toward the blank shutters of the poulterer's shop where they jutted out against our window. Then one clear line came:—

> The hare, in spite of fur, was very cold.

The head, moving machine-like, turned right to the advertisement where the Blaudett's Cathedral pastille reeked abominably. He grunted, and went on:—

> Incense in a censer—
> Before her darling picture framed in gold—
> Maiden's picture—angel's portrait—

'Hsh!' said Mr. Cashell guardedly from the inner office, as though in the presence of spirits. 'There's something coming through from somewhere; but it isn't Poole.' I heard the crackle of sparks as he depressed the keys of the transmitter. In my own brain, too, something crackled, or it might have been the hair on my head. Then I heard my own voice, in a harsh whisper: 'Mr. Cashell, there is something coming through here, too. Leave me alone till I tell you.'

'But I thought you'd come to see this wonderful thing—sir,' indignantly at the end.

'Leave me alone till I tell you. Be quiet.'

I watched—I waited. Under the blue-veined hand—the dry hand of the consumptive—came away clear, without erasure:—

> And my weak spirit fails
> To think how the dead must freeze—

he shivered as he wrote—

> Beneath the churchyard mould.

Then he stopped, laid the pen down, and leaned back.

For an instant, that was half an eternity, the shop spun before me in a rainbow-tinted whirl, in and through which my own soul most dispassionately considered my own soul as that fought with an over-mastering fear. Then I smelt the strong smell of cigarettes from Mr. Shaynor's clothing, and heard, as though it had been the rending of trumpets, the rattle of his breathing. I was still in my place of observation, much as one would watch a rifle-shot at the butts, half-bent, hands on my knees, and head within a few inches of the black, red, and yellow blanket of his shoulder. I was whispering encouragement, evidently to my other self, sounding sentences, such as men pronounce in dreams.

'If he has read Keats, it proves nothing. If he hasn't—like causes *must* beget like effects. There is no escape from this law. *You* ought to be grateful that you know "St. Agnes' Eve" without the book; because, given the circumstances, such as Fanny Brand, who is the key of the enigma, and approximately represents the latitude and longitude of

Fanny Brawne; allowing also for the bright red colour of the arterial blood upon the handkerchief, which was just what you were puzzling over in the shop just now; and counting the effect of the professional environment, here almost perfectly duplicated—the result is logical and inevitable. As inevitable as induction.'

Still, the other half of my soul refused to be comforted. It was cowering in some minute and inadequate corner—at an immense distance.

Hereafter, I found myself one person again, my hands still gripping my knees, and my eyes glued on the page before Mr. Shaynor. As dreamers accept and explain the upheaval of landscapes and the resurrection of the dead, with excerpts from the evening hymn or the multiplication-table, so I had accepted the facts, whatever they might be, that I should witness, and had devised a theory, sane and plausible to my mind, that explained them all. Nay, I was even in advance of my facts, walking hurriedly before them, assured that they would fit my theory. And all that I now recall of that epoch-making theory are the lofty words: 'If he has read Keats it's the chloric-ether. If he hasn't, it's the identical bacillus, or Hertzian wave of tuberculosis, *plus* Fanny Brand and the professional status which, in conjunction with the main-stream of subconscious thought common to all mankind, has thrown up temporarily an induced Keats.'

Mr. Shaynor returned to his work, erasing and rewriting as before with swiftness. Two or three blank pages he tossed aside. Then he wrote, muttering:—

The little smoke of a candle that goes out.

'No,' he muttered. 'Little smoke—little smoke—little smoke. What else?' He thrust his chin forward toward the advertisement, whereunder the last of the Blaudett's Cathedral pastilles fumed in its holder. 'Ah!' Then with relief:—

The little smoke that dies in moonlight cold.

Evidently he was snared by the rhymes of his first verse, for he wrote and rewrote 'gold—cold—mould' many times. Again he sought inspiration from the advertisement, and set down, without erasure, the line I had overheard:—

And threw warm gules on Madeleine's young breast.

As I remembered the original it is 'fair'—a trite word—instead of 'young,' and I found myself nodding approval, though I admitted that the attempt to reproduce 'Its little smoke in pallid moonlight died' was a failure.

Followed without a break ten or fifteen lines of bald prose—the naked soul's confession of its physical yearning for its beloved—unclean as we count uncleanliness; unwholesome, but human exceedingly; the raw material, so it seemed to me in that hour and in that place, whence Keats wove the twenty-sixth, seventh, and eighth stanzas of his poem. Shame I had none in overseeing this revelation; and my fear had gone with the smoke of the pastille.

'That's it,' I murmured. 'That's how it's blocked out. Go on! Ink it in, man. Ink it in!'

Mr. Shaynor returned to broken verse wherein 'loveliness' was made to rhyme with a desire to look upon 'her empty dress.' He picked up a fold of the gay, soft blanket, spread it over one hand, caressed it with infinite tenderness, thought, muttered, traced some snatches which I could not decipher, shut his eyes drowsily, shook his head, and dropped the stuff. Here I found myself at fault, for I could not then see (as I do now) in what manner a red, black, and yellow Austrian blanket coloured his dreams.

In a few minutes he laid aside his pen, and, chin on hand, considered the shop with thoughtful and intelligent eyes. He threw down the blanket, rose, passed along a line of drug-drawers, and read the names on the labels aloud. Returning, he took from his desk Christy's *New Commercial Plants* and the old Culpepper that I had given him, opened and laid them side by side with a clerky air, all trace of passion gone from his face, read first in one and then in the other, and paused with pen behind his ear.

'What wonder of Heaven's coming now?' I thought.

'Manna—manna—manna,' he said at last, under wrinkled brows. 'That's what I wanted. Good! Now then! Now then! Good! Good! Oh, by God, that's good!' His voice rose and he spoke rightly and fully without a falter:—

> 'Candied apple, quince and plum and gourd,
>   With jellies smoother than the creamy curd,
>   And lucent syrops tinct with cinnamon;
>   Manna and dates in argosy transferred
>   From Fez; and spicèd dainties, every one
>   From silken Samarcand to cedared Lebanon.'

He repeated it once more, using 'blander' for 'smoother' in the second line; then wrote it down without erasure, but this time (my set eyes missed no stroke of any word) he substituted 'soother' for his atrocious second thought, so that it came away under his hand as it is written in the book— as it is written in the book.

A wind went shouting down the street, and on the heels of the wind followed a spurt and rattle of rain.

After a smiling pause—and good right had he to smile— he began anew, always tossing the last sheet over his shoulder:—

> The sharp rain falling on the window-pane,
>   Rattling sleet—the wind-blown sleet.

Then prose: 'It is very cold of mornings when the wind brings rain and sleet with it. I heard the sleet on the window-pane outside, and thought of you, my darling. I am always thinking of you. I wish we could both run away like two lovers into the storm and get that little cottage by the sea which we are always thinking about, my own dear darling. We could sit and watch the sea beneath our windows. It would be a fairyland all of our own—a fairy sea—a fairy sea. . . .'

He stopped, raised his head, and listened. The steady drone of the Channel along the sea-front that had borne us company so long leaped up a note to the sudden fuller surge that signals the change from ebb to flood. It beat in like the change of step throughout an army—this renewed pulse of the sea—and filled our ears till they, accepting it, marked it no longer.

> A fairyland for you and me
> Across the foam—beyond . . .
> A magic foam, a perilous sea.

He grunted again with effort and bit his underlip. My throat dried, but I dared not gulp to moisten it lest I should break the spell that was drawing him nearer and nearer to the high-water mark but two of the sons of Adam have reached. Remember that in all the millions permitted there are no more than five—five little lines—of which one can say: 'These are the pure Magic. These are the clear Vision. The rest is only poetry.' And Mr. Shaynor was playing hot and cold with two of them!

I vowed no unconscious thought of mine should influence the blindfold soul, and pinned myself desperately to the other three, repeating and re-repeating:—

> 'A savage place! as holy and enchanted
> As e'er beneath a waning moon was haunted
> By woman wailing for her demon-lover.'

But though I believed my brain thus occupied, my every sense hung upon the writing under the dry, bony hand, all brown-fingered with chemicals and cigarette-smoke.

> Our windows fronting on the dangerous foam,

(he wrote, after long, irresolute snatches), and then—

> Our open casements facing desolate seas
> Forlorn—forlorn—

Here again his face grew peaked and anxious with that sense of loss I had first seen when the Power snatched him. But this time the agony was tenfold keener. As I watched it mounted like mercury in the tube. It lighted his face from within till I thought the visibly scourged soul must leap forth naked between his jaws, unable to endure. A drop of sweat trickled from my forehead down my nose and splashed on the back of my hand.

> Our windows facing on the desolate seas
> And pearly foam of magic fairyland—

'Not yet—not yet,' he muttered, 'wait a minute. *Please* wait a minute. I shall get it then—

> Our magic windows fronting on the sea,
> The dangerous foam of desolate seas . . .
>   For aye.

Ouh, my God!'

From head to heel he shook—shook from the marrow of his bones outwards—then leaped to his feet with raised arms, and slid the chair screeching across the tiled floor where it struck the drawers behind and fell with a jar. Mechanically, I stooped to recover it.

As I rose, Mr. Shaynor was stretching and yawning at leisure.

'I've had a bit of a doze,' he said. 'How did I come to knock the chair over? You look rather——'

'The chair startled me,' I answered. 'It was so sudden in this quiet.'

Young Mr. Cashell behind his shut door was offendedly silent.

'I suppose I must have been dreaming,' said Mr. Shaynor.

'I suppose you must,' I said. 'Talking of dreams—I—I noticed you writing—before——'

He flushed consciously.

'I meant to ask you if you've ever read anything written by a man called Keats.'

'Oh! I haven't much time to read poetry, and I can't say that I remember the name exactly. Is he a popular writer?'

'Middling. I thought you might know him because he's the only poet who was ever a druggist. And he's rather what's called the lover's poet.'

'Indeed. I must dip into him. What did he write about?'

'A lot of things. Here's a sample that may interest you.'

Then and there, carefully, I repeated the verse he had twice spoken and once written not ten minutes ago.

'Ah! Anybody could see he was a druggist from that line about the tinctures and syrups. It's a fine tribute to our profession.'

'I don't know,' said young Mr. Cashell, with icy politeness, opening the door one half-inch, 'if you still happen to be interested in our trifling experiments. But, should such be the case——'

I drew him aside, whispering, 'Shaynor seemed going off into some sort of fit when I spoke to you just now. I thought, even at the risk of being rude, it wouldn't do to take you off your instruments just as the call was coming through. Don't you see?'

'Granted—granted as soon as asked,' he said, unbending. 'I *did* think it a shade odd at the time. So that was why he knocked the chair down?'

'I hope I haven't missed anything,' I said.

'I'm afraid I can't say that, but you're just in time for the end of a rather curious performance. You can come in too, Mr. Shaynor. Listen, while I read it off.'

The Morse instrument was ticking furiously. Mr. Cashell interpreted: ' "*K.K.V. Can make nothing of your signals.*" ' A pause. ' "*M.M.V. M.M.V. Signals unintelligible. Purpose anchor Sandown Bay. Examine instruments to-morrow.*" Do you know what that means? It's a couple of men-o'-war working Marconi signals off the Isle of Wight. They are trying to talk to each other. Neither can read the other's messages, but all their messages are being taken in by our receiver here. They've been going on for ever so long. I wish you could have heard it.'

'How wonderful!' I said. 'Do you mean we're overhearing Portsmouth ships trying to talk to each other—that we're eavesdropping across half South England?'

'Just that. Their transmitters are all right, but their receivers are out of order, so they only get a dot here and a dash there. Nothing clear.'

'Why is that?'

'God knows—and Science will know tomorrow. Perhaps the induction is faulty; perhaps the receivers aren't tuned to receive just the number of vibrations per second that the transmitter sends. Only a word here and there. Just enough to tantalise.'

Again the Morse sprang to life.

'That's one of 'em complaining now. Listen: *"Disheartening—most disheartening."* It's quite pathetic. Have you ever seen a spiritualistic séance? It reminds me of that sometimes—odds and ends of messages coming out of nowhere—a word here and there—no good at all.'

'But mediums are all impostors,' said Mr. Shaynor, in the doorway, lighting an asthma-cigarette. 'They only do it for the money they can make. I've seen 'em.'

'Here's Poole, at last—clear as a bell. L.L.L. *Now* we shan't be long.' Mr. Cashell rattled the keys merrily. 'Anything you'd like to tell 'em?'

'No, I don't think so,' I said. 'I'll go home and get to bed. I'm feeling a little tired.'

'THEY'

One view called me to another; one hill-top to its fellow, half across the county, and since I could answer at no more trouble than the snapping forward of a lever, I let the county flow under my wheels. The orchid-studded flats of the East gave way to the thyme, ilex, and grey grass of the Downs; these again to the rich cornland and fig-trees of the lower coast, where you carry the beat of the tide on your left hand for fifteen level miles; and when at last I turned inland through a huddle of rounded hills and woods I had run myself clean out of my known marks. Beyond that precise hamlet which stands godmother to the capital of the United States, I found hidden villages where bees, the only things awake, boomed in eighty-foot lindens that overhung grey Norman churches; miraculous brooks diving under stone bridges built for heavier traffic than would ever vex them again; tithe-barns larger than their churches, and an old smithy that cried out aloud how it had once been a hall of the Knights of the Temple. Gipsies I found on a common where the gorse, bracken, and heath fought it out together up a mile of Roman road; and a little farther on I disturbed a red fox rolling dog-fashion in the naked sunlight.

As the wooded hills closed about me I stood up in the car to take the bearings of that great Down whose ringed head is a landmark for fifty miles across the low countries. I judged that the lie of the country would bring me across some westward-running road that went to his feet, but I did not allow for the confusing veils of the woods. A quick turn plunged me first into a green cutting brim-full of liquid sunshine, next into a gloomy tunnel where last year's dead leaves whispered and scuffled about my tyres. The strong hazel stuff meeting overhead had not been cut for a couple of generations at least, nor had any axe helped the moss-cankered oak and beech to spring above them. Here the road changed frankly into a carpeted ride on whose brown velvet spent primrose-clumps showed like jade, and a few sickly, white-stalked bluebells nodded together. As the slope favoured I shut off the power and slid over the whirled leaves, expecting every moment to meet a keeper; but I only heard a jay, far off, arguing against the silence under the twilight of the trees.

Still the track descended. I was on the point of reversing and working my way back on the second speed ere I ended in some swamp, when I saw sunshine through the tangle ahead and lifted the brake.

It was down again at once. As the light beat across my face my fore-wheels took the turf of a great still lawn from which sprang horsemen ten feet high with levelled lances, monstrous peacocks, and sleek round-headed maids of honour—blue, black, and glistening—all of clipped yew. Across the lawn—the marshalled woods besieged it on three sides—stood an ancient house of lichened and weather-worn stone, with mullioned windows and roofs of rose-red tile. It was flanked by semi-circular walls, also rose-red, that closed the lawn on the fourth side, and at their feet a box hedge grew man-high. There were doves on the roof about the slim brick chimneys, and I caught a glimpse of an octagonal dove-house behind the screening wall.

Here, then, I stayed; a horseman's green spear laid at my breast; held by the exceeding beauty of that jewel in that setting.

'If I am not packed off for a trespasser, or if this knight does not ride a wallop at me,' thought I, 'Shakespeare and Queen Elizabeth at least must come out of that half-open garden door and ask me to tea.'

A child appeared at an upper window, and I thought the little thing waved a friendly hand. But it was to call a companion, for presently another bright head showed. Then I heard a laugh among the yew-peacocks, and turning to make sure (till then I had been watching the house only) I saw the silver of a fountain behind a hedge thrown up against the sun. The doves on the roof cooed to the cooing water; but between the two notes I caught the utterly happy chuckle of a child absorbed in some light mischief.

The garden door—heavy oak sunk deep in the thickness of the wall—opened further: a woman in a big garden hat set her foot slowly on the time-hollowed stone step and as slowly walked across the turf. I was forming some apology when she lifted up her head and I saw that she was blind.

'I heard you,' she said. 'Isn't that a motor car?'

'I'm afraid I've made a mistake in my road. I should have turned off up above—I never dreamed——' I began.

'But I'm very glad. Fancy a motor car coming into the garden! It will be such a treat——' She turned and made as though looking about her. 'You—you haven't seen any one, have you—perhaps?'

'No one to speak to, but the children seemed interested at a distance.'

'Which?'

'I saw a couple up at the window just now, and I think I heard a little chap in the grounds.'

'Oh, lucky you!' she cried, and her face brightened. 'I hear them, of course, but that's all. You've seen them and heard them?'

'Yes,' I answered. 'And if I know anything of children, one of them's having a beautiful time by the fountain yonder. Escaped, I should imagine.'

'You're fond of children?'

I gave her one or two reasons why I did not altogether hate them.

'Of course, of course,' she said. 'Then you understand. Then you won't think it foolish if I ask you to take your car through the gardens, once or twice—quite slowly. I'm sure they'd like to see it. They see so little, poor things. One tries to make their life pleasant, but——' she threw out her hands towards the woods. 'We're so out of the world here.'

'That will be splendid,' I said. 'But I can't cut up your grass.'

She faced to the right. 'Wait a minute,' she said. 'We're at the South gate, aren't we? Behind those peacocks there's a flagged path. We call it the Peacocks' Walk. You can't see it from here, they tell me, but if you squeeze along by the edge of the wood you can turn at the first peacock and get on to the flags.'

It was sacrilege to wake that dreaming house-front with the clatter of machinery, but I swung the car to clear the turf, brushed along the edge of the wood and turned in on the broad stone path where the fountain-basin lay like one star-sapphire.

'May I come too?' she cried. 'No, please don't help me. They'll like it better if they see me.'

She felt her way lightly to the front of the car, and with one foot on the step she called: 'Children, oh, children! Look and see what's going to happen!'

The voice would have drawn lost souls from the Pit, for the yearning that underlay its sweetness, and I was not surprised to hear an answering shout behind the yews. It must have been the child by the fountain, but he fled at our approach, leaving a little toy boat in the water. I saw the glint of his blue blouse among the still horsemen.

Very disposedly we paraded the length of the walk and at her request backed again. This time the child had got the better of his panic, but stood far off and doubting.

'The little fellow's watching us,' I said. 'I wonder if he'd like a ride.'

'They're very shy still. Very shy. But, oh, lucky you to be able to see them! Let's listen.'

I stopped the machine at once, and the humid stillness, heavy with the scent of box, cloaked us deep. Shears I could hear where some gardener was clipping; a mumble of bees and broken voices that might have been the doves.

'Oh, unkind!' she said weariedly.

'Perhaps they're only shy of the motor. The little maid at the window looks tremendously interested.'

'Yes?' She raised her head. 'It was wrong of me to say that. They are really fond of me. It's the only thing that makes life worth living—when they're fond of you, isn't it? I daren't think what the place would be without them. By the way, is it beautiful?'

'I think it is the most beautiful place I have ever seen.'

'So they all tell me. I can feel it, of course, but that isn't quite the same thing.'

'Then have you never——?' I began, but stopped abashed.

'Not since I can remember. It happened when I was only a few months old, they tell me. And yet I must remember something, else how could I dream about colours? I see light in my dreams, and colours, but I never see *them*. I only hear them just as I do when I'm awake.'

'It's difficult to see faces in dreams. Some people can, but most of us haven't the gift,' I went on, looking up at the window where the child stood all but hidden.

'I've heard that too,' she said. 'And they tell me that one never sees a dead person's face in a dream. Is that true?'

'I believe it is—now I come to think of it.'

'But how is it with yourself—yourself?' The blind eyes turned towards me.

'I have never seen the faces of my dead in any dream,' I answered.

'Then it must be as bad as being blind.'

The sun had dipped behind the woods and the long shades were possessing the insolent horsemen one by one. I saw the light die from off the top of a glossy-leafed lance and all the brave hard green turn to soft black. The house, accepting another day at end, as it had accepted an hundred thousand gone, seemed to settle deeper into its rest among the shadows.

'Have you ever wanted to?' she said after the silence.

'Very much sometimes,' I replied. The child had left the window as the shadows closed upon it.

'Ah! So've I, but I don't suppose it's allowed. . . . Where d'you live?'

'Quite the other side of the county—sixty miles and more, and I must be going back. I've come without my big lamps.'

'But it's not dark yet. I can feel it.'

'I'm afraid it will be by the time I get home. Could you lend me someone to set me on my road at first? I've utterly lost myself.'

'I'll send Madden with you to the cross-roads. We are so out of the world, I don't wonder you were lost! I'll guide you round to the front of the house; but you will go slowly, won't you, till you're out of the grounds? It isn't foolish, do you think?'

'I promise you I'll go like this,' I said, and let the car start herself down the flagged path.

We skirted the left wing of the house, whose elaborately cast lead guttering alone was worth a day's journey; passed under a great rose-grown gate in the red wall, and so round to the high front of the house, which in beauty and stateliness as much excelled the back as that all others I had seen.

'Is it so very beautiful?' she said wistfully when she heard my raptures. 'And you like the lead figures too? There's the old azalea garden behind. They say that this place must have been made for children. Will you help me out, please? I should like to come with you as far as the cross-roads, but I mustn't leave them. Is that you, Madden? I want you to show this gentleman the way to the cross-roads. He has lost his way, but—he has seen them.'

A butler appeared noiselessly at the miracle of old oak that must be called the front door, and slipped aside to put on his hat. She stood looking at me with open blue eyes in which no sight lay, and I saw for the first time that she was beautiful.

'Remember,' she said quietly, 'if you are fond of them you will come again,' and disappeared within the house.

The butler in the car said nothing till we were nearly at the lodge gates, where catching a glimpse of a blue blouse in a shrubbery I swerved amply lest the devil that leads little boys to play should drag me into child-murder.

'Excuse me,' he asked of a sudden, 'but why did you do that, sir?'

'The child yonder.'

'Our young gentleman in blue?'

'Of course.'

'He runs about a good deal. Did you see him by the fountain, sir?'

'Oh, yes, several times. Do we turn here?'

'Yes, sir. And did you 'appen to see them upstairs too?'

'At the upper window? Yes.'

'Was that before the mistress come out to speak to you, sir?'

'A little before that. Why d'you want to know?'

He paused a little. 'Only to make sure that—that they had seen the car, sir, because with children running about, though I'm sure you're driving particularly careful, there might be an accident. That was all, sir. Here are the cross-roads. You can't miss your way from now on. Thank you, sir, but that isn't *our* custom, not with——'

'I beg your pardon,' I said, and thrust away the British silver.

'Oh, it's quite right with the rest of 'em as a rule. Good-bye, sir.'

He retired into the armour-plated conning-tower of his caste and walked away. Evidently a butler solicitous for the honour of his house, and interested, probably through a maid, in the nursery.

Once beyond the signposts at the cross-roads I looked back, but the crumpled hills interlaced so jealously that I could not see where the house had lain. When I asked its name at a cottage along the road, the fat woman who sold sweetmeats there gave me to understand that people with motor cars had small right to live—much less to 'go about talking like carriage folk.' They were not a pleasant-mannered community.

When I retraced my route on the map that evening I was little wiser. Hawkin's Old Farm appeared to be the Survey title of the place, and the old County Gazetteer, generally so ample, did not allude to it. The big house of those parts was Hodnington Hall, Georgian with early Victorian embellishments, as an atrocious steel engraving attested. I carried my difficulty to a neighbour—a deep-rooted tree of that soil—and he gave me a name of a family which conveyed no meaning.

A month or so later—I went again, or it may have been that my car took the road of her own volition. She over-ran the fruitless Downs, threaded every turn of the maze of lanes below the hills, drew through the high-walled woods, impenetrable in their full leaf, came out at the cross-roads where the butler had left me, and a little farther on developed an internal trouble which forced me to turn her in on a grass way-waste that cut into a summer-silent hazel wood. So far as I could make sure by the sun and a six-inch Ordnance map, this should be the road flank of that wood which I had first explored from the heights above. I made a mightly serious business of my repairs and a glittering shop of my repair kit, spanners, pump, and the like, which I spread out orderly upon a rug. It was a trap to catch all childhood, for on such a day, I argued, the children would not be far off. When I paused in my work I listened, but the wood was so full of the noises of summer (though the birds had mated) that I could not at first distinguish these from the tread of small cautious feet stealing across the dead leaves. I rang my bell in an alluring manner, but the feet fled, and I repented, for to a child a sudden noise is very real terror. I must have been at work half an hour when I heard in the wood the voice of the blind woman crying: 'Children, oh, children! Where are you?' and the stillness made slow to close on the perfection of that cry. She came towards me, half feeling her way between the tree boles, and though a child, it seemed, clung to her skirt, it swerved into the leafage like a rabbit as she drew nearer.

'Is that you?' she said, 'from the other side of the county?'

'Yes, it's me from the other side of the county.'

'Then why didn't you come through the upper woods? They were there just now.'

'They were here a few minutes ago. I expect they knew my car had broken down, and came to see the fun.'

'Nothing serious, I hope? How do cars break down?'

'In fifty different ways. Only mine has chosen the fifty-first.'

She laughed merrily at the tiny joke, cooed with delicious laughter, and pushed her hat back.

'Let me hear,' she said.

'Wait a moment,' I cried, 'and I'll get you a cushion.'

She set her foot on the rug all covered with spare parts, and stooped above it eagerly. 'What delightful things!' The hands through which she saw glanced in the chequered sunlight. 'A box here—another box! Why, you've arranged them like playing shop!'

'I confess now that I put it out to attract them. I don't need half those things really.'

'How nice of you! I heard your bell in the upper wood. You say they were here before that?'

'I'm sure of it. Why are they so shy? That little fellow in blue who was with you just now ought to have got over his fright. He's been watching me like a Red Indian.'

'It must have been your bell,' she said. 'I heard one of them go past me in trouble when I was coming down. They're shy—so shy even with me.' She turned her face over her shoulder and cried again: 'Children, oh, children! Look and see!'

'They must have gone off together on their own affairs,' I suggested, for there was a murmur behind us of lowered voices broken by the sudden squeaking giggles of childhood. I returned to my tinkerings and she leaned forward, her chin on her hand, listening interestedly.

'How many are they?' I said at last. The work was finished, but I saw no reason to go.

Her forehead puckered a little in thought. 'I don't quite know,' she said simply. 'Sometimes more—sometimes less. They come and stay with me because I love them, you see.'

'That must be very jolly,' I said, replacing a drawer, and as I spoke I heard the inanity of my answer.

'You—you aren't laughing at me?' she cried. 'I—I haven't any of my own. I never married. People laugh at me sometimes about them because—because——'

'Because they're savages,' I returned. 'It's nothing to fret for. That sort laugh at everything that isn't in their own fat lives.'

'I don't know. How should I? I only don't like being laughed at about *them*. It hurts; and when one can't see. . . . I don't want to seem silly,' her chin quivered like a child's as she spoke, 'but we blindies have only one skin, I think. Everything outside hits straight at our souls. It's different with you. You've such good defences in your eyes —looking out—before anyone can really pain you in your soul. People forget that with us.'

I was silent, reviewing that inexhaustible matter—the more than inherited (since it is also carefully taught) brutality of the Christian peoples, beside which the mere heathendom of the West Coast nigger is clean and restrained. It led me a long distance into myself.

'Don't do that!' she said of a sudden, putting her hands before her eyes.

'What?'

She made a gesture with her hand.

'That! It's—it's all purple and black. Don't! That colour hurts.'

'But how in the world do you know about colours?' I exclaimed, for here was a revelation indeed.

'Colours as colours?' she asked.

'No. *Those* Colours which you saw just now.'

'You know as well as I do,' she laughed, 'else you wouldn't have asked that question. They aren't in the world at all. They're in *you*—when you went so angry.'

'D'you mean a dull purplish patch, like port wine mixed with ink?' I said.

'I've never seen ink or port wine, but the colours aren't mixed. They are separate—all separate.'

'Do you mean black streaks and jags across the purple?'

She nodded. 'Yes—if they are like this,' and zig-zagged her finger again, 'but it's more red than purple—that bad colour.'

'And what are the colours at the top of the—whatever you see?'

Slowly she leaned forward and traced on the rug the figure of the Egg itself.

'I see them so,' she said, pointing with a grass stem, 'white, green, yellow, red, purple, and when people are angry or bad, black across the red—as you were just now.'

'Who told you anything about it—in the beginning?' I demanded.

'About the Colours? No one. I used to ask what Colours were when I was little—in table-covers and curtains and carpets, you see—because some colours hurt me and some made me happy. People told me; and when I got older that was how I saw people.' Again she traced the outline of the Egg which it is given to very few of us to see.

'All by yourself?' I repeated.

'All by myself. There wasn't anyone else. I only found out afterwards that other people did not see the Colours.'

She leaned against the tree-bole plaiting and unplaiting chance-plucked grass stems. The children in the wood had drawn nearer. I could see them with the tail of my eye frolicking like squirrels.

'Now I am sure you will never laugh at me,' she went on after a long silence. 'Nor at *them*.'

'Goodness! No!' I cried, jolted out of my train of thought. 'A man who laughs at a child—unless the child is laughing too—is a heathen!'

'I didn't mean that, of course. You'd never laugh *at* children, but I thought—I used to think—that perhaps you might laugh about *them*. So now I beg your pardon. . . . What are you going to laugh at?'

I had made no sound, but she knew.

'At the notion of your begging my pardon. If you had done your duty as a pillar of the State and a landed proprietress you ought to have summoned me for trespass when I barged through your woods the other day. It was disgraceful of me—inexcusable.'

She looked at me, her head against the tree-trunk—long and steadfastly—this woman who could see the naked soul.

'How curious,' she half whispered. 'How very curious.'

'Why, what have I done?'

'You don't understand . . . and yet you understood about the Colours. Don't you understand?'

She spoke with a passion that nothing had justified, and I faced her bewilderedly as she rose. The children had gathered themselves in a roundel behind a bramble bush. One sleek head bent over something smaller, and the set of the little shoulders told me that fingers were on lips. They, too, had some child's tremendous secret. I alone was hopelessly astray there in the broad sunlight.

'No,' I said, and shook my head as though the dead eyes could note. 'Whatever it is, I don't understand yet. Perhaps I shall later—if you'll let me come again.'

'You will come again,' she answered. 'You will surely come again and walk in the wood.'

'Perhaps the children will know me well enough by that time to let me play with them—as a favour. You know what children are like.'

'It isn't a matter of favour but of right,' she replied, and while I wondered what she meant, a dishevelled woman plunged round the bend of the road, loose-haired, purple, almost lowing with agony as she ran. It was my rude, fat friend of the sweetmeat shop. The blind woman heard and stepped forward. 'What is it, Mrs. Madehurst?' she asked.

The woman flung her apron over her head and literally grovelled in the dust, crying that her grandchild was sick to death, that the local doctor was away fishing, that Jenny the mother was at her wits' end, and so forth, with repetitions and bellowings.

'Where's the next nearest doctor?' I asked between paroxysms.

'Madden will tell you. Go round to the house and take him with you. I'll attend to this. Be quick!' She half supported the fat woman into the shade. In two minutes I was blowing all the horns of Jericho under the front of the House Beautiful, and Madden, in the pantry, rose to the crisis like a butler and a man.

A quarter of an hour at illegal speeds caught us a doctor

five miles away. Within the half-hour we had decanted him, much interested in motors, at the door of the sweetmeat shop, and drew up the road to await the verdict.

'Useful things cars,' said Madden, all man and no butler. 'If I'd had one when mine took sick she wouldn't have died.'

'How was it?' I asked.

'Croup. Mrs. Madden was away. No one knew what to do. I drove eight miles in a tax-cart for the doctor. She was choked when we came back. This car 'd ha' saved her. She'd have been close on ten now.'

'I'm sorry,' I said. 'I thought you were rather fond of children from what you told me going to the cross-roads the other day.'

'Have you seen 'em again, sir—this mornin'?'

'Yes, but they're well broke to cars. I couldn't get any of them within twenty yards of it.'

He looked at me carefully as a scout considers a stranger —not as a menial should lift his eyes to his divinely appointed superior.

'I wonder why,' he said just above the breath that he drew.

We waited on. A light wind from the sea wandered up and down the long lines of the woods, and the wayside grasses, whitened already with summer dust, rose and bowed in sallow waves.

A woman, wiping the suds off her arms, came out of the cottage next the sweetmeat shop.

'I've be'n listenin' in de back-yard,' she said cheerily. 'He says Arthur's unaccountable bad. Did ye hear him shruck just now? Unaccountable bad. I reckon t'will come Jenny's turn to walk in de wood nex' week along, Mr. Madden.'

'Excuse me, sir, but your lap-robe is slipping,' said Madden deferentially. The woman started, dropped a curtsey, and hurried away.

'What does she mean by "walking in the wood"?' I asked.

'It must be some saying they use hereabouts. I'm from Norfolk myself,' said Madden. 'They're an independent lot in this county. She took you for a chauffeur, sir.'

I saw the Doctor come out of the cottage followed by a draggletailed wench who clung to his arm as though he could make treaty for her with Death. 'Dat sort,' she wailed —'dey're just as much to us dat has 'em as if dey was lawful born. Just as much—just as much! An' God, He'd be just as pleased if you saved 'un, Doctor. Don't take it from me. Miss Florence will tell ye de very same. Don't leave 'im, Doctor!'

'I know, I know,' said the man; 'but he'll be quiet for a while now. We'll get the nurse and the medicine as fast as we can.' He signalled me to come forward with the car, and I strove not to be privy to what followed; but I saw the girl's face, blotched and frozen with grief, and I felt the hand without a ring clutching at my knees when we moved away.

The Doctor was a man of some humour, for I remember he claimed my car under the Oath of Æsculapius, and used it and me without mercy. First we convoyed Mrs. Madehurst and the blind woman to wait by the sick-bed till the nurse should come. Next we invaded a neat county town for prescriptions (the Doctor said the trouble was cerebro-spinal meningitis), and when the County Institute, banked and flanked with scared market cattle, reported itself out of nurses for the moment we literally flung ourselves loose upon the county. We conferred with the owners of great houses—magnates at the ends of overarching avenues whose big-boned womenfolk strode away from their tea-tables to listen to the imperious Doctor. At last a white-haired lady sitting under a cedar of Lebanon and surrounded by a court of magnificent Borzois—all hostile to motors—gave the Doctor, who received them as from a princess, written orders which we bore many miles at top speed, through a park, to a French nunnery, where we took over in exchange a pallid-faced and trembling Sister. She knelt at the bottom of the tonneau telling her beads without

pause till, by short cuts of the Doctor's invention, we had
her to the sweetmeat shop once more. It was a long afternoon crowded with mad episodes that rose and dissolved
like the dust of our wheels; cross-sections of remote and
incomprehensible lives through which we raced at right
angles; and I went home in the dusk, wearied out, to dream
of the clashing horns of cattle; round-eyed nuns walking in
a garden of graves; pleasant tea-parties beneath shady
trees; the carbolic-scented, grey-painted corridors of the
County Institute; the steps of shy children in the wood, and
the hands that clung to my knees as the motor began to
move.

. . . . . .

I had intended to return in a day or two, but it pleased
Fate to hold me from that side of the county, on many
pretexts, till the elder and the wild rose had fruited. There
came at last a brilliant day, swept clear from the south-
west, that brought the hills within hand's reach—a day of
unstable airs and high filmy clouds. Through no merit of
my own I was free, and set the car for the third time on
that known road. As I reached the crest of the Downs I
felt the soft air change, saw it glaze under the sun; and,
looking down at the sea, in that instant beheld the blue of
the Channel turn through polished silver and dulled steel to
dingy pewter. A laden collier hugging the coast steered
outward for deeper water, and, across copper-coloured
haze, I saw sails rise one by one on the anchored fishing-
fleet. In a deep dene behind me an eddy of sudden wind
drummed through sheltered oaks, and spun aloft the first
dry sample of autumn leaves. When I reached the beach
road the sea-fog fumed over the brickfields, and the tide
was telling all the groynes of the gale beyond Ushant. In
less than an hour summer England vanished in chill grey.
We were again the shut island of the North, all the ships of
the world bellowing at our perilous gates; and between
their outcries ran the piping of bewildered gulls. My cap
dripped moisture, the folds of the rug held it in pools or

sluiced it away in runnels, and the salt-rime stuck to my lips.

Inland the smell of autumn loaded the thickened fog among the trees, and the drip became a continuous shower. Yet the late flowers—mallow of the wayside, scabious of the field, and dahlia of the garden—showed gay in the mist, and beyond the sea's breath there was little sign of decay in the leaf. Yet in the villages the house doors were all open, and bare-legged, bare-headed children sat at ease on the damp doorsteps to shout 'pip-pip' at the stranger.

I made bold to call at the sweetmeat shop, where Mrs. Madehurst met me with a fat woman's hospitable tears. Jenny's child, she said, had died two days after the nun had come. It was, she felt, best out of the way, even though insurance offices, for reasons which she did not pretend to follow, would not willingly insure such stray lives. 'Not but what Jenny didn't tend to Arthur as though he'd come all proper at de end of de first year—like Jenny herself.' Thanks to Miss Florence, the child had been buried with a pomp which, in Mrs. Madehurst's opinion, more than covered the small irregularity of its birth. She described the coffin, within and without, the glass hearse, and the evergreen lining of the grave.

'But how's the mother?' I asked.

'Jenny? Oh, she'll get over it. I've felt dat way with one or two o' my own. She'll get over. She's walkin' in de wood now.'

'In this weather?'

Mrs. Madehurst looked at me with narrowed eyes across the counter.

'I dunno but it opens de 'eart like. Yes, it opens de 'eart. Dat's where losin' and bearin' comes so alike in de long run, we do say.'

Now the wisdom of the old wives is greater than that of all the Fathers, and this last oracle sent me thinking so extendedly as I went up the road, that I nearly ran over a woman and a child at the wooded corner by the lodge gates of the House Beautiful.

'Awful weather!' I cried, as I slowed dead for the turn.
'Not so bad,' she answered placidly out of the fog.
'Mine's used to 'un. You'll find yours indoors, I reckon.'

Indoors, Madden received me with professional cour-
tesy, and kind inquiries for the health of the motor, which
he would put under cover.

I waited in a still, nut-brown hall, pleasant with late
flowers and warmed with a delicious wood fire—a place of
good influence and great peace. (Men and women may
sometimes, after great effort, achieve a creditable lie; but
the house, which is their temple, cannot say anything save
the truth of those who have lived in it.) A child's cart and
a doll lay on the black-and-white floor, where a rug had
been kicked back. I felt that the children had only just
hurried away—to hide themselves, most like—in the many
turns of the great adzed staircase that climbed statelily out
of the hall, or to crouch at gaze behind the lions and roses
of the carven gallery above. Then I heard her voice above
me, singing as the blind sing—from the soul:—

'In the pleasant orchard-closes.'

And all my early summer came back at the call.

'In the pleasant orchard-closes,
    God bless all our gains, say we—
But may God bless all our losses,
    Better suits with our degree.'

She dropped the marring fifth line, and repeated—

'Better suits with our degree!'

I saw her lean over the gallery, her linked hands white
as pearl against the oak.

'Is that you—from the other side of the county?' she
called.

'Yes, me—from the other side of the county,' I answered,
laughing.

'What a long time before you had to come here again.'
She ran down the stairs, one hand lightly touching the

broad rail. 'It's two months and four days. Summer's gone!'

'I meant to come before, but Fate prevented.'

'I knew it. Please do something to that fire. They won't let me play with it, but I can feel it's behaving badly. Hit it!'

I looked on either side of the deep fireplace, and found but a half-charred hedge-stake with which I punched a black log into flame.

'It never goes out, day or night,' she said, as though explaining. 'In case any one comes in with cold toes, you see.'

'It's even lovelier inside than it was out,' I murmured. The red light poured itself along the age-polished dusky panels till the Tudor roses and lions of the gallery took colour and motion. An old eagle-topped convex mirror gathered the picture into its mysterious heart, distorting afresh the distorted shadows, and curving the gallery lines into the curves of a ship. The day was shutting down in half a gale as the fog turned to stringy scud. Through the uncurtained mullions of the broad window I could see the valiant horsemen of the lawn rear and recover against the wind that taunted them with legions of dead leaves.

'Yes, it must be beautiful,' she said. 'Would you like to go over it? There's still light enough upstairs.'

I followed her up the unflinching, wagon-wide staircase to the gallery whence opened the thin fluted Elizabethan doors.

'Feel how they put the latch low down for the sake of the children.' She swung a light door inward.

'By the way, where are they?' I asked. 'I haven't even heard them to-day.'

She did not answer at once. Then, 'I can only hear them,' she replied softly. 'This is one of their rooms—everything ready, you see.'

She pointed into a heavily-timbered room. There were little low gate tables and children's chairs. A dolls' house, its hooked front half open, faced a great dappled rocking-horse, from whose padded saddle it was but a child's scram-

ble to the broad window-seat overlooking the lawn. A toy
gun lay in a corner beside a gilt wooden cannon.

'Surely they've only just gone,' I whispered. In the failing
light a door creaked cautiously. I heard the rustle of a
frock and the patter of feet—quick feet through a room
beyond.

'I heard that,' she cried triumphantly. 'Did you? Children, oh, children! Where are you?'

The voice filled the walls that held it lovingly to the last
perfect note, but there came no answering shout such as I
had heard in the garden. We hurried on from room to oak-
floored room; up a step here, down three steps there;
among a maze of passages; always mocked by our quarry.
One might as well have tried to work an unstopped warren
with a single ferret. There were bolt-holes innumerable—
recesses in walls, embrasures of deep-slitted windows now
darkened, whence they could start up behind us; and abandoned fireplaces, six feet deep in the masonry, as well as
the tangle of communicating doors. Above all, they had
the twilight for their helper in our game. I had caught one
or two joyous chuckles of evasion, and once or twice had
seen the silhouette of a child's frock against some darken-
ing window at the end of a passage; but we returned empty-
handed to the gallery, just as a middle-aged woman was
setting a lamp in its niche.

'No, I haven't seen her either this evening, Miss Florence,' I heard her say, 'but that Turpin he says he wants
to see you about his shed.'

'Oh, Mr. Turpin must want to see me very badly. Tell
him to come to the hall, Mrs. Madden.'

I looked down into the hall whose only light was the
dulled fire, and deep in the shadow I saw them at last. They
must have slipped down while we were in the passages, and
now thought themselves perfectly hidden behind an old gilt
leather screen. By child's law, my fruitless chase was as
good as an introduction, but since I had taken so much
trouble I resolved to force them to come forward later by
the simple trick, which children detest, of pretending not to

notice them. They lay close, in a little huddle, no more
than shadows except when a quick flame betrayed an outline.

'And now we'll have some tea,' she said. 'I believe I
ought to have offered it you at first, but one doesn't arrive
at manners somehow when one lives alone and is considered—h'm—peculiar.' Then with very pretty scorn,
'Would you like a lamp to see to eat by?'

'The firelight's much pleasanter, I think.' We descended
into that delicious gloom and Madden brought tea.

I took my chair in the direction of the screen ready to
surprise or be surprised as the game should go, and at her
permission, since a hearth is always sacred, bent forward
to play with the fire.

'Where do you get these beautiful short faggots from?' I
asked idly. 'Why, they are tallies!'

'Of course,' she said. 'As I can't read or write I'm driven
back on the early English tally for my accounts. Give me
one and I'll tell you what it meant.'

I passed her an unburned hazel-tally, about a foot long,
and she ran her thumb down the nicks.

'This is the milk-record for the home farm for the month
of April last year, in gallons,' said she. 'I don't know what
I should have done without tallies. An old forester of mine
taught me the system. It's out of date now for every one
else; but my tenants respect it. One of them's coming now
to see me. Oh, it doesn't matter. He has no business here
out of office hours. He's a greedy, ignorant man—very
greedy, or—he wouldn't come here after dark.'

'Have you much land then?'

'Only a couple of hundred acres in hand, thank goodness. The other six hundred are nearly all let to folk who
knew my folk before me, but this Turpin is quite a new
man—and a highway robber.'

'But are you sure I shan't be——?'

'Certainly not. You have the right. He hasn't any children.'

'Ah, the children!' I said, and slid my low chair back till it nearly touched the screen that hid them. 'I wonder whether they'll come out for me.'

There was a murmur of voices—Madden's and a deeper note—at the low, dark side door, and a ginger-headed, canvas-gaitered giant of the unmistakable tenant-farmer type stumbled or was pushed in.

'Come to the fire, Mr. Turpin,' she said.

'If—if you please, Miss, I'll—I'll be quite as well by the door.' He clung to the latch as he spoke like a frightened child. Of a sudden I realised that he was in the grip of some almost overpowering fear.

'Well?'

'About that new shed for the young stock—that was all. These first autumn storms settin' in . . . but I'll come again, Miss.' His teeth did not chatter much more than the door-latch.

'I think not,' she answered levelly. 'The new shed—m'm. What did my agent write you on the 15th?'

'I—fancied p'raps that if I came to see you—ma—man to man like, Miss. But——'

His eyes rolled into every corner of the room wide with horror. He half opened the door through which he had entered, but I noticed it shut again—from without and firmly.

'He wrote what I told him,' she went on. 'You are over-stocked already. Dunnett's Farm never carried more than fifty bullocks—even in Mr. Wright's time. And *he* used cake. You've sixty-seven and you don't cake. You've broken the lease in that respect. You're dragging the heart out of the farm.'

'I'm—I'm getting some minerals—superphosphates—next week. I've as good as ordered a truck-load already. I'll go down to the station to-morrow about 'em. Then I can come and see you man to man like, Miss, in the daylight. . . . That gentleman's not going away, is he?' He almost shrieked.

I had only slid the chair a little farther back, reaching behind me to tap on the leather of the screen, but he jumped like a rat.

'No. Please attend to me, Mr. Turpin.' She turned in her chair and faced him with his back to the door. It was an old and sordid little piece of scheming that she forced from him—his plea for the new cow-shed at his landlady's expense, that he might with the covered manure pay his next year's rent out of the valuation after, as she made clear, he had bled the enriched pastures to the bone. I could not but admire the intensity of his greed, when I saw him outfacing for its sake whatever terror it was that ran wet on his forehead.

I ceased to tap the leather—was, indeed, calculating the cost of the shed—when I felt my relaxed hand taken and turned softly between the soft hands of a child. So at last I had triumphed. In a moment I would turn and acquaint myself with those quick-footed wanderers. . . .

The little brushing kiss fell in the centre of my palm—as a gift on which the fingers were, once, expected, to close: as the all-faithful, half-reproachful signal of a waiting child not used to neglect even when grown-ups were busiest—a fragment of the mute code devised very long ago.

Then I knew. And it was as though I had known from the first day when I looked across the lawn at the high window.

I heard the door shut. The woman turned to me in silence, and I felt that she knew.

What time passed after this I cannot say. I was roused by the fall of a log, and mechanically rose to put it back. Then I returned to my place in the chair very close to the screen.

'Now you understand,' she whispered, across the packed shadows.

'Yes, I understand—now. Thank you.'

'I—I only hear them.' She bowed her head in her hands. 'I have no right, you know—no other right. I have neither borne nor lost—neither borne nor lost!'

'Be very glad then,' said I, for my soul was torn open within me.

'Forgive me!'

She was still, and I went back to my sorrow and my joy.

'It was because I loved them so,' she said at last, brokenly. '*That* was why it was, even from the first—even before I knew that they—they were all I should ever have. And I loved them so!'

She stretched out her arms to the shadows and the shadows within the shadow.

'They came because I loved them—because I needed them. I—I must have made them come. Was that wrong, think you?'

'No—no.'

'I—I grant you that the toys and—and all that sort of thing were nonsense, but—but I used to so hate empty rooms myself when I was little.' She pointed to the gallery. 'And the passages all empty. . . . And how could I ever bear the garden door shut? Suppose——'

'Don't! For pity's sake, don't!' I cried. The twilight had brought a cold rain with gusty squalls that plucked at the leaded windows.

'And the same thing with keeping the fire in all night. *I* don't think it so foolish—do you?'

I looked at the broad brick hearth, saw, through tears, I believe, that there was no unpassable iron on or near it, and bowed my head.

'I did all that and lots of other things—just to make believe. Then they came. I heard them, but I didn't know that they were not mine by right till Mrs. Madden told me——'

'The butler's wife? What?'

'One of them—I heard—she saw. And knew Hers! *Not* for me. I didn't know at first. Perhaps I was jealous. Afterwards, I began to understand that it was only because I loved them, not because—— . . . Oh, you *must* bear or lose,' she said piteously. 'There is no other way—and yet they love me. They must! Don't they?'

There was no sound in the room except the lapping voices of the fire, but we two listened intently, and she at least took comfort from what she heard. She recovered herself and half rose. I sat still in my chair by the screen.

'Don't think me a wretch to whine about myself like this, but—but I'm all in the dark, you know, and *you* can see.'

In truth I could see, and my vision confirmed me in my resolve, though that was like the very parting of spirit and flesh. Yet a little longer I would stay since it was the last time.

'You think it is wrong, then?' she cried sharply, though I had said nothing.

'Not for you. A thousand times no. For you it is right. . . . I am grateful to you beyond words. For me it would be wrong. For me only. . . .'

'Why?' she said, but passed her hand before her face as she had done at our second meeting in the wood. 'Oh, I see,' she went on simply as a child. 'For you it would be wrong.' Then with a little indrawn laugh, 'And, d'you remember, I called you lucky—once—at first. You who must never come here again!'

She left me to sit a little longer by the screen, and I heard the sound of her feet die out along the gallery above.

REGULUS

(1908)

Regulus, a Roman general, defeated the Cartha-
ginians 256 B.C., but was next year defeated and
taken prisoner by the Carthaginians, who sent him to
Rome with an embassy to ask for peace or an ex-
change of prisoners. Regulus strongly advised the
Roman Senate to make no terms with the enemy. He
then returned to Carthage and was put to death.

The Fifth Form had been dragged several times in its collective life, from one end of the school Horace to the other.
Those were the years when Army examiners gave thousands of marks for Latin, and it was Mr. King's hated business to defeat them.

Hear him, then, on a raw November morning at second
lesson.

'Aha!' he began, rubbing his hands. '*Cras ingens itera-*
bimus aequor. Our portion to-day is the Fifth Ode of the
Third Book, I believe—concerning one Regulus, a gentleman. And how often have we been through it?'

'Twice, sir,' said Malpass, head of the Form.

Mr. King shuddered. 'Yes, twice, quite literally,' he said.
'To-day, with an eye to your Army *viva-voce* examinations
—ugh!—I shall exact somewhat freer and more florid rendi-
tions. With feeling and comprehension if that be possible.
I except'—here his eye swept the back benches—'our friend
and companion Beetle, from whom, now as always, I demand an absolutely literal translation.' The form laughed
subserviently.

'Spare his blushes! Beetle charms us first.'

Beetle stood up, confident in the possession of a guaranteed construe, left behind by M'Turk, who had that day gone into the sick-house with a cold. Yet he was too wary a hand to show confidence.

'*Credidimus*, we—believe—we have believed,' he opened in hesitating slow time, '*tonantem Fovem*, thundering Jove —*regnare*, to reign—*caelo*, in heaven. *Augustus*, Augustus —*habebitur*, will be held or considered—*praesens divus*, a present God—*adjectis Britannis*, the Britons being added— *imperio*, to the Empire—*gravibusque Persis*, with the heavy —er, stern Persians.'

'What?'

'The grave or stern Persians.' Beetle pulled up with the 'Thank-God-I-have-done-my-duty' air of Nelson in the cockpit.

'I am quite aware,' said King, 'that the first stanza is about the extent of your knowledge, but continue, sweet one, continue. *Gravibus*, by the way, is usually translated as "troublesome." '

Beetle drew a long and tortured breath. The second stanza (which carries over to the third) of that Ode is what is technically called a 'stinker.' But M'Turk had done him handsomely.

'*Milesne Crassi*, had—has the soldier of Crassus—*vixit*, lived—*turpis maritus*, a disgraceful husband——'

'You slurred the quantity of the word after *turpis*,' said King. 'Let's hear it.'

Beetle guessed again, and for a wonder hit the correct quantity. 'Er—a disgraceful husband—*conjuge barbara*, with a barbarous spouse.'

'Why do you select *that* disgustful equivalent out of all the dictionary?' King snapped. 'Isn't "wife" good enough for you?'

'Yes, sir. But what do I do about this bracket, sir? Shall I take it now?'

'Confine yourself at present to the soldier of Crassus.'

'Yes, sir. *Et*, and—*consenuit*, has he grown old—*in armis*, in the—er—arms—*hostium socerorum,* of his father-in-law's enemies.'

'Who? How? Which?'

'Arms of his enemies' fathers-in-law, sir.'

'Tha-anks. By the way, what meaning might you attach to *in armis?*'

'Oh, weapons—weapons of war, sir.' There was a virginal note in Beetle's voice as though he had been falsely accused of uttering indecencies. 'Shall I take the bracket now, sir?'

'Since it seems to be troubling you.'

'*Pro Curia,* O for the Senate House—*inversique mores,* and manners upset—upside down.'

'Ve-ry like your translation. Meantime, the soldier of Crassus?'

'*Sub rege Medo,* under a Median King—*Marsus et Apulus,* he being a Marsian and an Apulian.'

'Who? The Median King?'

'No, sir. The soldier of Crassus. *Oblittus* agrees with *milesne Crassi,* sir,' volunteered too hasty Beetle.

'Does it? It doesn't with *me.*'

'*Oh-blight-us,*' Beetle corrected hastily, 'forgetful—*anciliorum,* of the shields, or trophies—*et nominis,* and the—his name—*et togae,* and the toga—*eternaeque Vestae,* and eternal Vesta—*incolumi Jove,* Jove being safe—*et urbe Roma,* and the Roman city.' With an air of hardly restrained zeal —'Shall I go on, sir?'

Mr. King winced. 'No, thank you. You have indeed given us a translation! May I ask if it conveys any meaning whatever to your so-called mind?'

'Oh, I think so, sir.' This with gentle toleration for Horace and all his works.

'We envy you. Sit down.'

Beetle sat down relieved, well knowing that a reef of uncharted genitives stretched ahead of him, on which in spite of M'Turk's sailing-directions he would infallibly have been wrecked.

Rattray, who took up the task, steered neatly through them and came unscathed to port.

'Here we require drama,' said King. 'Regulus himself is speaking now. Who shall represent the provident-minded Regulus? Winton, will you kindly oblige?'

Winton of King's House, a long, heavy, towheaded Second Fifteen forward, overdue for his First Fifteen colours, and in aspect like an earnest, elderly horse, rose up, and announced, among other things, that he had seen 'signs affixed to Punic deluges.' Half the Form shouted for joy, and the other half for joy that there was something to shout about.

Mr. King opened and shut his eyes with great swiftness. 'Signa adfixa delubris,' he gasped. 'So *delubris* is "deluges" is it? Winton, in all our dealings, have I ever suspected you of a jest?'

'No, sir,' said the rigid and angular Winton, while the Form rocked about him.

'And yet you assert *delubris* means "deluges." Whether I am a fit subject for such a jape is, of course, a matter of opinion, but. . . . Winton, you are normally conscientious. May we assume you looked out *delubris*?'

'No, sir.' Winton was privileged to speak that truth dangerous to all who stand before Kings.

' 'Made a shot at it then?'

Every line of Winton's body showed he had done nothing of the sort. Indeed, the very idea that 'Pater' Winton (and a boy is not called 'Pater' by companions for his frivolity) would make a shot at anything was beyond belief. But he replied, 'Yes,' and all the while worked with his right heel as though he were heeling a ball at punt-about.

Though none dared to boast of being a favourite with King, the taciturn, three-cornered Winton stood high in his House-Master's opinion. It seemed to save him neither rebuke nor punishment, but the two were in some fashion sympathetic.

'Hm!' said King drily. 'I was going to say—*Flagitio additis damnum,* but I think—I think I see the process. Beetle, the translation of *delubris*, please.'

Beetle raised his head from his shaking arm long enough to answer: 'Ruins, sir.'

There was an impressive pause while King checked off crimes on his fingers. Then to Beetle the much-enduring man addressed winged words:

'Guessing,' said he. 'Guessing, Beetle, as usual, from the look of *delubris* that it bore some relation to *diluvium* or deluge, you imparted the result of your half-baked lucubrations to Winton who seems to have been lost enough to have accepted it. Observing next, your companion's fall, from the presumed security of your undistinguished position in the rear-guard, you took another pot-shot. The turbid chaos of your mind threw up some memory of the word "dilapidations" which you have pitifully attempted to disguise under the synonym of "ruins." '

As this was precisely what Beetle had done he looked hurt but forgiving. 'We will attend to this later,' said King. 'Go on, Winton, and retrieve yourself.'

Delubris happened to be the one word which Winton had not looked out and had asked Beetle for, when they were settling into their places. He forged ahead with no further trouble. Only when he rendered *scilicet* as 'forsooth,' King erupted.

'Regulus,' he said, 'was not a leader-writer for the penny press, nor, for that matter, was Horace. Regulus says: "The soldier ransomed by gold will come keener for the fight—will he by—by gum!" *That's* the meaning of *scilicet*. It indicates contempt—bitter contempt. "Forsooth," forsooth! You'll be talking about "speckled beauties" and "eventually transpire" next. Howell, what do you make of that doubled "Vidi ego—ego vidi"? It wasn't put in to fill up the metre, you know.'

'Isn't it intensive, sir?' said Howell, afflicted by a genuine interest in what he read. 'Regulus was a bit in earnest about Rome making no terms with Carthage—and he wanted to let the Romans understand it, didn't he, sir?'

'Less than your usual grace, but the fact. Regulus *was* in earnest. He was also engaged at the same time in cutting his own throat with every word he uttered. He knew Carthage which (your examiners won't ask you this so you needn't take notes) was a sort of God-forsaken nigger Manchester. Regulus was not thinking about his own life. He was telling Rome the truth. He was playing for his side. Those lines from the eighteenth to the fortieth ought to be written in blood. Yet there are things in human garments which will tell you that Horace was a flaneur—a man about town. Avoid such beings. Horace knew a very great deal. *He* knew! *Erit ille fortis*—"will he be brave who once to faithless foes has knelt?" And again (stop pawing with your hooves, Thornton!) *hic unde vitam sumeret inscius.* That means roughly—but I perceive I am ahead of my translators. Begin at *hic unde,* Vernon, and let us see if you have the spirit of Regulus.'

Now no one expected fireworks from gentle Paddy Vernon, sub-prefect of Hartopp's House, but, as must often be the case with growing boys, his mind was in abeyance for the time being, and he said, all in a rush, on behalf of Regulus: *'O magna Carthago probrosis altior Italiae ruinis,* O Carthage, thou wilt stand forth higher than the ruins of Italy.'

Even Beetle, most lenient of critics, was interested at this point, though he did not join the half-groan of reprobation from the wiser heads of the Form.

'Please don't mind me,' said King, and Vernon very kindly did not. He ploughed on thus: 'He (Regulus) is related to have removed from himself the kiss of the shameful wife and of his small children as less by the head, and, being stern, to have placed his virile visage on the ground.'

Since King loved 'virile' about as much as he did 'spouse' or 'forsooth' the Form looked up hopefully. But Jove thundered not.

'Until,' Vernon continued, 'he should have confirmed the sliding fathers as being the author of counsel never given under an alias.'

He stopped, conscious of stillness round him like the dread calm of the typhoon's centre. King's opening voice was sweeter than honey.

'I am painfully aware by bitter experience that I cannot give you any idea of the passion, the power, the—the essential guts of the lines which you have so foully outraged in our presence. But——' the note changed, 'so far as in me lies, I will strive to bring home to you, Vernon, the fact that there exist in Latin a few pitiful rules of grammar, of syntax, nay, even of declension, which were not created for your incult sport—your Bœotian diversion. You will, therefore, Vernon, write out and bring to me to-morrow a word-for-word English-Latin translation of the Ode, together with a full list of all adjectives—an adjective is not a verb, Vernon, as the Lower Third will tell you—all adjectives, their number, case, and gender. Even now I haven't begun to deal with you faithfully.'

'I—I'm very sorry, sir,' Vernon stammered.

'You mistake the symptoms, Vernon. You are possibly discomfited by the imposition, but sorrow postulates some sort of mind, intellect, *nous*. Your rendering of *probrosis* alone stamps you as lower than the beasts of the field. Will some one take the taste out of our mouths? And—talking of tastes——' He coughed. There was a distinct flavour of chlorine gas in the air. Up went an eyebrow, though King knew perfectly well what it meant.

'Mr. Hartopp's st—science class next door,' said Malpass.

'Oh yes. I had forgotten. Our newly established Modern Side, of course. Perowne, open the windows; and Winton, go on once more from *interque maerentes*.'

'And hastened away,' said Winton, 'surrounded by his mourning friends, into—into illustrious banishment. But I got that out of Conington, sir,' he added in one conscientious breath.

'I am aware. The master generally knows his ass's crib, though I acquit *you* of any intention that way. Can you suggest anything for *egregius exul*? Only "egregious exile"? I fear "egregious" is a good word ruined. No! You can't in this case improve on Conington. Now then for *atqui sciebat quae sibi barbarus tortor pararet*. The whole force of it lies in the *atqui*.'

'Although he knew,' Winton suggested.

'Stronger than that, I think.'

'He who knew well,' Malpass interpolated.

'Ye-es. "Well though he knew." I don't like Conington's "well-witting." It's Wardour Street.'

'Well though he knew what the savage torturer was—was getting ready for him,' said Winton.

'Ye-es. Had in store for him.'

'Yet he brushed aside his kinsmen and the people delaying his return.'

'Ye-es; but then how do you render *obstantes?*'

'If it's a free translation mightn't *obstantes* and *morantem* come to about the same thing, sir?'

'Nothing comes to "about the same thing" with Horace, Winton. As I have said, Horace was not a journalist. No, I take it that his kinsmen bodily withstood his departure, whereas the crowd—*populumque*—the democracy stood about futilely pitying him and getting in the way. Now for that noblest of endings—*quam si clientum,*' and King ran off into the quotation:

> 'As though some tedious business o'er
> Of clients' court, his journey lay
> Towards Venafrum's grassy floor
> Or Sparta-built Tarentum's bay.

All right, Winton. Beetle, when you've quite finished dodging the fresh air yonder, give me the meaning of *tendens*—and turn down your collar.'

'Me, sir? *Tendens,* sir? Oh! Stretching away in the direction of, sir.'

'Idiot! Regulus was not a feature of the landscape. He was a man, self-doomed to death by torture. *Atqui sciebat* —knowing it—having achieved it for his country's sake— can't you hear that *atqui* cut like a knife?—he moved off with some dignity. That is why Horace out of the whole golden Latin tongue chose the one word "tendens"—which is utterly untranslatable.'

The gross injustice of being asked to translate it, converted Beetle into a young Christian martyr, till King buried his nose in his handkerchief again.

'I think they've broken another gas-bottle next door, sir,' said Howell. 'They're always doing it.' The Form coughed as more chlorine came in.

'Well, I suppose we must be patient with the Modern Side,' said King. 'But it is almost insupportable for this Side. Vernon, what are you grinning at?'

Vernon's mind had returned to him glowing and inspired. He chuckled as he underlined his Horace.

'It appears to amuse you,' said King. 'Let us participate. What is it?'

'The last two lines of the Tenth Ode, in this book, sir,' was Vernon's amazing reply.

'What? Oh, I see. *Non hoc semper erit liminis aut aquae caelestis patiens latus.*'[1] King's mouth twitched to hide a grin. 'Was that done with intention?'

'I—I thought it fitted, sir.'

'It does. It's distinctly happy. What put it into your thick head, Paddy?'

'I don't know, sir, except we did the Ode last term.'

'And you remembered? The same head that minted *probrosis* as a verb! Vernon, you are an enigma. No! This Side will *not* always be patient of unheavenly gases and waters. I will make representations to our so-called Moderns. Meantime (who shall say I am not just?) I remit you your accrued pains and penalties in regard to *probrosim, probrosis, probrosit* and other enormities. I oughtn't to do it, but this Side is occasionally human. By no means bad, Paddy.'

'Thank you, sir,' said Vernon, wondering how inspiration had visited him.

[1] 'This side will not always be patient of rain and waiting on the threshold.'

Then King, with a few brisk remarks about Science, headed them back to Regulus, of whom and of Horace and Rome and evil-minded commercial Carthage and of the democracy eternally futile, he explained, in all ages and climes, he spoke for ten minutes; passing thence to the next Ode—*Delicta majorum*—where he fetched up, full-voiced, upon—'*Dis te minorem quod geris imperas*' (Thou rulest because thou bearest thyself as lower than the Gods) —making it a text for a discourse on manners, morals, and respect for authority as distinct from bottled gases, which lasted till the bell rang. Then Beetle, concertinaing his books, observed to Winton, 'When King's really on tap he's an interestin' dog. Hartopp's chlorine uncorked him.'

'Yes; but why did you tell me *delubris* was "deluges," you silly ass?' said Winton.

'Well, that uncorked him too. Look out, you hoof-handed old owl!' Winton had cleared for action as the Form poured out like puppies at play and was scragging Beetle. Stalky from behind collared Winton low. The three fell in confusion.

'*Dis te minorem quod geris imperas*,' quoth Stalky, ruffling Winton's lint-white locks. ' 'Mustn't jape with Number Five study. Don't be too virtuous. Don't brood over it. 'Twon't count against you in your future caree-ah. Cheer up, Pater.'

'Pull him off my—er—essential guts, will you?' said Beetle from beneath. 'He's squashin' 'em.'

They dispersed to their studies.

. . . . .

No one, the owner least of all, can explain what is in a growing boy's mind. It might have been the blind ferment of adolescence; Stalky's random remarks about virtue might have stirred him; like his betters he might have sought popularity by way of clowning; or, as the Head asserted years later, the only known jest of his serious life might have worked on him, as a sober-sided man's one love colours and dislocates all his after days. But, at the next lesson, mechanical drawing with Mr. Lidgett who as draw-ing-master had very limited powers of punishment, Winton fell suddenly from grace and let loose a live mouse in the form-room. The whole form, shrieking and leaping high, threw at it all the plaster cones, pyramids, and fruit in high relief—not to mention ink-pots—that they could lay hands on. Mr. Lidgett reported at once to the Head; Winton owned up to his crime, which, venial in the Upper Third, pardonable at a price in the Lower Fourth, was, of course, rank ruffianism on the part of a Fifth Form boy; and so, by graduated stages, he arrived at the Head's study just before lunch, penitent, perturbed, annoyed with himself and—as the Head said to King in the corridor after the meal—more human than he had known him in seven years.

'You see,' the Head drawled on, 'Winton's only fault is a certain costive and unaccommodating virtue. So this comes very happily.'

'I've never noticed any sign of it,' said King. Winton was in King's House, and though King as pro-consul might, and did, infernally oppress his own Province, once a black and yellow cap was in trouble at the hands of the Imperial authority King fought for him to the very last steps of Caesar's throne.

'Well, you yourself admitted just now that a mouse was beneath the occasion,' the Head answered.

'It was.' Mr. King did not love Mr. Lidgett. 'It should have been a rat. But—but—I hate to plead it—it's the lad's first offence.'

'Could you have damned him more completely, King?'

'Hm. What is the penalty?' said King, in retreat, but keeping up a rear-guard action.

'Only my usual few lines of Virgil to be shown up by tea-time.'

The Head's eyes turned slightly to that end of the cor-ridor where Mullins, Captain of the Games ('Pot,' 'old Pot,' or 'Potiphar' Mullins), was pinning up the usual Wednes-day notice—'Big, Middle, and Little Side Football—A to K, L to Z, 3 to 4.45 P.M.

You cannot write out the Head's usual few (which means five hundred) Latin lines and play football for one hour and three-quarters between the hours of 1.30 and 5 P.M. Winton had evidently no intention of trying to do so, for he hung about the corridor with a set face and an uneasy foot. Yet it was law in the school, compared with which that of the Medes and Persians was no more than a non-committal resolution, that any boy, outside the First Fifteen, who missed his football for any reason whatever, and had not a written excuse, duly signed by competent authority to explain his absence, would receive not less than three strokes with a ground-ash from the Captain of the Games, generally a youth between seventeen and eighteen years, rarely under eleven stone ('Pot' was nearer thirteen), and always in hard condition.

King knew without inquiry that the Head had given Winton no such excuse.

'But he is practically a member of the First Fifteen. He has played for it all this term,' said King. 'I believe his Cap should have arrived last week.'

'His Cap has not been given him. Officially, therefore, he is naught. I rely on old Pot.'

'But Mullins is Winton's study-mate,' King persisted.

Pot Mullins and Pater Winton were cousins and rather close friends.

'That will make no difference to Mullins—or Winton, if I know 'em,' said the Head.

'But—but,' King played his last card desperately, 'I was going to recommend Winton for extra sub-prefect in my House, now Carton has gone.'

'Certainly,' said the Head. 'Why not? He will be excellent by tea-time, I hope.'

At that moment they saw Mr. Lidgett, tripping down the corridor, waylaid by Winton.

'It's about that mouse-business at mechanical drawing,' Winton opened, swinging across his path.

'Yes, yes, highly disgraceful,' Mr. Lidgett panted.

'I know it was,' said Winton. 'It—it was a cad's trick because——'

'Because you knew I couldn't give you more than fifty lines,' said Mr. Lidgett.

'Well, anyhow I've come to apologise for it.'

'Certainly,' said Mr. Lidgett, and added, for he was a kindly man, 'I think that shows quite right feeling. I'll tell the Head at once I'm satisfied.'

'No—no!' The boy's still unmended voice jumped from the growl to the squeak. 'I didn't mean *that!* I—I did it on principle. Please don't—er—do anything of that kind.'

Mr. Lidgett looked him up and down and, being an artist, understood.

'Thank you, Winton,' he said. 'This shall be between ourselves.'

'You heard?' said King, indecent pride in his voice.

'Of course. You thought he was going to get Lidgett to beg him off the impot.'

King denied this with so much warmth that the Head laughed and King went away in a huff.

'By the way,' said the Head, 'I've told Winton to do his lines in your form-room—not in his study.'

'Thanks,' said King over his shoulder, for the Head's orders had saved Winton and Mullins, who was doing extra Army work in the study, from an embarrassing afternoon together.

An hour later, King wandered into his still form-room as though by accident. Winton was hard at work.

'Aha!' said King, rubbing his hands. 'This does not look like games, Winton. Don't let me arrest your facile pen. Whence this sudden love for Virgil?'

'Impot from the Head, sir, for that mouse-business this morning.'

'Rumours thereof have reached us. That was a lapse on your part into Lower Thirdery which I don't quite understand.'

The 'tump-tump' of the puntabouts before the sides settled to games came through the open window. Winton, like his House-master, loved fresh air. Then they heard Paddy Vernon, sub-prefect on duty, calling the roll in the field and marking defaulters. Winton wrote steadily. King curled himself up on a desk, hands round knees. One would have said that the man was gloating over the boy's misfortune, but the boy understood.

'*Dis te minorem quod geris imperas,*' King quoted presently. 'It is necessary to bear oneself as lower than the local gods—even than drawing-masters who are precluded from effective retaliation. I *do* wish you'd tried that mouse-game with me, Pater.'

Winton grinned; then sobered. 'It was a cad's trick, sir, to play on Mr. Lidgett.' He peered forward at the page he was copying.

'Well, "the sin *I* impute to each frustrate ghost"——' King stopped himself. 'Why do you goggle like an owl? Hand me the Mantuan and I'll dictate. No matter. Any rich Virgilian measures will serve. I may peradventure recall a few.' He began:

'Tu regere imperio populos Romane memento
Hae tibi erunt artes pacisque imponere morem,
Parcere subjectis et debellare superbos.

There you have it all, Winton. Write that out twice and yet once again.'

For the next forty minutes, with never a glance at the book, King paid out the glorious hexameters (and King could read Latin as though it were alive), Winton hauling them in and coiling them away behind him as trimmers in a telegraph-ship's hold coil away deep-sea cable. King broke from the Aeneid to the Georgics and back again, pausing now and then to translate some specially loved line or to dwell on the treble-shot texture of the ancient fabric. He did not allude to the coming interview with Mullins except at the last, when he said, 'I think at this juncture, Pater, I need not ask you for the precise significance of *atqui sciebat quae sibi barbarus tortor.*'

The ungrateful Winton flushed angrily, and King loafed

out to take five o'clock call-over, after which he invited little Hartopp to tea and a talk on chlorine-gas. Hartopp accepted the challenge like a bantam, and the two went up to King's study about the same time as Winton returned to the form-room beneath it to finish his lines.

Then half a dozen of the Second Fifteen who should have been washing strolled in to condole with 'Pater' Winton, whose misfortune and its consequences were common talk. No one was more sincere than the long, red-headed, knotty-knuckled 'Paddy' Vernon, but, being a careless animal, he joggled Winton's desk.

'Curse you for a silly ass!' said Winton. 'Don't do that.'

No one is expected to be polite while under punishment, so Vernon, sinking his sub-prefectship, replied peacefully enough:

'Well, don't be wrathy, Pater.'

'I'm not,' said Winton. 'Get out! This ain't your House form-room.'

' 'Form-room don't belong to you. Why don't you go to your own study?' Vernon replied.

'Because Mullins is there waitin' for the victim,' said Stalky delicately, and they all laughed. 'You ought to have shaken that mouse out of your trouser-leg, Pater. That's the way *I* did in my youth. Pater's revertin' to his second childhood. Never mind, Pater, we all respect you and your future caree-ah.'

Winton, still writhing, growled. Vernon leaning on the desk somehow shook it again. Then he laughed.

'What are you grinning at?' Winton asked.

'I was only thinkin' of *you* being sent up to take a lickin' from Pot. I swear I don't think it's fair. You've never shirked a game in your life, and you're as good as in the First Fifteen already. Your Cap ought to have been delivered last week, oughtn't it?'

It was law in the school that no man could by any means enjoy the privileges and immunities of the First Fifteen till the black velvet cap with the gold tassel, made by dilatory Exeter outfitters, had been actually set on his head. Ages ago, a large-built and unruly Second Fifteen had attempted to change this law, but the prefects of that age were still larger, and the lively experiment had never been repeated.

'Will you,' said Winton very slowly, 'kindly mind your own damned business, you cursed, clumsy, fat-headed fool?'

The form-room was as silent as the empty field in the darkness outside. Vernon shifted his feet uneasily.

'Well, *I* shouldn't like to take a lickin' from Pot,' he said.

'Wouldn't you?' Winton asked, as he paged the sheets of lines with hands that shook.

'No, I shouldn't,' said Vernon, his freckles growing more distinct on the bridge of his white nose.

'Well, I'm going to take it'—Winton moved clear of the desk as he spoke. 'But *you're* going to take a lickin' from me first.' Before any one realised it, he had flung himself neighing against Vernon. No decencies were observed on either side, and the rest looked on amazed. The two met confusedly, Vernon trying to do what he could with his longer reach; Winton, insensible to blows, only concerned to drive his enemy into a corner and batter him to pulp. This he managed over against the fireplace, where Vernon dropped half-stunned. 'Now I'm going to give you your lickin',' said Winton. 'Lie there till I get a ground-ash and I'll cut you to pieces. If you move, I'll chuck you out of the window.' He wound his hands into the boy's collar and waistband, and had actually heaved him half off the ground before the others with one accord dropped on his head, shoulders, and legs. He fought them crazily in an awful hissing silence. Stalky's sensitive nose was rubbed along the floor; Beetle received a jolt in the wind that sent him whistling and crowing against the wall; Perowne's forehead was cut, and Malpass came out with an eye that explained itself like a dying rainbow through a whole week.

'Mad! Quite mad!' said Stalky, and for the third time wriggled back to Winton's throat. The door opened and King came in, Hartopp's little figure just behind him. The mound on the floor panted and heaved but did not rise, for

Winton still squirmed vengefully. 'Only a little play, sir,' said Perowne. ''Only hit my head against a form.' This was quite true.

'Oh,' said King. '*Dimovit obstantes propinquos.* You, I presume, are the *populus* delaying Winton's return to— Mullins, eh?'

'No, sir,' said Stalky behind his claret-coloured handkerchief. 'We're the *maerentes amicos.*'

'Not bad! You see, some of it sticks after all,' King chuckled to Hartopp, and the two masters left without further inquiries.

The boys sat still on the now passive Winton.

'Well,' said Stalky at last, 'of all the putrid he-asses, Pater, you are *the*——'

'I'm sorry. I'm awfully sorry,' Winton began, and they let him rise. He held out his hand to the bruised and bewildered Vernon. 'Sorry, Paddy. I—I must have lost my temper. I—I don't know what's the matter with me.'

''Fat lot of good that'll do my face at tea,' Vernon grunted. 'Why couldn't you say there was something wrong with you instead of lamming out like a lunatic? Is my lip puffy?'

'Just a trifle. Look at my beak! Well, we got all these pretty marks at footer—owin' to the zeal with which we played the game,' said Stalky, dusting himself. 'But d'you think you're fit to be let loose again, Pater? 'Sure you don't want to kill another sub-prefect? I wish *I* was Pot. I'd cut your sprightly young soul out.'

'I s'pose I ought to go to Pot now,' said Winton.

'And let all the other asses see you lookin' like this! Not much. We'll all come up to Number Five Study and wash off in hot water. Beetle, you aren't damaged. Go along and light the gas-stove.'

'There's a tin of cocoa in my study somewhere,' Perowne shouted after him. 'Rootle round till you find it, and take it up.'

Separately, by different roads, Vernon's jersey pulled half over his head, the boys repaired to Number Five

Study. Little Hartopp and King, I am sorry to say, leaned over the banisters of King's landing and watched.

'Ve-ry human,' said little Hartopp. 'Your virtuous Winton, having got himself into trouble, takes it out of my poor old Paddy. I wonder what precise lie Paddy will tell about his face.'

'But surely you aren't going to embarrass him by asking?' said King.

'*Your* boy won,' said Hartopp.

'To go back to what we were discussing,' said King quickly, 'do you pretend that your modern system of inculcating unrelated facts about chlorine, for instance, all of which may be proved fallacies by the time the boys grow up, can have any real bearing on education—even the low type of it that examiners expect?'

'I maintain nothing. But is it any worse than your Chinese reiteration of uncomprehended syllables in a dead tongue?'

'Dead, forsooth!' King fairly danced. 'The only living tongue on earth! Chinese! On my word, Hartopp!'

'And at the end of seven years—how often have I said it?' Hartopp went on,—'seven years of two hundred and twenty days of six hours each, your victims go away with nothing, absolutely nothing, except, perhaps, if they've been very attentive, a dozen—no, I'll grant you twenty—one score of totally unrelated Latin tags which any child of twelve could have absorbed in two terms.'

'But—but can't you realise that if our system brings later —at any rate—at a pinch—a simple understanding—grammar and Latinity apart—a mere glimpse of the significance (foul word!) of, we'll say, one Ode of Horace, one twenty lines of Virgil, we've got what we poor devils of ushers are striving after?'

'And what might that be?' said Hartopp.

'Balance, proportion, perspective—life. Your scientific man is the unrelated animal—the beast without background. Haven't you ever realised *that* in your atmosphere of stinks?'

'Meantime you make them lose life for the sake of living, eh?'

'Blind again, Hartopp! I told you about Paddy's quotation this morning. (But he made *probrosis* a verb, he did!) You yourself heard young Corkran's reference to *maerentes amicos*. It sticks—a little of it sticks among the barbarians.'

'Absolutely and essentially Chinese,' said little Hartopp, who, alone of the common-room, refused to be outfaced by King. 'But I don't yet understand how Paddy came to be licked by Winton. Paddy's supposed to be something of a boxer.'

'Beware of vinegar made from honey,' King replied. 'Pater, like some other people, is patient and long-suffering, but he has his limits. The Head is oppressing him damnably, too. As I pointed out, the boy has practically been in the First Fifteen since term began.'

'But, my dear fellow, I've known you give a boy an impot and refuse him leave off games, again and again.'

'Ah, but that was when there was real need to get at some oaf who couldn't be sensitised in any other way. Now, in our esteemed Head's action I see nothing but——'

The conversation from this point does not concern us.

Meantime Winton, very penitent and especially polite towards Vernon, was being cheered with cocoa in Number Five Study. They had some difficulty in stemming the flood of his apologies. He himself pointed out to Vernon that he had attacked a sub-prefect for no reason whatever, and, therefore, deserved official punishment.

'I can't think what was the matter with me to-day,' he mourned. 'Ever since that blasted mouse business——'

'Well, then, don't think,' said Stalky. 'Or do you want Paddy to make a row about it before all the school?'

Here Vernon was understood to say that he would see Winton and all the school somewhere else.

'And if you imagine Perowne and Malpass and me are goin' to give evidence at a prefects' meeting just to soothe your beastly conscience, you jolly well err,' said Beetle. 'I know what you did.'

'What?' croaked Pater, out of the valley of his humiliation.

'You went Berserk. I've read all about it in *Hypatia*.'

'What's "going Berserk"?' Winton asked.

'Never you mind,' was the reply. 'Now, don't you feel awfully weak and seedy?'

'I *am* rather tired,' said Winton, sighing.

'That's what you ought to be. You've gone Berserk and pretty soon you'll go to sleep. But you'll probably be liable to fits of it all your life,' Beetle concluded. ' 'Shouldn't wonder if you murdered some one some day.'

'Shut up—you and your Berserks!' said Stalky. 'Go to Mullins now and get it over, Pater.'

'I call it filthy unjust of the Head,' said Vernon. 'Anyhow, you've given me my lickin', old man. I hope Pot'll give you yours.'

'I'm awfully sorry—awfully sorry,' was Winton's last word.

It was the custom in that consulship to deal with games' defaulters between five o'clock call-over and tea. Mullins, who was old enough to pity, did not believe in letting boys wait through the night till the chill of the next morning for their punishments. He was finishing off the last of the small fry and their excuses when Winton arrived.

'But, please, Mullins'—this was Babcock tertius, a dear little twelve-year-old mother's darling—'I had an awful hack on the knee. I've been to the Matron about it and she gave me some iodine. I've been rubbing it in all day. I thought that would be an excuse off.'

'Let's have a look at it,' said the impassive Mullins. 'That's a shin-bruise—about a week old. Touch your toes. I'll give you the iodine.'

Babcock yelled loudly as he had many times before. The face of Jevons, aged eleven, a new boy that dark wet term, low in the House, low in the Lower School, and lowest of all in his homesick little mind, turned white at the horror of the sight. They could hear his working lips part stickily as Babcock wailed his way out of hearing.

'Hullo, Jevons! What brings you here?' said Mullins.

'Pl-ease, sir, I went for a walk with Babcock tertius.'

'Did you? Then I bet you went to the tuckshop—and you paid, didn't you?'

A nod. Jevons was too terrified to speak.

'Of course, and I bet Babcock told you that old Pot 'ud let you off because it was the first time.'

Another nod with a ghost of a smile in it.

'All right.' Mullins picked Jevons up before he could guess what was coming, laid him on the table with one hand, with the other gave him three emphatic spanks, then held him high in air.

'Now you tell Babcock tertius that he's got you a licking from me, and see you jolly well pay it back to him. And when you're prefect of games don't you let any one shirk his footer without a written excuse. Where d'you play in your game?'

'Forward, sir.'

'You can do better than that. I've seen you run like a young buck-rabbit. Ask Dickson from me to try you as three-quarter next game, will you? Cut along.'

Jevons left, warm for the first time that day, enormously set up in his own esteem, and very hot against the deceitful Babcock.

Mullins turned to Winton. 'Your name's on the list, Pater.' Winton nodded.

'I know it. The Head landed me with an impot for that mouse-business at mechanical drawing. No excuse.'

'He meant it then?' Mullins jerked his head delicately towards the ground-ash on the table. 'I heard something about it.'

Winton nodded. 'A rotten thing to do,' he said. 'Can't think what I was doing ever to do it. It counts against a fellow so; and there's some more too——'

'All right, Pater. Just stand clear of our photobracket, will you?'

The little formality over, there was a pause. Winton swung round, yawned in Pot's astonished face and staggered towards the window-seat.

'What's the matter with you, Dick? Ill?'

'No. Perfectly all right, thanks. Only—only a little sleepy.' Winton stretched himself out, and then and there fell deeply and placidly asleep.

'It isn't a faint,' said the experienced Mullins, 'or his pulse wouldn't act. 'Tisn't a fit or he'd snort and twitch. It can't be sunstroke, this term, and he hasn't been over-training for anything.' He opened Winton's collar, packed a cushion under his head, threw a rug over him and sat down to listen to the regular breathing. Before long Stalky arrived, on pretence of borrowing a book. He looked at the window-seat.

''Noticed anything wrong with Winton lately?' said Mullins.

''Notice anything wrong with my beak?' Stalky replied. 'Pater went Berserk after call-over, and fell on a lot of us for jesting with him about his impot. You ought to see Malpass's eye.'

'You mean that Pater fought?' said Mullins.

'Like a devil. Then he nearly went to sleep in our study just now. I expect he'll be all right when he wakes up. Rummy business! Conscientious old bargee. You ought to have heard his apologies.'

'But Pater can't fight one little bit,' Mullins repeated.

''Twasn't fighting. He just tried to murder every one.' Stalky described the affair, and when he left Mullins went off to take counsel with the Head, who, out of a cloud of blue smoke, told him that all would yet be well.

'Winton,' said he, 'is a little stiff in his moral joints. He'll get over that. If he asks you whether to-day's doings will count against him in his——'

'But you know it's important to him, sir. His people aren't—very well off,' said Mullins.

'That's why I'm taking all this trouble. You must reassure him, Pot. I have overcrowded him with new experiences. Oh, by the way, has his Cap come?'

'It came at dinner, sir.' Mullins laughed.

Sure enough, when he waked at tea-time, Winton proposed to take Mullins all through every one of his day's lapses from grace, and 'Do you think it will count against me?' said he.

'Don't you fuss so much about yourself and your silly career,' said Mullins. 'You're all right. And oh—here's your First Cap at last. Shove it up on the bracket and come on to tea.'

They met King on their way, stepping statelily and rubbing his hands. 'I have applied,' said he, 'for the services of an additional sub-prefect in Carton's unlamented absence. Your name, Winton, seems to have found favour with the powers that be, and—and all things considered—I am disposed to give my support to the nomination. You are therefore a quasi-lictor.'

'Then it didn't count against me,' Winton gasped as soon as they were out of hearing.

A Captain of Games can jest with a sub-prefect publicly.

'You utter ass!' said Mullins, and caught him by the back of his stiff neck and ran him down to the hall where the sub-prefects, who sit below the salt, made him welcome with the economical bloater-paste of mid-term.

. . . . .

King and little Hartopp were sparring in the Reverend John Gillett's study at 10 P.M.—classical *versus* modern as usual.

'Character — proportion — background,' snarled King. 'That is the essence of the Humanities.'

'Analects of Confucius,' little Hartopp answered.

'Time,' said the Reverend John behind the soda-water. 'You men oppress me. Hartopp, what did you say to Paddy in your dormitories to-night? Even *you* couldn't have overlooked his face.'

'But I did,' said Hartopp calmly. 'I wasn't even humorous about it, as some clerics might have been. I went straight through and said naught.'

'Poor Paddy! Now, for my part,' said King, 'and you know I am not lavish in my praises, I consider Winton a first-class type; absolutely first-class.'

'Ha-ardly,' said the Reverend John. 'First-class of the second class, I admit. The very best type of second class but' —he shook his head—'it should have been a rat. Pater'll never be anything more than a Colonel of Engineers.'

'What do you base that verdict on?' said King stiffly.

'He came to me after prayers—with all his conscience.'

'Poor old Pater. Was it the mouse?' said little Hartopp.

'That, and what he called his uncontrollable temper, and his responsibilities as sub-prefect.'

'And you?'

'If we had had what is vulgarly called a pi-jaw he'd have had hysterics. So I recommended a dose of Epsom salts. He'll take it, too—conscientiously. Don't eat me, King. Perhaps he'll be a K.C.B.'

Ten o'clock struck and the Army class boys in the further studies coming to their houses after an hour's extra work passed along the gravel path below. Some one was chanting, to the tune of 'White sand and grey sand,' *Dis te minorem quod geris imperas*. He stopped outside Mullins' study. They heard Mullins' window slide up and then Stalky's voice:

'Ah! Good-evening, Mullins, my *barbarus tortor*. We're the waits. We have come to inquire after the local Berserk. Is he doin' as well as can be expected in his new caree-ah?'

'Better than you will, in a sec, Stalky,' Mullins grunted.

''Glad of that. We thought he'd like to know that Paddy has been carried to the sick-house in ravin' delirium. They think it's concussion of the brain.'

'Why, he was all right at prayers,' Winton began earnestly, and they heard a laugh in the background as Mullins slammed down the window.

''Night, Regulus,' Stalky sang out, and the light footsteps went on.

'You see. It sticks. A little of it sticks among the barbarians,' said King.

'Amen,' said the Reverend John. 'Go to bed.'

FRIENDLY BROOK

(MARCH 1914)

The valley was so choked with fog that one could scarcely
see a cow's length across a field. Every blade, twig,
bracken-frond, and hoof-print carried water, and the air
was filled with the noise of rushing ditches and field-drains,
all delivering to the brook below. A week's November rain
on water-logged land had gorged her to full flood, and she
proclaimed it aloud.

Two men in sackcloth aprons were considering an un-
trimmed hedge that ran down the hillside and disappeared
into mist beside those roarings. They stood back and took
stock of the neglected growth, tapped an elbow of hedge-
oak here, a mossed beech-stub there, swayed a stooled ash
back and forth, and looked at each other.

'I reckon she's about two rod thick,' said Jabez the
younger, 'an' she hasn't felt iron since—when has she,
Jesse?'

'Call it twenty-five year, Jabez, an' you won't be far out.'

'Umm!' Jabez rubbed his wet handbill on his wetter coat-
sleeve. 'She ain't a hedge. She's all manner o' trees. We'll
just about have to——' He paused, as professional etiquette
required.

'Just about have to side her up an' see what she'll bear.
But hadn't we best——?' Jesse paused in his turn, both men
being artists and equals.

'Get some kind o' line to go by.' Jabez ranged up and
down till he found a thinner place, and with clean snicks of
the handbill revealed the original face of the fence. Jesse
took over the dripping stuff as it fell forward, and, with a

grasp and a kick, made it to lie orderly on the bank till it should be faggoted.

By noon a length of unclean jungle had turned itself into a cattle-proof barrier, tufted here and there with little plumes of the sacred holly which no woodman touches without orders.

'Now we've a witness-board to go by!' said Jesse at last.

'She won't be as easy as this all along,' Jabez answered. 'She'll need plenty stakes and binders when we come to the brook.'

'Well, ain't we plenty?' Jesse pointed to the ragged perspective ahead of them that plunged downhill into the fog. 'I lay there's a cord an' a half o' firewood, let alone faggots, 'fore we get anywheres anigh the brook.'

'The brook's got up a piece since morning,' said Jabez. 'Sounds like's if she was over Wickenden's door-stones.'

Jesse listened, too. There was a growl in the brook's roar as though she worried something hard.

'Yes. She's over Wickenden's door-stones,' he replied. 'Now she'll flood acrost Alder Bay an' that'll ease her.'

'She won't ease Jim Wickenden's hay none if she do,' Jabez grunted. 'I told Jim he'd set that liddle hay-stack o' his too low down in the medder. I *told* him so when he was drawin' the bottom for it.'

'I told him so, too,' said Jesse. 'I told him 'fore ever you did. I told him when the County Council tarred the roads up along.' He pointed up-hill, where unseen automobiles and road-engines droned past continually. 'A tarred road, she shoots every drop o' water into a valley same's a slate roof. 'Tisn't as 'twas in the old days, when the waters soaked in and soaked out in the way o' nature. It rooshes off they tarred roads all of a lump, and naturally every drop is bound to descend into the valley. And there's tar roads both two sides this valley for ten mile. That's what I told Jim Wickenden when they tarred the roads last year. But he's a valley-man. He don't hardly ever journey up-hill.'

'What did he say when you told him that?' Jabez demanded, with a little change of voice.

'Why? What did he say to you when *you* told him?' was the answer.

'What he said to you, I reckon, Jesse.'

'Then, you don't need me to say it over again, Jabez.'

'Well, let be how 'twill, what was he gettin' *after* when he said what he said to me?' Jabez insisted.

'*I* dunno; unless you tell me what manner o' words he said to *you*.'

Jabez drew back from the hedge—all hedges are nests of treachery and eavesdropping—and moved to an open cattle-lodge in the centre of the field.

'No need to go ferretin' around,' said Jesse. 'None can't see us here 'fore we see them.'

'What was Jim Wickenden gettin' at when I said he'd set his stack too near anigh the brook?' Jabez dropped his voice. 'He was in his mind.'

'He ain't never been out of it yet to my knowledge,' Jesse drawled, and uncorked his teabottle.

'But then Jim says: "I ain't goin' to shift my stack a yard," he says. "The Brook's been good friends to me, and if she be minded," he says, "to take a snatch at my hay, *I* ain't settin' out to withstand her." That's what Jim Wickenden says to me last—last June-end 'twas,' said Jabez.

'Nor he hasn't shifted his stack, neither,' Jesse replied. 'An' if there's more rain, the brook she'll shift it for him.'

'No need tell *me!* But I want to know what Jim was gettin' *at?*'

Jabez opened his clasp-knife very deliberately; Jesse as carefully opened his. They unfolded the newspapers that wrapped their dinners, coiled away and pocketed the string that bound the packages, and sat down on the edge of the lodge manger. The rain began to fall again through the fog, and the brook's voice rose.

. . . . . .

'But I always allowed Mary was his lawful child, like,' said Jabez, after Jesse had spoken for a while.

''Tain't so. . . . Jim Wickenden's woman she never

made nothing. She come out o' Lewes with her stockin's round her heels, an' she never made nor mended aught till she died. *He* had to light fire an' get breakfast every mornin' except Sundays, while she sowed it abed. Then she took an' died, sixteen, seventeen, year back; but she never had no childern.'

'They was valley-folk,' said Jabez apologetically. 'I'd no call to go in among 'em, but I always allowed Mary——'

'No. Mary come out o' one o' those Lunnon Childern Societies. After his woman died, Jim got his mother back from his sister over to Peasmarsh, which she'd gone to house with when Jim married. His mother kept house for Jim after his woman died. They do say 'twas his mother led him on toward adoptin' of Mary—to furnish out the house with a child, like, and to keep him off of gettin' a noo woman. He mostly done what his mother contrived. 'Cardenly, twixt 'em, they asked for a child from one o' those Lunnon societies—same as it might ha' been these Barnardo childern—an' Mary was sent down to 'em, in a candle-box, I've heard.'

'Then Mary is chance-born. I never knowed that,' said Jabez. 'Yet I must ha' heard it some time or other . . .'

'No. She ain't. 'Twould ha' been better for some folk if she had been. She come to Jim in a candle-box with all the proper papers—lawful child o' some couple in Lunnon somewheres—mother dead, father drinkin'. *And* there was that Lunnon society's five shillin's a week for her. Jim's mother she wouldn't despise week-end money, but I never heard Jim was much of a muck-grubber. Let be how 'twill, they two mothered up Mary no bounds, till it looked at last like they'd forgot she wasn't their own flesh an' blood. Yes, I reckon they forgot Mary wasn't their'n by rights.'

'That's no new thing,' said Jabez. 'There's more'n one or two in this parish wouldn't surrender back their Bernarders. You ask Mark Copley an' his woman an' that Bernarder cripple-babe o' theirs.'

'Maybe they need the five shillin',' Jesse suggested.

'It's handy,' said Jabez. 'But the child's more. "Dada" he

says, an' "Mumma" he says, with his great rollin' head-piece all hurdled up in that iron collar. *He* won't live long —his backbone's rotten, like. But they Copleys do just about set store by him—five bob or no five bob.'

'Same way with Jim an' his mother,' Jesse went on. 'There was talk betwixt 'em after a few years o' not takin' any more week-end money for Mary; but let alone *she* never passed a farden in the mire 'thout longin's, Jim didn't care, like, to push himself forward into the Society's re-membrance. So naun came of it. The week-end money would ha' made no odds to Jim—not after his uncle willed him they four cottages at Eastbourne *an'* money in the bank.'

'That was true, too, then? I heard something in a scad-derin' word-o'-mouth way,' said Jabez.

'I'll answer for the house property, because Jim he ree-quested my signed name at the foot o' some papers con-cernin' it. Regardin' the money in the bank, he nature-ally wouldn't like such things talked about all round the parish, so he took strangers for witnesses.'

'Then 'twill make Mary worth seekin' after?'

'She'll need it. Her Maker ain't done much for her out-side nor yet in.'

'That ain't no odds.' Jabez shook his head till the water showered off his hat-brim. 'If Mary has money, she'll be wed before any likely pore maid. She's cause to be grateful to Jim.'

'She hides it middlin' close, then,' said Jesse. 'It don't sometimes look to me as if Mary has her natural rightful feelin's. She don't put on an apron o' Mondays 'thout being druv to it—in the kitchen *or* the hen-house. She's studyin' to be a school-teacher. She'll make a beauty! I never knowed her show any sort o' kindness to nobody—not even when Jim's mother was took dumb. No! 'Twadn't no stroke. It stifled the old lady in the throat here. First she couldn't shape her words no shape; then she clucked, like, an' lastly she couldn't more than suck down spoonmeat an' hold her peace. Jim took her to Doctor Harding, an' Harding he bundled her off to Brighton Hospital on a ticket, but they couldn't make no stay to her afflictions there; and she was bundled off to Lunnon, an' they lit a great old lamp inside her, and Jim told me they couldn't make out nothing in no sort there; and, along o' one thing an' another, an' all their spyin's and pryin's, she come back a hem sight worse than when she started. Jim said he'd have no more hospitalizin', so he give her a slate, which she tied to her waist-string, and what she was minded to say she writ on it.'

'Now, I never knowed that! But they're valley-folk,' Jabez repeated.

' 'Twadn't particular noticeable, for she wasn't a talkin' woman any time o' her days. Mary had all three's tongue. . . . Well, then, two years this summer, come what I'm tellin' you. Mary's Lunnon father, which they'd put clean out o' their minds, arrived down from Lunnon with the law on his side, sayin' he'd take his daughter back to Lunnon, after all. I was working for Mus' Dockett at Pounds Farm that summer, but I was obligin' Jim that evenin' muckin' out his pigpen. I seed a stranger come traipsin' over the bridge agin' Wickenden's door-stones. 'Twadn't the new County Council bridge with the handrail. They hadn't given it in for a public right o' way then. 'Twas just a bit o' lathy old plank which Jim had throwed acrost the brook for his own conveniences. The man wasn't drunk— only a little concerned in liquor, like—an' his back was a mask where he'd slipped in the muck comin' along. He went up the bricks past Jim's mother, which was feedin' the ducks, an' set himself down at the table inside—Jim was just changin' his socks—an' the man let Jim know all his rights and aims regardin' Mary. Then there just about *was* a hurly-bulloo? Jim's fust mind was to pitch him forth, but he'd done that once in his young days, an' got six months up to Lewes jail along o' the man fallin' on his head. So he swallowed his spittle an' let him talk. The law about Mary *was* on the man's side from fust to last, for he showed us all the papers. Then Mary come downstairs—she'd been studyin' for an examination—an' the man tells her who he

was, an' she says he had ought to have took proper care of
his own flesh and blood while he had it by him, an' not to
think he could ree-claim it when it suited. He says somethin' or other, but she looks him up an' down, front an'
backwent, an' she just tongues him scadderin' out o' doors,
and he went away stuffin' all the papers back into his hat,
talkin' most abusefully. Then she come back an' freed her
mind against Jim an' his mother for not havin' warned her
of her upbringin's, which it come out she hadn't ever been
told. They didn't say naun to her. They never did. *I*'d ha'
packed her off with any man that would ha' took her—an'
God's pity on him!'

'Umm!' said Jabez, and sucked his pipe.

'So then, that was the beginnin'. The man come back
again next week or so, an' he catched Jim alone, 'thout his
mother this time, an' he fair beazled him with his papers
an' his talk—for the law *was* on his side—till Jim went down
into his money-purse an' give him ten shillings hush-money
—he told me—to withdraw away for a bit an' leave Mary
with 'em.'

'But that's no way to get rid o' man or woman,' Jabez
said.

'No more 'tis. I told Jim so. "What can I do?" Jim says.
"The law's *with* the man. I walk about daytimes thinkin' o'
it till I sweats my underclothes wringin', an' I lie abed
nights thinkin' o' it till I sweats my sheets all of a sop. 'Tisn't
as if I was a young man," he says, "nor yet as if I was a
pore man. Maybe he'll drink hisself to death." I e'en a'most
told him outright what foolishness he was enterin' into, but
he knowed it—he knowed it—because he said next time the
man come t'would be fifteen shillin's. An' next time 'twas.
Just fifteen shillin's!'

'An' *was* the man her father?' asked Jabez.

'He had the proofs an' the papers. Jim showed me what
that Lunnon Childern's Society had answered when Mary
writ up to 'em an' taxed 'em with it. I lay she hadn't been
proper polite in her letters to 'em, for they answered middlin' short. They said the matter was out o' their hands, but

—let's see if I remember—oh, yes,—they ree-gretted there
had been an oversight. I reckon they had sent Mary out in
the candle-box as a orphan instead o' havin' a father. Terrible awkward! Then, when he'd drinked up the money, the
man come again—in his usuals—an' he kept hammerin' on
and hammerin' on about his duty to his pore dear wife, an'
what he'd do for his dear daughter in Lunnon, till the tears
runned down his two dirty cheeks an' he come away with
more money. Jim used to slip it into his hand behind the
door; but his mother she heard the chink. She didn't hold
with hush-money. She'd write out all her feelin's on the
slate, an' Jim 'ud be settin' up half the night answerin' back
an' showing that the man had the law with him.'

'Hadn't that man no trade nor business, then?'

'He told me he was a printer. I reckon, though, he lived
on the rates like the rest of 'em up there in Lunnon.'

'An' how did Mary take it?'

'She said she'd sooner go into service than go with the
man. I reckon a mistress 'ud be middlin' put to it for a maid
'fore she put Mary into cap an' gown. She was studyin' to
be a schoo-ool-teacher. A beauty she'll make! . . . Well,
that was how things went that fall. Mary's Lunnon father
kep' comin' an' comin' 'carden as he'd drinked out the
money Jim gave him; an' each time he'd put up his price
for not takin' Mary away. Jim's mother, she didn't like
partin' with no money, an' bein' obliged to write her feelin's
on the slate instead o' givin' 'em vent by mouth, she was
just about mad. Just about she *was* mad!

'Come November, I lodged with Jim in the outside room
over 'gainst his hen-house. I paid *her* my rent. I was workin'
for Dockett at Pounds—gettin' chestnut-bats out o' Perry
Shaw. Just such weather as this be—rain atop o' rain after a
wet October. (An' I remember it ended in dry frostes right
away up to Christmas.) Dockett he'd sent up to Perry
Shaw for me—no, he comes puffin' up to me himself—because a big cornerpiece o' the bank had slipped into the
brook where she makes that elber at the bottom o' the
Seventeen Acre, an' all the rubbishy alders an' sallies which

he ought to have cut out when he took the farm, they'd slipped with the slip, an' the brook was comin' rooshin' down atop of 'em, an' they'd just about back an' spill the waters over his winter wheat. The water was lyin' in the flats already. "Gor a-mighty, Jesse!" he bellers out at me, "get that rubbish away all manners you can. Don't stop for no fagottin', but give the brook play or my wheat's past salvation. I can't lend you no help," he says, "but work an' I'll pay ye." '

'You had him there,' Jabez chuckled.

'Yes. I reckon I had ought to have drove my bargain, but the brook was backin' up on good bread-corn. So 'cardenly, I laid into the mess of it, workin' off the bank where the trees was drownin' themselves head-down in the roosh—just such weather as this—an' the brook creepin' up on me all the time. 'Long toward noon, Jim comes mow-chin' along with his toppin' axe over his shoulder.

' "Be you minded for an extra hand at your job?" he says.

' "Be you minded to turn to?" I ses, an'—no more talk to it—Jim laid in alongside o' me. He's no bunger with a toppin' axe.'

'Maybe, but I've seed him at a job o' throwin' in the woods, an' he didn't seem to make out no shape,' said Jabez. 'He haven't got the shoulders, nor yet the judgment —my opinion—when he's dealin' with full-girt timber. He don't rightly make up his mind where he's goin' to throw her.'

'We wasn't throwin' nothin'. We was cuttin' out they soft alders, an' haulin' 'em up the bank 'fore they could back the waters on the wheat. Jim didn't say much, 'less it was that he'd had a post-card from Mary's Lunnon father, night before, sayin' he was comin' down that mornin'. Jim, he'd sweated all night, an' he didn't reckon hisself equal to the talkin' an' the swearin' an' the cryin', an' his mother blamin' him afterwards on the slate. "It spiled my day to think of it," he ses, when we was eatin' our pieces. "So I've fair cried dunghill an' run. Mother'll have to tackle him by herself. I lay *she* won't give him no hush-money," he ses. "I lay he'll be surprised by the time he's done with *her*," he ses. An' that was e'en a'most all the talk we had concernin' it. But he's no bunger with the toppin' axe.

'The brook she'd crep' up an' up on us, an' she kep' creepin' upon us till we was workin' knee-deep in the shallers, cuttin' an' pookin' an' pullin' what we could get to o' the rubbish. There was a middlin' lot comin' down-stream, too—cattle-bars an' hop-poles an' odds-ends bats, all poltin' down together; but they rooshed round the elber good shape by the time we'd backed out they drowned trees. Come four o'clock we reckoned we'd done a proper day's work, an' she'd take no harm if we left her. We couldn't puddle about there in the dark an' wet to no more advantage. Jim he was pourin' the water out of his boots— no, I was doin' that. Jim was kneelin' to unlace his'n. "Damn it all, Jesse," he ses, standin' up; "the flood must be over my doorsteps at home, for here comes my old white-top bee-skep!"'

'Yes. I allus heard he paints his bee-skeps,' Jabez put in. 'I dunno paint don't tarrify bees more'n it keeps 'em dry.'

' "I'll have a pook at it," he ses, an' he pooks at it as it comes round the elber. The roosh nigh jerked the pooker out of his hand-grips, an' he calls to me, an' I come runnin' barefoot. Then we pulled on the pooker, an' it reared up on eend in the roosh, an' we guessed what 'twas. 'Cardenly we pulled it in into a shaller, an' it rolled a piece, an' a great old stiff man's arm nigh hit me in the face. Then we was sure. " 'Tis a man," ses Jim. But the face was all a mask. "I reckon it's Mary's Lunnon father," he ses presently. "Lend me a match and I'll make sure." He never used baccy. We lit three matches one by another, well's we could in the rain, an' he cleaned off some o' the slob with a tussick o' grass. "Yes," he ses. "It's Mary's Lunnon father. He won't tarrify us no more. D'you want him, Jesse?" he ses.

' "No," I ses. "If this was Eastbourne beach like, he'd be half-a-crown apiece to us 'fore the coroner; but now we'd only lose a day havin' to 'tend the inquest. I lay he fell into the brook."

'"I lay he did," ses Jim. "I wonder if he saw mother." He turns him over, an' opens his coat an' puts his fingers in the waistcoat pocket an' starts laughin'. "He's seen mother, right enough," he ses. "An' he's got the best of her, too. *She* won't be able to crow no more over *me* 'bout givin' him money. *I* never give him more than a sovereign. She's give him two!" an' he trousers 'em, laughin' all the time. "An' now we'll pook him back again, for I've done with him," he ses.

'So we pooked him back into the middle of the brook, an' we saw he went round the elber 'thout balkin', an' we walked quite a piece beside of him to set him on his ways. When we couldn't see no more, we went home by the high road, because we knowed the brook 'u'd be out acrost the medders, an' we wasn't goin' to hunt for Jim's little rotten old bridge in that dark—an' rainin' Heavens' hard, too. I was middlin' pleased to see light an' vittles again when we got home. Jim he pressed me to come insides for a drink. He don't drink in a generality, but he was rid of all his troubles that evenin', d'ye see? "Mother," he ses so soon as the door ope'd, "have you seen him?" She whips out her slate an' writes down—"No." "Oh, no," ses Jim. "You don't get out of it that way, mother. I lay you *have* seen him, an' I lay he's bested you for all your talk, same as he bested me. Make a clean breast of it, mother," he ses. "He got round you too." She was goin' for the slate again, but he stops her. "It's all right, mother," he ses. "I've seen him sense you have, an' he won't trouble us no more." The old lady looks up quick as a robin, an' she writes, "Did he say so?" "No," ses Jim, laughin'. "He didn't say so. That's how I know. But he bested *you*, mother. You can't have it in at *me* for bein' soft-hearted. You're twice as tender-hearted as what I be. Look!" he ses, an' he shows her the two sovereigns. "Put 'em away where they belong," he ses. "He won't never come for no more; an' now we'll have our drink," he ses, "for we've earned it."

'Nature-ally they weren't goin' to let me see where they kep' their monies. She went upstairs with it—for the whisky.'

'I never knowed Jim was a drinkin' man—in his own house, like,' said Jabez.

'No more he isn't; but what he takes he likes good. He won't tech no publican's hogwash acrost the bar. Four shillin's he paid for that bottle o' whisky. I know, because when the old lady brought it down there wasn't more'n jest a liddle few dreenin's an' dregs in it. Nothin' to set before neighbours, I do assure you.'

' "Why, 'twas half full last week, mother," he ses. "You don't mean," he ses, "you've given him all that as well? It's two shillin's worth," he ses. (That's how I knowed he paid four.) "Well, well, mother, you be too tender-'earted to live. But I don't grudge it to him," he ses. "I don't grudge him nothin' he can keep." So, 'cardenly, we drinked up what little sup was left.'

'An' what come to Mary's Lunnon father?' said Jabez, after a full minute's silence.

'I be too tired to go readin' papers of evenin's; but Dockett he told me, that very week, I think, that they'd inquested on a man down at Roberts-bridge which had polted and polted up agin' so many bridges an' banks, like, they couldn't make naun out of him.'

'An' what did Mary say to all these doin's?'

'The old lady bundled her off to the village 'fore her Lunnon father come, to buy week-end stuff (an' she forgot the half o' it). When we come in she was upstairs studyin' to be a school-teacher. None told her naun about it. 'Twadn't girls' affairs.'

' 'Reckon *she* knowed?' Jabez went on.

'She? She must have guessed it middlin' close when she saw her money come back. But she never mentioned it in writing so far's I know. She were more worritted that night on account of two-three her chickens bein' drowned, for the flood had skewed their old hen-house round on her postes. I cobbled her up next mornin' when the brook shrinked.'

'An' where did you find the bridge? Some fur down-stream, didn't ye?'

'Just where she allus was. She hadn't shifted but very little. The brook had gulled out the bank a piece under one eend o' the plank, so's she was liable to tilt ye sideways if you wasn't careful. But I pooked three-four bricks under her, an' she was all plumb again.'

'Well, I dunno how it *looks* like, but let be how 'twill,' said Jabez, 'he hadn't no business to come down from Lunnon tarrifyin' people, an' threatenin' to take away childern which they'd hobbed up for their lawful own—even if 'twas Mary Wickenden.'

'He had the business right enough, an' he had the law with him—no gettin' over that,' said Jesse. 'But he had the drink with him, too, an' that was where he failed, like.'

'Well, well! Let be how 'twill, the brook was a good friend to Jim. I see it now. I allus *did* wonder what he was gettin' at when he said that, when I talked to him about shiftin' the stack. "You dunno everythin'," he ses. "The Brook's been a good friend to me," he ses, "an' if she's minded to have a snatch at my hay, *I* ain't settin' out to withstand her."'

'I reckon she's about shifted it, too, by now,' Jesse chuckled. 'Hark! That ain't any slip off the bank which she's got hold of.'

The Brook had changed her note again. It sounded as though she were mumbling something soft.

THE WISH HOUSE

The new Church Visitor had just left after a twenty minutes' call. During that time, Mrs. Ashcroft had used such English as an elderly, experienced, and pensioned cook should, who had seen life in London. She was the readier, therefore, to slip back into easy, ancient Sussex ('t's softening to 'd's as one warmed) when the 'bus brought Mrs. Fettley from thirty miles away for a visit, that pleasant March Saturday. The two had been friends since childhood; but, of late, destiny had separated their meetings by long intervals.

Much was to be said, and many ends, loose since last time, to be ravelled up on both sides, before Mrs. Fettley, with her bag of quilt-patches, took the couch beneath the window commanding the garden, and the football-ground in the valley below.

'Most folk got out at Bush Tye for the match there,' she explained, 'so there weren't no one for me to cushion agin, the last five mile. An' she *do* just-about bounce ye.'

'You've took no hurt,' said her hostess. 'You don't brittle by ageìn', Liz.'

Mrs. Fettley chuckled and made to match a couple of patches to her liking. 'No, or I'd ha' broke twenty year back. You can't ever mind when I was so's to be called round, can ye?'

Mrs. Ashcroft shook her head slowly—she never hurried—and went on stitching a sack-cloth lining into a list-bound rush tool-basket. Mrs. Fettley laid out more patches in the Spring light through the geraniums on the window-sill, and they were silent awhile.

'What like's this new Visitor o' yourn?' Mrs. Fettley inquired, with a nod towards the door. Being very short-sighted, she had, on her entrance, almost bumped into the lady.

Mrs. Ashcroft suspended the big packing-needle judicially on high, ere she stabbed home. 'Settin' aside she don't bring much news with her yet, I dunno as I've anythin' special agin her.'

'Ourn, at Keyneslade,' said Mrs. Fettley, 'she's full o' words an' pity, but she don't stay for answers. Ye can get on with your thoughts while she clacks.'

'This 'un don't clack. She's aimin' to be one o' those High Church nuns, like.'

'Ourn's married, but, by what they say, she've made no great gains of it . . .' Mrs. Fettley threw up her sharp chin. 'Lord! How they dam' cherubim do shake the very bones o' the place!'

The tile-sided cottage trembled at the passage of two specially chartered forty-seat charabancs on their way to the Bush Tye match; a regular Saturday 'shopping' 'bus, for the county's capital, fumed behind them; while, from one of the crowded inns, a fourth car backed out to join the procession, and held up the stream of through pleasure-traffic.

'You're as free-tongued as ever, Liz,' Mrs. Ashcroft observed.

'Only when I'm with you. Otherwhiles, I'm Granny—three times over. I lay that basket's for one o' your gran'chiller —ain't it?'

' 'Tis for Arthur—my Jane's eldest.'

'But he ain't workin' nowheres, is he?'

'No. 'Tis a picnic-basket.'

'You're let off light. My Willie, he's allus at me for money for them aireated wash-poles folk puts up in their gardens to draw the music from Lunnon, like. An' I give it 'im—pore fool me!'

'An' he forgets to give you the promise-kiss after, don't he?' Mrs. Ashcroft's heavy smile seemed to strike inwards.

'He do. 'No odds 'twixt boys now an' forty year back.

'Take all an' give naught—an' we to put up with it! Pore fool we! Three shillin' at a time Willie'll ask me for!'

'They don't make nothin' o' money these days,' Mrs. Ashcroft said.

'An' on'y last week,' the other went on, 'me daughter, she ordered a quarter pound suet at the butchers's; an' she sent it back to 'im to be chopped. She said she couldn't bother with choppin' it.'

'I lay he charged her, then.'

'I lay he did. She told me there was a whisk-drive that afternoon at the Institute, an' she couldn't bother to do the choppin'.'

'Tck!'

Mrs. Ashcroft put the last firm touches to the basket-lining. She had scarcely finished when her sixteen-year-old grandson, a maiden of the moment in attendance, hurried up the garden-path shouting to know if the thing were ready, snatched it, and made off without acknowledgment. Mrs. Fettley peered at him closely.

'They're goin' picnickin' somewheres,' Mrs. Ashcroft explained.

'Ah,' said the other, with narrowed eyes. 'I lay *he* won't show much mercy to any he comes across, either. Now 'oo the dooce do he remind me of, all of a sudden?'

'They must look arter theirselves—'same as we did.' Mrs. Ashcroft began to set out the tea.

'No denyin' *you* could, Gracie,' said Mrs. Fettley.

'What's in your head now?'

'Dunno . . . But it come over me, sudden-like—about dat woman from Rye—I've slipped the name—Barnsley, wadn't it?'

'Batten—Polly Batten, you're thinkin' of.'

'That's it—Polly Batten. That day she had it in for you with a hay-fork—'time we was all hayin' at Smalldene—for stealin' her man.'

'But you heered me tell her she had my leave to keep him?' Mrs. Ashcroft's voice and smile were smoother than ever.

'I did—an' we was all looking that she'd prod the fork
spang through your breastes when you said it.'

'No-oo. She'd never go beyond bounds—Polly. She shruck
too much for reel doin's.'

'Allus seems to *me*,' Mrs. Fettley said after a pause, 'that
a man 'twixt two fightin' women is the foolishest thing on
earth. 'Like a dog bein' called two ways.'

'Mebbe. But what set ye off on those times, Liz?'

'That boy's fashion o' carryin' his head an' arms. I haven't
rightly looked at him since he's growed. Your Jane never
showed it, but—*him!* Why, 'tis Jim Batten and his tricks
come to life again! . . . Eh?'

'Mebbe. There's some that would ha' made it out so—
bein' barren-like, themselves.'

'Oho! Ah well! Dearie, dearie me, now! . . . An' Jim
Batten's been dead this——'

'Seven and twenty year,' Mrs. Ashcroft answered briefly.
'Won't ye draw up, Liz?'

Mrs. Fettley drew up to buttered toast, currant bread,
stewed tea, bitter as leather, some home-preserved pears,
and a cold boiled pig's tail to help down the muffins. She
paid all the proper compliments.

'Yes. I dunno as I've ever owed me belly much,' said
Mrs. Ashcroft thoughtfully. 'We only go through this world
once.'

'But don't it lay heavy on ye, sometimes?' her guest
suggested.

'Nurse says I'm a sight liker to die o' me indigestion than
me leg.' For Mrs. Ashcroft had a long-standing ulcer on her
shin, which needed regular care from the Village Nurse,
who boasted (or others did, for her) that she had dressed
it one hundred and three times already during her term of
office.

'An' you that *was* so able, too! It's all come on ye before
your full time, like. *I*'ve watched ye goin'.' Mrs. Fettley
spoke with real affection.

'Somethin's bound to find ye sometimes. I've me 'eart left
me still,' Mrs. Ashcroft returned.

'You was always big-hearted enough for three. That's somethin' to look back on at the day's eend.'

'I reckon you've *your* back-lookin's, too,' was Mrs. Ashcroft's answer.

'You know it. But I don't think much regardin' such matters excep' when I'm along with you, Gra'. 'Takes two sticks to make a fire.'

Mrs. Fettley stared, with jaw half-dropped, at the grocer's bright calendar on the wall. The cottage shook again to the roar of the motor-traffic, and the crowded football-ground below the garden roared almost as loudly; for the village was well set to its Saturday leisure.

.   .   .   .   .

Mrs. Fettley had spoken very precisely for some time without interruption, before she wiped her eyes. 'And,' she concluded, 'they read 'is death-notice to me, out o' the paper last month. O' course it wadn't any o' *my* becomin' concerns—let be I 'adn't set eyes on him for so long. O' course *I* couldn't say nor show nothin'. Nor I've no rightful call to go to Eastbourne to see 'is grave, either. I've been schemin' to slip over there by the 'bus some day; but they'd ask questions at 'ome past endurance. So I 'aven't even *that* to stay me.'

'But you've 'ad your satisfactions?'

'Godd! Yess! Those four years 'e was workin' on the rail near us. An' the other drivers they gave him a brave funeral, too.'

'Then you've naught to cast-up about. 'Nother cup o' tea?'

.   .   .   .   .

The light and air had changed a little with the sun's descent, and the two elderly ladies closed the kitchen-door against chill. A couple of jays squealed and skirmished through the undraped apple-trees in the garden. This time, the word was with Mrs. Ashcroft, her elbows on the tea-table, and her sick leg propped on a stool. . . .

'Well I never! But what did your 'usband say to that?'
Mrs. Fettley asked, when the deep-toned recital halted.

''E said I might go where I pleased for all of 'im. But
seein' 'e was bedrid, I said I'd 'tend 'im out. 'E knowed I
wouldn't take no advantage of 'im in that state. 'E lasted
eight or nine week. Then he was took with a seizure-like;
an' laid stone-still for days. Then 'e propped 'imself up abed
an' says: "You pray no man'll ever deal with you like
you've dealed with some." "An' you?" I says, for *you* know,
Liz, what a rover 'e was. "It cuts both ways," says 'e, "but
I'm death-wise, an' I can see what's comin' to you." He died
a-Sunday an' was buried a-Thursday . . . An' yet I'd set a
heap by him—one time or—did I ever?'

'You never told me that before,' Mrs. Fettley ventured.

'I'm payin' ye for what ye told me just now. Him bein'
dead, I wrote up, sayin' I was free for good, to that Mrs.
Marshall in Lunnon—which gave me my first place as
kitchen-maid—Lord, how long ago! She was well pleased,
for they two was both gettin' on, an' I knowed their ways.
You remember, Liz, I used to go to 'em in service between
whiles, for years—when we wanted money, or—or my 'usband was away—on occasion.'

''E *did* get that six months at Chichester, didn't 'e?' Mrs.
Fettley whispered. 'We never rightly won to the bottom of
it.'

''E'd ha' got more, but the man didn't die.'

''None o' your doin's, was it, Gra'?'

'No! 'Twas the woman's husband this time. An' so, my
man bein' dead, I went back to them Marshall's, as cook, to
get me legs under a gentleman's table again, and be called
with a handle to me name. That was the year you shifted to
Portsmouth.'

'Cosham,' Mrs. Fettley corrected. 'There was a middlin'
lot o' new buildin' bein' done there. My man went first, an'
got the room, an' I follered.'

'Well, then, I was a year-abouts in Lunnon, all at a breath,
like, four meals a day an' livin' easy. Then, 'long towards
autumn, they two went travellin', like, to France; keepin'

me on, for they couldn't do without me. I put the house to
rights for the caretaker, an' then I slipped down 'ere to me
sister Bessie—me wages in me pockets, an' all 'ands glad to
be'old of me.'

'That would be when I was at Cosham,' said Mrs. Fettley.

'*You* know, Liz, there wasn't no cheap-dog pride to folk,
those days, no more than there was cinemas nor whisk-
drives. Man or woman 'ud lay hold o' any job that promised a shillin' to the backside of it, didn't they? I was all
peaked up after Lunnon, an' I thought the fresh airs 'ud
serve me. So I took on at Smalldene, obligin' with a hand
at the early potato-liftin', stubbin' hens, an' such-like. They'd
ha' mocked me sore in my kitchen in Lunnon, to see me in
men's boots, an' me petticoats all shorted.'

'Did it bring ye any good?' Mrs. Fettley asked.

''Twadn't for that I went. You know, 's'well's me, that
na'un happens to ye till it '*as* 'appened. Your mind don't
warn ye before'and of the road ye've took, till you're at the
far eend of it. We've only a backwent view of our pro-
ceedin's.'

''Oo was it?'

''Arry Mockler.' Mrs. Ashcroft's face puckered to the
pain of her sick leg.

Mrs. Fettley gasped. ''Arry? Bert Mockler's son! An' *I*
never guessed!'

Mrs. Ashcroft nodded. 'An' I told myself—*an'* I beleft it
—that I wanted field-work.'

'What did ye get out of it?'

'The usuals. Everythin' at first—worse than naught after. I
had signs an' warnings a-plenty, but I took no heed of 'em.
For we was burnin' rubbish one day, just when we'd come
to know how 'twas with—with both of us. 'Twas early in the
year for burnin', an' I said so. "No!" says he. "The sooner
dat old stuff's off an' done with," 'e says, "the better." 'Is
face was harder'n rocks when he spoke. Then it come over
me that I'd found me master, which I 'adn't ever before. I'd
allus owned 'em, like.'

'Yes! Yes! They're yourn or you're theirn,' the other sighed. 'I like the right way best.'

'I didn't. But 'Arry did . . . 'Long then, it come time for me to go back to Lunnon. I couldn't. I clean couldn't! So, I took an' tipped a dollop o' scaldin' water out o' the copper one Monday mornin' over me left 'and and arm. Dat stayed me where I was for another fortnight.'

'Was it worth it?' said Mrs. Fettley, looking at the silvery scar on the wrinkled fore-arm.

Mrs. Ashcroft nodded. 'An' after that, we two made it up 'twixt us so's 'e could come to Lunnon for a job in a liv'ry-stable not far from me. 'E got it. *I* 'tended to that. There wadn't no talk nowhere. His own mother never suspicioned how 'twas. He just slipped up to Lunnon, an' there we abode that winter, not 'alf a mile 'tother from each.'

'Ye paid 'is fare an' all, though'; Mrs. Fettley spoke convincedly.

Again Mrs. Ashcroft nodded. 'Dere wadn't much I didn't do for him. 'E was me master, an'—O God, help us!—we'd laugh over it walkin' together after dark in them paved streets, an' me corns fair wrenchin' in me boots! I'd never been like that before. Ner he! Ner he!'

Mrs. Fettley clucked sympathetically.

'An' when did ye come to the eend?' she asked.

'When 'e paid it all back again, every penny. Then I knowed, but I wouldn't *suffer* meself to know. "You've been mortal kind to me," he says. "Kind!" I said. " 'Twixt *us?*" But 'e kep' all on tellin' me 'ow kind I'd been an' 'e'd never forget it all his days. I held it from off o' me for three evenin's, because I would *not* believe. Then 'e talked about not bein' satisfied with 'is job in the stables, an' the men there puttin' tricks on 'im, an' all they lies which a man tells when 'e's leavin' ye. I heard 'im out, neither 'elpin' nor 'inderin'. At the last, I took off a liddle brooch which he'd give me an' I says: "Dat'll do. *I* ain't askin' na'un'." An' I turned me round an' walked off to me own sufferin's. 'E didn't make 'em worse. 'E didn't come nor write after that. 'E slipped off 'ere back 'ome to 'is mother again.'

'An' 'ow often did ye look for 'en to come back?' Mrs. Fettley demanded mercilessly.

'More'n once—more'n once! Goin' over the streets we'd used, I thought de very pave-stones 'ud shruck out under me feet.'

'Yes,' said Mrs. Fettley. 'I dunno but dat don't 'urt as much as aught else. An' dat was all ye got?'

'No. 'Twadn't. That's the curious part, if you'll believe it, Liz.'

'I do. I lay you're further off lyin' now than in all your life, Gra'.'

'I am . . . An' I suffered, like I'd not wish my most arrantest enemies to. God's Own Name! I went through the hoop that spring! One part of it was 'eddicks which I'd never known all me days before. Think o' *me* with an 'eddick! But I come to be grateful for 'em. They kep' me from thinkin' . . .'

''Tis like a tooth,' Mrs. Fettley commented. 'It must rage an' rugg till it tortures itself quiet on ye; an' then—then there's na'un left.'

'*I* got enough lef' to last me all *my* days on earth. It come about through our charwoman's liddle girl—Sophy Ellis was 'er name—all eyes an' elbers an' hunger. I used to give 'er vittles. Otherwhiles, I took no special notice of 'er, an' a sight less, o' course, when me trouble about 'Arry was on me. But—you know how liddle maids first feel it sometimes—she come to be crazy-fond o' me, pawin' an' cuddlin' all whiles; an' I 'adn't the 'eart to beat 'er off . . . One afternoon, early in spring 'twas, 'er mother 'ad sent 'er round to scutchel up what vittles she could off of us. I was settin' by the fire, me apern over me head, half-mad with the 'eddick, when she slips in. I reckon I was middlin' short with 'er. "Lor'!" she says. "Is *that* all? I'll take it off you in two-twos!" I told her not to lay a finger on me, for I thought she'd want to stroke my forehead; an'—I ain't that make. "*I* won't tech ye," she says, an' slips out again. She 'adn't been gone ten minutes 'fore me old 'eddick took off quick as bein' kicked. So I went about my work. Prasin'ly, Sophy

comes back, an' creeps into my chair quiet as a mouse.
'Er eyes was deep in 'er 'ead an' 'er face all drawed. I
asked 'er what 'ad 'appened. "Nothin'," she says. "On'y *I*'ve
got it now." "Got what?" I says. "Your 'eddick," she says,
all hoarse an' sticky-lipped. "I've took it on me." "Nonsense," I says, "it went of itself when you was out. Lay still
an' I'll make ye a cup o' tea." " 'Twon't do no good," she
says, "till your time's up. 'Ow long do *your* 'eddicks last?"
"Don't talk silly," I says, "or I'll send for the Doctor." It
looked to me like she might be hatchin' de measles. "Oh,
Mrs. Ashcroft," she says, stretchin' out 'er liddle thin arms.
"I *do* love ye." There wasn't any holdin' agin that. I took
'er into me lap an' made much of 'er. "Is it truly gone?" she
says. "Yes," I says, "an' if 'twas you took it away, I'm truly
grateful." " '*Twas* me," she says, layin' 'er cheek to mine.
"No one but me knows how." An' then she said she'd
changed me 'eddick for me at a Wish 'Ouse.'

'Whatt?' Mrs. Fettley spoke sharply.

'A Wish House. No! *I* 'adn't 'eard o' such things, either. I
couldn't get it straight at first, but, puttin' all together, I
made out that a Wish 'Ouse 'ad to be a house which 'ad
stood unlet an' empty long enough for Some One, like, to
come an' in'abit there. She said a liddle girl that she'd played
with in the livery-stables where 'Arry worked 'ad told 'er so.
She said the girl 'ad belonged in a caravan that laid up, o'
winters, in Lunnon. Gipsy, I judge.'

'Ooh! There's no sayin' what Gippos know, but *I*'ve never
'eard of a Wish 'Ouse, an' I know—some things,' said Mrs.
Fettley.

'Sophy said there was a Wish 'Ouse in Wadloes Road—
just a few streets off, on the way to our green-grocer's. All
you 'ad to do, she said, was to ring the bell an' wish your
wish through the slit o' the letter-box. I asked 'er if the
fairies give it 'er? "Don't ye know," she says, "there's no
fairies in a Wish 'Ouse? There's on'y a Token." '

'Goo' Lord A'mighty! Where did she come by *that* word?'
cried Mrs. Fettley; for a Token is a wraith of the dead or,
worse still, of the living.

'The caravan-girl 'ad told 'er, she said. Well, Liz, it troubled me to 'ear 'er, an' lyin' in me arms she must ha' felt it. "That's very kind o' you," I says, holdin' 'er tight, "to wish me 'eddick away. But why didn't ye ask somethin' nice for yourself?" "You can't do that," she says. "All you'll get at a Wish 'Ouse is leave to take some one else's trouble. I've took Ma's 'eddicks, when she's been kind to me; but this is the first time I've been able to do aught for you. Oh, Mrs. Ashcroft, I *do* just-about love you." An' she goes on all like that. Liz, I tell you my 'air e'en a'most stood on end to 'ear 'er. I asked 'er what like a Token was. "I dunno," she says, "but after you've ringed the bell, you'll 'ear it run up from the basement, to the front door. Then say your wish," she says, "an' go away." "The Token don't open de door to ye, then?" I says. "Oh no," she says. "You on'y 'ear gig-glin', like, be'ind the front door. Then you say you'll take the trouble off of 'oo ever 'tis you've chose for your love; an' ye'll get it," she says. I didn't ask no more—she was too 'ot an' fevered. I made much of 'er till it come time to light de gas, an' a liddle after that, 'er 'eddick—mine, I suppose— took off, an' she got down an' played with the cat.'

'Well, I never!' said Mrs. Fettley. 'Did—did ye foller it up, anyways?'

'She askt me to, but I wouldn't 'ave no such dealin's with a child.'

'What *did* ye do, then?'

' 'Sat in me own room 'stid o' the kitchen when me 'ed-dicks come on. But it lay at de back o' me mind.'

' 'Twould. Did she tell ye more, ever?'

'No. Besides what the Gippo girl 'ad told 'er, she knew naught, 'cept that the charm worked. An', next after that— in May 'twas—I suffered the summer out in Lunnon. 'Twas hot an' windy for weeks, an' the streets stinkin' o' dried 'orse-dung blowin' from side to side an' lyin' level with the kerb. We don't get that nowadays. I 'ad my 'ol'day just before hoppin',[1] an' come down 'ere to stay with Bessie

[1] Hop-picking.

again. She noticed I'd lost flesh, an' was all poochy under
the eyes.'

'Did ye see 'Arry?'

Mrs. Ashcroft nodded. 'The fourth—no, the fifth day.
Wednesday 'twas. I knowed 'e was workin' at Smalldene
again. I asked 'is mother in the street, bold as brass. She
'adn't room to say much, for Bessie—you know 'er tongue—
was talkin' full-clack. But that Wednesday, I was walkin'
with one o' Bessie's chillern hangin' on me skirts, at de
back o' Chanter's Tot. Prasin'ly, I felt 'e was be'ind me on
the footpath, an' I knowed by 'is tread 'e'd changed 'is nature. I slowed, an' I heard 'im slow. Then I fussed a piece
with the child, to force him past me, like. So 'e *ad* to come
past. 'E just says "Good-evenin'," and goes on, tryin' to pull
'isself together.'

'Drunk, was he?' Mrs. Fettley asked.

'Never! S'runk an' wizen; 'is clothes 'angin' on 'im like
bags, an' the back of 'is neck whiter'n chalk. 'Twas all I
could do not to oppen my arms an' cry after 'im. But I
swallered me spittle till I was back 'ome again an' the
chillern abed. Then I says to Bessie, after supper, "What in
de world's come to 'Arry Mockler?" Bessie told me 'e'd
been a-Hospital for two months, 'long o' cuttin' 'is foot wid
a spade, muckin' out the old pond at Smalldene. There was
poison in de dirt, an' it rooshed up 'is leg, like, an' come
out all over him. 'E 'adn't been back to 'is job—carterin' at
Smalldene—more'n a fortnight. She told me the Doctor said
he'd go off, likely, with the November frostes; an' 'is mother
'ad told 'er that 'e didn't rightly eat nor sleep, an' sweated
'imself into pools, no odds 'ow chill 'e lay. An' spit terrible
o' mornin's. "Dearie me," I says. "But, mebbe, hoppin' 'll set
'im right again," an' I licked me thread-point an' I fetched
me needle's eye up to it an' I threads me needle under de
lamp, steady as rocks. An' dat night (me bed was in de
wash-house) I cried an' I cried. An' *you* know, Liz—for
you've been with me in my throes—it takes summat to make
me cry.'

'Yes; but chile-bearin' is on'y just pain,' said Mrs. Fettley.

'I come round by cock-crow, an' dabbed cold tea on me eyes to take away the signs. Long towards nex' evenin'—I was settin' out to lay some flowers on me 'usband's grave, for the look o' the thing—I met 'Arry over against where the War Memorial is now. 'E was comin' back from 'is 'orses, so 'e couldn't *not* see me. I looked 'im all over, an' " 'Arry," I says twix' me teeth, "come back an' rest-up in Lunnon." "I won't take it," he says, "for I can give ye naught." "I don't ask it," I says. "By God's Own Name, I don't ask na'un! On'y come up an' see a Lunnon doctor." 'E lifts 'is two 'eavy eyes at me: " 'Tis past that, Gra'," 'e says. "I've but a few months left." " 'Arry!" I says. "*My* man!" I says. I couldn't say no more. 'Twas all up in me throat. "Thank ye kindly, Gra'," 'e says (but 'e never says "my woman"), an' 'e went on up-street an' 'is mother—Oh, damn 'er!—she was watchin' for 'im, an' she shut de door be'ind 'im.'

Mrs. Fettley stretched an arm across the table, and made to finger Mrs. Ashcroft's sleeve at the wrist, but the other moved it out of reach.

'So I went on to the churchyard with my flowers, an' I remembered my 'usband's warnin' that night he spoke. 'E *was* death-wise, an' it *'ad* 'appened as 'e said. But as I was settin' down de jam-pot on the grave-mound, it come over me there was one thing I *could* do for 'Arry. Doctor or no Doctor, I thought I'd make a trial of it. So I did. Nex' mornin', a bill came down from our Lunnon green-grocer. Mrs. Marshall, she'd lef' me petty cash for suchlike—o' course—but I tole Bess 'twas for me to come an' open the 'ouse. So I went up, afternoon train.'

'An'—but I know you 'adn't—'adn't you no fear?'

'What for? There was nothin' front o' me but my own shame an' God's croolty. I couldn't ever get 'Arry—'ow *could* I? I knowed it must go on burnin' till it burned me out.'

'Aie!' said Mrs. Fettley, reaching for the wrist again, and this time Mrs. Ashcroft permitted it.

'Yit 'twas a comfort to know I could try *this* for 'im. So I went an' I paid the green-grocer's bill, an' put 'is receipt in me 'and-bag, an' then I stepped round to Mrs. Ellis—our char—an' got the 'ouse-keys an' opened the 'ouse. First, I made me bed to come back to (God's Own Name! Me bed to lie upon!). Nex' I made me a cup o' tea an' sat down in the kitchen thinkin', till 'long towards dusk. Terrible close, 'twas. Then I dressed me an' went out with the receipt in me 'and-bag, feignin' to study it for an address, like. Fourteen, Wadloes Road, was the place—a liddle basement-kitchen 'ouse, in a row of twenty-thirty such, an' tiddy strips o' walled garden in front—the paint off the front doors, an' na'un done to na'un since ever so long. There wasn't 'ardly no one in the streets 'cept the cats. *'Twas* 'ot, too! I turned into the gate bold as brass; up de steps I went an' I ringed the front-door bell. She pealed loud, like it do in an empty house. When she'd all ceased, I 'eard a cheer, like, pushed back on de floor o' the kitchen. Then I 'eard feet on de kitchen-stairs, like it might ha' been a heavy woman in slippers. They come up to de stairhead, acrost the hall—I 'eard the bare boards creak under 'em—an' at de front door dey stopped. I stooped me to the letter-box slit, an' I says: "Let me take everythin' bad that's in store for my man, 'Arry Mockler, for love's sake." Then, whatever it was 'tother side de door let its breath out, like, as if it 'ad been holdin' it for to 'ear better.'

'Nothin' was *said* to ye?' Mrs. Fettley demanded.

'Na'un. She just breathed out—a sort of *A-ah*, like. Then the steps went back an' downstairs to the kitchen—all draggy —an' I heard the cheer drawed up again.'

'An' you abode on de doorstep, throughout all, Gra'?' Mrs. Ashcroft nodded.

'Then I went away, an' a man passin' says to me: "Didn't you know that house was empty?" "No," I says. "I must ha' been give the wrong number." An' I went back to our 'ouse, an' I went to bed; for I was fair flogged out. 'Twas too 'ot to sleep more'n snatches, so I walked me about, lyin' down betweens, till crack o' dawn. Then I went to the kitchen to make me a cup o' tea, an' I hitted meself just above the ankle on an old roastin'-jack o' mine that Mrs. Ellis had moved out from the corner, her last cleanin'. An' so—nex' after that—I waited till the Marshalls come back o' their holiday.'

'Alone there? I'd ha' thought you'd 'ad enough of empty houses,' said Mrs. Fettley, horrified.

'Oh, Mrs. Ellis an' Sophy was runnin' in an' out soon's I was back, an' 'twixt us we cleaned de house again top-to-bottom. There's allus a hand's turn more to do in every house. An' that's 'ow 'twas with me that autumn an' winter, in Lunnon.'

'Then na'un hap—overtook ye for your doin's?'

Mrs. Ashcroft smiled. 'No. Not then. 'Long in November I sent Bessie ten shillin's.'

'You was allus free-'anded,' Mrs. Fettley interrupted.

'An' I got what I paid for, with the rest o' the news. She said the hoppin' 'ad set 'im up wonderful. 'E'd 'ad six weeks of it, and now 'e was back again carterin' at Smalldene. No odds to me *'ow* it 'ad 'appened—'slong's it *'ad*. But I dunno as my ten shillin's eased me much. 'Arry bein' *dead*, like, 'e'd ha' been mine, till Judgment. 'Arry bein' alive, 'e'd like as not pick up with some woman middlin' quick. I raged over that. Come spring, I 'ad somethin' else to rage for. I'd growed a nasty little weepin' boil, like, on me shin, just above the boot-top, that wouldn't heal no shape. It made me sick to look at it, for I'm clean-fleshed by nature. Chop me all over with a spade, an' I'd heal like turf. Then Mrs. Marshall she set 'er own doctor at me. 'E said I ought to ha' come to him at first go-off, 'stead o' drawin' all manner o' dyed stockin's over it for months. 'E said I'd stood up too much to me work, for it was settin' very close atop of a big swelled vein, like, behither the small o' me ankle. "Slow come, slow go," 'e says. "Lay your leg up on high an' rest it," he says, "an' 'twill ease off. Don't let it close up too soon. You've got a very fine leg, Mrs. Ashcroft," 'e says. An' he put wet dressin's on it.'

''E done right.' Mrs. Fettley spoke firmly. 'Wet dressin's

to wet wounds. They draw de humours, same's a lamp-wick draws de oil.'

'That's true. An' Mrs. Marshall was allus at me to make me set down more, an' dat nigh healed it up. An' then after a while they packed me off down to Bessie's to finish the cure; for I ain't the sort to sit down when I ought to stand up. You was back in the village then, Liz.'

'I was. I was, but—never did I guess!'

'I didn't desire ye to.' Mrs. Ashcroft smiled. 'I saw 'Arry once or twice in de street, wonnerful fleshed up an' restored back. Then, one day I didn't see 'im, an' 'is mother told me one of 'is 'orses 'ad lashed out an' caught 'im on the 'ip. So 'e was abed an' middlin' painful. An' Bessie, she says to his mother, 'twas a pity 'Arry 'adn't a woman of 'is own to take the nursin' off 'er. And the old lady *was* mad! She told us that 'Arry 'ad never looked after any woman in 'is born days, an' as long as she was atop the mowlds, she'd con-trive for 'im till 'er two 'ands dropped off. So I knowed she'd do watch-dog for me, 'thout askin' for bones.'

Mrs. Fettley rocked with small laughter.

'That day,' Mrs. Ashcroft went on, 'I'd stood on me feet nigh all the time, watchin' the doctor go in an' out; for they thought it might be 'is ribs, too. That made my boil break again, issuin' an' weepin'. But it turned out 'twadn't ribs at all, an' 'Arry 'ad a good night. When I heard that, nex' mornin', I says to meself, "I won't lay two an' two together *yit*. I'll keep me leg down a week, an' see what comes of it." It didn't hurt me that day, to speak of—'seemed more to draw the strength out o' me like—an' 'Arry 'ad another good night. That made me persevere; but I didn't dare lay two an' two together till the week-end, an' then, 'Arry come forth e'en a'most 'imself again—na'un hurt outside ner in of him. I nigh fell on me knees in de wash-house when Bessie was up-street. "I've got ye now, my man," I says. "You'll take your good from me 'thout knowin' it till my life's end. O God, send me long to live for 'Arry's sake!" I says. An' I dunno that didn't still me ragin's.'

'For good?' Mrs. Fettley asked.

'They come back, plenty times, but, let be how 'twould, I knowed I was doin' for 'im. I *knowed* it. I took an' worked me pains on an' off, like regulatin' my own range, till I learned to 'ave 'em at my commandments. An' that was funny, too. There was times, Liz, when my trouble 'ud all s'rink an' dry up, like. First, I used to try an' fetch it on again; bein' fearful to leave 'Arry alone too long for anythin' to lay 'old of. Prasin'ly I come to see that was a sign he'd do all right awhile, an' so I saved myself.'

' 'Ow long for?' Mrs. Fettley asked, with deepest interest.

'I've gone de better part of a year onct or twice with na'un more to show than the liddle weepin' core of it, like. *All* s'rinked up an' dried off. Then he'd inflame up—for a warnin'—an' I'd suffer it. When I couldn't no more—an' I *'ad* to keep on goin' with my Lunnon work—I'd lay me leg high on a cheer till it eased. Not too quick. I knowed by the feel of it, those times, dat 'Arry was in need. Then I'd send another five shillin's to Bess, or somethin' for the chillern, to find out if, mebbe, 'e'd took any hurt through my neglects. 'Twas *so!* Year in, year out, I worked it dat way, Liz, an' 'e got 'is good from me 'thout knowin'—for years and years.'

'But what did *you* get out of it, Gra'?' Mrs. Fettley almost wailed. 'Did ye see 'im reg'lar?'

'Times—when I was 'ere on me 'ol'days. An' more, now that I'm 'ere for good. But 'e's never looked at me, ner any other woman 'cept 'is mother. 'Ow I used to watch an' listen! So did she.'

'Years an' years!' Mrs. Fettley repeated. 'An' where's 'e workin' at now?'

'Oh, 'e's give up carterin' quite a while. He's workin' for one o' them big tractorisin' firms—plowin' sometimes, an' sometimes off with lorries—fur as Wales, I've 'eard. He comes 'ome to 'is mother 'tween whiles; but I don't set eyes on 'im now, fer weeks on end. No odds! 'Is job keeps 'im from continuin' in one stay anywheres.'

'But—just for de sake o' sayin' somethin'—s'pose 'Arry *did* get married?' said Mrs. Fettley.

Mrs. Ashcroft drew her breath sharply between her still even and natural teeth. '*Dat* ain't been required of me,' she answered. 'I reckon my pains 'ull be counted agin that. Don't *you*, Liz?'

'It ought to be, dearie. It ought to be.'

'It *do* 'urt sometimes. You shall see it when Nurse comes. She thinks I don't know it's turned.'

Mrs. Fettley understood. Human nature seldom walks up to the word 'cancer.'

'Be ye certain sure, Gra'?' she asked.

'I was sure of it when old Mr. Marshall 'ad me up to 'is study an' spoke a long piece about my faithful service. I've obliged 'em on an' off for a goodish time, but not enough for a pension. But they give me a weekly 'lowance for life. I knew what *that* sinnified—as long as three years ago.'

'Dat don't *prove* it, Gra'.'

'To give fifteen bob a week to a woman 'oo'd live twenty year in the course o' nature? It *do!*'

'You're mistook! You're mistook!' Mrs. Fettley insisted.

'Liz, there's *no* mistakin' when the edges are all heaped up, like—same as a collar. You'll see it. An' I laid out Dora Wickwood, too. *She* 'ad it under the arm-pit, like.'

Mrs. Fettley considered awhile, and bowed her head in finality.

''Ow long d'you reckon 'twill allow ye, countin' from now, dearie?'

'Slow come, slow go. But if I don't set eyes on ye 'fore next hoppin', this'll be good-bye, Liz.'

'Dunno as I'll be able to manage by then—not 'thout I have a liddle dog to lead me. For de chillern, dey won't be troubled, an'—O Gra'!—I'm blindin' up—I'm blindin' up!'

'Oh, *dat* was why you didn't more'n finger with your quilt-patches all this while! I was wonderin' . . . But the pain *do* count, don't ye think, Liz? The pain *do* count to keep 'Arry—where I want 'im. Say it can't be wasted, like.'

'I'm sure of it—sure of it, dearie. You'll 'ave your reward.'

'I don't want no more'n this—*if* de pain is taken into de reckonin'.'

' 'Twill be—'twill be, Gra'.'

There was a knock on the door.

'That's Nurse. She's before 'er time,' said Mrs. Ashcroft. 'Open to 'er.'

The young lady entered briskly, all the bottles in her bag clicking. 'Evenin', Mrs. Ashcroft,' she began. 'I've come raound a little earlier than usual because of the Institute dance to-na-ite. You won't ma-ind, will you?'

'Oh, no. Me dancin' days are over.' Mrs. Ashcroft was the self-contained domestic at once. 'My old friend, Mrs. Fettley 'ere, has been settin' talkin' with me a while.'

'I hope she 'asn't been fatiguing you?' said the Nurse a little frostily.

'Quite the contrary. It 'as been a pleasure. Only—only—just at the end I felt a bit—a bit flogged out like.'

'Yes, yes.' The Nurse was on her knees already, with the washes to hand. 'When old ladies get together they talk a deal too much, I've noticed.'

'Mebbe we do,' said Mrs. Fettley, rising. 'So now I'll make myself scarce.'

'Look at it first, though,' said Mrs. Ashcroft feebly. 'I'd like ye to look at it.'

Mrs. Fettley looked, and shivered. Then she leaned over, and kissed Mrs. Ashcroft once on the waxy yellow forehead, and again on the faded grey eyes.

'It *do* count, don't it—de pain?' The lips that still kept trace of their original moulding hardly more than breathed the words.

Mrs. Fettley kissed them and moved towards the door.

'MY SON'S WIFE'

(1913)

He had suffered from the disease of the century since his early youth, and before he was thirty he was heavily marked with it. He and a few friends had rearranged Heaven very comfortably, but the reorganisation of Earth, which they called Society, was even greater fun. It demanded Work in the shape of many taxi-rides daily; hours of brilliant talk with brilliant talkers; some sparkling correspondence; a few silences (but on the understanding that their own turn should come soon) while other people expounded philosophies; and a fair number of picture-galleries, tea-fights, concerts, theatres, music-halls, and cinema shows; the whole trimmed with love-making to women whose hair smelt of cigarette-smoke. Such strong days sent Frankwell Midmore back to his flat assured that he and his friends had helped the World a step nearer the Truth, the Dawn, and the New Order.

His temperament, he said, led him more towards concrete data than abstract ideas. People who investigate detail are apt to be tired at the day's end. The same temperament, or it may have been a woman, made him early attach himself to the Immoderate Left of his Cause in the capacity of an experimenter in Social Relations. And since the Immoderate Left contains plenty of women anxious to help earnest inquirers with large independent incomes to arrive at evaluations of essentials, Frankwell Midmore's lot was far from contemptible.

At that hour Fate chose to play with him. A widowed aunt, widely separated by nature, and more widely by marriage, from all that Midmore's mother had ever been or desired to be, died and left him possessions. Mrs. Midmore, having that summer embraced a creed which denied the existence of death, naturally could not stoop to burial; but Midmore had to leave London for the dank country at a season when Social Regeneration works best through long, cushioned conferences, two by two, after tea. There he faced the bracing ritual of the British funeral, and was wept at across the raw grave by an elderly coffin-shaped female with a long nose, who called him 'Master Frankie'; and there he was congratulated behind an echoing top-hat by a man he mistook for a mute, who turned out to be his aunt's lawyer. He wrote his mother next day, after a bright account of the funeral:

'So far as I can understand, she has left me between four and five hundred a year. It all comes from Ther Land, as they call it down here. The unspeakable attorney, Sperrit, and a green-eyed daughter, who hums to herself as she tramps but is silent on all subjects except "huntin'," insisted on taking me to see it. Ther Land is brown and green in alternate slabs like chocolate and pistachio cakes, speckled with occasional peasants who do not utter. In case it should not be wet enough there is a wet brook in the middle of it. Ther House is by the brook. I shall look into it later. If there should be any little memento of Jenny that you care for, let me know. Didn't you tell me that mid-Victorian furniture is coming into the market again? Jenny's old maid —it is called Rhoda Dolbie—tells me that Jenny promised it thirty pounds a year. The will does not. Hence, I suppose, the tears at the funeral. But that is close on ten per cent of the income. I fancy Jenny has destroyed all her private papers and records of her *vie intime,* if, indeed, life be possible in such a place. The Sperrit man told me that if I had means of my own I might come and live on Ther Land. I didn't tell him how much I would pay not to! I cannot think it right that any human being should exercise mastery over others in the merciless fashion our tom-fool social system permits; so, as it is all mine, I intend to sell it whenever the unholy Sperrit can find a purchaser.'

And he went to Mr. Sperrit with the idea next day, just before returning to town.

'Quite so,' said the lawyer. 'I see your point, of course. But the house itself is rather old-fashioned—hardly the type purchasers demand nowadays. There's no park, of course, and the bulk of the land is let to a life-tenant, a Mr. Sidney. As long as he pays his rent, he can't be turned out, and even if he didn't'—Mr. Sperrit's face relaxed a shade—'you might have a difficulty.'

'The property brings four hundred a year, I understand,' said Midmore.

'Well, hardly—ha-ardly. Deducting land and income tax, tithes, fire insurance, cost of collection and repairs of course, it returned two hundred and eighty-four pounds last year. The repairs are rather a large item—owing to the brook. I call it Liris—out of Horace, you know.'

Midmore looked at his watch impatiently.

'I suppose you can find somebody to buy it?' he repeated.

'We will do our best, of course, if those are your instructions. Then, that is all except'—here Midmore half rose, but Mr. Sperrit's little grey eyes held his large brown ones firmly—'except about Rhoda Dolbie, Mrs. Werf's maid. I may tell you that we did not draw up your aunt's last will. She grew secretive towards the last—elderly people often do —and had it done in London. I expect her memory failed her, or she mislaid her notes. She used to put them in her spectacle-case. . . . My motor only takes eight minutes to get to the station, Mr. Midmore . . . but, as I was saying, whenever she made her will with *us,* Mrs. Werf always left Rhoda thirty pounds per annum. Charlie, the wills!' A clerk with a baldish head and a long nose dealt documents on to the table like cards, and breathed heavily behind Midmore. 'It's in no sense a legal obligation, of course,' said Mr. Sperrit. 'Ah, that one is dated January the 11th, eighteen eighty-nine.'

Midmore looked at his watch again and found himself saying with no good grace: 'Well, I suppose she'd better have it—for the present at any rate.'

He escaped with an uneasy feeling that two hundred and fifty-four pounds a year was not exactly four hundred, and that Charlie's long nose annoyed him. Then he returned, first-class, to his own affairs.

Of the two, perhaps three, experiments in Social Relations which he had then in hand, one interested him acutely. It had run for some months and promised most variegated and interesting developments, on which he dwelt luxuriously all the way to town. When he reached his flat he was not well prepared for a twelve-page letter explaining, in the diction of the Immoderate Left which rubricates its I's and illuminates its T's, that the lady had realised greater attractions in another Soul. She re-stated, rather than pleaded, the gospel of the Immoderate Left as her justification, and ended in an impassioned demand for her right to express herself in and on her own life, through which, she pointed out, she could pass but once. She added that if, later, she should discover Midmore was 'essentially complementary to her needs,' she would tell him so. That Midmore had himself written much the same sort of epistle—barring the hint of return—to a woman of whom his needs for self-expression had caused him to weary three years before, did not assist him in the least. He expressed himself to the gas-fire in terms essential but not complimentary. Then he reflected on the detached criticism of his best friends and her best friends, male and female, with whom he and she and others had talked so openly while their gay adventure was in flower. He recalled, too—this must have been about midnight—her analysis from every angle, remote and most intimate, of the mate to whom she had been adjudged under the base convention which is styled marriage. Later, at that bad hour when the cattle wake for a little, he remembered her in other aspects and went down into the hell appointed; desolate, desiring, with no God to call upon. About eleven o'clock next morning Eliphaz the Temanite, Bildad the Shuhite, and Zophar the Naamathite called upon him 'for they had made appointment together' to see how he took it; but the janitor told them that Job had gone—into the country, he believed.

Midmore's relief when he found his story was not written across his aching temples for Mr. Sperrit to read—the defeated lover, like the successful one, believes all earth privy to his soul—was put down by Mr. Sperrit to quite different causes. He led him into a morning-room. The rest of the house seemed to be full of people, singing to a loud piano idiotic songs about cows, and the hall smelt of damp cloaks.

'It's our evening to take the winter cantata,' Mr. Sperrit explained. 'It's "High Tide on the Coast of Lincolnshire." I hoped you'd come back. There are scores of little things to settle. As for the house, of course, it stands ready for you at any time. I couldn't get Rhoda out of it—nor could Charlie for that matter. She's the sister, isn't she, of the nurse who brought you down here when you were four, she says, to recover from measles?'

'Is she? Was I?' said Midmore through the bad tastes in his mouth. 'D'you suppose I could stay there the night?'

Thirty joyous young voices shouted appeal to some one to leave their 'pipes of parsley 'ollow—'ollow—'ollow!' Mr. Sperrit had to raise his voice above the din.

'Well, if I asked you to stay *here,* I should never hear the last of it from Rhoda. She's a little cracked, of course, but the soul of devotion and capable of anything. *Ne sit ancillae,* you know.'

'Thank you. Then I'll go. I'll walk.' He stumbled out dazed and sick into the winter twilight, and sought the square house by the brook.

It was not a dignified entry, because when the door was unchained and Rhoda exclaimed, he took two valiant steps into the hall and then fainted—as men sometimes will after twenty-two hours of strong emotion and little food.

'I'm sorry,' he said when he could speak. He was lying at the foot of the stairs, his head on Rhoda's lap.

'Your 'ome is your castle, sir,' was the reply in his hair. 'I smelt it wasn't drink. You lay on the sofa till I get your supper.'

She settled him in a drawing-room hung with yellow silk, heavy with the smell of dead leaves and oil lamp. Something murmured soothingly in the background and overcame the noises in his head. He thought he heard horses' feet on wet gravel and a voice singing about ships and flocks and grass. It passed close to the shuttered bay-window.

> But each will mourn his own, she saith,
> And sweeter woman ne'er drew breath
> Than my son's wife, Elizabeth . . .
> Cusha—cusha—cusha—calling.

The hoofs broke into a canter as Rhoda entered with the tray. 'And then I'll put you to bed,' she said. 'Sidney's coming in the morning.' Midmore asked no questions. He dragged his poor bruised soul to bed and would have pitied it all over again, but the food and warm sherry and water drugged him to instant sleep.

Rhoda's voice wakened him, asking whether he would have ''ip, foot, or sitz,' which he understood were the baths of the establishment. 'Suppose you try all three,' she suggested. 'They're all yours, you know, sir.'

He would have renewed his sorrows with the daylight, but her words struck him pleasantly. Everything his eyes opened upon was his very own to keep for ever. The carved four-post Chippendale bed, obviously worth hundreds; the wavy walnut William and Mary chairs—he had seen worse ones labelled twenty guineas apiece; the oval medallion mirror; the delicate eighteenth-century wire fireguard; the heavy brocaded curtains were his—all his. So, too, a great garden full of birds that faced him when he shaved; a mulberry tree, a sun-dial, and a dull, steel-coloured brook that murmured level with the edge of a lawn a hundred yards away. Peculiarly and privately his own was the smell of sausages and coffee that he sniffed at the head of the wide square landing, all set round with mysterious doors and Bartolozzi prints. He spent two hours after breakfast in exploring his new possessions. His heart leaped up at such things as sewing-machines, a rubber-tyred bath-chair in a tiled passage, a malachite-headed Malacca cane, boxes and boxes of unopened stationery, seal-rings, bunches of keys, and at the bottom of a steel-net reticule a little leather purse with seven pounds ten shillings in gold and eleven shillings in silver.

'You used to play with that when my sister brought you down here after your measles,' said Rhoda as he slipped the money into his pocket. 'Now, this was your pore dear auntie's business-room.' She opened a low door. 'Oh, I forgot about Mr. Sidney! There he is.' An enormous old man with rheumy red eyes that blinked under downy white eyebrows sat in an Empire chair, his cap in his hands. Rhoda withdrew sniffing. The man looked Midmore over in silence, then jerked a thumb towards the door. 'I reckon she told you who I be,' he began. 'I'm the only farmer you've got. Nothin' goes off my place 'thout it walks on its own feet. What about my pig-pound?'

'Well, what about it?' said Midmore.

'That's just what I be come about. The County Councils are getting more particular. Did ye know there was swine fever at Pashell's? There *be*. It'll 'ave to be in brick.'

'Yes,' said Midmore politely.

'I've bin at your aunt that was, plenty times about it. I don't say she wasn't a just woman, but she didn't read the lease same way I did. I be used to bein' put upon, but there's no doing any longer 'thout that pig-pound.'

'When would you like it?' Midmore asked. It seemed the easiest road to take.

'Any time or other suits me, I reckon. He ain't thrivin' where he is, an' I paid eighteen shillin' for him.' He crossed his hands on his stick and gave no further sign of life.

'Is that all?' Midmore stammered.

'All now—excep' '—he glanced fretfully at the table beside him—'excep' my usuals. Where's that Rhoda?'

Midmore rang the bell. Rhoda came in with a bottle and a glass. The old man helped himself to four stiff fingers, rose in one piece, and stumped out. At the door he cried ferociously: 'Don't suppose it's any odds to you whether I'm drowned or not, but them floodgates want a wheel and winch, they do. I be too old for liftin' 'em with the bar—my time o' life.'

'Good riddance if 'e was drowned,' said Rhoda. 'But don't you mind him. He's only amusin' himself. Your pore dear auntie used to give 'im 'is usual—'tisn't the whisky *you* drink—an' send 'im about 'is business.'

'I see. Now, is a pig-pound the same thing as a pig-sty?'

Rhoda nodded. ''E needs one, too, but 'e ain't entitled to it. You look at 'is lease—third drawer on the left in that Bombay cab'net—an' next time 'e comes you ask 'im to read it. That'll choke 'im off, because 'e can't!'

There was nothing in Midmore's past to teach him the message and significance of a hand-written lease of the late 'eighties, but Rhoda interpreted.

'It don't mean anything reelly,' was her cheerful conclusion, 'excep' you mustn't get rid of him anyhow, an' 'e can do what 'e likes always. Lucky for us 'e *do* farm; and if it wasn't for 'is woman——'

'Oh, there's a Mrs. Sidney, is there?'

'Lor, *no!* The Sidneys don't marry. They keep. That's his fourth since—to my knowledge. He was a takin' man from the first.'

'Any families?'

'They'd be grown up by now if there was, wouldn't they? But you can't spend all your days considerin' 'is interests. That's what gave your pore aunt 'er indigestion. 'Ave you seen the gun-room?'

Midmore held strong views on the immorality of taking life for pleasure. But there was no denying that the late Colonel Werf's seventy-guinea breechloaders were good at their filthy job. He loaded one, took it out and pointed—merely pointed—it at a cock-pheasant which rose out of a shrubbery behind the kitchen, and the flaming bird came down in a long slant on the lawn, stone dead. Rhoda from the scullery said it was a lovely shot, and told him lunch was ready.

He spent the afternoon gun in one hand, a map in the other, beating the bounds of his lands. They lay altogether in a shallow, uninteresting valley, flanked with woods and bisected by a brook. Up stream was his own house; down stream, less than half a mile, a low red farm-house squatted in an old orchard, beside what looked like small lock-gates on the Thames. There was no doubt as to ownership. Mr. Sidney saw him while yet far off, and bellowed at him about pig-pounds and flood-gates. These last were two great sliding shutters of weedy oak across the brook, which were prised up inch by inch with a crowbar along a notched strip of iron, and when Sidney opened them they at once let out half the water. Midmore watched it shrink between its aldered banks like some conjuring trick. This, too, was his very own.

'I see,' he said. 'How interesting! Now, what's that bell for?' he went on, pointing to an old ship's bell in a rude belfry at the end of an outhouse. 'Was that a chapel once?' The red-eyed giant seemed to have difficulty in expressing himself for the moment and blinked savagely.

'Yes,' he said at last. 'My chapel. When you 'ear that bell ring you'll 'ear something. Nobody but me ud put up with it—but I reckon it don't make any odds to you.' He slammed the gates down again, and the brook rose behind them with a suck and a grunt.

Midmore moved off, conscious that he might be safer with Rhoda to hold his conversational hand. As he passed the front of the farm-house a smooth fat woman, with neatly parted grey hair under a widow's cap, curtsied to him deferentially through the window. By every teaching of the Immoderate Left she had a perfect right to express herself in any way she pleased, but the curtsey revolted him. And on his way home he was hailed from behind a hedge by a manifest idiot with no roof to his mouth, who hallooed and danced round him.

'What did that beast want?' he demanded of Rhoda at tea.

'Jimmy? He only wanted to know if you 'ad any telegrams to send. 'E'll go anywhere so long as 'tisn't across running water. That gives 'im 'is seizures. Even talkin' about it for fun like makes 'im shake.'

'But why isn't he where he can be properly looked after?'

'What 'arm's 'e doing? 'E's a love-child, but 'is family can pay for 'im. If 'e was locked up 'e'd die all off at once, like a wild rabbit. Won't you, please, look at the drive, sir?'

Midmore looked in the fading light. The neat gravel was pitted with large roundish holes, and there was a punch or two of the same sort on the lawn.

'That's the 'unt comin' 'ome,' Rhoda explained. 'Your pore dear auntie always let 'em use our drive for a short cut after the Colonel died. The Colonel wouldn't so much because he preserved; but your auntie was always an 'orse-woman till 'er sciatica.'

'Isn't there some one who can rake it over or—or something?' said Midmore vaguely.

'Oh yes. You'll never see it in the morning, but—you was out when they came 'ome an' Mister Fisher—he's the Master—told me to tell you with 'is compliments that if you wasn't preservin' and cared to 'old to the old understandin', 'is gravel-pit is at your service same as before. 'E thought, perhaps, you mightn't know, and it 'ad slipped my mind to tell you. It's good gravel, Mister Fisher's, and it binds beautiful on the drive. We 'ave to draw it, o' course, from the pit, but——'

Midmore looked at her helplessly.

'Rhoda,' said he, 'what am I supposed to do?'

'Oh, let 'em come through,' she replied. 'You never know. You may want to 'unt yourself some day.'

That evening it rained and his misery returned on him, the worse for having been diverted. At last he was driven to paw over a few score books in a panelled room called the library, and realised with horror what the late Colonel Werf's mind must have been in his prime. The volumes smelt of a dead world as strongly as they did of mildew. He opened and thrust them back, one after another, till

crude coloured illustrations of men on horses held his eye.
He began at random and read a little, moved into the
drawing-room with the volume, and settled down by the fire
still reading. It was a foul world into which he peeped for
the first time—a heavy-eating, hard-drinking hell of horse-
copers, swindlers, matchmaking mothers, economically dependent virgins selling themselves blushingly for cash and
lands: Jews, tradesmen, and an ill-considered spawn of
Dickens-and-horsedung characters (I give Midmore's own
criticism), but he read on, fascinated, and behold, from
the pages leaped, as it were, the brother to the red-eyed
man of the brook, bellowing at a landlord (here Midmore
realised that *he* was that very animal) for new barns; and
another man who, like himself again, objected to hoof-
marks on gravel. Outrageous as thought and conception
were, the stuff seemed to have the rudiments of observation. He dug out other volumes by the same author, till
Rhoda came in with a silver candlestick.

'Rhoda,' said he, 'did you ever hear about a character
called James Pigg—and Batsey?'

'Why, o' course,' said she. 'The Colonel used to come
into the kitchen in 'is dressin'-gown an' read us all those
Jorrockses.'

'Oh, Lord!' said Midmore, and went to bed with a book
called *Handley Cross* under his arm, and a lonelier Co-
lumbus into a stranger world the wet-ringed moon never
looked upon.

• • • • •

Here we omit much. But Midmore never denied that for
the epicure in sensation the urgent needs of an ancient
house, as interpreted by Rhoda pointing to daylight through
attic-tiles held in place by moss, gives an edge to the pleasure of Social Research elsewhere. Equally he found that the
reaction following prolonged research loses much of its
grey terror if one knows one can at will bathe the soul in
the society of plumbers (all the water-pipes had chronic
appendicitis), village idiots (Jimmy had taken Midmore

under his weak wing and camped daily at the drive-gates), and a giant with red eyelids whose every action is an unpredictable outrage.

Towards spring Midmore filled his house with a few friends of the Immoderate Left. It happened to be the day when, all things and Rhoda working together, a cartload of bricks, another of sand, and some bags of lime had been despatched to build Sidney his almost daily-demanded pig-pound. Midmore took his friends across the flat fields with some idea of showing them Sidney as a type of 'the peasantry.' They hit the minute when Sidney, hoarse with rage, was ordering bricklayer, mate, carts and all off his premises. The visitors disposed themselves to listen.

'You never give me no notice about changin' the pig,' Sidney shouted. The pig—at least eighteen inches long—reared on end in the old sty and smiled at the company.

'But, my good man——' Midmore opened.

'I ain't! For aught you know I be a dam' sight worse than you be. You can't come and be'ave arbit'ry with me. You *are* be'avin' arbit'ry! All you men go clean away an' don't set foot on my land till I bid ye.'

'But you asked'—Midmore felt his voice jump up—'to have the pig-pound built.'

' 'Spose I did. That's no reason you shouldn't send me notice to change the pig. 'Comin' down on me like this 'thout warnin'! That pig's got to be got into the cowshed an' all.'

'Then open the door and let him run in,' said Midmore.

'Don't you be'ave arbit'ry with *me!* Take all your dam' men 'ome off my land. I won't be treated arbit'ry.'

The carts moved off without a word, and Sidney went into the house and slammed the door.

'Now, I hold that is enormously significant,' said a visitor. 'Here you have the logical outcome of centuries of feudal oppression—the frenzy of fear.' The company looked at Midmore with grave pain.

'But he *did* worry my life out about his pig-sty,' was all Midmore found to say.

Others took up the parable and proved to him if he only held true to the gospels of the Immoderate Left the earth would soon be covered with 'jolly little' pig-sties, built in the intervals of morris-dancing by 'the peasant' himself.

Midmore felt grateful when the door opened again and Mr. Sidney invited them all to retire to the road which, he pointed out, was public. As they turned the corner of the house, a smooth-faced woman in a widow's cap curtsied to each of them through the window.

Instantly they drew pictures of that woman's lot, deprived of all vehicle for self-expression—'the set grey life and apathetic end,' one quoted—and they discussed the tremendous significance of village theatricals. Even a month ago Midmore would have told them all that he knew and Rhoda had dropped about Sidney's forms of self-expression. Now, for some strange reason, he was content to let the talk run on from village to metropolitan and world drama.

Rhoda advised him after the visitors left that 'if he wanted to do that again' he had better go up to town.

'But we only sat on cushions on the floor,' said her master.

'They're too old for romps,' she retorted, 'an' it's only the beginning of things. I've seen what I've seen. Besides, they talked and laughed in the passage going to their baths —such as took 'em.'

'Don't be a fool, Rhoda,' said Midmore. No man—unless he has loved her—will casually dismiss a woman on whose lap he has laid his head.

'Very good,' she snorted, 'but that cuts both ways. An' now, you go down to Sidney's this evenin' and put him where he ought to be. He was in his right about you givin' 'im notice about changin' the pig, but he 'adn't any right to turn it up before your company. No manners, no pig-pound. He'll understand.'

Midmore did his best to make him. He found himself reviling the old man in speech and with a joy quite new in all his experience. He wound up—it was a plagiarism from a plumber—by telling Mr. Sidney that he looked like a turkey-cock, had the morals of a parish bull, and need never hope for a new pig-pound as long as he or Midmore lived.

'Very good,' said the giant. 'I reckon you thought you 'ad something against me, and now you've come down an' told it me like man to man. Quite right. I don't bear malice. Now, you send along those bricks an' sand, an' I'll make a do to build the pig-pound myself. If you look at my lease you'll find out you're bound to provide me materials for the repairs. Only—only I thought there'd be no 'arm in my askin' you to do it throughout like.'

Midmore fairly gasped. 'Then, why the devil did you turn my carts back when—when I sent them up here to do it throughout for you?'

Mr. Sidney sat down on the floodgates, his eyebrows knitted in thought.

'I'll tell you,' he said slowly. ' 'Twas too dam' like cheatin' a suckin' baby. My woman, she said so too.'

For a few seconds the teachings of the Immoderate Left, whose humour is all their own, wrestled with those of Mother Earth, who has her own humours. Then Midmore laughed till he could scarcely stand. In due time Mr. Sidney laughed too—crowing and wheezing crescendo till it broke from him in roars. They shook hands, and Midmore went home grateful that he had held his tongue among his companions.

When he reached his house he met three or four men and women on horseback, very muddy indeed, coming down the drive. Feeling hungry himself, he asked them if they were hungry. They said they were, and he bade them enter. Jimmy took their horses, who seemed to know him. Rhoda took their battered hats, led the women upstairs for hairpins, and presently fed them all with tea-cakes, poached eggs, anchovy toast, and drinks from a coromandel-wood liqueur case which Midmore had never known that he possessed.

'And I *will* say,' said Miss Connie Sperrit, her spurred foot on the fender and a smoking muffin in her whip hand, 'Rhoda does one top-hole. She always did since I was eight.'

'Seven, Miss, was when you began to 'unt,' said Rhoda, setting down more buttered toast.

'And so,' the M.F.H. was saying to Midmore, 'when he got to your brute Sidney's land, we had to whip 'em off. It's a regular Alsatia for 'em. They know it. Why'—he dropped his voice—'I don't want to say anything against Sidney as your tenant, of course, but I do believe the old scoundrel's perfectly capable of putting down poison.'

'Sidney's capable of anything,' said Midmore with immense feeling; but once again he held his tongue. They were a queer community; yet when they had stamped and jingled out to their horses again, the house felt hugely big and disconcerting.

This may be reckoned the conscious beginning of his double life. It ran in odd channels that summer—a riding school, for instance, near Hayes Common and a shooting ground near Wormwood Scrubs. A man who has been saddle-galled or shoulder-bruised for half the day is not at his London best of evenings; and when the bills for his amusements come in he curtails his expenses in other directions. So a cloud settled on Midmore's name. His London world talked of a hardening of heart and a tightening of purse-strings which signified disloyalty to the Cause. One man, a confidant of the old expressive days, attacked him robustiously and demanded account of his soul's progress. It was not furnished, for Midmore was calculating how much it would cost to repave stables so dilapidated that even the village idiot apologised for putting visitors' horses into them. The man went away, and served up what he had heard of the pig-pound episode as a little newspaper sketch, calculated to annoy. Midmore read it with an eye as practical as a woman's, and since most of his experiences had been among women, at once sought out a woman to whom he might tell his sorrow at the disloyalty of his own familiar friend. She was so sympathetic that he went on to confide how his bruised heart—she knew all about it—had found so-lace, with a long O, in another quarter which he indicated rather carefully in case it might be betrayed to other loyal friends. As his hints pointed directly towards facile Hampstead, and as his urgent business was the purchase of a horse from a dealer, Beckenham way, he felt he had done good work. Later, when his friend, the scribe, talked to him alluringly of 'secret gardens' and those so-laces to which every man who follows the Wider Morality is entitled, Midmore lent him a five-pound note which he had got back on the price of a ninety-guinea bay gelding. So true it is, as he read in one of the late Colonel Werf's books, that 'the young man of the present day would sooner lie under an imputation against his morals than against his knowledge of horse-flesh.'

Midmore desired more than he desired anything else at that moment to ride and, above all, to jump on a ninety-guinea bay gelding with black points and a slovenly habit of hitting his fences. He did not wish many people except Mr. Sidney, who very kindly lent his soft meadow behind the flood-gates, to be privy to the matter, which he rightly foresaw would take him to the autumn. So he told such friends as hinted at country week-end visits that he had practically let his newly inherited house. The rent, he said, was an object to him, for he had lately lost large sums through ill-considered benevolences. He would name no names, but they could guess. And they guessed loyally all round the circle of his acquaintance as they spread the news that explained so much.

There remained only one couple of his once intimate associates to pacify. They were deeply sympathetic and utterly loyal, of course, but as curious as any of the apes whose diet they had adopted. Midmore met them in a suburban train, coming up to town, not twenty minutes after he had come off two hours' advanced tuition (one guinea an hour) over hurdles in a hall. He had, of course, changed his kit, but his too heavy bridle-hand shook a little among the newspapers. On the inspiration of the moment, which is your natural liar's best hold, he told them that he was condemned to a rest-cure. He would lie in semi-darkness drinking milk, for weeks and weeks, cut off even from letters. He was astonished and delighted at the ease with which the usual lie confounds the unusual intellect. They swallowed it as swiftly as they recommended him to live on nuts and fruit; but he saw in the woman's eyes the exact reason she would set forth for his retirement. After all, she had as much right to express herself as he purposed to take for himself; and Midmore believed strongly in the fullest equality of the sexes.

That retirement made one small ripple in the strenuous world. The lady who had written the twelve-page letter ten months before sent him another of eight pages, analysing all the motives that were leading her back to him—should she come?—now that he was ill and alone. Much might yet be retrieved, she said, out of the waste of jarring lives and piteous misunderstandings. It needed only a hand.

But Midmore needed two, next morning very early, for a devil's diversion, among wet coppices, called 'cubbing.'

'You haven't a bad seat,' said Miss Sperrit through the morning-mists. 'But you're worrying him.'

'He pulls so,' Midmore grunted.

'Let him alone, then. Look out for the branches,' she shouted, as they whirled up a splashy ride. Cubs were plentiful. Most of the hounds attached themselves to a straight-necked youngster of education who scuttled out of the woods into the open fields below.

'Hold on!' some one shouted. 'Turn 'em, Midmore. That's your brute Sidney's land. It's all wire.'

'Oh, Connie, stop!' Mrs. Sperrit shrieked as her daughter charged at a boundary-hedge.

'Wire be damned! I had it all out a fortnight ago. Come on!' This was Midmore, buffeting into it a little lower down.

'I knew that!' Connie cried over her shoulder, and she flitted across the open pasture, humming to herself.

'Oh, of course! If some people have private information,

they can afford to thrust.' This was a snuff-coloured habit into which Miss Sperrit had cannoned down the ride.

'What! Midmore got Sidney to heel? *You* never did that, Sperrit.' This was Mr. Fisher, M.F.H., enlarging the breach Midmore had made.

'No, confound him!' said the father testily. 'Go on, sir! *Injecto ter pulvere*—you've kicked half the ditch into my eye already.'

They killed that cub a little short of the haven his mother had told him to make for—a two-acre Alsatia of a gorse-patch to which the M.F.H. had been denied access for the last fifteen seasons. He expressed his gratitude before all the field and Mr. Sidney, at Mr. Sidney's farm-house door.

'And if there should be any poultry claims——' he went on.

'There won't be,' said Midmore. 'It's too like cheating a sucking child, isn't it, Mr. Sidney?'

'You've got me!' was all the reply. 'I be used to bein' put upon, but you've got me, Mus' Midmore.'

Midmore pointed to a new brick pig-pound built in strict disregard of the terms of the life-tenant's lease. The gesture told the tale to the few who did not know, and they shouted.

Such pagan delights as these were followed by pagan sloth of evenings when men and women elsewhere are at their brightest. But Midmore preferred to lie out on a yellow silk couch, reading works of a debasing vulgarity; or, by invitation, to dine with the Sperrits and savages of their kidney. These did not expect flights of fancy or phrasing. They lied, except about horses, grudgingly and of necessity, not for art's sake; and, men and women alike, they expressed themselves along their chosen lines with the serene indifference of the larger animals. Then Midmore would go home and identify them, one by one, out of the natural-history books by Mr. Surtees, on the table beside the sofa. At first they looked upon him coolly, but when the tale of the removed wire and the recaptured gorse had gone the rounds, they accepted him for a person willing to play their games. True, a faction suspended judgment for a

while, because they shot, and hoped that Midmore would
serve the glorious mammon of pheasant-raising rather than
the unkempt god of fox-hunting. But after he had shown
his choice, they did not ask by what intellectual process he
had arrived at it. He hunted three, sometimes four, times
a week, which necessitated not only one bay gelding
(£94: 10s.), but a mannerly white-stockinged chestnut
(£114), and a black mare, rather long in the back but
with a mouth of silk (£150), who so evidently preferred to
carry a lady that it would have been cruel to have balked
her. Besides, with that handling she could be sold at a profit.
And besides, the hunt was a quiet, intimate, kindly little
hunt, not anxious for strangers, of good report in the
Field, the servant of one M.F.H., given to hospitality, riding well its own horses, and, with the exception of Midmore, not novices. But as Miss Sperrit observed, after the
M.F.H. had said some things to him at a gate: 'It *is* a pity
you don't know as much as your horse, but you will in
time. It takes years and yee-ars. I've been at it for fifteen
and I'm only just learning. But you've made a decent
kick-off.'

So he kicked off in wind and wet and mud, wondering
quite sincerely why the bubbling ditches and sucking pastures held him from day to day, or what so-lace he could
find on off days in chasing grooms and bricklayers round
outhouses.

To make sure he up-rooted himself one week-end of
heavy mid-winter rain, and re-entered his lost world in the
character of Galahad fresh from a rest-cure. They all
agreed, with an eye over his shoulder for the next comer,
that he was a different man; but when they asked him for
the symptoms of nervous strain, and led him all through
their own, he realised he had lost much of his old skill in
lying. His three months' absence, too, had put him hopelessly behind the London field. The movements, the allu-
sions, the slang of the game had changed. The couples had
rearranged themselves or were re-crystallizing in fresh
triangles, whereby he put his foot in it badly. Only one

great soul (he who had written the account of the pig-pound episode) stood untouched by the vast flux of time, and Midmore lent him another fiver for his integrity. A woman took him, in the wet forenoon, to a pronouncement on the Oneness of Impulse in Humanity, which struck him as a polysyllabic *résumé* of Mr. Sidney's domestic arrangements, plus a clarion call to 'shock civilisation into common-sense.'

'And you'll come to tea with me to-morrow?' she asked, after lunch, nibbling cashew nuts from a saucer. Midmore replied that there were great arrears of work to overtake when a man had been put away for so long.

'But you've come back like a giant refreshed. . . . I hope that Daphne'—this was the lady of the twelve and the eight-page letter—'will be with us too. She has misunderstood herself, like so many of us,' the woman murmured, 'but I think eventually . . .' she flung out her thin little hands. 'However, these are things that each lonely soul must adjust for itself.'

'Indeed, yes,' said Midmore with a deep sigh. The old tricks were sprouting in the old atmosphere like mushrooms in a dung-pit. He passed into an abrupt reverie, shook his head, as though stung by tumultuous memories, and departed without any ceremony of farewell to—catch a mid-afternoon express where a man meets associates who talk horse, and weather as it affects the horse, all the way down. What worried him most was that he had missed a day with the hounds.

He met Rhoda's keen old eyes without flinching; and the drawing-room looked very comfortable that wet evening at tea. After all, his visit to town had not been wholly a failure. He had burned quite a bushel of letters at his flat. A flat—here he reached mechanically toward the worn volumes near the sofa—a flat was a consuming animal. As for Daphne . . . he opened at random on the words: 'His lordship then did as desired and disclosed a *tableau* of considerable strength and variety.' Midmore reflected: 'And I used to think . . . But she wasn't . . . We were all babblers and skirters together . . . I didn't babble much—thank goodness—but I skirted.' He turned the pages backward for more *Sortes Surteesianae,* and read: 'When at length they rose to go to bed it struck each man as he followed his neighbour upstairs, that the man before him walked very crookedly.' He laughed aloud at the fire.

'What about to-morrow?' Rhoda asked, entering with garments over her shoulder. 'It's never stopped raining since you left. You'll be plastered out of sight an' all in five minutes. You'd better wear your next best, 'adn't you? I'm afraid they've shrank. 'Adn't you best try 'em on?'

'Here?' said Midmore.

' 'Suit yourself. I bathed you when you wasn't larger than a leg o' lamb,' said the ex-ladies'-maid.

'Rhoda, one of these days I shall get a valet, and a married butler.'

'There's many a true word spoke in jest. But nobody's huntin' to-morrow.'

'Why? Have they cancelled the meet?'

'They say it only means slipping and overreaching in the mud, and they all 'ad enough of that to-day. Charlie told me so just now.'

'Oh!' It seemed that the word of Mr. Sperrit's confidential clerk had weight.

'Charlie came down to help Mr. Sidney lift the gates,' Rhoda continued.

'The flood-gates? They are perfectly easy to handle now. I've put in a wheel and a winch.'

'When the brook's really up they must be took clean out on account of the rubbish blockin' 'em. That's why Charlie came down.'

Midmore grunted impatiently. 'Everybody has talked to me about that brook ever since I came here. It's never done anything yet.'

'This 'as been a dry summer. If you care to look now, sir, I'll get you a lantern.'

She paddled out with him into a large wet night. Half-way down the lawn her light was reflected on shallow brown water, pricked through with grass blades at the edges. Beyond that light, the brook was strangling and kicking among hedges and tree-trunks.

'What on earth will happen to the big rosebed?' was Midmore's first word.

'It generally 'as to be restocked after a flood. Ah!' she raised her lantern. 'There's two garden-seats knockin' against the sun-dial. Now, that won't do the roses any good.'

'This is too absurd. There ought to be some decently thought-out system—for—for dealing with this sort of thing.' He peered into the rushing gloom. There seemed to be no end to the moisture and the racket. In town he had noticed nothing.

'It can't be 'elped,' said Rhoda. 'It's just what it does do once in just so often. We'd better go back.'

All earth under foot was sliding in a thousand liquid noises towards the hoarse brook. Somebody wailed from the house: ''Fraid o' the water! Come 'ere! 'Fraid o' the water!'

'That's Jimmy. Wet always takes 'im that way,' she explained. The idiot charged into them, shaking with terror.

'Brave Jimmy! How brave of Jimmy! Come into the hall. What Jimmy got now?' she crooned. It was a sodden note which ran: 'Dear Rhoda—Mr. Lotten, with whom I rode home this afternoon, told me that if this wet keeps up, he's afraid the fish-pond he built last year, where Coxen's old mill-dam was, will go, as the dam did once before, he says. If it does it's bound to come down the brook. It may be all right, but perhaps you had better look out. C. S.'

'If Coxen's dam goes, that means . . . I'll 'ave the drawing-room carpet up at once to be on the safe side. The claw-'ammer is in the libery.'

'Wait a minute. Sidney's gates are out, you said?'

'Both. He'll need it if Coxen's pond goes. . . . I've seen it once.'

'I'll just slip down and have a look at Sidney. Light the lantern again, please, Rhoda.'

'You won't get *him* to stir. He's been there since he was born. But *she* don't know anything. I'll fetch your waterproof and some top-boots.'

''Fraid o' the water! 'Fraid o' the water!' Jimmy sobbed, pressed against a corner of the hall, his hands to his eyes.

'All right, Jimmy. Jimmy can help play with the carpet,' Rhoda answered, as Midmore went forth into the darkness and the roarings all round. He had never seen such an utterly unregulated state of affairs. There was another lantern reflected on the streaming drive.

'Hi! Rhoda! Did you get my note? I came down to make sure. I thought, afterwards, Jimmy might funk the water!'

'It's me—Miss Sperrit,' Midmore cried. 'Yes, we got it, thanks.'

'You're back, then. Oh, good! . . . Is it bad down with you?'

'I'm going to Sidney's to have a look.'

'You won't get *him* out. 'Lucky I met Bob Lotten. I told him he hadn't any business impounding water for his idiotic trout without rebuilding the dam.'

'How far up is it? I've only been there once.'

'Not more than four miles as the water will come. He says he's opened all the sluices.'

She had turned and fallen into step beside him, her hooded head bowed against the thinning rain. As usual she was humming to herself.

'Why on earth did you come out in this weather?' Midmore asked.

'It was worse when you were in town. The rain's taking off now. If it wasn't for that pond, I wouldn't worry so much. There's Sidney's bell. Come on!' She broke into a run. A cracked bell was jangling feebly down the valley.

'Keep on the road!' Midmore shouted. The ditches were snorting bank-full on either side, and towards the brookside the fields were afloat and beginning to move in the darkness.

'Catch me going off it! There's his light burning all right.' She halted undistressed at a little rise. 'But the flood's in

the orchard. Look!' She swung her lantern to show a front
rank of old apple-trees reflected in still, out-lying waters
beyond the half-drowned hedge. They could hear above the
thud-thud of the gorged flood-gates, shrieks in two keys as
monotonous as a steam-organ.

'The high one's the pig.' Miss Sperrit laughed.

'All right! I'll get *her* out. You stay where you are, and
I'll see you home afterwards.'

'But the water's only just over the road,' she objected.

'Never mind. Don't you move. Promise?'

'All right. You take my stick, then, and feel for holes in
case anything's washed out anywhere. This *is* a lark!'

Midmore took it, and stepped into the water that moved
sluggishly as yet across the farm road which ran to Sidney's
front door from the raised and metalled public road. It
was half way up to his knees when he knocked. As he
looked back Miss Sperrit's lantern seemed to float in mid-
ocean.

'You can't come in or the water'll come with you. I've
bunged up all the cracks,' Mr. Sidney shouted from within.
'Who be ye?'

'Take me out! Take me out!' the woman shrieked, and
the pig from his sty behind the house urgently seconded
the motion.

'I'm Midmore! Coxen's old mill-dam is likely to go, they
say. Come out!'

'I told 'em it would when they made a fish-pond of it.
'Twasn't ever puddled proper. But it's a middlin' wide
valley. She's got room to spread. . . . Keep still, or I'll
take and duck you in the cellar! . . . You go 'ome, Mus'
Midmore, an' take the law o' Mus' Lotten soon's you've
changed your socks.'

'Confound you, aren't you coming out?'

'To catch my death o' cold? I'm all right where I be.
I've seen it before. But you can take *her*. She's no sort o'
use or sense. . . . Climb out through the window. Didn't
I tell you I'd plugged the door-cracks, you fool's daughter?'
The parlour window opened, and the woman flung herself

into Midmore's arms, nearly knocking him down. Mr. Sidney leaned out of the window, pipe in mouth.

'Take her 'ome,' he said, and added oracularly:

> 'Two women in one house,
> Two cats an' one mouse,
> Two dogs an' one bone—
> Which I will leave alone.

I've seen it before.' Then he shut and fastened the window.

'A trap! A trap! You had ought to have brought a trap for me. I'll be drowned in this wet,' the woman cried.

'Hold up! You can't be any wetter than you are. Come along!' Midmore did not at all like the feel of the water over his boot-tops.

'Hooray! Come along!' Miss Sperrit's lantern, not fifty yards away, waved cheerily.

The woman threshed towards it like a panic-stricken goose, fell on her knees, was jerked up again by Midmore, and pushed on till she collapsed at Miss Sperrit's feet.

'But you won't get bronchitis if you go straight to Mr. Midmore's house,' said the unsympathetic maiden.

'O Gawd! O Gawd! I wish our 'eavenly Father 'ud forgive me my sins an' call me 'ome,' the woman sobbed. 'But I won't go to 'is 'ouse! I won't.'

'All right, then. Stay here. Now, if we run,' Miss Sperrit whispered to Midmore, 'she'll follow us. Not too fast!'

They set off at a considerate trot, and the woman lumbered behind them, bellowing, till they met a third lantern —Rhoda holding Jimmy's hand. She had got the carpet up, she said, and was escorting Jimmy past the water that he dreaded.

'That's all right,' Miss Sperrit pronounced. 'Take Mrs. Sidney back with you, Rhoda, and put her to bed. I'll take Jimmy with me. You aren't afraid of the water now, are you, Jimmy?'

'Not afraid of anything now.' Jimmy reached for her hand. 'But get away from the water quick.'

'I'm coming with you,' Midmore interrupted.

'You most certainly are not. You're drenched. She threw you twice. Go home and change. You may have to be out again all night. It's only half-past seven now. I'm perfectly safe.' She flung herself lightly over a stile, and hurried uphill by the footpath, out of reach of all but the boasts of the flood below.

Rhoda, dead silent, herded Mrs. Sidney to the house.

'You'll find your things laid out on the bed,' she said to Midmore as he came up. 'I'll attend to—to this. *She's* got nothing to cry for.'

Midmore raced into dry kit, and raced uphill to be rewarded by the sight of the lantern just turning into the Sperrits' gate. He came back by way of Sidney's farm, where he saw the light twinkling across three acres of shining water, for the rain had ceased and the clouds were stripping overhead, though the brook was noisier than ever. Now there was only that doubtful mill-pond to look after —that and his swirling world abandoned to himself alone.

'We shall have to sit up for it,' said Rhoda after dinner. And as the drawing-room commanded the best view of the rising flood, they watched it from there for a long time, while all the clocks of the house bore them company.

''Tisn't the water, it's the mud on the skirting-board after it goes down that I mind,' Rhoda whispered. 'The last time Coxen's mill broke, I remember it came up to the second—no, third—step o' Mr. Sidney's stairs.'

'What did Sidney do about it?'

'He made a notch on the step. 'E said it was a record. Just like 'im.'

'It's up to the drive now,' said Midmore after another long wait. 'And the rain stopped before eight, you know.'

'Then Coxen's dam 'as broke, and that's the first of the flood-water.' She stared out beside him. The water was rising in sudden pulses—an inch or two at a time, with great sweeps and lagoons and a sudden increase of the brook's proper thunder.

'You can't stand all the time. Take a chair,' Midmore said presently.

Rhoda looked back into the bare room. 'The carpet bein'
up *does* make a difference. Thank you, sir, I *will* 'ave a
set-down.'

''Right over the drive now,' said Midmore. He opened
the window and leaned out. 'Is that wind up the valley,
Rhoda?'

'No, that's *it!* But I've seen it before.'

There was not so much a roar as the purposeful drive of
a tide across a jagged reef, which put down every other
sound for twenty minutes. A wide sheet of water hurried
up to the little terrace on which the house stood, pushed
round either corner, rose again and stretched, as it were,
yawning beneath the moonlight, joined other sheets waiting
for them in unsuspected hollows, and lay out all in one. A
puff of wind followed.

'It's right up to the wall now. I can touch it with my
finger.' Midmore bent over the window-sill.

'I can 'ear it in the cellars,' said Rhoda dolefully. 'Well,
we've done what we can! I think I'll 'ave a look.' She left
the room and was absent half an hour or more, during
which time he saw a full-grown tree hauling itself across
the lawn by its naked roots. Then a hurdle knocked against
the wall, caught on an iron foot-scraper just outside, and
made a square-headed ripple. The cascade through the
cellar-windows diminished.

'It's dropping,' Rhoda cried, as she returned. 'It's only
tricklin' into my cellars now.'

'Wait a minute. I believe—I believe I can see the scraper
on the edge of the drive just showing!'

In another ten minutes the drive itself roughened and
became gravel again, tilting all its water towards the shrubbery.

'The pond's gone past,' Rhoda announced. 'We shall only
'ave the common flood to contend with now. You'd better
go to bed.'

'I ought to go down and have another look at Sidney
before daylight.'

'No need. You can see 'is light burnin' from all the up-stairs windows.'

'By the way. I forgot about *her*. Where've you put her?'

'In my bed.' Rhoda's tone was ice. 'I wasn't going to undo a room for *that* stuff.'

'But it—it couldn't be helped,' said Midmore. 'She was half drowned. One mustn't be narrowminded, Rhoda, even if her position isn't quite—er—regular.'

'Pfff! I wasn't worryin' about that.' She leaned forward to the window. 'There's the edge of the lawn showin' now. It falls as fast as it rises. Dearie'—the change of tone made Midmore jump—'didn't you know that I was 'is first? *That's* what makes it so hard to bear.' Midmore looked at the long lizard-like back and had no words.

She went on, still talking through the black window-pane:

'Your pore dear auntie was very kind about it. She said she'd make all allowances for one, but no more. Never any more. . . . Then, you didn't know 'oo Charlie was all this time?'

'Your nephew, I always thought.'

'Well, well,' she spoke pityingly. 'Everybody's business being nobody's business, I suppose no one thought to tell you. But Charlie made 'is own way for 'imself from the beginnin'! . . . But *her* upstairs, she never produced anything. Just an 'ousekeeper, as you might say. 'Turned over an' went to sleep straight off. She 'ad the impudence to ask me for 'ot sherry-gruel.'

'Did you give it to her,' said Midmore.

'Me? Your sherry? No!'

The memory of Sidney's outrageous rhyme at the window, and Charlie's long nose (he thought it looked interested at the time) as he passed the copies of Mrs. Werf's last four wills, overcame Midmore without warning.

'This damp is givin' you a cold,' said Rhoda, rising. 'There you go again! Sneezin's a sure sign of it. Better go to bed. You can't do anythin' excep' '—she stood rigid, with crossed arms—'about me.'

'Well. What about you?' Midmore stuffed the handkerchief into his pocket.

'Now you know about it, what are you goin' to do—sir?'

She had the answer on her lean cheek before the sentence was finished.

'Go and see if you can get us something to eat, Rhoda. And beer.'

'I expec' the larder'll be in a swim,' she replied, 'but old bottled stuff don't take any harm from wet.' She returned with a tray, all in order, and they ate and drank together, and took observations of the falling flood till dawn opened its bleared eyes on the wreck of what had been a fair garden. Midmore, cold and annoyed, found himself humming:

'That flood strewed wrecks upon the grass,
    That ebb swept out the flocks to sea.

There isn't a rose left, Rhoda!

An awesome ebb and flow it was
To many more than mine and me.
But each will mourn his . . .

It'll cost me a hundred.'

'Now we know the worst,' said Rhoda, 'we can go to bed. I'll lay on the kitchen sofa. His light's burnin' still.'

'And *she?*'

'Dirty old cat! You ought to 'ear 'er snore!'

At ten o'clock in the morning, after a maddening hour in his own garden on the edge of the retreating brook, Midmore went off to confront more damage at Sidney's. The first thing that met him was the pig, snowy white, for the water had washed him out of his new sty, calling on high heaven for breakfast. The front door had been forced open, and the flood had registered its own height in a brown dado on the walls. Midmore chased the pig out and called up the stairs.

'I be abed o' course. Which step 'as she rose to?' Sidney
cried from above. 'The fourth? Then it's beat all records.
Come up.'

'Are you ill?' Midmore asked as he entered the room.
The red eyelids blinked cheerfully. Mr. Sidney, beneath a
sumptuous patch-work quilt, was smoking.

'Nah! I'm only thankin' God I ain't my own landlord.
Take that cheer. What's she done?'

'It hasn't gone down enough for me to make sure.'

'Them floodgates o' yourn 'll be middlin' far down the
brook by now; an' your rose-garden have gone after 'em.
I saved my chickens, though. You'd better get Mus' Sperrit
to take the law o' Lotten an' 'is fish-pond.'

'No, thanks. I've trouble enough without that.'

'Hev ye?' Mr. Sidney grinned. 'How did ye make out
with those two women o' mine last night? I lay they fought.'

'You infernal old scoundrel!' Midmore laughed.

'I be—an' then again I bain't,' was the placid answer.
'But, Rhoda, *she* wouldn't ha' left me last night. Fire or
flood, she wouldn't.'

'Why didn't you ever marry her?' Midmore asked.

'Waste of good money. She was willin' without.'

There was a step on the gritty mud below, and a voice
humming. Midmore rose quickly saying: 'Well, I suppose
you're all right now.'

'I be. I ain't a landlord, nor I ain't young—nor anxious.
Oh, Mus' Midmore! Would it make any odds about her
thirty pounds comin' regular if I married her? Charlie said
maybe 'twould.'

'Did he?' Midmore turned at the door. 'And what did
Jimmy say about it?'

'Jimmy?' Mr. Sidney chuckled as the joke took him.
'Oh, *he's* none o' mine. He's Charlie's look-out.'

Midmore slammed the door and ran downstairs.

'Well, this is a—sweet—mess,' said Miss Sperrit in shortest
skirts and heaviest riding-boots. 'I had to come down and
have a look at it. "The old mayor climbed the belfry
tower." 'Been up all night nursing your family?'

'Nearly that! Isn't it cheerful?' He pointed through the door to the stairs with small twig-drift on the last three treads.

'It's a record, though,' said she, and hummed to herself:

'That flood strewed wrecks upon the grass,
That ebb swept out the flocks to sea.'

'You're always singing that, aren't you?' Midmore said suddenly as she passed into the parlour where slimy chairs had been stranded at all angles.

'Am I? Now I come to think of it I believe I do. They say I always hum when I ride. Have you noticed it?'

'Of course I have. I notice every——'

'Oh,' she went on hurriedly. 'We had it for the village cantata last winter—"The Brides of Enderby." '

'No! "High Tide on the Coast of Lincolnshire." ' For some reason Midmore spoke sharply.

'Just like that.' She pointed to the befouled walls. 'I say. . . . Let's get this furniture a little straight. . . . You know it too?'

'Every word, since you sang it, of course.'

'When?'

'The first night I ever came down. You rode past the drawing-room window in the dark singing it—"And sweeter woman——" '

'I thought the house was empty then. Your aunt always let us use that short cut. Ha-hadn't we better get this out into the passage? It'll all have to come out anyhow. You take the other side.' They began to lift a heavyish table. Their words came jerkily between gasps and their faces were as white as—a newly washed and very hungry pig.

'Look out!' Midmore shouted. His legs were whirled from under him, as the table, grunting madly, careened and knocked the girl out of sight.

The wild boar of Asia could not have cut down a couple more scientifically, but this little pig lacked his ancestor's nerve and fled shrieking over their bodies.

'Are you hurt, darling?' was Midmore's first word, and 'No—I'm only winded—dear,' was Miss Sperrit's, as he lifted her out of her corner, her hat over one eye and her right cheek a smear of mud.

. . . . .

They fed him a little later on some chickenfeed that they found in Sidney's quiet barn, a pail of buttermilk out of the dairy, and a quantity of onions from a shelf in the back-kitchen.

'Seed-onions, most likely,' said Connie. 'You'll hear about this.'

'What does it matter? They ought to have been gilded. We must buy him.'

'And keep him as long as he lives,' she agreed. 'But I think I ought to go home now. You see, when I came out I didn't expect . . . Did you?'

'No! Yes. . . . It had to come. . . . But if any one had told me an hour ago! . . . Sidney's unspeakable parlour—and the mud on the carpet.'

'Oh, I say! Is my cheek clean now?'

'Not quite. Lend me your hanky again a minute, darling. . . . What a purler you came!'

'You can't talk. 'Remember when your chin hit that table and you said "blast"! I was just going to laugh.'

'You didn't laugh when I picked you up. You were going "oo-oo-oo" like a little owl.'

'My dear child——'

'Say that again!'

'My dear child. (Do you really like it? I keep it for my best friends.) My dee-ar child, I thought I was going to be sick there and then. He knocked every ounce of wind out of me—the angel! But I must really go.'

They set off together, very careful not to join hands or take arms.

'Not across the fields,' said Midmore at the stile. 'Come round by—by your own place.'

She flushed indignantly.

'It will be yours in a little time,' he went on, shaken with his own audacity.

'Not so much of your little times, if you please!' She shied like a colt across the road; then instantly, like a colt, her eyes lit with new curiosity as she came in sight of the drive-gates.

'And not quite so much of your airs and graces, Madam,' Midmore returned, 'or I won't let you use our drive as a short cut any more.'

'Oh, I'll be good. I'll be good.' Her voice changed suddenly. 'I swear I'll try to be good, dear. I'm not much of a thing at the best. What made *you* . . .'

'I'm worse—worse! Miles and oceans worse. But what does it matter now?'

They halted beside the gate-pillars.

'I see!' she said, looking up the sodden carriage sweep to the front door porch where Rhoda was slapping a wet mat to and fro. '*I* see. . . . Now, I really must go home. No! Don't you come. I must speak to Mother first all by myself.'

He watched her up the hill till she was out of sight.

THE VORTEX

(AUGUST 1914)

'Thy Lord spoke by inspiration to the Bee.'
                                        AL KORAN.

I have, to my grief and loss, suppressed several notable stories of my friend, the Hon. A. M. Penfentenyou, once Minister of Woods and Waysides in De Thouar's first administration; later, Premier in all but name of one of Our great and growing Dominions; and now, as always, the idol of his own Province, which is two and one-half the size of England.

For this reason I hold myself at liberty to deal with some portion of the truth concerning Penfentenyou's latest visit to Our shores. He arrived at my house by car, on a hot summer day, in a white waistcoat and spats, sweeping black frock-coat and glistening top-hat—a little rounded, perhaps, at the edges, but agile as ever in mind and body.

'What is the trouble now?' I asked, for the last time we had met, Penfentenyou was floating a three-million pound loan for his beloved but unscrupulous Province, and I did not wish to entertain any more of his financial friends.

'We,' Penfentenyou replied ambassadorially, 'have come to have a Voice in Your Councils. By the way, the Voice is coming down on the evening train with my Agent-General. I thought you wouldn't mind if I invited 'em. You know We're going to share Your burdens henceforward. You'd better get into training.'

'Certainly,' I replied. 'What's the Voice like?'

'He's in earnest,' said Penfentenyou. 'He's got It, and he's got It bad. He'll give It to you,' he said.

'What's his name?'

'We call him all sorts of names, but I think you'd better call him Mr. Lingnam. You won't have to do it more than once.'

'What's he suffering from?'

'The Empire. He's pretty nearly cured us all of Imperialism at home. P'raps he'll cure you.'

'Very good. What am I to do with him?'

'Don't you worry,' said Penfentenyou. 'He'll do it.'

And when Mr. Lingnam appeared half-an-hour later with the Agent-General for Penfentenyou's Dominion, he did just that.

He advanced across the lawn eloquent as all the tides. He said he had been observing to the Agent-General that it was both politically immoral and strategically unsound that forty-four million people should bear the entire weight of the defences of Our mighty Empire, but, as he had observed (here the Agent-General evaporated), we stood now upon the threshold of a new era in which the self-governing *and* self-respecting (bis) Dominions would rightly and righteously, as copartners in Empery, shoulder their share of any burden which the Pan-Imperial Council of the Future should allot. The Agent-General was already arranging for drinks with Penfentenyou at the other end of the garden. Mr. Lingnam swept me on to the most remote bench and settled to his theme.

We dined at eight. At nine Mr. Lingnam was only drawing abreast of things Imperial. At ten the Agent-General, who earns his salary, was shamelessly dozing on the sofa. At eleven he and Penfentenyou went to bed. At midnight Mr. Lingnam brought down his big-bellied despatch box with the newspaper clippings and set to federating the Empire in earnest. I remember that he had three alternative plans. As a dealer in words, I plumped for the resonant third—'Reciprocally co-ordinated Senatorial Hegemony'—which he then elaborated in detail for three-quarters of an hour. At half-past one he urged me to have faith and to remember that nothing mattered except the Idea. Then he retired to his room, accompanied by one glass of cold water, and I went into the dawn-lit garden and prayed to any Power that might be off duty for the blood of Mr. Lingnam, Penfentenyou, and the Agent-General.

To me, as I have often observed elsewhere, the hour of earliest dawn is fortunate, and the wind that runs before it has ever been my most comfortable counsellor.

'Wait!' it said, all among the night's expectant rosebuds. 'To-morrow is also a day. Wait upon the Event!'

I went to bed so at peace with God and Man and Guest that when I waked I visited Mr. Lingnam in pyjamas, and he talked to me Pan-Imperially for half-an-hour before his bath. Later, the Agent-General said he had letters to write, and Penfentenyou invented a Cabinet crisis in his adored Dominion which would keep him busy with codes and cables all the forenoon. But I said firmly, 'Mr. Lingnam wishes to see a little of the country round here. You are coming with us in your own car.'

'It's a hired one,' Penfentenyou objected.

'Yes. Paid for by me as a taxpayer,' I replied.

'And yours has a top, and the weather looks thundery,' said the Agent-General. 'Ours hasn't a wind-screen. Even our goggles were hired.'

'I'll lend you goggles,' I said. 'My car is under repairs.'

The hireling who had looked to be returned to London spat and growled on the drive. She was an open car, capable of some eighteen miles on the flat, with tetanic gears and a perpetual palsy.

'It won't make the least difference,' sighed the Agent-General. 'He'll only raise his voice. He did it all the way coming down.'

'I say,' said Penfentenyou suspiciously, 'what are you doing all this *for?*'

'Love of the Empire,' I answered, as Mr. Lingnam tripped up in dust-coat and binoculars. 'Now, Mr. Lingnam will tell us exactly what he wants to see. He probably knows more about England than the rest of us put together.'

'I read it up yesterday,' said Mr. Lingnam simply. While

we stowed the lunch-basket (one can never make too sure with a hired car) he outlined a very pretty and instructive little day's run.

'You'll drive, of course?' said Penfentenyou to him. 'It's the only thing you know anything about.'

This astonished me, for your greater Federationists are rarely mechanicians, but Mr. Lingnam said he would prefer to be inside for the present and enjoy our conversation.

Well settled on the back seat, he did not once lift his eyes to the mellow landscape around him, or throw a word at the life of the English road which to me is one renewed and unreasoned orgy of delight. The mustard-coloured scouts of the Automobile Association; their natural enemies, the unjust police; our natural enemies, the deliberate market-day cattle, broadside-on at all corners, the bicycling butcher-boy a furlong behind; road-engines that pulled giddy-go-rounds, rifle galleries, and swings, and sucked snortingly from wayside ponds in defiance of the notice-board; traction-engines, their trailers piled high with road metal; uniformed village nurses, one per seven statute miles, flitting by on their wheels; governess-carts full of pink children jogging unconcernedly past roaring, brazen touring-cars; the wayside rector with virgins in attendance, their faces screwed up against our dust; motor-bicycles of every shape charging down at every angle; red flags of rifle-ranges; detachments of dusty-putteed Territorials; coveys of flagrant children playing in mid-street, and the wise, educated English dog safe and quite silent on the pavement if his fool-mistress would but cease from trying to save him, passed and repassed us in sunlit or shaded settings. But Mr. Lingnam only talked. He talked—we all sat together behind so that we could not escape him—and he talked above the worn gears and a certain maddening swish of one badly patched tire—*and* he talked of the Federation of the Empire against all conceivable dangers except himself. Yet I was neither brutally rude like Penfentenyou, nor swooningly bored like the Agent-General. I remembered a certain Joseph Finsbury who delighted the Tregonwell Arms on the borders of the New Forest with 'nine'—it should have been ten—'versions of a single income of two hundred pounds' placing the imaginary person in—but I could not recall the list of towns further than 'London, Paris, Bagdad, and Spitzbergen.' This last I must have murmured aloud, for the Agent-General suddenly became human and went on: 'Bussorah, Heligoland, and the Scilly Islands——'

'What?' growled Penfentenyou.

'Nothing,' said the Agent-General, squeezing my hand affectionately. 'Only we have just found out that we are brothers.'

'Exactly,' said Mr. Lingnam. 'That's what I've been trying to lead up to. We're *all* brothers. D'you realise that fifteen years ago such a conversation as we're having would have been unthinkable? The Empire wouldn't have been ripe for it. To go back, even ten years——'

'I've got it,' cried the Agent-General. ' "Brighton, Cincinnati, and Nijni-Novgorod!" God bless R.L.S.! Go on, Uncle Joseph. I can endure much now.'

Mr. Lingnam went on like our shandrydan, slowly and loudly. He admitted that a man obsessed with a Central Idea—and, after all, the only thing that mattered was the Idea—might become a bore, but the World's Work, he pointed out, had been done by bores. So he laid his bones down to that work till we abandoned ourselves to the passage of time and the Mercy of Allah, Who Alone closes the Mouths of His Prophets. And we wasted more than fifty miles of summer's vivid own England upon him the while.

About two o'clock we topped Sumtner Rising and looked down on the village of Sumtner Barton, which lies just across a single railway line, spanned by a red brick bridge. The thick, thunderous June airs brought us gusts of melody from a giddy-go-round steam-organ in full blast near the pond on the village green. Drums, too, thumped and banners waved and regalia flashed at the far end of the broad village street. Mr. Lingnam asked why.

'Nothing Imperial, I'm afraid. It looks like a Foresters'

Fête—one of our big Mutual Benefit Societies,' I explained.

'The Idea only needs to be co-ordinated to Imperial scale——' he began.

'But it means that the pub. will be crowded,' I went on.

'What's the matter with lunching by the roadside here?' said Penfentenyou. 'We've got the lunch-basket.'

'Haven't you ever heard of Sumtner Barton ales?' I demanded, and he became the administrator at once, saying, '*I* see! Lingnam can drive us in and we'll get some, while Holford'—this was the hireling chauffeur, whose views on beer we knew not—'lays out lunch here. That'll be better than eating at the pub. We can take in the Foresters' Fête as well, and perhaps I can buy some newspapers at the station.'

'True,' I answered. 'The railway station is just under that bridge, and we'll come back and lunch here.'

I indicated a terrace of cool clean shade beneath kindly beeches at the head of Sumtner Rise. As Holford got out the lunch-basket, a detachment of Regular troops on manœuvres swung down the baking road.

'Ah!' said Mr. Lingnam, the monthly-magazine roll in his voice. 'All Europe is an armed camp, groaning, as I remember I once wrote, under the weight of its accoutrements.'

'Oh, hop in and drive,' cried Penfentenyou. 'We want that beer!'

It made no difference. Mr. Lingnam could have federated the Empire from a tight rope. He continued his oration at the wheel as we trundled.

'The danger to the Younger Nations is of being drawn into this vortex of Militarism,' he went on, dodging the rear of the soldiery.

'Slow past troops,' I hinted. 'It saves 'em dust. And we overtake on the right as a rule in England.'

'Thanks!' Mr. Lingnam slued over. 'That's another detail which needs to be co-ordinated throughout the Empire. But to go back to what I was saying. My idea has always been that the component parts of the Empire should take counsel among themselves on the approach of war, so that, after we have decided on the merits of the *casus belli,* we can co-ordinate what part each Dominion shall play whenever war is, unfortunately, a possibility.'

We neared the hog-back railway bridge, and the hireling knocked piteously at the grade. Mr. Lingnam changed gears, and she hoisted herself up to a joyous *Youp-i-addy-i-ay!* from the steam-organ. As we topped the arch we saw a Foresters' band with banners marching down the street.

'That's all very fine,' said the Agent-General, 'but in real life things have a knack of happening without approaching——'

(Some schools of Thought hold that Time is not; and that when we attain complete enlightenment we shall behold past, present, and future as One Awful Whole. I myself have nearly achieved this.)

We dipped over the bridge into the village. A boy on a bicycle, loaded with four paper bonnet-boxes, pedalled towards us, out of an alley on our right. He bowed his head the better to overcome the ascent, and naturally took his left. Mr. Lingnam swerved frantically to the right. Penfen-tenyou shouted. The boy looked up, saw the car was like to squeeze him against the bridge wall, flung himself off his machine and across the narrow pavement into the nearest house. He slammed the door at the precise moment when the car, all brakes set, bunted the abandoned bicycle, shattering three of the bonnet-boxes and jerking the fourth over the unscreened dashboard into Mr. Lingnam's arms.

There was a dead stillness, then a hiss like that of escaping steam, and a man who had been running towards us ran the other way.

'Why! I think that those must be bees,' said Mr. Lingnam.

They were—four full swarms—and the first living objects which he had remarked upon all day.

Some one said, 'Oh, God!' The Agent-General went out over the back of the car, crying resolutely: 'Stop the traffic!

Stop the traffic, there!' Penfentenyou was already on the pavement ringing a door-bell, so I had both their rugs, which—for I am an apiarist—I threw over my head. While I was tucking my trousers into my socks—for I am an apiarist of experience—Mr. Lingnam picked up the unexploded bonnet-box and with a single magnificent gesture (he told us afterwards he thought there was a river beneath) hurled it over the parapet of the bridge, ere he ran across the road toward the village green. Now, the station platform immediately below was crowded with Foresters and their friends waiting to welcome a delegation from a sister Court. I saw the box burst on the flint edging of the station garden and the contents sweep forward cone-wise like shrapnel. But the result was stimulating rather than sedative. All those well-dressed people below shouted like Sodom and Gomorrah. Then they moved as a unit into the booking-office, the waiting-rooms, and other places, shut doors and windows and declaimed aloud, while the incoming train whistled far down the line.

I pivoted round cross-legged on the back seat, like a Circassian beauty beneath her veil, and saw Penfentenyou, his coat-collar over his ears, dancing before a shut door and holding up handfuls of currency to a silver-haired woman at an upper window, who only mouthed and shook her head. A little child, carrying a kitten, came smiling round a corner. Suddenly (but these things moved me no more than so many yards of threepenny cinematograph-film) the kitten leaped spitting from her arms, the child burst into tears, Penfentenyou, still dancing, snatched her up and tucked her under his coat, the woman's countenance blanched, the front door opened, Penfentenyou and the child pressed through, and I was alone in an inhospitable world where every one was shutting windows and calling children home.

A voice cried: 'You've frowtened 'em! You've frowtened 'em! Throw dust on 'em and they'll settle!'

I did not desire to throw dust on any created thing. I needed both hands for my draperies and two more for my stockings. Besides, the bees were doing me no hurt. They recognised me as a member of the County Bee-keepers' Association who had paid his annual subscription and was entitled to a free seat at all apicultural exhibitions. The quiver and the churn of the hireling car, or it might have been the lurching banners and the arrogant big drum, inclined many of them to go up street, and pay court to the advancing Foresters' band. So they went, such as had not followed Mr. Lingnam in his flight toward the green, and I looked out of two goggled eyes instead of half a one at the approaching musicians, while I listened with both ears to the delayed train's second whistle down the line beneath me.

The Foresters' band no more knew what was coming than do troops under sudden fire. Indeed, there were the same extravagant gestures and contortions as attend wounds and deaths in war; the very same uncanny cessations of speech—for the trombone was cut off at midslide, even as a man drops with a syllable on his tongue. They clawed, they slapped, they fled, leaving behind them a trophy of banners and brasses crudely arranged round the big drum. Then that end of the street also shut its windows, and the village, stripped of life, lay round me like a reef at low tide. Though I am, as I have said, an apiarist in good standing, I never realised that there were so many bees in the world. When they had woven a flashing haze from one end of the desert street to the other, there remained reserves enough to form knops and pendules on all window-sills and gutter-ends, without diminishing the multitudes in the three oozing bonnet-boxes, or drawing on the Fourth (Railway) Battalion in charge of the station below. The prisoners in the waiting-rooms and other places there cried out a great deal (I argued that they were dying of the heat), and at regular intervals the stationmaster called and called to a signalman who was not on duty, and the train whistled as it drew nearer.

Then Penfentenyou, venal and adaptable politician of the type that survives at the price of all the higher emotions, appeared at the window of the house on my right, broken and congested with mirth, the woman beside him, and the child in his arms. I saw his mouth open and shut, he hollowed his hands round it, but the churr of the motor and the bees drowned his words. He pointed dramatically across the street many times and fell back, tears running down his face. I turned like a hooded barbette in a heavy seaway (not knowing when my trousers would come out of my socks again) through one hundred and eighty degrees, and in due time bore on the village green. There was a salmon in the pond, rising short at a cloud of midges to the tune of *Yip-i-addy;* but there was none to gaff him. The swing-boats were empty, cocoanuts sat still on their red sticks before white screens, and the gay-painted horses of the giddy-go-rounds revolved riderless. All was melody, green turf, bright water, and this greedy gambolling fish. When I had identified it by its grey gills and binoculars as Lingnam, I prostrated myself before Allah in that mirth which is more truly labour than any prayer. Then I turned to the purple Penfentenyou at the window, and wiped my eyes on the rug edge.

He raised the window half one cautious inch and bellowed through the crack: 'Did you see *him?* Have they got *you?* I can see lots of things from here. It's like a three-ring circus!'

'Can you see the station?' I replied, nodding toward the right rear mudguard.

He twisted and craned sideways, but could not command that beautiful view.

'No! What's it like?' he cried.

'Hell!' I shouted. The silvery-haired woman frowned; so did Penfentenyou, and, I think, apologised to her for my language.

'You're always so extreme,' he fluted reproachfully. 'You forget that nothing matters except the Idea. Besides, they are this lady's bees.'

He closed the window, and introduced us through it in dumb show; but he contrived to give the impression that *I* was the specimen under glass.

A spurt of damp steam saved me from apoplexy. The

train had lost patience at last, and was coming into the
station directly beneath me to see what was the matter.
Happy voices sang and heads were thrust out all along the
compartments, but none answered their songs or greetings.
She halted, and the people began to get out. Then they began to get in again, as their friends in the waiting-rooms
advised. All did not catch the warning, so there was congestion at the doors, but those whom the bees caught got
in first.

Still the bees, more bent on their own business than wan-
ton torture, kept to the south end of the platform by the
bookstall, and that was why the completely exposed engine-
driver at the north end of the train did not at first understand the hermetically sealed stationmaster when the latter
shouted to him many times to 'get on out o' this.'

'Where are you?' was the reply. 'And what for?'

'It don't matter where I am, an' you'll get what-for in a
minute if you don't shift,' said the stationmaster. 'Drop 'em
at Parson's Meadow and they can walk up over the fields.'

That bare-armed, thin-shirted idiot, leaning out of the
cab, took the stationmaster's orders as an insult to his dignity, and roared at the shut offices: 'You'll give me what
for, will you? Look 'ere, I'm not in the 'abit of——' His outstretched hand flew to his neck. . . . Do you know that if
you sting an engine-driver it is the same as stinging his
train? She starts with a jerk that nearly smashes the cou-
plings, and runs, barking like a dog, till she is out of sight.
Nor does she think about spilled people and parted families
on the platform behind her. I had to do all that. There was
a man called Fred, and his wife Harriet—a cheery, full-
blooded couple—who interested me immensely before they
battered their way into a small detached building, already
densely occupied. There was also a nameless bachelor who
sat under a half-opened umbrella and twirled it dizzily,
which was so new a game that I applauded aloud.

When they had thoroughly cleared the ground, the bees
set about making comb for publication at the bookstall
counter. Presently some bold hearts tiptoed out of the wait-

ing-rooms over the loud gravel with the consciously modest air of men leaving church, climbed the wooden staircase to the bridge, and so reached my level, where the inexhaustible bonnet-boxes were still vomiting squadrons and platoons. There was little need to bid them descend. They had wrapped their heads in handkerchiefs, so that they looked like the disappointed dead scuttling back to Purgatory. Only one old gentleman, pontifically draped in a banner embroidered 'Temperance and Fortitude,' ran the gauntlet up-street, shouting as he passed me, 'It's night or Blücher, Mister.' They let him in at the White Hart, the pub. where I should have bought the beer.

After this the day sagged. I fell to reckoning how long a man in a Turkish bath, weakened by excessive laughter, could live without food, and specially drink; and how long a disenfranchised bee could hold out under the same conditions.

Obviously, since her one practical joke costs her her life, the bee can have but small sense of humour; but her fundamentally dismal and ungracious outlook on life impressed me beyond words. She had paralysed locomotion, wiped out trade, social intercourse, mutual trust, love, friendship, sport, music (the lonely steam-organ had run down at last), all that gives substance, colour or savour to life, and yet, in the barren desert she had created, was not one whit more near to the evolution of a saner order of things. The Heavens were darkened with the swarms' divided counsels; the street shimmered with their purposeless sallies. They clotted on tiles and gutter-pipes, and began frenziedly to build a cell or two of comb ere they discovered that their queen was not with them; then flung off to seek her, or whirled, dishevelled and insane, into another hissing nebula on the false rumour that she was there. I scowled upon them with disfavour, and a massy, blue thunderhead rose majestically from behind the elm-trees of Sumtner Barton Rectory, arched over and scowled with me. Then I realised that it was not bees nor locusts that had darkened the skies, but the oncoming of the malignant English thunderstorm—the one thing before which even Deborah the bee cannot express her silly little self.

'Aha! *Now* you'll catch it,' I said, as the herald gusts set the big drum rolling down the street like a box-kite. Up and up yearned the dark cloud, till the first lightning quivered and cut. Deborah cowered. Where she flew, there she fled; where she was, there she sat still; and the solid rain closed in on her as a book that is closed when the chapter is finished. By the time it had soaked to my second rug, Penfentenyou appeared at the window, wiping his false mouth on a napkin.

'Are you all right?' he inquired. 'Then *that's* all right! Mrs. Bellamy says that her bees don't sting in the wet. You'd better fetch Lingman over. He's got to pay for them and the bicycle.'

I had no words which the silver-haired lady could listen to, but paddled across the flooded street between flashes to the pond on the green. Mr. Lingnam, scarcely visible through the sheeting downpour, trotted round the edge. He bore himself nobly, and lied at the mere sight of me.

'Isn't this wet?' he cried. 'It has drenched me to the skin. I shall need a change.'

'Come along,' I said. 'I don't know what you'll get, but you deserve more.'

Penfentenyou, dry, fed, and in command, let us in. 'You,' he whispered to me, 'are to wait in the scullery. Mrs. Bellamy didn't like the way you talked about her bees. Hsh! Hsh! She's a kind-hearted lady. She's a widow, Lingnam, but she's kept *his* clothes, and as soon as you've paid for the damage she'll rent you a suit. I've arranged it all!'

'Then tell him he mustn't undress in my hall,' said a voice from the stair-head.

'Tell *her*——' Lingnam began.

'Come and look at the pretty suit I've chosen,' Penfentenyou cooed, as one cajoling a maniac.

I staggered out-of-doors again, and fell into the car, whose ever-running machinery masked my yelps and hiccups. When I raised my forehead from the wheel, I saw that traffic through the village had been resumed, after, as my watch showed, one and one-half hour's suspension. There were two limousines, one landau, one doctor's car, three touring-cars, one patent steam-laundry van, three tri-cars, one traction-engine, some motorcycles, one with a side-car, and one brewery lorry. It was the allegory of my own imperturbable country, delayed for a short time by un-foreseen external events but now going about her business, and I blessed Her with tears in my eyes, even though I knew She looked upon me as drunk and incapable.

Then troops came over the bridge behind me—a company of dripping wet Regulars without any expression. In their rear, carrying the lunch-basket, marched the Agent-General and Holford the hired chauffeur.

'I say,' said the Agent-General, nodding at the darkened khaki backs. 'If *that's* what we've got to depend on in event of war they're a broken reed. They ran like hares—ran like hares, I tell you.'

'And you?' I asked.

'Oh, I just sauntered back over the bridge and stopped the traffic that end. Then I had lunch. 'Pity about the beer, though. I say—these cushions are sopping wet!'

'I'm sorry,' I said. 'I haven't had time to turn 'em.'

'Nor there wasn't any need to 'ave kept the engine run-nin' all this time,' said Holford sternly. 'I'll 'ave to account for the expenditure of petrol. It exceeds the mileage indi-cated, you see.'

'I'm sorry,' I repeated. After all, that is the way that tax-payers regard most crises.

The house-door opened and Penfentenyou and another came out into the now thinning rain.

'Ah! There you both are! Here's Lingnam,' he cried. 'He's got a little wet. He's had to change.'

We saw that. I was too sore and weak to begin another laugh, but the Agent-General crumpled up where he stood. The late Mr. Bellamy must have been a man of tremendous personality, which he had impressed on every angle of his garments. I was told later that he had died in delirium tre-

mens, which at once explained the pattern, and the reason
why Mr. Lingnam, writhing inside it, swore so inspiredly.
Of the deliberate and diffuse Federationist there remained
no trace, save the binoculars and two damp whiskers. We
stood on the pavement, before Elemental Man calling on
Elemental Powers to condemn and incinerate Creation.

'Well, hadn't we better be getting back?' said the Agent-
General.

'Look out!' I remarked casually. 'Those bonnet-boxes are
full of bees still!'

'Are they?' said the livid Mr. Lingnam, and tilted them
over with the late Mr. Bellamy's large boots. Deborah
rolled out in drenched lumps into the swilling gutter. There
was a muffled shriek at the window where Mrs. Bellamy
gesticulated.

'It's all right. I've paid for them,' said Mr. Lingnam. He
dumped out the last dregs like mould from a pot-bound
flower-pot.

'What? Are you going to take 'em home with you?' said
the Agent-General.

'No!' He passed a wet hand over his streaky forehead.
'Wasn't there a bicycle that was the beginning of this trouble?' said he.

'It's under the fore-axle, sir,' said Holford promptly. 'I
can fish it out from 'ere.'

'Not till I've done with it, please.' Before we could stop
him, he had jumped into the car and taken charge. The
hireling leaped into her collar, surged, shrieked (less loudly
than Mrs. Bellamy at the window), and swept on. That
which came out behind her was, as Holford truely observed,
no joy-wheel. Mr. Lingnam swung round the big drum in
the market-place and thundered back, shouting: 'Leave it
alone. It's my meat!'

'Mince-meat, 'e means,' said Holford after this second
trituration. 'You couldn't say now it 'ad ever *been* one,
could you?'

Mrs. Bellamy opened the window and spoke. It appears
she had only charged for damage to the bicycle, not for the

entire machine which Mr. Lingnam was ruthlessly gleaning, spoke by spoke, from the highway and cramming into the slack of the hood. At last he answered, and I have never seen a man foam at the mouth before. 'If you don't stop, I shall come into your house—in this car—and drive upstairs and—kill you!'

She stopped; he stopped. Holford took the wheel, and we got away. It was time, for the sun shone after the storm, and Deborah beneath the tiles and the eaves already felt its reviving influence compel her to her interrupted labours of federation. We warned the village policeman at the far end of the street that he might have to suspend traffic again. The proprietor of the giddy-go-round, swings, and cocoanut-shies wanted to know from whom, in this world or another, he could recover damages. Mr. Lingnam referred him most directly to Mrs. Bellamy. . . . Then we went home.

After dinner that evening Mr. Lingnam rose stiffly in his place to make a few remarks on the Federation of the Empire on the lines of Co-ordinated, Offensive Operations, backed by the Entire Effective Forces, Moral, Military and Fiscal, of Permanently Mobilised Communities, the whole brought to bear, without any respect to the merits of any *casus belli*, instantaneously, automatically, and remorselessly at the first faint buzz of war.

'The trouble with Us,' said he, 'is that We take such an infernally long time making sure that We are right that We don't go ahead when things happen. For instance, *I* ought to have gone ahead instead of pulling up when I hit that bicycle.'

'But you were in the wrong, Lingnam, when you turned to the right,' I put in.

'I don't want to hear any more of your damned, detached, mugwumping excuses for the other fellow,' he snapped.

'Now you're beginning to see things,' said Penfentenyou. 'I hope you won't backslide when the swellings go down.'

THE VILLAGE THAT VOTED THE EARTH WAS FLAT

Our drive till then had been quite a success. The other men in the car were my friend Woodhouse, young Ollyett, a distant connection of his, and Pallant, the M.P. Woodhouse's business was the treatment and cure of sick journals. He knew by instinct the precise moment in a newspaper's life when the impetus of past good management is exhausted and it fetches up on the dead-centre between slow and expensive collapse and the new start which can be given by gold injections—and genius. He was wisely ignorant of journalism; but when he stooped on a carcase there was sure to be meat. He had that week added a half-dead, halfpenny evening paper to his collection, which consisted of a prosperous London daily, one provincial ditto, and a limp-bodied weekly of commercial leanings. He had also, that very hour, planted me with a large block of the evening paper's common shares, and was explaining the whole art of editorship to Ollyett, a young man three years from Oxford, with coir-matting-coloured hair and a face harshly modelled by harsh experiences, who, I understood, was assisting in the new venture. Pallant, the long, wrinkled M.P., whose voice is more like a crane's than a peacock's, took no shares, but gave us all advice.

'You'll find it rather a knacker's yard,' Woodhouse was saying. 'Yes, I know they call me The Knacker; but it will pay inside a year. All my papers do. I've only one motto: Back your luck and back your staff. It'll come out all right.'

Then the car stopped, and a policeman asked our names and addresses for exceeding the speed-limit. We pointed out that the road ran absolutely straight for half a mile

ahead without even a side-lane. 'That's just what we depend on,' said the policeman unpleasantly.

'The usual swindle,' said Woodhouse under his breath.
'What's the name of this place?'

'Huckley,' said the policeman. 'H-u-c-k-l-e-y,' and wrote
something in his note-book at which young Ollyett protested. A large red man on a grey horse who had been
watching us from the other side of the hedge shouted an
order we could not catch. The policeman laid his hand on
the rim of the right driving-door (Woodhouse carries his
spare tyre aft), and it closed on the button of the electric
horn. The grey horse at once bolted, and we could hear
the rider swearing all across the landscape.

'Damn it, man, you've got your silly fist on it! Take it
off!' Woodhouse shouted.

'Ho!' said the constable, looking carefully at his fingers as
though we had trapped them. 'That won't do you any good
either,' and he wrote once more in his note-book before he
allowed us to go.

This was Woodhouse's first brush with motor law, and
since I expected no ill consequences to myself, I pointed
out that it was very serious. I took the same view myself
when in due time I found that I, too, was summonsed on
charges ranging from the use of obscene language to en-
dangering traffic.

Judgment was done in a little pale-yellow market-town
with a small Jubilee clock-tower and a large corn-exchange.
Woodhouse drove us there in his car. Pallant, who had not
been included in the summons, came with us as moral
support. While we waited outside, the fat man on the grey
horse rode up and entered into loud talk with his brother
magistrates. He said to one of them—for I took the trouble
to note it down—'It falls away from my lodge-gates, dead
straight, three-quarters of a mile. I'd defy any one to resist
it. We rooked seventy pounds out of 'em last month. No
car can resist the temptation. You ought to have one your
side the county, Mike. They simply can't resist it.'

'Whew!' said Woodhouse. 'We're in for trouble. Don't

you say a word—or Ollyett either! I'll pay the fines and we'll get it over as soon as possible. Where's Pallant?'

'At the back of the court somewhere,' said Ollyett. 'I saw him slip in just now.'

The fat man then took his seat on the Bench, of which he was chairman, and I gathered from a bystander that his name was Sir Thomas Ingell, Bart., M.P., of Ingell Park, Huckley. He began with an allocution pitched in a tone that would have justified revolt throughout empires. Evidence, when the crowded little court did not drown it with applause, was given in the pauses of the address. They were all very proud of their Sir Thomas, and looked from him to us, wondering why we did not applaud too.

Taking its time from the chairman, the Bench rollicked with us for seventeen minutes. Sir Thomas explained that he was sick and tired of processions of cads of our type, who would be better employed breaking stones on the road than in frightening horses worth more than themselves or their ancestors. This was after it had been proved that Woodhouse's man had turned on the horn purposely to annoy Sir Thomas, who 'happened to be riding by'! There were other remarks too—primitive enough,—but it was the unspeakable brutality of the tone, even more than the quality of the justice, or the laughter of the audience that stung our souls out of all reason. When we were dismissed —to the tune of twenty-three pounds, twelve shillings and sixpence—we waited for Pallant to join us, while we listened to the next case—one of driving without a licence. Ollyett, with an eye to his evening paper, had already taken very full notes of our own, but we did not wish to seem prejudiced.

'It's all right,' said the reporter of the local paper soothingly. 'We never report Sir Thomas *in extenso*. Only the fines and charges.'

'Oh, thank you,' Ollyett replied, and I heard him ask who every one in court might be. The local reporter was very communicative.

The new victim, a large, flaxen-haired man in somewhat

striking clothes, to which Sir Thomas, now thoroughly warmed, drew public attention, said that he had left his licence at home. Sir Thomas asked him if he expected the police to go to his home address at Jerusalem to find it for him; and the court roared. Nor did Sir Thomas approve of the man's name, but insisted on calling him 'Mr. Masquerader,' and every time he did so, all his people shouted. Evidently this was their established *auto-da-fé*.

'He didn't summons me—because I'm in the House, I suppose. I think I shall have to ask a Question,' said Pallant, reappearing at the close of the case.

'I think *I* shall have to give it a little publicity too,' said Woodhouse. 'We can't have this kind of thing going on, you know.' His face was set and quite white. Pallant's, on the other hand, was black, and I know that my very stomach had turned with rage. Ollyett was dumb.

'Well, let's have lunch,' Woodhouse said at last. 'Then we can get away before the show breaks up.'

We drew Ollyett from the arms of the local reporter, crossed the Market Square to the Red Lion and found Sir Thomas's 'Mr. Masquerader' just sitting down to beer, beef and pickles.

'Ah!' said he, in a large voice. 'Companions in misfortune. Won't you gentlemen join me?'

'Delighted,' said Woodhouse. 'What did you get?'

'I haven't decided. It might make a good turn, but—the public aren't educated up to it yet. It's beyond 'em. If it wasn't, that red dub on the Bench would be worth fifty a week.'

'Where?' said Woodhouse. The man looked at him with unaffected surprise.

'At any one of My places,' he replied. 'But perhaps you live here?'

'Good heavens!' cried young Ollyett suddenly. 'You *are* Masquerier, then? I thought you were!'

'Bat Masquerier.' He let the words fall with the weight of an international ultimatum. 'Yes, that's all I am. But you have the advantage of me, gentlemen.'

For the moment, while we were introducing ourselves, I was puzzled. Then I recalled prismatic music-hall posters —of enormous acreage—that had been the unnoticed background of my visits to London for years past. Posters of men and women, singers, jongleurs, impersonators and audacities of every draped and undraped brand, all moved on and off in London and the Provinces by Bat Masquerier —with the long wedge-tailed flourish following the final 'r'.

'*I* knew you at once,' said Pallant, the trained M.P., and I promptly backed the lie. Woodhouse mumbled excuses. Bat Masquerier was not moved for or against us any more than the frontage of one of his own palaces.

'I always tell My people there's a limit to the size of the lettering,' he said. 'Overdo that and the ret'na doesn't take it in. Advertisin' is the most delicate of all the sciences.'

'There's one man in the world who is going to get a little of it if I live for the next twenty-four hours,' said Woodhouse, and explained how this would come about.

Masquerier stared at him lengthily with gun-metal-blue eyes.

'You mean it?' he drawled; the voice was as magnetic as the look.

'I *do*,' said Ollyett. 'That business of the horn alone ought to have him off the Bench in three months.' Masquerier looked at him even longer than he had looked at Woodhouse.

'He told *me*,' he said suddenly, 'that my home-address was Jerusalem. You heard that?'

'But it was the tone—the tone,' Ollyett cried.

'You noticed that, too, did you?' said Masquerier. 'That's the artistic temperament. You can do a lot with it. And I'm Bat Masquerier,' he went on. He dropped his chin in his fists and scowled straight in front of him. . . . 'I made the Silhouettes—I made the Trefoil and the Jocunda. I made 'Dal Benzaguen.' Here Ollyett sat straight up, for in common with the youth of that year he worshipped Miss Vidal Benzaguen of the Trefoil immensely and unreservedly.

' "*Is* that a dressing-gown or an ulster you're supposed to

be wearing?" You heard *that?* . . . "And I suppose you
hadn't time to brush your hair either?" You heard *that?*
. . . Now, you hear *me!*' His voice filled the coffee-room,
then dropped to a whisper as dreadful as a surgeon's before
an operation. He spoke for several minutes. Pallant muttered 'Hear! hear!' I saw Ollyett's eye flash—it was to Ollyett
that Masquerier addressed himself chiefly,—and Woodhouse
leaned forward with joined hands.

'Are you *with* me?' he went on, gathering us all up in
one sweep of the arm. 'When I begin a thing I see it
through, gentlemen. What Bat can't break, breaks him!
But I haven't struck that thing yet. This is no one-turn
turn-it-down show. This is business to the dead finish. Are
you with me, gentlemen? Good! Now, we'll pool our assets.
One London morning, and one provincial daily, didn't you
say? One weekly commercial ditto and one M.P.'

'Not much use, I'm afraid,' Pallant smirked.

'But privileged. *But* privileged,' he returned. 'And we
have also my little team—London, Blackburn, Liverpool,
Leeds—I'll tell you about Manchester later—and Me! Bat
Masquerier.' He breathed the name reverently into his
tankard. 'Gentlemen, when our combination has finished
with Sir Thomas Ingell, Bart., M.P., and everything else
that is his, Sodom and Gomorrah will be a winsome bit of
Merrie England beside 'em. I must go back to town now,
but I trust you gentlemen will give me the pleasure of your
company at dinner to-night at the Chop Suey—the Red
Amber Room—and we'll block out the scenario.' He laid
his hand on young Ollyett's shoulder and added: 'It's your
brains I want.' Then he left, in a good deal of astrakhan
collar and nickel-plated limousine, and the place felt less
crowded.

We ordered our car a few minutes later. As Woodhouse,
Ollyett and I were getting in, Sir Thomas Ingell, Bart.,
M.P., came out of the Hall of Justice across the square
and mounted his horse. I have sometimes thought that if he
had gone in silence he might even then have been saved,
but as he settled himself in the saddle he caught sight of us

and must needs shout: 'Not off yet? You'd better get away and you'd better be careful.' At that moment Pallant, who had been buying picture-postcards, came out of the inn, took Sir Thomas's eye and very leisurely entered the car. It seemed to me that for one instant there was a shade of uneasiness on the baronet's grey-whiskered face.

'I hope,' said Woodhouse after several miles, 'I hope he's a widower.'

'Yes,' said Pallant. 'For his poor, dear wife's sake I hope that, very much indeed. I suppose he didn't see me in Court. Oh, here's the parish history of Huckley written by the Rector and here's your share of the picture-postcards. Are we all dining with this Mr. Masquerier to-night?'

'Yes!' said we all.

* * * * * *

If Woodhouse knew nothing of journalism, young Ollyett, who had graduated in a hard school, knew a good deal. Our halfpenny evening paper, which we will call *The Bun* to distinguish her from her prosperous morning sister, *The Cake,* was not only diseased but corrupt. We found this out when a man brought us the prospectus of a new oil-field and demanded sub-leaders on its prosperity. Ollyett talked pure Brasenose to him for three minutes. Otherwise he spoke and wrote trade-English—a toothsome amalgam of Americanisms and epigrams. But though the slang changes, the game never alters, and Ollyett and I and, in the end, some others enjoyed it immensely. It was weeks ere we could see the wood for the trees, but so soon as the staff realised that they had proprietors who backed them right or wrong, and specially when they were wrong (which is the sole secret of journalism), and that their fate did not hang on any passing owner's passing mood, they did miracles.

But we did not neglect Huckley. As Ollyett said our first care was to create an 'arresting atmosphere' round it. He used to visit the village of week-ends, on a motor-bicycle with a side-car; for which reason I left the actual place

alone and dealt with it in the abstract. Yet it was I who
drew first blood. Two inhabitants of Huckley wrote to
contradict a small, quite solid paragraph in *The Bun* that a
hoopoe had been seen at Huckley and had, 'of course, been
shot by the local sportsmen.' There was some heat in their
letters, both of which we published. Our version of how the
hoopoe got his crest from King Solomon was, I grieve to
say, so inaccurate that the Rector himself—no sportsman, as
he pointed out, but a lover of accuracy—wrote to us to
correct it. We gave his letter good space and thanked him.

'This priest is going to be useful,' said Ollyett. 'He has
the impartial mind. I shall vitalise him.'

Forthwith he created M. L. Sigden, a recluse of refined
tastes who in *The Bun* demanded to know whether this
Huckley-of-the-Hoopoe was the Hugly of his boyhood and
whether, by any chance, the fell change of name had been
wrought by collusion between a local magnate and the
railway, in the mistaken interests of spurious refinement.
'For I knew it and loved it with the maidens of my day
—*eheu ab angulo!*—as Hugly,' wrote M. L. Sigden from
Oxford.

Though other papers scoffed, *The Bun* was gravely sympathetic. Several people wrote to deny that Huckley had
been changed at birth. Only the Rector—no philosopher, as
he pointed out, but a lover of accuracy—had his doubts,
which he laid publicly before Mr. M. L. Sigden, who suggested, through *The Bun,* that the little place might have
begun life in Anglo-Saxon days as 'Hogslea' or among the
Normans as 'Argilé,' on account of its much clay. The
Rector had his own ideas too (he said it was mostly
gravel), and M. L. Sigden had a fund of reminiscences.
Oddly enough—which is seldom the case with free reading-
matter—our subscribers rather relished the correspondence,
and contemporaries quoted freely.

'The secret of power,' said Ollyett, 'is not the big stick.
It's the liftable stick.' (This means the 'arresting' quotation
of six or seven lines.) 'Did you see the *Spec.* had a middle

on "Rural Tenacities" last week? That was all Huckley. I'm doing a "Mobiquity" on Huckley next week.'

Our 'Mobiquities' were Friday evening accounts of easy motor-bike-*cum*-side-car trips round London, illustrated (we could never get that machine to work properly) by smudgy maps. Ollyett wrote the stuff with a fervour and a delicacy which I always ascribed to the side-car. His account of Epping Forest, for instance, was simply young love with its soul at its lips. But his Huckley 'Mobiquity' would have sickened a soap-boiler. It chemically combined loathsome familiarity, leering suggestion, slimy piety and rancid 'social service' in one fuming compost that fairly lifted me off my feet.

'Yes,' said he, after compliments. 'It's the most vital, arresting and dynamic bit of tump I've done up to date. *Non nobis gloria!* I met Sir Thomas Ingell in his own park. He talked to me again. He inspired most of it.'

'Which? The "glutinous native drawl," or "the neglected adenoids of the village children"?' I demanded.

'Oh, no! That's only to bring in the panel doctor. It's the last flight we—I'm proudest of.'

This dealt with 'the crepuscular penumbra spreading her dim limbs over the boskage'; with 'jolly rabbits'; with a herd of 'gravid polled Angus'; and with the 'arresting, gipsy-like face of their swart, scholarly owner—as well known at the Royal Agricultural Shows as that of our late King-Emperor.'

' "Swart" is good and so's "gravid," ' said I, 'but the panel doctor will be annoyed about the adenoids.'

'Not half as much as Sir Thomas will about his face,' said Ollyett. 'And if you only knew what I've left out!'

He was right. The panel doctor spent his week-end (this is the advantage of Friday articles) in overwhelming us with a professional counterblast of no interest whatever to our subscribers. We told him so, and he, then and there, battered his way with it into the *Lancet* where they are keen on glands, and forgot us altogether. But Sir Thomas Ingell was of sterner stuff. He must have spent a happy week-end too. The letter which we received from him on Monday proved him to be a kinless loon of upright life, for no woman, however remotely interested in a man, would have let it pass the home wastepaper-basket. He objected to our references to his own herd, to his own labours in his own village, which he said was a Model Village, and to our infernal insolence; but he objected most to our invoice of his features. We wrote him courteously to ask whether the letter was meant for publication. He, remembering, I presume, the Duke of Wellington, wrote back, 'Publish and be damned.'

'Oh! This is too easy,' Ollyett said as he began heading the letter.

'Stop a minute,' I said. 'The game is getting a little beyond us. To-night's the Bat dinner.' (I may have forgotten to tell you that our dinner with Bat Masquerier in the Red Amber Room of the Chop Suey had come to be a weekly affair.) 'Hold it over till they've all seen it.'

'Perhaps you're right,' he said. 'You might waste it.'

At dinner, then, Sir Thomas's letter was handed round. Bat seemed to be thinking of other matters, but Pallant was very interested.

'I've got an idea,' he said presently. 'Could you put something into *The Bun* to-morrow about foot-and-mouth disease in that fellow's herd?'

'Oh, plague if you like,' Ollyett replied. 'They're only five measly Shorthorns. I saw one lying down in the park. She'll serve as a substratum of fact.'

'Then, do that; and hold the letter over meanwhile. I think *I* come in here,' said Pallant.

'Why?' said I.

'Because there's something coming up in the House about foot-and-mouth, and because he wrote me a letter after that little affair when he fined you. 'Took ten days to think it over. Here you are,' said Pallant. 'House of Commons paper, you see.'

We read:

DEAR PALLANT—Although in the past our paths have not lain much together, I am sure you will agree with me that on the floor of the House all members are on a footing of equality. I make bold, therefore, to approach you in a matter which I think capable of a very different interpretation from that which perhaps was put upon it by your friends. Will you let them know that that was the case and that I was in no way swayed by animus in the exercise of my magisterial duties, which as you, as a brother magistrate, can imagine are frequently very distasteful to—Yours very sincerely,

T. INGELL.

P.S.—I have seen to it that the motor vigilance to which your friends took exception has been considerably relaxed in my district.

'What did you answer?' said Ollyett, when all our opinions had been expressed.

'I told him I couldn't do anything in the matter. And I couldn't—then. But you'll remember to put in that foot-and-mouth paragraph. I want something to work upon.'

'It seems to me *The Bun* has done all the work up to date,' I suggested. 'When does *The Cake* come in?'

'*The Cake,*' said Woodhouse, and I remembered afterwards that he spoke like a Cabinet Minister on the eve of a Budget, 'reserves to itself the fullest right to deal with situations as they arise.'

'Ye-eh!' Bat Masquerier shook himself out of his thoughts. ' "Situations as they arise." I ain't idle either. But there's no use fishing till the swim's baited. You'—he turned to Ollyett—'manufacture very good ground-bait. . . . I always tell My people—— What the deuce is that?'

There was a burst of song from another private dining-room across the landing. 'It ees some ladies from the Trefoil,' the waiter began.

'Oh, I know that. What are they singing, though?'

He rose and went out, to be greeted by shouts of applause from that merry company. Then there was silence, such as one hears in the form-room after a master's entry. Then a voice that we loved began again: 'Here we go gathering nuts in May—nuts in May—nuts in May!'

'It's only 'Dal—and some nuts,' he explained when he returned. 'She says she's coming in to dessert.' He sat down, humming the old tune to himself, and till Miss Vidal Benzaguen entered, he held us speechless with tales of the artistic temperament.

We obeyed Pallant to the extent of slipping into *The Bun* a wary paragraph about cows lying down and dripping at the mouth, which might be read either as an unkind libel or, in the hands of a capable lawyer, as a piece of faithful nature-study.

'And besides,' said Ollyett, 'we allude to "gravid polled Angus." I am advised that no action can lie in respect of virgin Shorthorns. Pallant wants us to come to the House to-night. He's got us places for the Strangers' Gallery. I'm beginning to like Pallant.'

'Masquerier seems to like you,' I said.

'Yes, but I'm afraid of him,' Ollyett answered with perfect sincerity. 'I am. He's the Absolutely Amoral Soul. I've never met one yet.'

We went to the House together. It happened to be an Irish afternoon, and as soon as I had got the cries and the faces a little sorted out, I gathered there were grievances in the air, but how many of them was beyond me.

'It's all right,' said Ollyett of the trained ear. 'They've shut their ports against—oh yes—export of Irish cattle! Foot-and-mouth disease at Ballyhellion. *I* see Pallant's idea!'

The House was certainly all mouth for the moment, but, as I could feel, quite in earnest. A Minister with a piece of typewritten paper seemed to be fending off volleys of insults. He reminded me somehow of a nervous huntsman breaking up a fox in the face of rabid hounds.

'It's question-time. They're asking questions,' said Ollyett. 'Look! Pallant's up.'

There was no mistaking it. His voice, which his enemies said was his one parliamentary asset, silenced the hubbub as toothache silences mere singing in the ears. He said:

'Arising out of that, may I ask if any special consideration has recently been shown in regard to any suspected outbreak of this disease on *this* side of the Channel?'

He raised his hand; it held a noon edition of *The Bun*. We had thought it best to drop the paragraph out of the later ones. He would have continued, but something in a grey frock-coat roared and bounded on a bench opposite, and waved another *Bun*. It was Sir Thomas Ingell.

'As the owner of the herd so dastardly implicated——' His voice was drowned in shouts of 'Order!'—the Irish leading.

'What's wrong?' I asked Ollyett. 'He's got his hat on his head, hasn't he?'

'Yes, but his wrath should have been put as a question.'

'Arising out of that, Mr. Speaker, Sirrr!' Sir Thomas bellowed through a lull, 'are you aware that—that all this is a conspiracy—part of a dastardly conspiracy to make Huckley ridiculous—to make *us* ridiculous? Part of a deep-laid plot to make *me* ridiculous, Mr. Speaker, Sir!'

The man's face showed almost black against his white whiskers, and he struck out swimmingly with his arms. His vehemence puzzled and held the House for an instant, and the Speaker took advantage of it to lift his pack from Ireland to a new scent. He addressed Sir Thomas Ingell in tones of measured rebuke, meant also, I imagine, for the whole House, which lowered its hackles at the word. Then Pallant, shocked and pained: 'I can only express my profound surprise that in response to my simple question the honourable member should have thought fit to indulge in a personal attack. If I have in any way offended——'

Again the Speaker intervened, for it appeared that he regulated these matters.

He, too, expressed surprise, and Sir Thomas sat back in

a hush of reprobation that seemed to have the chill of the centuries behind it. The Empire's work was resumed.

'Beautiful!' said I, and I felt hot and cold up my back.

'And now we'll publish his letter,' said Ollyett.

We did—on the heels of his carefully reported outburst. We made no comment. With that rare instinct for grasping the heart of a situation which is the mark of the Anglo-Saxon, all our contemporaries and, I should say, two-thirds of our correspondents demanded how such a person could be made more ridiculous than he had already proved himself to be. But beyond spelling his name 'Injle,' we alone refused to hit a man when he was down.

'There's no need,' said Ollyett. 'The whole Press is on the huckle from end to end.'

Even Woodhouse was a little astonished at the ease with which it had come about, and said as much.

'Rot!' said Ollyett. 'We haven't really begun. Huckley isn't news yet.'

'What do you mean?' said Woodhouse, who had grown to have great respect for his young but by no means distant connection.

'Mean? By the grace of God, Master Ridley, I mean to have it so that when Huckley turns over in its sleep, Reuters and the Press Association jump out of bed to cable.' Then he went off at score about certain restorations in Huckley Church which, he said—and he seemed to spend his every week-end there—had been perpetrated by the Rector's predecessor, who had abolished a 'leper-window' or a 'squinch-hole' (whatever these may be) to institute a lavatory in the vestry. It did not strike me as stuff for which Reuters or the Press Association would lose much sleep, and I left him declaiming to Woodhouse about a fourteenth-century font which, he said, he had unearthed in the sexton's tool-shed.

My methods were more on the lines of peaceful penetration. An odd copy, in The Bun's rag-and-bone library, of Hone's Every-Day Book had revealed to me the existence of a village dance founded, like all village dances, on Druidical mysteries connected with the Solar Solstice (which is always unchallengeable) and Midsummer Morning, which is dewy and refreshing to the London eye. For this I take no credit—Hone being a mine any one can work —but that I rechristened that dance, after I had revised it, 'The Gubby' is my title to immortal fame. It was still to be witnessed, I wrote, 'in all its poignant purity at Huckley, that last home of significant mediæval survivals'; and I fell so in love with my creation that I kept it back for days, enamelling and burnishing.

'You'd better put it in,' said Ollyett at last. 'It's time we asserted ourselves again. The other fellows are beginning to poach. You saw that thing in the *Pinnacle* about Sir Thomas's Model Village? He must have got one of their chaps down to do it.'

''Nothing like the wounds of a friend,' I said. 'That account of the non-alcoholic pub alone was——'

'I liked the bit best about the white-tiled laundry and the Fallen Virgins who wash Sir Thomas's dress shirts. Our side couldn't come within a mile of that, you know. We haven't the proper flair for sexual slobber.'

'That's what I'm always saying,' I retorted. 'Leave 'em alone. The other fellows are doing our work for us now. Besides I want to touch up my "Gubby Dance" a little more.'

'No. You'll spoil it. Let's shove it in to-day. For one thing it's Literature. I don't go in for compliments as you know, but, etc. etc.'

I had a healthy suspicion of young Ollyett in every aspect, but though I knew that I should have to pay for it, I fell to his flattery, and my priceless article on the 'Gubby Dance' appeared. Next Saturday he asked me to bring out *The Bun* in his absence, which I naturally assumed would be connected with the little maroon side-car. I was wrong.

On the following Monday I glanced at *The Cake* at breakfast-time to make sure, as usual, of her inferiority to my beloved but unremunerative *Bun*. I opened on a heading: 'The Village that Voted the Earth was Flat.' I read . . . I read that the Geoplanarian Society—a society devoted to the proposition that the earth is flat—had held its Annual Banquet and Exercises at Huckley on Saturday, when after convincing addresses, amid scenes of the greatest enthusiasm, Huckley village had decided by an unanimous vote of 438 that the earth was flat. I do not remember that I breathed again till I had finished the two columns of description that followed. Only one man could have written them. They were flawless—crisp, nervous, austere yet human, poignant, vital, arresting—most distinctly arresting—dynamic enough to shift a city—and quotable by whole sticks at a time. And there was a leader, a grave and poised leader, which tore me in two with mirth, until I remembered that I had been left out—infamously and unjustifiably dropped. I went to Ollyett's rooms. He was breakfasting, and, to do him justice, looked conscience-stricken.

'It wasn't my fault,' he began. 'It was Bat Masquerier. I swear *I* would have asked you to come if——'

'Never mind that,' I said. 'It's the best bit of work you've ever done or will do. Did any of it happen?'

'Happen? Heavens! D'you think even *I* could have invented it?'

'Is it exclusive to *The Cake?*' I cried.

'It cost Bat Masquerier two thousand,' Ollyett replied. 'D'you think he'd let any one else in on that? But I give you my sacred word I knew nothing about it till he asked me to come down and cover it. He had Huckley posted in three colours, "The Geoplanarians' Annual Banquet and Exercises." Yes, he invented "Geoplanarians." He wanted Huckley to think it meant aeroplanes. Yes, I know that there is a real Society that thinks the world's flat—they ought to be grateful for the lift—but Bat made his own. He did! He created the whole show, I tell you. He swept out half his Halls for the job. Think of that—on a Saturday! They—we went down in motor char-à-bancs—three of 'em —one pink, one primrose, and one forget-me-not blue— twenty people in each one and "The Earth *is* Flat" on each side and across the back. I went with Teddy Rickets and Lafone from the Trefoil, and both the Silhouette Sisters, and—wait a minute!—the Crossleigh Trio. You know the Every-Day Dramas Trio at the Jocunda—Ada Crossleigh, "Bunt" Crossleigh, and little Victorine? Them. And there was Hoke Ramsden, the lightning-change chap in *Morgiana and Drexel*—and there was Billy Turpeen. Yes, you know him! The North London Star. "I'm the Referee that got himself disliked at Blackheath." *That* chap! And there was Mackaye—that one-eyed Scotch fellow that all Glasgow is crazy about. Talk of subordinating yourself for Art's sake! Mackaye was the earnest inquirer who got converted at the end of the meeting. And there was quite a lot of girls I didn't know, and—oh, yes—there was 'Dal! 'Dal Benzaguen herself! We sat together, going and coming. She's all the darling there ever was. She sent you her love, and she told me to tell you that she won't forget about Nellie Farren. She says you've given her an ideal to work for. She? Oh, she was the Lady Secretary to the Geoplanarians, of course. I forget who were in the other brakes—provincial stars mostly—but they played up gorgeously. The art of the music-hall's changed since your day. They didn't overdo it a bit. You see, people who believe the earth is flat don't dress quite like other people. You may have noticed that I hinted at that in my account. It's a rather flat-fronted Ionic style —neo-Victorian, except for the bustles, 'Dal told me,—but 'Dal looked heavenly in it! So did little Victorine. And there was a girl in the blue brake—she's a provincial—but she's coming to town this winter and she'll knock 'em— Winnie Deans. Remember that! She told Huckley how she had suffered for the Cause as a governess in a rich family where they believed that the world is round, and how she threw up her job sooner than teach immoral geography. That was at the overflow meeting outside the Baptist chapel. She knocked 'em to sawdust! We must look out for Winnie. . . . But Lafone! Lafone was beyond everything. Impact, personality—conviction—the whole bag o' tricks! He sweated conviction. Gad, he convinced *me* while he was speaking! (Him? He was President of the Geoplanarians, of course. Haven't you read my account?) It *is* an infer-

nally plausible theory. After all, no one has actually proved
the earth is round, have they?'

'Never mind the earth. What about Huckley?'

'Oh, Huckley got tight. That's the worst of these model
villages if you let 'em smell fire-water. There's one alcoholic
pub in the place that Sir Thomas can't get rid of. Bat made
it his base. He sent down the banquet in two motor lorries
—dinner for five hundred and drinks for ten thousand.
Huckley voted all right. Don't you make any mistake about
that. No vote, no dinner. A unanimous vote—exactly as I've
said. At least, the Rector and the Doctor were the only
dissentients. We didn't count them. Oh yes, Sir Thomas was
there. He came and grinned at us through his park gates.
He'll grin worse to-day. There's an aniline dye that you rub
through a stencil-plate that eats about a foot into any stone
and wears good to the last. Bat had both the lodge-gates
stencilled "The Earth *is* flat!" and all the barns and walls
they could get at. . . . Oh Lord, but Huckley was drunk!
We had to fill 'em up to make 'em forgive us for not being
aeroplanes. Unthankful yokels! D'you realise that Emper-
ors couldn't have commanded the talent Bat decanted on
'em? Why, 'Dal alone was. . . . And by eight o'clock not
even a bit of paper left! The whole show packed up and
gone, and Huckley hoo-raying for the earth being flat.'

'Very good,' I began. 'I am, as you know, a one-third
proprietor of *The Bun*.'

'I didn't forget that,' Ollyett interrupted. 'That was up-
permost in my mind all the time. I've got a special account
for *The Bun* to-day—it's an idyll—and just to show how I
thought of you, I told 'Dal, coming home, about your
Gubby Dance, and she told Winnie. Winnie came back in
our char-à-banc. After a bit we had to get out and dance
it in a field. It's quite a dance the way we did it—and Lafone
invented a sort of gorilla lockstep procession at the end.
Bat had sent down a film-chap on the chance of getting
something. He was the son of a clergyman—most dynamic
personality. He said there isn't anything for the cinema in
meetings *qua* meetings—they lack action. Films are a

branch of art by themselves. But he went wild over the Gubby. He said it was like Peter's vision at Joppa. He took about a million feet of it. Then I photoed it exclusive for *The Bun*. I've sent 'em in already, only remember we must eliminate Winnie's left leg in the first figure. It's too arresting. . . . And there you are! But I tell you I'm afraid of Bat. That man's the Personal Devil. He did it all. He didn't even come down himself. He said he'd distract his people.'

'Why didn't he ask me to come?' I persisted.

'Because he said you'd distract me. He said he wanted my brains on ice. He got 'em. I believe it's the best thing I've ever done.' He reached for *The Cake* and re-read it luxuriously. 'Yes, out and away the best—supremely quotable,' he concluded, and—after another survey—'By God, what a genius I was yesterday!'

I would have been angry, but I had not the time. That morning, Press agencies grovelled to me in *The Bun* office for leave to use certain photos, which, they understood, I controlled, of a certain village dance. When I had sent the fifth man away on the edge of tears, my self-respect came back a little. Then there was *The Bun's* poster to get out. Art being elimination, I fined it down to two words (one too many, as it proved)—'The Gubby!' in red, at which our manager protested; but by five o'clock he told me that I was *the* Napoleon of Fleet Street. Ollyett's account in *The Bun* of the Geoplanarians' Exercises and Love Feast lacked the supreme shock of his version in *The Cake* but it bruised more; while the photos of 'The Gubby' (which, with Winnie's left leg, was why I had set the doubtful press to work so early) were beyond praise and next day, beyond price. But even then I did not understand.

A week later, I think it was, Bat Masquerier telephoned to me to come to the Trefoil.

'It's your turn now,' he said. 'I'm not asking Ollyett. Come to the stage-box.'

I went, and, as Bat's guest, was received as Royalty is not. We sat well back and looked out on the packed thousands. It was *Morgiana and Drexel,* that fluid and electric review which Bat—though he gave Lafone the credit—really created.

'Ye-es,' said Bat dreamily, after Morgiana had given 'the nasty jar' to the Forty Thieves in their forty oil 'combinations.' 'As you say, I've got 'em and I can hold 'em. What a man does doesn't matter much; and how he does it don't matter either. It's the *when*—the psychological moment. 'Press can't make up for it; money can't; brains can't. A lot's luck, but all the rest is genius. I'm not speaking about My people now. I'm talking of Myself.'

Then 'Dal—she was the only one who dared—knocked at the door and stood behind us all alive and panting as Morgiana. Lafone was carrying the police-court scene, and the house was ripped up crossways with laughter.

'Ah! Tell a fellow now,' she asked me for the twentieth time, 'did you love Nellie Farren when you were young?'

'Did we love her?' I answered. ' "If the earth and the sky and the sea"—There were three million of us, 'Dal, and we worshipped her.'

'How did she get it across?' 'Dal went on.

'She was Nellie. The houses used to coo over her when she came on.'

'I've had a good deal, but I've never been cooed over yet,' said 'Dal wistfully.

'It isn't the how, it's the when,' Bat repeated. 'Ah!'

He leaned forward as the house began to rock and peal full-throatedly. 'Dal fled. A sinuous and silent procession was filing into the police-court to a scarcely audible accompaniment. It was dressed—but the world and all its picture-palaces know how it was dressed. It danced and it danced, and it danced the dance which bit all humanity in the leg for half a year, and it wound up with the lockstep finale that mowed the house down in swathes, sobbing and aching. Somebody in the gallery moaned, 'Oh Gord, the Gubby!' and we heard the word run like a shudder, for they had not a full breath left among them. Then 'Dal came on, an electric star in her dark hair, the diamonds flashing in her three-inch heels—a vision that made no sign for thirty counted seconds while the police-court scene dissolved behind her into Morgiana's Manicure Palace, and they recovered themselves. The star on her forehead went out, and a soft light bathed her as she took—slowly, slowly to the croon of adoring strings—the eighteen paces forward. We saw her first as a queen alone; next as a queen for the first time conscious of her subjects, and at the end, when her hands fluttered, as a woman delighted, awed not a little, but transfigured and illuminated with sheer, compelling affection and goodwill. I caught the broken mutter of welcome—the coo which is more than tornadoes of applause. It died and rose and died again lovingly.

'She's got it across,' Bat whispered. 'I've never seen her like this. I told her to light up the star, but I was wrong, and she knew it. She's an artist.'

''Dal, you darling!' some one spoke, not loudly but it carried through the house.

'Thank *you!*' 'Dal answered, and in that broken tone one heard the last fetter riveted. 'Good evening, boys! I've just come from—now—where the dooce was it I have come from?' She turned to the impassive files of the Gubby dancers, and went on: 'Ah, so good of you to remind me, you dear, bun-faced things. I've just come from the village—The Village that Voted the Earth was Flat.'

She swept into that song with the full orchestra. It devastated the habitable earth for the next six months. Imagine, then, what its rage and pulse must have been at the incandescent hour of its birth! She only gave the chorus once. At the end of the second verse, 'Are you *with* me, boys?' she cried, and the house tore it clean away from her—'*Earth* was flat—*Earth* was flat. Flat as my hat—Flatter than that'—drowning all but the bassoons and double-basses that marked the word.

'Wonderful,' I said to Bat. 'And it's only "Nuts in May" with variations.'

'Yes—but *I* did the variations,' he replied.

At the last verse she gestured to Carlini the conductor, who threw her up his baton. She caught it with a boy's ease. 'Are you *with* me?' she cried once more, and—the maddened house behind her—abolished all the instruments except the guttural belch of the double-basses on '*Earth*'— '*The* Village that voted the *Earth* was flat—*Earth* was flat!' It was delirium. Then she picked up the Gubby dancers and led them in a clattering improvised lockstep thrice round the stage till her last kick sent her diamond-hilted shoe catherine-wheeling to the electrolier.

I saw the forest of hands raised to catch it, heard the roaring and stamping pass through hurricanes to full typhoon; heard the song, pinned down by the faithful double-basses as the bull-dog pins down the bellowing bull, over-bear even those; till at last the curtain fell and Bat took me round to her dressing-room, where she lay spent after her seventh call. Still the song, through all those whitewashed walls, shook the reinforced concrete of the Trefoil as steam pile-drivers shake the flanks of a dock.

'I'm all out—first time in my life. Ah! Tell a fellow now, did I get it across?' she whispered huskily.

'You know you did,' I replied as she dipped her nose deep in a beaker of barley-water. 'They cooed over you.'

Bat nodded. 'And poor Nellie's dead—in Africa, ain't it?'

'I hope I'll die before they stop cooing,' said 'Dal.

' "*Earth* was flat—*Earth* was flat!" ' Now it was more like mine-pumps in flood.

'They'll have the house down if you don't take another,' some one called.

'Bless 'em!' said 'Dal, and went out for her eighth, when in the face of that cataract she said yawning, 'I don't know how *you* feel, children, but *I*'m dead. You be quiet.'

'Hold a minute,' said Bat to me. 'I've got to hear how it went in the provinces. Winnie Deans had it in Manchester, and Ramsden at Glasgow—and there are all the films too. I had rather a heavy week-end.'

The telephones presently reassured him.

'It'll do,' said he. 'And *he* said my home address was Jerusalem.' He left me humming the refrain of 'The Holy City.' Like Ollyett I found myself afraid of that man.

When I got out into the street and met the disgorging picture-palaces capering on the pavements and humming it (for he had put the gramophones on with the films), and when I saw far to the south the red electrics flash 'Guppy' across the Thames, I feared more than ever.

. . . . .

A few days passed which were like nothing except, perhaps, a suspense of fever in which the sick man perceives the searchlights of the world's assembled navies in act to converge on one minute fragment of wreckage—one only in all the black and agony-strewn sea. Then those beams focused themselves. Earth as we knew it—the full circuit of our orb—laid the weight of its impersonal and searing curiosity on this Huckley which had voted that it was flat. It asked for news about Huckley—where and what it might be, and how it talked—it knew how it danced—and how it thought in its wonderful soul. And then, in all the zealous, merciless press, Huckley was laid out for it to look at, as a drop of pond water is exposed on the sheet of a magic-lantern show. But Huckley's sheet was only coterminous with the use of type among mankind. For the precise moment that was necessary, Fate ruled it that there should be nothing of first importance in the world's idle eye. One atrocious murder, a political crisis, an incautious or heady continental statesman, the mere catarrh of a king, would have wiped out the significance of our message, as a passing cloud annuals the urgent helio. But it was halcyon weather in every respect. Ollyett and I did not need to lift our little fingers any more than the Alpine climber whose last sentence has unkeyed the arch of the avalanche. The thing roared and pulverised and swept beyond eyesight all by itself—all by itself. And once well away, the fall of kingdoms could not have diverted it.

Ours is, after all, a kindly earth. While The Song ran and raped it with the cataleptic kick of 'Ta-ra-ra-boom-de-ay,' multiplied by the West African significance of 'Everybody's doing it,' plus twice the infernal elemen-

tality of a certain tune in *Dona et Gamma;* when for all
practical purposes, literary, dramatic, artistic, social, mu-
nicipal, political, commercial, and administrative, the Earth
was flat, the Rector of Huckley wrote to us—again as a
lover of accuracy—to point out that the Huckley vote on
'the alleged flatness of this scene of our labours here below' was *not* unanimous; he and the doctor having voted
against it. And the great Baron Reuter himself (I am sure it
could have been none other) flashed that letter in full to
the front, back, and both wings of this scene of our labours.
For Huckley was News. *The Bun* also contributed a
photograph which cost me some trouble to fake.

'We are a vital nation,' said Ollyett while we were discussing affairs at a Bat dinner 'Only an Englishman could
have written that letter at this present juncture.'

'It reminded me of a tourist in the Cave of the Winds
under Niagara. Just one figure in a mackintosh. But perhaps you saw our photo?' I said proudly.

'Yes,' Bat replied. 'I've been to Niagara, too. And how's
Huckley taking it?'

'They don't quite understand, of course,' said Ollyett.
'But it's bringing pots of money into the place. Ever since
the motor-bus excursions were started——'

'I didn't know they had been,' said Pallant.

'Oh yes. Motor char-à-bancs—uniformed guides and key-
bugles included. They're getting a bit fed up with the tune
there nowadays,' Ollyett added.

'They play it under his windows, don't they?' Bat asked.
'He can't stop the right of way across his park.'

'He cannot,' Ollyett answered. 'By the way, Woodhouse,
I've bought that font for you from the sexton. I paid fifteen
pounds for it.'

'What am I supposed to do with it?' asked Woodhouse.

'You give it to the Victoria and Albert Museum. It is
fourteenth-century work all right. You can trust me.'

'Is it worth it—now?' said Pallant. 'Not that I'm weaken-
ing, but merely as a matter of tactics?'

'But this is true,' said Ollyett. 'Besides, it is my hobby, I always wanted to be an architect. I'll attend to it myself. It's too serious for *The Bun* and miles too good for *The Cake*.'

He broke ground in a ponderous architectural weekly, which had never heard of Huckley. There was no passion in his statement, but mere fact backed by a wide range of authorities. He established beyond doubt that the old font at Huckley had been thrown out, on Sir Thomas's instigation, twenty years ago, to make room for a new one of Bath stone adorned with Limoges enamels; and that it had lain ever since in a corner of the sexton's shed. He proved, with learned men to support him, that there was only one other font in all England to compare with it. So Woodhouse bought it and presented it to a grateful South Kensington which said it would see the earth still flatter before it returned the treasure to purblind Huckley. Bishops by the benchful and most of the Royal Academy, not to mention 'Margaritas ante Porcos,' wrote fervently to the papers. *Punch* based a political cartoon on it; the *Times* a third leader, 'The Lust of Newness'; and the *Spectator* a scholarly and delightful middle, 'Village Hausmania.' The vast amused outside world said in all its tongues and types: 'Of course! This is just what Huckley would do!' And neither Sir Thomas nor the Rector nor the sexton nor any one else wrote to deny it.

'You see,' said Ollyett, 'this is much more of a blow to Huckley than it looks—because every word of it's true. Your Gubby Dance was inspiration, I admit, but it hadn't its roots in——'

'Two hemispheres and four continents so far,' I pointed out.

'Its roots in the hearts of Huckley was what I was going to say. Why don't you ever come down and look at the place? You've never seen it since we were stopped there.'

'I've only my week-ends free,' I said, 'and you seem to spend yours there pretty regularly—with the side-car. I was afraid——'

'Oh, *that's* all right,' he said cheerily. 'We're quite an old engaged couple now. As a matter of fact, it happened after the "gravid polled Angus" business. Come along this Saturday. Woodhouse says he'll run us down after lunch. He wants to see Huckley too.'

Pallant could not accompany us, but Bat took his place.

'It's odd,' said Bat, 'that none of us except Ollyett has ever set eyes on Huckley since that time. That's what I always tell My people. Local colour is all right after you've got your idea. Before that, it's a mere nuisance.' He regaled us on the way down with panoramic views of the success— geographical and financial—of 'The Gubby' and The Song.

'By the way,' said he, 'I've assigned 'Dal all the gramophone rights of "The Earth." She's a born artist. Hadn't sense enough to hit me for triple-dubs the morning after. She'd have taken it out in coos.'

'Bless her! And what'll she make out of the gramophone rights?' I asked.

'Lord knows!' he replied. 'I've made fifty-four thousand my little end of the business, and it's only just beginning. Hear *that!*'

A shell-pink motor-brake roared up behind us to the music on a key-bugle of 'The Village that Voted the Earth was Flat.' In a few minutes we overtook another, in natural wood, whose occupants were singing it through their noses.

'I don't know that agency. It must be Cook's,' said Ollyett. 'They *do* suffer.' We were never out of earshot of the tune the rest of the way to Huckley.

Though I knew it would be so, I was disappointed with the actual aspect of the spot we had—it is not too much to say—created in the face of the nations. The alcoholic pub; the village green; the Baptist chapel; the church; the sexton's shed; the Rectory whence the so-wonderful letters had come; Sir Thomas's park gate-pillars still violently declaring 'The Earth *is* flat,' were as mean, as average, as ordinary as the photograph of a room where a murder has been committed. Ollyett, who, of course, knew the place specially well, made the most of it to us. Bat, who had employed it

as a back-cloth to one of his own dramas, dismissed it as a
thing used and emptied, but Woodhouse expressed my feelings when he said: 'Is that all—after all we've done?'

'*I* know,' said Ollyett soothingly. ' "Like that strange song
I heard Apollo sing: When Ilion like a mist rose into tow-
ers." I've felt the same sometimes, though it has been Para-
dise for me. But they *do* suffer.'

The fourth brake in thirty minutes had just turned into
Sir Thomas's park to tell the Hall that 'The *Earth* was flat';
a knot of obviously American tourists were kodaking his
lodge gates; while the tea-shop opposite the lych-gate was
full of people buying postcards of the old font as it had lain
twenty years in the sexton's shed. We went to the alcoholic
pub and congratulated the proprietor.

'It's bringin' money to the place,' said he. 'But in a sense
you can buy money too dear. It isn't doin' us any good.
People are laughin' at us. That's what they're doing. . . .
Now, with regard to that Vote of ours you may have heard
talk about. . . .'

'For Gorze sake, chuck that votin' business,' cried an
elderly man at the door. 'Money-gettin' or no money-gettin',
we're fed up with it.'

'Well, I do think,' said the publican, shifting his ground,
'I do think Sir Thomas might ha' managed better in some
things.'

'He tole me,'—the elderly man shouldered his way to the
bar—'he tole me twenty years ago to take an' lay that font in
my tool-shed. He *tole* me so himself. An' now, after twenty
years, me own wife makin' me out little better than the
common 'angman!'

'That's the sexton,' the publican explained. 'His good lady
sells the postcards—if you 'aven't got some. But we feel Sir
Thomas might ha' done better.'

'What's he got to do with it?' said Woodhouse.

'There's nothin' we can trace 'ome to 'im in so many
words, but we think he might 'ave saved us the font business. Now, in regard to that votin' business——'

'Chuck it! Oh, chuck it!' the sexton roared, 'or you'll 'ave me cuttin' my throat at cock-crow. 'Ere's another parcel of funmakers!'

A motor-brake had pulled up at the door and a multitude of men and women immediately descended. We went out to look. They bore rolled banners, a reading-desk in three pieces, and, I specially noticed, a collapsible harmonium, such as is used on ships at sea.

'Salvation Army?' I said, though I saw no uniforms.

Two of them unfurled a banner between poles which bore the legend: 'The Earth *is* flat.' Woodhouse and I turned to Bat. He shook his head. 'No, no! Not me. . . . If I had only seen their costumes in advance!'

'Good Lord!' said Ollyett. 'It's the genuine Society!'

The company advanced on the green with the precision of people well broke to these movements. Scene-shifters could not have been quicker with the three-piece rostrum, nor stewards with the harmonium. Almost before its cross-legs had been kicked into their catches, certainly before the tourists by the lodge-gates had begun to move over, a woman sat down to it and struck up a hymn:

> 'Hear ther truth our tongues are telling,
>   Spread ther light from shore to shore,
> God hath given man a dwelling
>   Flat and flat for evermore.
>
> 'When ther Primal Dark retreated,
>   When ther deeps were undesigned,
> He with rule and level meted
>   Habitation for mankind!'

I saw sick envy on Bat's face. 'Curse Nature,' he muttered. 'She gets ahead of you every time. To think *I* forgot hymns and a harmonium!'

Then came the chorus:

> 'Hear ther truth our tongues are telling,
>   Spread ther light from shore to shore—
> Oh, be faithful! Oh, be truthful!
>   Earth is flat for evermore.'

They sang several verses with the fervour of Christians awaiting their lions. Then there were growlings in the air. The sexton, embraced by the landlord, two-stepped out of the pub-door. Each was trying to outroar the other. 'Apologising in advarnce for what he says,' the landlord shouted, 'you'd better go away' (here the sexton began to speak words). 'This isn't the time nor yet the place for—for any more o' this chat.'

The crowd thickened. I saw the village police-sergeant come out of his cottage buckling his belt.

'But surely,' said the woman at the harmonium, 'there must be some mistake. We are not suffragettes.'

'Damn it! They'd be a change,' cried the sexton. 'You get out of this! Don't talk! *I* can't stand it for one! Get right out, or we'll font you!'

The crowd which was being recruited from every house in sight echoed the invitation. The sergeant pushed forward. A man beside the reading-desk said: 'But surely we are among dear friends and sympathisers. Listen to me for a moment.'

It was the moment that a passing char-à-banc chose to strike into The Song. The effect was instantaneous. Bat, Ollyett, and I, who by divers roads have learned the psychology of crowds, retreated towards the tavern door. Woodhouse, the newspaper proprietor, anxious, I presume, to keep touch with the public, dived into the thick of it. Every one else told the Society to go away at once. When the lady at the harmonium (I began to understand why it is sometimes necessary to kill women) pointed at the stencilled park pillars and called them 'the cromlechs of our common faith,' there was a snarl and a rush. The police-sergeant checked it, but advised the Society to keep on going. The Society withdrew into the brake fighting, as it were, a rearguard action of oratory up each step. The collapsed harmonium was hauled in last, and with the perfect unreason of crowds, they cheered it loudly till the chauffeur slipped in his clutch and sped away. Then the crowd broke up, congratulating all concerned except the sexton, who

was held to have disgraced his office by having sworn at
ladies. We strolled across the green towards Woodhouse,
who was talking to the police-sergeant near the park-gates.
We were not twenty yards from him when we saw Sir
Thomas Ingell emerge from the lodge and rush furiously at
Woodhouse with an uplifted stick, at the same time shrieking: 'I'll teach you to laugh, you——' but Ollyett has the
record of the language. By the time we reached them, Sir
Thomas was on the ground; Woodhouse, very white, held
the walking-stick and was saying to the sergeant:

'I give this person in charge for assault.'

'But, good Lord!' said the sergeant, whiter than Woodhouse. 'It's Sir Thomas.'

'Whoever it is, it isn't fit to be at large,' said Woodhouse.
The crowd suspecting something wrong began to reassem-
ble, and all the English horror of a row in public moved us,
headed by the sergeant, inside the lodge. We shut both park-
gates and lodge-door.

'You saw the assault, sergeant,' Woodhouse went on.
'You can testify I used no more force than was necessary to
protect myself. You can testify that I have not even damaged this person's property. (Here! take your stick, you!)
You heard the filthy language he used.'

'I—I can't say I did,' the sergeant stammered.

'Oh, but we did!' said Ollyett, and repeated it, to the
apron-veiled horror of the lodge-keeper's wife.

Sir Thomas on a hard kitchen chair began to talk. He
said he had 'stood enough of being photographed like a
wild beast,' and expressed loud regret that he had not killed
'that man,' who was 'conspiring with the sergeant to laugh
at him.'

''Ad you ever seen 'im before, Sir Thomas?' the sergeant
asked.

'No! But it's time an example was made here. I've never
seen the sweep in my life.'

I think it was Bat Masquerier's magnetic eye that recalled the past to him, for his face changed and his jaw
dropped. 'But I have!' he groaned. 'I remember now.'

Here a writhing man entered by the back door. He was,

he said, the village solicitor. I do not assert that he licked Woodhouse's boots, but we should have respected him more if he had and been done with it. His notion was that the matter could be accommodated, arranged and compromised for gold, and yet more gold. The sergeant thought so too. Woodhouse undeceived them both. To the sergeant he said, 'Will you or will you not enter the charge?' To the village solicitor he gave the name of his lawyers, at which the man wrung his hands and cried, 'Oh, Sir T., Sir T.!' in a miserable falsetto, for it was a Bat Masquerier of a firm. They conferred together in tragic whispers.

'I don't dive after Dickens,' said Ollyett to Bat and me by the window, 'but every time *I* get into a row I notice the police-court always fills up with his characters.'

'I've noticed that too,' said Bat. 'But the odd thing is you mustn't give the public straight Dickens—not in My business. I wonder why that is.'

Then Sir Thomas got his second wind and cursed the day that he, or it may have been we, were born. I feared that though he was a Radical he might apologise and, since he was an M.P., might lie his way out of the difficulty. But he was utterly and truthfully beside himself. He asked foolish questions—such as what we were doing in the village at all, and how much blackmail Woodhouse expected to make out of him. But neither Woodhouse nor the sergeant nor the writhing solicitor listened. The upshot of their talk, in the chimney-corner, was that Sir Thomas stood engaged to appear next Monday before his brother magistrates on charges of assault, disorderly conduct, and language calculated, etc. Ollyett was specially careful about the language.

Then we left. The village looked very pretty in the late light—pretty and tuneful as a nest of nightingales.

'You'll turn up on Monday, I hope,' said Woodhouse, when we reached town. That was his only allusion to the affair.

So we turned up—through a world still singing that the Earth was flat—at the little clay-coloured market-town with the large Corn Exchange and the small Jubilee memorial.

We had some difficulty in getting seats in the court. Wood-house's imported London lawyer was a man of command-ing personality, with a voice trained to convey blasting im-putations by tone. When the case was called, he rose and stated his client's intention not to proceed with the charge. His client, he went on to say, had not entertained, and, of course, in the circumstances could not have entertained, any suggestion of accepting on behalf of public charities any moneys that might have been offered to him on the part of Sir Thomas's estate. At the same time, no one ac-knowledged more sincerely than his client the spirit in which those offers had been made by those entitled to make them. But, as a matter of fact—here he became the man of the world colloguing with his equals—certain—er—details had come to his client's knowledge *since* the lamentable outburst, which . . . He shrugged his shoulders. Nothing was served by going into them, but he ventured to say that, had those painful circumstances only been known earlier, his client would—again 'of course'—never have dreamed—— A gesture concluded the sentence, and the ensnared Bench looked at Sir Thomas with new and withdrawing eyes. Frankly, as they could see, it would be nothing less than cruelty to proceed further with this—er—unfortunate affair. He asked leave, therefore, to withdraw the charge *in toto*, and at the same time to express his client's deepest sym-pathy with all who had been in any way distressed, as his client had been, by the fact and the publicity of proceedings which he could, of course, again assure them that his client would never have dreamed of instituting if, as he hoped he had made plain, certain facts had been before his client at the time when . . . But he had said enough. For his fee it seemed to me that he had.

Heaven inspired Sir Thomas's lawyer—all of a sweat lest his client's language should come out—to rise up and thank him. Then, Sir Thomas—not yet aware what leprosy had been laid upon him, but grateful to escape on any terms— followed suit. He was heard in interested silence, and peo-ple drew back a pace as Gehazi passed forth.

'You hit hard,' said Bat to Woodhouse afterwards. 'His own people think he's mad.'

'You don't say so? I'll show you some of his letters to-night at dinner,' he replied.

He brought them to the Red Amber Room of the Chop Suey. We forgot to be amazed, as till then we had been amazed, over the Song or 'The Gubby,' or the full tide of Fate that seemed to run only for our sakes. It did not even interest Ollyett that the verb 'to huckle' had passed into the English leader-writers' language. We were studying the interior of a soul, flash-lighted to its grimiest corners by the dread of 'losing its position.'

'And then it thanked you, didn't it, for dropping the case?' said Pallant.

'Yes, and it sent me a telegram to confirm.' Woodhouse turned to Bat. 'Now d'you think I hit too hard?' he asked.

'No—o!' said Bat. 'After all—I'm talking of every one's business now—one can't ever do anything in Art that comes up to Nature in any game in life. Just think how this thing has——'

'Just let me run through that little case of yours again,' said Pallant, and picked up *The Bun* which had it set out in full.

'Any chance of 'Dal looking in on us to-night?' Ollyett began.

'She's occupied with her Art too,' Bat answered bitterly. 'What's the use of Art? Tell me, some one!' A barrel-organ outside promptly pointed out that the *Earth* was flat. 'The gramophone's killing street organs, but I let loose a hundred-and-seventy-four of those hurdygurdys twelve hours after The Song,' said Bat. 'Not counting the Provinces.' His face brightened a little.

'Look here!' said Pallant over the paper. 'I don't suppose you or those asinine J.P.'s knew it—but your lawyer ought to have known that you've all put your foot in it most confoundedly over this assault case.'

'What's the matter?' said Woodhouse.

'It's ludicrous. It's insane. There isn't two penn'orth of

legality in the whole thing. Of course, you could have withdrawn the charge, but the way you went about it is childish
—besides being illegal. What on earth was the Chief Constable thinking of?'

'Oh, he was a friend of Sir Thomas's. They all were for
that matter,' I replied.

'He ought to be hanged. So ought the Chairman of the
Bench. I'm talking as a lawyer now.'

'Why, what have we been guilty of? Misprison of treason
or compounding a felony—or what?' said Ollyett.

'I'll tell you later.' Pallant went back to the paper with
knitted brows, smiling unpleasantly from time to time. At
last he laughed.

'Thank you!' he said to Woodhouse. 'It ought to be pretty
useful—for us.'

'What d'you mean?' said Ollyett.

'For our side. They are all Rads who are mixed up in
this—from the Chief Constable down. There must be a
Question. There must be a Question.'

'Yes, but I wanted the charge withdrawn in my own
way,' Woodhouse insisted.

'That's nothing to do with the case. It's the legality of
your silly methods. You wouldn't understand if I talked till
morning.' He began to pace the room, his hands behind
him. 'I wonder if I can get it through our Whip's thick head
that it's a chance. . . . That comes of stuffing the Bench
with Radical tinkers,' he muttered.

'Oh, sit down!' said Woodhouse.

'Where's your lawyer to be found now?' he jerked out.

'At the Trefoil,' said Bat promptly. 'I gave him the stage-
box for to-night. He's an artist too.'

'Then I'm going to see him,' said Pallant. 'Properly handled this ought to be a godsend for our side.' He withdrew
without apology.

'Certainly, this thing keeps on opening up, and up,' I remarked inanely.

'It's beyond me!' said Bat. 'I don't think if I'd known I'd
have ever . . . Yes, I would, though. He said my home
address was——'

'It was his tone—his tone!' Ollyett almost shouted. Wood-house said nothing, but his face whitened as he brooded.

'Well, anyway,' Bat went on, 'I'm glad I always believed in God and Providence and all those things. Else I should lose my nerve. We've put it over the whole world—the full extent of the geographical globe. We couldn't stop it if we wanted to now. It's got to burn itself out. I'm not in charge any more. What'd you expect'll happen next. Angels?'

I expected nothing. Nothing that I expected approached what I got. Politics are not my concern, but, for the moment, since it seemed that they were going to 'huckle' with the rest, I took an interest in them. They impressed me as a dog's life without a dog's decencies, and I was confirmed in this when an unshaven and unwashen Pallant called on me at ten o'clock one morning, begging for a bath and a couch.

'Bail too?' I asked. He was in evening dress and his eyes were sunk feet in his head.

'No,' he said hoarsely. 'All night sitting. Fifteen divisions. 'Nother to-night. Your place was nearer than mine, so——' He began to undress in the hall.

When he awoke at one o'clock he gave me lurid accounts of what he said was history, but which was obviously collective hysteria. There had been a political crisis. He and his fellow M.P.'s had 'done things'—I never quite got at the things—for eighteen hours on end, and the pitiless Whips were even then at the telephones to herd 'em up to another dog-fight. So he snorted and grew hot all over again while he might have been resting.

'I'm going to pitch in my question about that miscarriage of justice at Huckley this afternoon, if you care to listen to it,' he said. 'It'll be absolutely thrown away—in our present state. I told 'em so; but it's my only chance for weeks. P'raps Woodhouse would like to come.'

'I'm sure he would. Anything to do with Huckley interests us,' I said.

'It'll miss fire, I'm afraid. Both sides are absolutely cooked. The present situation has been working up for some time. You see, the row was bound to come, etc. etc.,' and he flew off the handle once more.

I telephoned to Woodhouse, and we went to the House together. It was a dull, sticky afternoon with thunder in the air. For some reason or other, each side was determined to prove its virtue and endurance to the utmost. I heard men snarling about it all round me. 'If they won't spare us, we'll show 'em no mercy.' 'Break the brutes up from the start. They can't stand late hours.' 'Come on! No shirking! I know *you*'ve had a Turkish bath,' were some of the sentences I caught on our way. The House was packed already, and one could feel the negative electricity of a jaded crowd wrenching at one's own nerves, and depressing the afternoon soul.

'This is bad!' Woodhouse whispered. 'There'll be a row before they've finished. Look at the Front Benches!' And he pointed out little personal signs by which I was to know that each man was on edge. He might have spared himself. The House was ready to snap before a bone had been thrown. A sullen Minister rose to reply to a staccato question. His supporters cheered defiantly. 'None o' that! None o' that!' came from the Back Benches. I saw the Speaker's face stiffen like the face of a helmsman as he humours a hard-mouthed yacht after a sudden following sea. The trouble was barely met in time. There came a fresh, apparently causeless gust a few minutes later—savage, threatening, but futile. It died out—one could hear the sigh—in sudden wrathful realisation of the dreary hours ahead, and the ship of state drifted on.

Then Pallant—and the raw House winced at the torture of his voice—rose. It was a twenty-line question, studded with legal technicalities. The gist of it was that he wished to know whether the appropriate Minister was aware that there had been a grave miscarriage of justice on such and such a date, at such and such a place, before such and such justices of the peace, in regard to a case which arose——

I heard one desperate, weary 'damn!' float up from the pit of that torment. Pallant sawed on—'out of certain events which occurred at the village of Huckley.'

The House came to attention with a parting of the lips

like a hiccough, and it flashed through my mind. . . . Pallant repeated, 'Huckley. The village——'

'That voted the *Earth* was flat.' A single voice from a back bench sang it once like a lone frog in a far pool.

'*Earth* was flat,' croaked another voice opposite.

'*Earth* was flat.' There were several. Then several more.

It was, you understand, the collective, over-strained nerve of the House, snapping, strand by strand, to various notes, as the hawser parts from its moorings.

'The Village that voted the *Earth* was flat.' The tune was beginning to shape itself. More voices were raised and feet began to beat time. Even so it did not occur to me that the thing would——

'The Village that voted the *Earth* was flat!' It was easier now to see who were not singing. There were still a few. Of a sudden (and this proves the fundamental instability of the cross-bench mind) a cross-bencher leaped on his seat and there played an imaginary double-bass with tremendous maestro-like wagglings of the elbow.

The last strand parted. The ship of state drifted out helpless on the rocking tide of melody.

'The Village that voted the *Earth* was flat!
The Village that voted the *Earth* was flat!'

The Irish first conceived the idea of using their order-papers as funnels wherewith to reach the correct '*vroom—vroom*' on '*Earth.*' Labour, always conservative and respectable at a crisis, stood out longer than any other section, but when it came in it was howling syndicalism. Then, without distinction of Party, fear of constituents, desire for office, or hope of emolument, the House sang at the tops and at the bottoms of their voices, swaying their stale bodies and epileptically beating with their swelled feet. They sang 'The Village that voted the *Earth* was flat': first, because they wanted to, and secondly—which is the terror of that song—because they could not stop. For no consideration could they stop.

Pallant was still standing up. Some one pointed at him

and they laughed. Others began to point, lunging, as it were, in time with the tune. At this moment two persons came in practically abreast from behind the Speaker's chair, and halted appalled. One happened to be the Prime Minister and the other a messenger. The House, with tears running down their cheeks, transferred their attention to the paralysed couple. They pointed six hundred fore-fingers at them. They rocked, they waved, and they rolled while they pointed, but still they sang. When they weak-ened for an instant, Ireland would yell: 'Are ye *with* me, bhoys?' and they all renewed their strength like Antaeus. No man could say afterwards what happened to the Press or the Strangers' Gallery. It was the House, the hysterical and abandoned House of Commons, that held all eyes, as it deafened all ears. I saw both Front Benches bend for-ward, some with their foreheads on their dispatch-boxes, the rest with their faces in their hands; and their moving shoulders jolted the House out of its last rag of decency. Only the Speaker remained unmoved. The entire Press of Great Britain bore witness next day that he had not even bowed his head. The Angel of the Constitution, for vain was the help of man, foretold him the exact moment at which the House would have broken into 'The Gubby.' He is reported to have said: 'I heard the Irish beginning to shuffle it. So I adjourned.' Pallant's version is that he added: 'And I was never so grateful to a private member in all my life as I was to Mr. Pallant.'

He made no explanation. He did not refer to orders or disorders. He simply adjourned the House till six that eve-ning. And the House adjourned—some of it nearly on all fours.

I was not correct when I said that the Speaker was the only man who did not laugh. Woodhouse was beside me all the time. His face was set and quite white—as white, they told me, as Sir Thomas Ingell's when he went, by re-quest, to a private interview with his Chief Whip.

BAA BAA, BLACK SHEEP

Baa Baa, Black Sheep,
Have you any wool?
Yes, Sir, yes, Sir, three bags full.
One for the Master, one for the Dame—
None for the Little Boy that cries down the lane.

Nursery Rhyme.

THE FIRST BAG

When I was in my father's house, I was in a better place.

They were putting Punch to bed—the *ayah* and the *hamal* and Meeta, the big *Surti* boy, with the red-and-gold turban. Judy, already tucked inside her mosquito-curtains, was nearly asleep. Punch had been allowed to stay up for dinner. Many privileges had been accorded to Punch within the last ten days, and a greater kindness from the people of his world had encompassed his ways and works, which were mostly obstreperous. He sat on the edge of his bed and swung his bare legs defiantly.

'Punch-*baba* going to bye-lo?' said the *ayah* suggestively.

'No,' said Punch. 'Punch-*baba* wants the story about the Ranee that was turned into a tiger. Meeta must tell it, and the *hamal* shall hide behind the door and make tiger-noises at the proper time.'

'But Judy-*baba* will wake up,' said the *ayah*.

'Judy-*baba* is waked,' piped a small voice from the mosquito-curtains. 'There was a Ranee that lived at Delhi. Go on, Meeta,' and she fell fast asleep again while Meeta began the story.

Never had Punch secured the telling of that tale with so little opposition. He reflected for a long time. The *hamal* made the tiger-noises in twenty different keys.

''Top!' said Punch authoritatively. 'Why doesn't Papa come in and say he is going to give me *put-put?*'

'Punch-*baba* is going away,' said the *ayah*. 'In another week there will be no Punch-*baba* to pull my hair any more.' She sighed softly, for the boy of the household was very dear to her heart.

'Up the Ghauts in a train?' said Punch, standing on his bed. 'All the way to Nassick where the Ranee-Tiger lives?'

'Not to Nassick this year, little Sahib,' said Meeta, lifting him on his shoulder. 'Down to the sea where the coconuts are thrown, and across the sea in a big ship. Will you take Meeta with you to *Belait?*'

'You shall all come,' said Punch, from the height of Meeta's strong arms. 'Meeta and the *ayah* and the *hamal* and Bhini-in-the-Garden, and the salaam-Captain-Sahib-snake-man.'

There was no mockery in Meeta's voice when he replied: 'Great is the Sahib's favour,' and laid the little man down in the bed, while the *ayah,* sitting in the moonlight at the doorway, lulled him to sleep with an interminable canticle such as they sing in the Roman Catholic Church at Parel. Punch curled himself into a ball and slept.

Next morning Judy shouted that there was a rat in the nursery, and thus he forgot to tell her the wonderful news. It did not much matter, for Judy was only three and she would not have understood. But Punch was five; and he knew that going to England would be much nicer than a trip to Nassick.

. . . . .

Papa and Mamma sold the brougham and the piano, and stripped the house, and curtailed the allowance of crockery for the daily meals, and took long counsel together over a bundle of letters bearing the Rocklington postmark.

'The worst of it is that one can't be certain of anything,' said Papa, pulling his moustache. 'The letters in themselves are excellent, and the terms are moderate enough.'

'The worst of it is that the children will grow up away from me,' thought Mamma; but she did not say it aloud.

'We are only one case among hundreds,' said Papa bitterly. 'You shall go Home again in five years, dear.'

'Punch will be ten then—and Judy eight. Oh, how long and long and long the time will be! And we have to leave them among strangers.'

'Punch is a cheery little chap. He's sure to make friends wherever he goes.'

'And who could help loving my Ju?'

They were standing over the cots in the nursery late at night, and I think that Mamma was crying softly. After Papa had gone away, she knelt down by the side of Judy's cot. The *ayah* saw her and put up a prayer that the Memsahib might never find the love of her children taken away from her and given to a stranger.

Mamma's own prayer was a slightly illogical one. Summarised it ran: 'Let strangers love my children and be as good to them as I should be, but let *me* preserve their love and their confidence for ever and ever. Amen.' Punch scratched himself in his sleep, and Judy moaned a little.

Next day they all went down to the sea, and there was a scene at the Apollo Bunder when Punch discovered that Meeta could not come too, and Judy learned that the *ayah* must be left behind. But Punch found a thousand fascinating things in the rope, block, and steam-pipe line on the big P. & O. steamer long before Meeta and the *ayah* had dried their tears.

'Come back, Punch-*baba*,' said the *ayah*.

'Come back,' said Meeta, 'and be a *Burra Sahib* [a big man].'

'Yes,' said Punch, lifted up in his father's arms to wave good-bye. 'Yes, I will come back, and I will be a *Burra Sahib Bahadur* [a very big man indeed]!'

At the end of the first day Punch demanded to be set down in England, which he was certain must be close at hand. Next day there was a merry breeze, and Punch was very sick. 'When I come back to Bombay,' said Punch on his recovery, 'I will come by the road—in a broom-*gharri*. This is a very naughty ship.'

The Swedish boatswain consoled him, and he modified his opinions as the voyage went on. There was so much to see and to handle and ask questions about that Punch nearly forgot the *ayah* and Meeta and the *hamal,* and with difficulty remembered a few words of the Hindustani once his second speech.

But Judy was much worse. The day before the steamer reached Southampton, Mamma asked her if she would not like to see the *ayah* again. Judy's blue eyes turned to the stretch of sea that had swallowed all her tiny past, and she said: '*Ayah!* What *ayah?*'

Mamma cried over her and Punch marvelled. It was then that he heard for the first time Mamma's passionate appeal to him never to let Judy forget Mamma. Seeing that Judy was young, ridiculously young, and that Mamma, every evening for four weeks past, had come into the cabin to sing her and Punch to sleep with a mysterious rune that he called 'Sonny, my soul,' Punch could not understand what Mamma meant. But he strove to do his duty; for, the moment Mamma left the cabin, he said to Judy: 'Ju, you bemember Mamma?'

' 'Torse I do,' said Judy.

'Then *always* bemember Mamma, 'r else I won't give you the paper ducks that the red-haired Captain Sahib cut out for me.'

So Judy promised always to 'bemember Mamma.'

Many and many a time was Mamma's command laid upon Punch, and Papa would say the same thing with an insistence that awed the child.

'You must make haste and learn to write, Punch,' said Papa, 'and then you'll be able to write letters to us in Bombay.'

'I'll come into your room,' said Punch, and Papa choked. Papa and Mamma were always choking in those days. If Punch took Judy to task for not 'bemembering,' they choked. If Punch sprawled on the sofa in the Southampton lodging-house and sketched his future in purple and gold, they choked; and so they did if Judy put up her mouth for a kiss.

Through many days all four were vagabonds on the face of the earth—Punch with no one to give orders to, Judy too young for anything, and Papa and Mamma grave, distracted, and choking.

'Where,' demanded Punch, wearied of a loathsome contrivance on four wheels with a mound of luggage atop— '*where* is our broom-*gharri*? This thing talks so much that *I* can't talk. Where is our *own* broom-*gharri*? When I was at Bandstand before we comed away, I asked Inverarity Sahib why he was sitting in it, and he said it was his own. And I said, "I will *give* it you"—I like Inverarity Sahib— and I said, "Can you put your legs through the pully-wag loops by the windows?" And Inverarity Sahib said No, and laughed. 'I can put my legs through the pully-wag loops. I can put my legs through *these* pully-wag loops. Look! Oh, Mamma's crying again! I didn't know I wasn't not to do *so*.'

Punch drew his legs out of the loops of the four-wheeler: the door opened and he slid to the earth, in a cascade of parcels, at the door of an austere little villa whose gates bore the legend 'Downe Lodge.' Punch gathered himself together and eyed the house with disfavour. It stood on a sandy road, and a cold wind tickled his knickerbockered legs.

'Let us go away,' said Punch. 'This is not a pretty place.'

But Mamma and Papa and Judy had left the cab, and all the luggage was being taken into the house. At the doorstep stood a woman in black, and she smiled largely, with dry chapped lips. Behind her was a man, big, bony, grey, and lame as to one leg—behind him a boy of twelve, black-haired and oily in appearance. Punch surveyed the trio, and advanced without fear, as he had been accustomed to do in Bombay when callers came and he happened to be playing in the veranda.

'How do you do?' said he. 'I am Punch.' But they were all looking at the luggage—all except the grey man, who shook hands with Punch, and said he was 'a smart little fellow.' There was much running about and banging of boxes, and Punch curled himself up on the sofa in the dining-room and considered things.

'I don't like these people,' said Punch. 'But never mind. We'll go away soon. We have always went away soon from everywhere. I wish we was gone back to Bombay *soon.*'

The wish bore no fruit. For six days Mamma wept at intervals, and showed the woman in black all Punch's clothes—a liberty which Punch resented. 'But p'raps she's a new white *ayah*,' he thought. 'I'm to call her Antirosa, but she doesn't call *me* Sahib. She says just Punch,' he confided to Judy. 'What is Antirosa?'

Judy didn't know. Neither she nor Punch had heard anything of an animal called an aunt. Their world had been Papa and Mamma, who knew everything, permitted everything, and loved everybody—even Punch when he used to go into the garden at Bombay and fill his nails with mould after the weekly nail-cutting, because, as he explained between two strokes of the slipper to his sorely-tried father, his fingers 'felt so new at the ends.'

In an undefined way Punch judged it advisable to keep both parents between himself and the woman in black and the boy with black hair. He did not approve of them. He liked the grey man, who had expressed a wish to be called 'Uncleharri.' They nodded at each other when they met, and the grey man showed him a little ship with rigging that took up and down.

'She is a model of the *Brisk*—the little *Brisk* that was sore exposed that day at Navarino.' The grey man hummed the last words and fell into a reverie. 'I'll tell you about Navarino, Punch, when we go for walks together; and you mustn't touch the ship, because she's the *Brisk*.'

Long before that walk, the first of many, was taken, they roused Punch and Judy in the chill dawn of a February morning to say Good-bye; and of all people in the wide earth to Papa and Mamma—both crying this time. Punch was very sleepy and Judy was cross.

'Don't forget us,' pleaded Mamma. 'Oh, my little son, don't forget us, and see that Judy remembers too.'

'I've told Judy to bemember,' said Punch, wriggling, for his father's beard tickled his neck. 'I've told Judy—ten—forty—'leven thousand times. But Ju's so young—quite a baby—isn't she?'

'Yes,' said Papa, 'quite a baby, and you must be good to Judy, and make haste to learn to write and—and—and——'

Punch was back in his bed again. Judy was fast asleep, and there was the rattle of a cab below. Papa and Mamma had gone away. Not to Nassick; that was across the sea. To some place much nearer, of course, and equally of course they would return. They came back after dinner-parties, and Papa had come back after he had been to a place called 'The Snows,' and Mamma with him, to Punch and Judy at Mrs. Inverarity's house in Marine Lines. Assuredly they would come back again. So Punch fell asleep till the true morning, when the black-haired boy met him with the information that Papa and Mamma had gone to Bombay, and that he and Judy were to stay at Downe Lodge 'for ever.' Antirosa, tearfully appealed to for a contradiction, said that Harry had spoken the truth, and that it behoved Punch to fold up his clothes neatly on going to bed. Punch went out and wept bitterly with Judy, into whose fair head he had driven some ideas of the meaning of separation.

When a matured man discovers that he has been deserted by Providence, deprived of his God, and cast without help, comfort, or sympathy, upon a world which is new and strange to him, his despair, which may find expression in evil living, the writing of his experiences, or the more satisfactory diversion of suicide, is generally supposed to be impressive. A child, under exactly similar circumstances as far as its knowledge goes, cannot very well curse God and die. It howls till its nose is red, its eyes are sore, and its head aches. Punch and Judy, through no fault of their own, had lost all their world. They sat in the hall and cried; the black-haired boy looking on from afar.

The model of the ship availed nothing, though the grey man assured Punch that he might pull the rigging up and down as much as he pleased; and Judy was promised free entry into the kitchen. They wanted Papa and Mamma, gone to Bombay beyond the seas, and their grief while it lasted was without remedy.

When the tears ceased the house was very still. Antirosa had decided that it was better to let the children 'have their cry out,' and the boy had gone to school. Punch raised his head from the floor and sniffed mournfully. Judy was nearly asleep. Three short years had not taught her how to bear sorrow with full knowledge. There was a distant, dull boom in the air—a repeated heavy thud. Punch knew that sound in Bombay in the monsoon. It was the sea—the sea that must be traversed before any one could get to Bombay.

'Quick, Ju!' he cried. 'We're close to the sea. I can hear it! Listen! That's where they've went. P'raps we can catch them if we was in time. They didn't mean to go without us. They've only forgot.'

'Iss,' said Judy. 'They've only forgotted. Less go to the sea.'

The hall-door was open and so was the garden-gate.

'It's very, very big, this place,' he said, looking cautiously down the road, 'and we will get lost. But *I* will find a man and order him to take me back to my house—like I did in Bombay.'

He took Judy by the hand, and the two ran hatless in the direction of the sound of the sea. Downe Lodge was almost the last of a range of newly-built houses running out, through a field of brick-mounds, to a heath where gipsies occasionally camped and where the Garrison Artillery of Rocklington practised. There were few people to be seen, and the children might have been taken for those of the soldiery who ranged far. Half an hour the wearied little legs tramped across heath, potato-patch, and sand-dune.

'I'se so tired,' said Judy, 'and Mamma will be angry.'

'Mamma's *never* angry. I suppose she is waiting at the sea now while Papa gets tickets. We'll find them and go along with them. Ju, you mustn't sit down. Only a little more and we'll come to the sea. Ju, if you sit down I'll *thmack* you!' said Punch.

They climbed another dune, and came upon the great grey sea at low tide. Hundreds of crabs were scuttling about the beach, but there was no trace of Papa and Mamma, not even of a ship upon the waters—nothing but sand and mud for miles and miles.

And 'Uncleharri' found them by chance—very muddy and very forlorn—Punch dissolved in tears, but trying to divert Judy with an 'ickle trab,' and Judy wailing to the pitiless horizon for 'Mamma, Mamma!'—and again 'Mamma!'

THE SECOND BAG

Ah, well-a-day, for we are souls bereaved!
Of all the creatures under Heaven's wide cope
We are most hopeless, who had once most hope,
And most beliefless, who had most believed.
A. H. Clough.

All this time not a word about Black Sheep. He came later, and Harry, the black-haired boy, was mainly responsible for his coming.

Judy—who could help loving little Judy?—passed, by special permit, into the kitchen and thence straight to Aunty Rosa's heart. Harry was Aunty Rosa's one child, and Punch was the extra boy about the house. There was no special place for him or his little affairs, and he was forbidden to sprawl on sofas and explain his ideas about the manufacture of this world and his hopes for his future. Sprawling was lazy and wore out sofas, and little boys were not expected to talk. They were talked to, and the talking-to was intended for the benefit of their morals. As the un-questioned despot of the house at Bombay, Punch could not quite understand how he came to be of no account in this his new life.

Harry might reach across the table and take what he wanted; Judy might point and get what she wanted. Punch was forbidden to do either. The grey man was his great hope and stand-by for many months after Mamma and Papa left, and he had forgotten to tell Judy to 'bemember Mamma.'

This lapse was excusable, because in the interval he had been introduced by Aunty Rosa to two very impressive things—an abstraction called God, the intimate friend and ally of Aunty Rosa, generally believed to live behind the kitchen-range because it was hot there—and a dirty brown book filled with unintelligible dots and marks. Punch was always anxious to oblige everybody. He therefore welded the story of the Creation on to what he could recollect of his Indian fairy tales, and scandalised Aunty Rosa by re-peating the result to Judy. It was a sin, a grievous sin, and Punch was talked to for a quarter of an hour. He could not understand where the iniquity came in, but was careful not to repeat the offence, because Aunty Rosa told him that God had heard every word he had said and was very angry. If this were true why didn't God come and say so, thought Punch, and dismissed the matter from his mind. Afterwards he learned to know the Lord as the only thing in the world more awful than Aunty Rosa—as a Creature that stood in the background and counted the strokes of the cane.

But the reading was, just then, a much more serious mat-ter than any creed. Aunty Rosa sat him upon a table and told him that A B meant ab.

'Why?' said Punch. 'A is a and B is bee. *Why* does A B mean ab?'

'Because I tell you it does,' said Aunty Rosa, 'and you've got to say it.'

Punch said it accordingly, and for a month, hugely against his will, stumbled through the brown book, not in the least comprehending what it meant. But Uncle Harry, who walked much and generally alone, was wont to come into the nursery and suggest to Aunty Rosa that Punch should walk with him. He seldom spoke, but he showed Punch all Rocklington, from the mudbanks and the sand of the back-bay to the great harbours where ships lay at anchor, and the dockyards where the hammers were never still, and the marine-store shops, and the shiny brass counters in the Offices where Uncle Harry went once every three months with a slip of blue paper and received sovereigns in exchange; for he held a wound-pension. Punch heard, too, from his lips the story of the battle of Navarino, where the sailors of the Fleet, for three days afterwards, were deaf as posts and could only sign to each other. 'That was because of the noise of the guns,' said Uncle Harry, 'and I have got the wadding of a bullet somewhere inside me now.'

Punch regarded him with curiosity. He had not the least idea what wadding was, and his notion of a bullet was a dockyard cannon-ball bigger than his own head. How could Uncle Harry keep a cannon-ball inside him? He was afraid to ask, for fear Uncle Harry might be angry.

Punch had never known what anger—real anger—meant until one terrible day when Harry had taken his paint-box to paint a boat with, and Punch had protested. Then Uncle Harry had appeared on the scene and, muttering something about 'strangers' children,' had with a stick smitten the black-haired boy across the shoulders till he wept and yelled, and Aunty Rosa came in and abused Uncle Harry for cruelty to his own flesh and blood, and Punch shuddered to the tips of his shoes. 'It wasn't my fault,' he explained to the boy, but both Harry and Aunty Rosa said that it was, and that Punch had told tales, and for a week there were no more walks with Uncle Harry.

But that week brought a great joy to Punch.

He had repeated till he was thrice weary the statement that 'The Cat lay on the Mat and the Rat came in.'

'Now I can truly read,' said Punch, 'and now I will never read anything in the world.'

He put the brown book in the cupboard where his school-books lived and accidentally tumbled out a venerable volume, without covers, labelled *Sharpe's Magazine*. There was the most portentous picture of a Griffin on the first page, with verses below. The Griffin carried off one sheep a day from a German village, till a man came with a 'falchion' and split the Griffin open. Goodness only knew what a falchion was, but there was the Griffin and his history was an improvement upon the eternal Cat.

'This,' said Punch, 'means things, and now I will know all about everything in all the world.' He read till the light failed, not understanding a tithe of the meaning, but tantalised by glimpses of new worlds hereafter to be revealed.

'What is a "falchion"? What is a "e-wee lamb"? What is a "base *uss*urper"? What is a "verdant mead"?' he demanded, with flushed cheeks, at bedtime, of the astonished Aunty Rosa.

'Say your prayers and go to sleep,' she replied, and that was all the help Punch then or afterwards found at her hands in the new and delightful exercise of reading.

'Aunty Rosa only knows about God and things like that,' argued Punch. 'Uncle Harry will tell me.'

The next walk proved that Uncle Harry could not help either; but he allowed Punch to talk, and even sat down on a bench to hear about the Griffin. Other walks brought other stories as Punch ranged farther afield, for the house held large store of old books that no one ever opened— from *Frank Fairlegh* in serial numbers, and the earlier poems of Tennyson, contributed anonymously to *Sharpe's Magazine*, to '62 Exhibition Catalogues, gay with colours and delightfully incomprehensible, and odd leaves of *Gulliver's Travels*.

As soon as Punch could string a few pot-hooks together he wrote to Bombay, demanding by return of post 'all the books in all the world.' Papa could not comply with this modest indent, but sent *Grimm's Fairy Tales* and a *Hans Andersen*. That was enough. If he were only left alone Punch could pass, at any hour he chose, into a land of his own, beyond reach of Aunty Rosa and her God, Harry and his teasements, and Judy's claims to be played with.

'Don't disturve me, I'm reading. Go and play in the kitchen,' grunted Punch. 'Aunty Rosa lets *you* go there.' Judy was cutting her second teeth and was fretful. She appealed to Aunty Rosa, who descended on Punch.

'I was reading,' he explained, 'reading a book. I *want* to read.'

'You're only doing that to show off,' said Aunty Rosa. 'But we'll see. Play with Judy now, and don't open a book for a week.'

Judy did not pass a very enjoyable playtime with Punch, who was consumed with indignation. There was a pettiness at the bottom of the prohibition which puzzled him.

'It's what I like to do,' he said, 'and she's found out that and stopped me. Don't cry, Ju—it wasn't your fault—*please* don't cry, or she'll say I made you.'

Ju loyally mopped up her tears, and the two played in their nursery, a room in the basement and half underground, to which they were regularly sent after the midday dinner while Aunty Rosa slept. She drank wine—that is to say, something from a bottle in the cellaret—for her stomach's sake, but if she did not fall asleep she would sometimes come into the nursery to see that the children were really playing. Now bricks, wooden hoops, ninepins, and chinaware cannot amuse for ever, especially when all Fairyland is to be won by the mere opening of a book, and, as often as not, Punch would be discovered reading to Judy or telling her interminable tales. That was an offence in the eyes of the law, and Judy would be whisked off by Aunty Rosa, while Punch was left to play alone, 'and be sure that I hear you doing it.'

It was not a cheering employ, for he had to make a playful noise. At last, with infinite craft, he devised an arrange-

ment whereby the table could be supported as to three legs
on toy bricks, leaving the fourth clear to bring down on the
floor. He could work the table with one hand and hold the
book with the other. This he did till an evil day when Aunty
Rosa pounced upon him unawares and told him that he
was 'acting a lie.'

'If you're old enough to do that,' she said—her temper
was always worst after dinner—'you're old enough to be
beaten.'

'But—I'm—I'm not a animal!' said Punch aghast. He remembered Uncle Harry and the stick, and turned white.
Aunty Rosa had hidden a light cane behind her, and Punch
was beaten then and there over the shoulders. It was a
revelation to him. The room-door was shut, and he was left
to weep himself into repentance and work out his own
gospel of life.

Aunty Rosa, he argued, had the power to beat him with
many stripes. It was unjust and cruel, and Mamma and
Papa would never have allowed it. Unless perhaps, as
Aunty Rosa seemed to imply, they had sent secret orders.
In which case he was abandoned indeed. It would be discreet in the future to propitiate Aunty Rosa, but then
again, even in matters in which he was innocent, he had
been accused of wishing to 'show off.' He had 'shown off'
before visitors when he had attacked a strange gentleman
—Harry's uncle, not his own—with requests for information
about the Griffin and the falchion, and the precise nature of
the Tilbury in which Frank Fairlegh rode—all points of
paramount interest which he was bursting to understand.
Clearly it would not do to pretend to care for Aunty Rosa.

At this point Harry entered and stood afar off, eyeing
Punch, a dishevelled heap in the corner of the room, with
disgust.

'You're a liar—a young liar,' said Harry, with great unc-
tion, 'and you're to have tea down here because you're not
fit to speak to us. And you're not to speak to Judy again
till Mother gives you leave. You'll corrupt her. You're only
fit to associate with the servant. Mother says so.'

Having reduced Punch to a second agony of tears, Harry departed upstairs with the news that Punch was still rebellious.

Uncle Harry sat uneasily in the dining-room. 'Damn it all, Rosa,' said he at last, 'can't you leave the child alone? He's a good enough little chap when I meet him.'

'He puts on his best manners with you, Henry,' said Aunty Rosa, 'but I'm afraid, I'm very much afraid, that he is the Black Sheep of the family.'

Harry heard and stored up the name for future use. Judy cried till she was bidden to stop, her brother not being worth tears; and the evening concluded with the return of Punch to the upper regions and a private sitting at which all the blinding horrors of Hell were revealed to Punch with such store of imagery as Aunty Rosa's narrow mind possessed.

Most grievous of all was Judy's round-eyed reproach, and Punch went to bed in the depths of the Valley of Humiliation. He shared his room with Harry and knew the torture in store. For an hour and a half he had to answer that young gentleman's questions as to his motives for telling a lie, and a grievous lie, the precise quantity of punishment inflicted by Aunty Rosa, and had also to profess his deep gratitude for such religious instruction as Harry thought fit to impart.

From that day began the downfall of Punch, now Black Sheep.

'Untrustworthy in one thing, untrustworthy in all,' said Aunty Rosa, and Harry felt that Black Sheep was delivered into his hands. He would wake him up in the night to ask him why he was such a liar.

'I don't know,' Punch would reply.

'Then don't you think you ought to get up and pray to God for a new heart?'

'Y-yess.'

'Get out and pray, then!' And Punch would get out of bed with raging hate in his heart against all the world, seen and unseen. He was always tumbling into trouble. Harry had a knack of cross-examining him as to his day's doings, which seldom failed to lead him, sleepy and savage, into half-a-dozen contradictions—all duly reported to Aunty Rosa next morning.

'But it *wasn't* a lie,' Punch would begin, charging into a laboured explanation that landed him more hopelessly in the mire. 'I said that I didn't say my prayers *twice* over in the day, and *that* was on Tuesday. *Once* I did. I *know* I did, but Harry said I didn't,' and so forth, till the tension brought tears, and he was dismissed from the table in disgrace.

'You usen't to be as bad as this,' said Judy, awestricken at the catalogue of Black Sheep's crimes. 'Why are you so bad now?'

'I don't know,' Black Sheep would reply. 'I'm not, if I only wasn't bothered upside-down. I knew what I *did,* and I want to say so; but Harry always makes it out different somehow, and Aunty Rosa doesn't believe a word I say. Oh, Ju! Don't *you* say I'm bad too.'

'Aunty Rosa says you are,' said Judy. 'She told the Vicar so when he came yesterday.'

'Why does she tell all the people outside the house about me? It isn't fair,' said Black Sheep. 'When I was in Bombay, and was bad—*doing* bad, not made-up bad like this— Mamma told Papa, and Papa told me he knew, and that was all. *Outside* people didn't know too—even Meeta didn't know.'

'I don't remember,' said Judy wistfully. 'I was all little then. Mamma was just as fond of you as she was of me, wasn't she?'

''Course she was. So was Papa. So was everybody.'

'Aunty Rosa likes me more than she does you. She says that you are a Trial and a Black Sheep, and I'm not to speak to you more than I can help.'

'Always? Not outside of the times when you mustn't speak to me at all?'

Judy nodded her head mournfully. Black Sheep turned away in despair, but Judy's arms were round his neck.

'Never mind, Punch,' she whispered. 'I *will* speak to you just the same as ever and ever. You're my own own brother though you are—though Aunty Rosa says you're bad, and Harry says you are a little coward. He says that if I pulled your hair hard, you'd cry.'

'Pull, then,' said Punch.

Judy pulled gingerly.

'Pull harder—as hard as you can! There! I don't mind how much you pull it *now*. If you'll speak to me same as ever I'll let you pull it as much as you like—pull it out if you like. But I know if Harry came and stood by and made you do it I'd cry.'

So the two children sealed the compact with a kiss, and Black Sheep's heart was cheered within him, and by extreme caution and careful avoidance of Harry he acquired virtue, and was allowed to read undisturbed for a week. Uncle Harry took him for walks, and consoled him with rough tenderness, never calling him Black Sheep. 'It's good for you, I suppose, Punch,' he used to say. 'Let us sit down. I'm getting tired.' His steps led him now not to the beach, but to the Cemetery of Rocklington, amid the potato-fields. For hours the grey man would sit on a tombstone, while Black Sheep would read epitaphs, and then with a sigh would stump home again.

'I shall lie there soon,' said he to Black Sheep, one winter evening, when his face showed white as a worn silver coin under the light of the lych gate. 'You needn't tell Aunty Rosa.'

A month later he turned sharp round, ere half a morning walk was completed, and stumped back to the house. 'Put me to bed, Rosa,' he muttered. 'I've walked my last. The wadding has found me out.'

They put him to bed, and for a fortnight the shadow of his sickness lay upon the house, and Black Sheep went to and fro unobserved. Papa had sent him some new books, and he was told to keep quiet. He retired into his own world, and was perfectly happy. Even at night his felicity was unbroken. He could lie in bed and string himself tales of travel and adventure while Harry was downstairs.

'Uncle Harry's going to die,' said Judy, who now lived almost entirely with Aunty Rosa.

'I'm very sorry,' said Black Sheep soberly. 'He told me that a long time ago.'

Aunty Rosa heard the conversation. 'Will nothing check your wicked tongue?' she said angrily. There were blue circles round her eyes.

Black Sheep retreated to the nursery and read *Cometh up as a Flower* with deep and uncomprehending interest. He had been forbidden to open it on account of its 'sinfulness,' but the bonds of the Universe were crumbling, and Aunty Rosa was in great grief.

'I'm glad,' said Black Sheep. 'She's unhappy now. It wasn't a lie, though. *I* knew. He told me not to tell.'

That night Black Sheep woke with a start. Harry was not in the room, and there was a sound of sobbing on the next floor. Then the voice of Uncle Harry, singing the song of the Battle of Navarino, came through the darkness:—

> 'Our vanship was the *Asia*—
> The *Albion* and *Genoa!*'

'He's getting well,' thought Black Sheep, who knew the song through all its seventeen verses. But the blood froze at his little heart as he thought. The voice leapt an octave, and ran shrill as a boatswain's pipe:—

> 'And next came on the lovely *Rose*,
> The *Philomel*, her fire-ship, closed,
> And the little *Brisk* was sore exposed
> That day at Navarino.'

'That day at Navarino, Uncle Harry!' shouted Black Sheep, half wild with excitement and fear of he knew not what.

A door opened, and Aunty Rosa screamed up the staircase: 'Hush! For God's sake hush, you little devil! Uncle Harry is *dead!*'

THE THIRD BAG

Journeys end in lovers' meeting,
Every wise man's son doth know.

'I wonder what will happen to me now,' thought Black
Sheep, when semi-pagan rites peculiar to the burial of the
Dead in middle-class houses had been accomplished, and
Aunty Rosa, awful in black crape, had returned to this life.
'I don't think I've done anything bad that she knows of. I
suppose I will soon. She will be very cross after Uncle
Harry's dying, and Harry will be cross too. I'll keep in the
nursery.'

Unfortunately for Punch's plans, it was decided that he
should be sent to a day-school which Harry attended. This
meant a morning walk with Harry, and perhaps an evening
one; but the prospect of freedom in the interval was refreshing. 'Harry'll tell everything I do, but I won't do anything,' said Black Sheep. Fortified with this virtuous resolution, he went to school only to find that Harry's version of
his character had preceded him, and that life was a burden
in consequence. He took stock of his associates. Some of
them were unclean, some of them talked in dialect, many
dropped their h's, and there were two Jews and a negro, or
some one quite as dark, in the assembly. 'That's a *hubshi*,'
said Black Sheep to himself. 'Even Meeta used to laugh at a
hubshi. I don't think this is a proper place.' He was indig-
nant for at least an hour, till he reflected that any expostula-
tion on his part would be by Aunty Rosa construed into
'showing off,' and that Harry would tell the boys.

'How do you like school?' said Aunty Rosa at the end
of the day.

'I think it is a very nice place,' said Punch quietly.

'I suppose you warned the boys of Black Sheep's character?' said Aunty Rosa to Harry.

'Oh yes,' said the censor of Black Sheep's morals. 'They know all about him.'

'If I was with my father,' said Black Sheep, stung to the quick, 'I shouldn't *speak* to those boys. He wouldn't let me. They live in shops. I saw them go into shops—where their fathers live and sell things.'

'You're too good for that school, are you?' said Aunty Rosa, with a bitter smile. 'You ought to be grateful, Black Sheep, that those boys speak to you at all. It isn't every school that takes little liars.'

Harry did not fail to make much capital out of Black Sheep's ill-considered remark; with the result that several boys, including the *hubshi*, demonstrated to Black Sheep the eternal equality of the human race by smacking his head, and his consolation from Aunty Rosa was that it 'served him right for being vain.' He learned, however, to keep his opinions to himself, and by propitiating Harry in carrying books and the like to get a little peace. His existence was not too joyful. From nine till twelve he was at school, and from two to four, except on Saturdays. In the evenings he was sent down into the nursery to prepare his lessons for the next day, and every night came the dreaded cross-questionings at Harry's hand. Of Judy he saw but little. She was deeply religious—at six years of age Religion is easy to come by—and sorely divided between her natural love for Black Sheep and her love for Aunty Rosa, who could do no wrong.

The lean woman returned that love with interest, and Judy, when she dared, took advantage of this for the remission of Black Sheep's penalties. Failures in lessons at school were punished at home by a week without reading other than schoolbooks, and Harry brought the news of such a failure with glee. Further, Black Sheep was then bound to repeat his lessons at bedtime to Harry, who generally succeeded in making him break down, and consoled him by gloomiest forebodings for the morrow. Harry was at once spy, practical joker, inquisitor, and Aunty Rosa's deputy executioner. He filled his many posts to admiration. From his actions, now that Uncle Harry was dead, there was no appeal. Black Sheep had not been permitted to keep any self-respect at school: at home he was, of course, utterly discredited, and grateful for any pity that the servant-girls—they changed frequently at Downe Lodge because they, too, were liars—might show. 'You're just fit to row in the same boat with Black Sheep,' was a sentiment that each new Jane or Eliza might expect to hear, before a month was over, from Aunty Rosa's lips; and Black Sheep was used to ask new girls whether they had yet been compared to him. Harry was 'Master Harry' in their mouths; Judy was officially 'Miss Judy'; but Black Sheep was never anything more than Black Sheep *tout court*.

As time went on and the memory of Papa and Mamma became wholly overlaid by the unpleasant task of writing them letters, under Aunty Rosa's eye, each Sunday, Black Sheep forgot what manner of life he had led in the beginning of things. Even Judy's appeals to 'try and remember about Bombay' failed to quicken him.

'I can't remember,' he said. 'I know I used to give orders and Mamma kissed me.'

'Aunty Rosa will kiss you if you are good,' pleaded Judy.

'Ugh! I don't want to be kissed by Aunty Rosa. She'd say I was doing it to get something more to eat.'

The weeks lengthened into months, and the holidays came; but just before the holidays Black Sheep fell into deadly sin.

Among the many boys whom Harry had incited to 'punch Black Sheep's head because he daren't hit back,' was one more aggravating than the rest, who, in an unlucky moment, fell upon Black Sheep when Harry was not near. The blows stung, and Black Sheep struck back at random with all the power at his command. The boy dropped and whimpered. Black Sheep was astounded at his own act, but, feeling the unresisting body under him, shook it with both his hands in blind fury and then began to throttle his enemy; meaning honestly to slay him. There was a scuffle, and Black Sheep was torn off the body by Harry and some colleagues, and cuffed home tingling but exultant. Aunty Rosa was out. Pending her arrival, Harry set himself to lecture Black Sheep on the sin of murder—which he described as the offence of Cain.

'Why didn't you fight him fair? What did you hit him when he was down for, you little cur?'

Black Sheep looked up at Harry's throat and then at a knife on the dinner-table.

'I don't understand,' he said wearily. 'You always set him on me and told me I was a coward when I blubbed. Will you leave me alone until Aunty Rosa comes in? She'll beat me if you tell her I ought to be beaten; so it's all right.'

'It's all wrong,' said Harry magisterially. 'You nearly killed him, and I shouldn't wonder if he dies.'

'Will he die?' said Black Sheep.

'I daresay,' said Harry, 'and then you'll be hanged, and go to Hell.'

'All right,' said Black Sheep, picking up the table-knife. 'Then I'll kill *you* now. You say things and do things and—and *I* don't know how things happen, and you never leave me alone—and I don't care *what* happens!'

He ran at the boy with the knife, and Harry fled upstairs to his room, promising Black Sheep the finest thrashing in the world when Aunty Rosa returned. Black Sheep sat at the bottom of the stairs, the table-knife in his hand, and wept for that he had not killed Harry. The servant-girl came up from the kitchen, took the knife away, and consoled him. But Black Sheep was beyond consolation. He would be badly beaten by Aunty Rosa; then there would be another beating at Harry's hands; then Judy would not be allowed to speak to him; then the tale would be told at school, and then—

There was no one to help and no one to care, and the best way out of the business was by death. A knife would hurt, but Aunty Rosa had told him, a year ago, that if he sucked paint he would die. He went into the nursery, unearthed the now disused Noah's Ark, and sucked the paint off as many animals as remained. It tasted abominably, but he had licked Noah's Dove clean by the time Aunty Rosa and Judy returned. He went upstairs and greeted them with: 'Please, Aunty Rosa, I believe I've nearly killed a boy at school, and I've tried to kill Harry, and when you've done all about God and Hell, will you beat me and get it over?'

The tale of the assault as told by Harry could only be explained on the ground of possession by the Devil. Wherefore Black Sheep was not only most excellently beaten, once by Aunty Rosa, and once, when thoroughly cowed down, by Harry, but he was further prayed for at family prayers, together with Jane, who had stolen a cold rissole from the pantry, and snuffled audibly as her sin was brought before the Throne of Grace. Black Sheep was sore and stiff but triumphant. He would die that very night and be rid of them all. No, he would ask for no forgiveness from Harry, and at bed-time would stand no questioning at Harry's hands, even though addressed as 'Young Cain.'

'I've been beaten,' said he, 'and I've done other things. I don't care what I do. If you speak to me to-night, Harry, I'll get out and try to kill you. Now you can kill me if you like.'

Harry took his bed into the spare room, and Black Sheep lay down to die.

It may be that the makers of Noah's Arks know that their animals are likely to find their way into young mouths, and paint them accordingly. Certain it is that the common, weary next morning broke through the windows and found Black Sheep quite well and a good deal ashamed of himself, but richer by the knowledge that he could, in extremity, secure himself against Harry for the future.

When he descended to breakfast on the first day of the holidays, he was greeted with the news that Harry, Aunty

Rosa, and Judy were going away to Brighton, while Black Sheep was to stay in the house with the servant. His latest outbreak suited Aunty Rosa's plans admirably. It gave her good excuse for leaving the extra boy behind. Papa in Bombay, who really seemed to know a young sinner's wants to the hour, sent, that week, a package of new books. And with these, and the society of Jane on board-wages, Black Sheep was left alone for a month.

The books lasted for ten days. They were eaten too quickly in long gulps of twelve hours at a time. Then came days of doing absolutely nothing, of dreaming dreams and marching imaginary armies up and down stairs, of counting the number of banisters, and of measuring the length and breadth of every room in handspans—fifty down the side, thirty across, and fifty back again. Jane made many friends, and, after receiving Black Sheep's assurance that he would not tell of her absences, went out daily for long hours. Black Sheep would follow the rays of the sinking sun from the kitchen to the dining-room and thence upward to his own bedroom until all was grey dark, and he ran down to the kitchen fire and read by its light. He was happy in that he was left alone and could read as much as he pleased. But, later, he grew afraid of the shadows of window curtains and the flapping of doors and the creaking of shutters. He went out into the garden, and the rustling of the laurel-bushes frightened him.

He was glad when they all returned—Aunty Rosa, Harry, and Judy—full of news, and Judy laden with gifts. Who could help loving loyal little Judy? In return for all her merry babblement, Black Sheep confided to her that the distance from the hall-door to the top of the first landing was exactly one-hundred and eighty-four handspans. He had found it out himself!

Then the old life recommenced; but with a difference, and a new sin. To his other iniquities Black Sheep had now added a phenomenal clumsiness—was as unfit to trust in action as he was in word. He himself could not account for spilling everything he touched, upsetting glasses as he put his hand out, and bumping his head against doors that were manifestly shut. There was a grey haze upon all his world, and it narrowed month by month, until at last it left Black Sheep almost alone with the flapping curtains that were so like ghosts, and the nameless terrors of broad daylight that were only coats on pegs after all.

Holidays came and holidays went, and Black Sheep was taken to see many people whose faces were all exactly alike; was beaten when occasion demanded, and tortured by Harry on all possible occasions; but defended by Judy through good and evil report, though she hereby drew upon herself the wrath of Aunty Rosa.

The weeks were interminable and Papa and Mamma were clean forgotten. Harry had left school and was a clerk in a Banking-Office. Freed from his presence, Black Sheep resolved that he should no longer be deprived of his allowance of pleasure-reading. Consequently when he failed at school he reported that all was well, and conceived a large contempt for Aunty Rosa as he saw how easy it was to deceive her. 'She says I'm a little liar when I don't tell lies, and now I do, she doesn't know,' thought Black Sheep. Aunty Rosa had credited him in the past with petty cunning and stratagem that had never entered into his head. By the light of the sordid knowledge that she had revealed to him he paid her back full tale. In a household where the most innocent of his motives, his natural yearning for a little affection, had been interpreted into a desire for more bread and jam, or to ingratiate himself with strangers and so put Harry into the background, his work was easy. Aunty Rosa could penetrate certain kinds of hypocrisy, but not all. He set his child's wits against hers and was no more beaten. It grew monthly more and more of a trouble to read the school-books, and even the pages of the open-print story-books danced and were dim. So Black Sheep brooded in the shadows that fell about him and cut him off from the world, inventing horrible punishments for 'dear Harry,' or plotting another line of the tangled web of deception that he wrapped round Aunty Rosa.

Then the crash came and the cobwebs were broken. It was impossible to foresee everything. Aunty Rosa made personal inquiries as to Black Sheep's progress and received information that startled her. Step by step, with a delight as keen as when she convicted an underfed housemaid of the theft of cold meats, she followed the trail of Black Sheep's delinquencies. For weeks and weeks, in order to escape banishment from the book-shelves, he had made a fool of Aunty Rosa, of Harry, of God, of all the world! Horrible, most horrible, and evidence of an utterly depraved mind.

Black Sheep counted the cost. 'It will only be one big beating and then she'll put a card with "Liar" on my back, same as she did before. Harry will whack me and pray for me, and she will pray for me at prayers and tell me I'm a Child of the Devil and give me hymns to learn. But I've done all my reading and she never knew. She'll say she knew all along. She's an old liar too,' said he.

For three days Black Sheep was shut in his own bed-room—to prepare his heart. 'That means two beatings. One at school and one here. *That* one will hurt most.' And it fell even as he thought. He was thrashed at school before the Jews and the *hubshi* for the heinous crime of carrying home false reports of progress. He was thrashed at home by Aunty Rosa on the same count, and then the placard was produced. Aunty Rosa stitched it between his shoulders and bade him go for a walk with it upon him.

'If you make me do that,' said Black Sheep very quietly, 'I shall burn this house down, and perhaps I'll kill you. I don't know whether I *can* kill you—you're so bony—but I'll try.'

No punishment followed this blasphemy, though Black Sheep held himself ready to work his way to Aunty Rosa's withered throat, and grip there till he was beaten off. Perhaps Aunty Rosa was afraid, for Black Sheep, having reached the Nadir of Sin, bore himself with a new reck-lessness.

In the midst of all the trouble there came a visitor from over the seas to Downe Lodge, who knew Papa and Mamma, and was commissioned to see Punch and Judy. Black Sheep was sent to the drawing-room and charged into a solid tea-table laden with china.

'Gently, gently, little man,' said the visitor, turning Black Sheep's face to the light slowly. 'What's that big bird on the palings?'

'What bird?' asked Black Sheep.

The visitor looked deep down into Black Sheep's eyes for half a minute, and then said suddenly: 'Good God, the little chap's nearly blind!'

It was a most businesslike visitor. He gave orders, on his own responsibility, that Black Sheep was not to go to school or open a book until Mamma came home. 'She'll be here in three weeks, as you know, of course,' said he, 'and I'm Inverarity Sahib. I ushered you into this wicked world, young man, and a nice use you seem to have made of your time. You must do nothing whatever. Can you do that?'

'Yes,' said Punch in a dazed way. He had known that Mamma was coming. There was a chance, then, of an-other beating. Thank Heaven, Papa wasn't coming too. Aunty Rosa had said of late that he ought to be beaten by a man.

For the next three weeks Black Sheep was strictly al-lowed to do nothing. He spent his time in the old nursery looking at the broken toys, for all of which account must be rendered to Mamma. Aunty Rosa hit him over the hands if even a wooden boat were broken. But that sin was of small importance compared to the other revelations, so darkly hinted at by Aunty Rosa. 'When your Mother comes, and hears what I have to tell her, she may appre-ciate you properly,' she said grimly, and mounted guard over Judy lest that small maiden should attempt to com-fort her brother, to the peril of her soul.

And Mamma came—in a four-wheeler—fluttered with tender excitement. Such a Mamma! She was young, frivolously young, and beautiful, with delicately flushed cheeks, eyes that shone like stars, and a voice that needed no appeal of outstretched arms to draw little ones to her heart. Judy ran straight to her, but Black Sheep hesitated. Could this wonder be 'showing off'? She would not put out her arms when she knew of his crimes. Meantime was it possible that by fondling she wanted to get anything out of Black Sheep? Only all his love and all his confidence; but that Black Sheep did not know. Aunty Rosa withdrew and left Mamma, kneeling between her children, half laughing, half crying, in the very hall where Punch and Judy had wept five years before.

'Well, chicks, do you remember me?'

'No,' said Judy frankly, 'but I said, "God bless Papa and Mamma" ev'vy night.'

'A little,' said Black Sheep. 'Remember I wrote to you every week, anyhow. That isn't to show off, but 'cause of what comes afterwards.'

'What comes after? What should come after, my darling boy?' And she drew him to her again. He came awkwardly, with many angles. 'Not used to petting,' said the quick Mothersoul. 'The girl is.'

'She's too little to hurt any one,' thought Black Sheep, 'and if I said I'd kill her, she'd be afraid. I wonder what Aunty Rosa will tell.'

There was a constrained late dinner, at the end of which Mamma picked up Judy and put her to bed with endearments manifold. Faithless little Judy had shown her defection from Aunty Rosa already. And that lady resented it bitterly. Black Sheep rose to leave the room.

'Come and say good-night,' said Aunty Rosa, offering a withered cheek.

'Huh!' said Black Sheep. 'I never kiss you, and I'm not going to show off. Tell that woman what I've done, and see what she says.'

Black Sheep climbed into bed feeling that he had lost

Heaven after a glimpse through the gates. In half an hour 'that woman' was bending over him. Black Sheep flung up his right arm. It wasn't fair to come and hit him in the dark. Even Aunty Rosa never tried that. But no blow followed.

'Are you showing off? I won't tell you anything more than Aunty Rosa has, and *she* doesn't know everything,' said Black Sheep as clearly as he could for the arms round his neck.

'Oh, my son—my little, little son! It was my fault—*my* fault, darling—and yet how could we help it? Forgive me, Punch.' The voice died out in a broken whisper, and two hot tears fell on Black Sheep's forehead.

'Has she been making you cry too?' he asked. 'You should see Jane cry. But you're nice, and Jane is a Born Liar—Aunty Rosa says so.'

'Hush, Punch, hush! My boy, don't talk like that. Try to love me a little bit—a little bit. You don't know how I want it. Punch-*baba,* come back to me! I am your Mother— your own Mother—and never mind the rest. I know—yes, I know, dear. It doesn't matter now. Punch, won't you care for me a little?'

It is astonishing how much petting a big boy of ten can endure when he is quite sure that there is no one to laugh at him. Black Sheep had never been made much of before, and here was this beautiful woman treating him— Black Sheep, the Child of the Devil and the inheritor of undying flame—as though he were a small God.

'I care for you a great deal, Mother dear,' he whispered at last, 'and I'm glad you've come back; but are you sure Aunty Rosa told you everything?'

'Everything. What *does* it matter? But——' the voice broke with a sob that was also laughter—'Punch, my poor, dear, half-blind darling, don't you think it was a little foolish of you?'

'*No.* It saved a lickin'.'

Mamma shuddered and slipped away in the darkness to write a long letter to Papa. Here is an extract:—

'. . . Judy is a dear, plump little prig who adores the woman, and wears with as much gravity as her religious opinions—only eight, Jack!—a venerable horse-hair atrocity which she calls her Bustle! I have just burnt it, and the child is asleep in my bed as I write. She will come to me at once. Punch I cannot quite understand. He is well nourished, but seems to have been worried into a system of small deceptions which the woman magnifies into deadly sins. Don't you recollect our own upbringing, dear, when the Fear of the Lord was so often the beginning of falsehood? I shall win Punch to me before long. I am taking the children away into the country to get them to know me, and, on the whole, I am content, or shall be when you come home, dear boy, and then, thank God, we shall be all under one roof again at last!'

Three months later, Punch, no longer Black Sheep, has discovered that he is the veritable owner of a real, live, lovely Mamma, who is also a sister, comforter, and friend, and that he must protect her till the Father comes home. Deception does not suit the part of a protector, and, when one can do anything without question, where is the use of deception?

'Mother would be awfully cross if you walked through that ditch,' says Judy, continuing a conversation.

'Mother's never angry,' says Punch. 'She'd just say, "You're a little *pagal* [idiot]"; and that's not nice, but I'll show.'

Punch walks through the ditch and mires himself to the knees. 'Mother dear,' he shouts, 'I'm just as dirty as I can pos-*sib*-ly be!'

'Then change your clothes as quickly as you pos-*sib*-ly can!' Mother's clear voice rings out from the house. 'And don't be a little *pagal!*'

'There! Told you so,' says Punch. 'It's all different now, and we are just as much Mother's as if she had never gone.'

Not altogether, O Punch, for when young lips have drunk deep of the bitter waters of Hate, Suspicion, and Despair, all the Love in the world will not wholly take away that knowledge; though it may turn darkened eyes for a while to the light, and teach Faith where no Faith was.

AN HABITATION ENFORCED

My friend, if cause doth wrest thee,
Ere folly hath much oppressed thee,
Far from acquaintance kest thee
Where country may digest thee . . .
Thank God that so hath blessed thee,
And sit down, Robin, and rest thee.

THOMAS TUSSER.

It came without warning, at the very hour his hand was
outstretched to crumple the Holtz and Gunsberg Combine.
The New York doctors called it overwork, and he lay in a
darkened room, one ankle crossed above the other, tongue
pressed into palate, wondering whether the next brain-
surge of prickly fires would drive his soul from all anchor-
ages. At last they gave judgment. With care he might in
two years return to the arena, but for the present he must
go across the water and do no work whatever. He accepted the terms. It was capitulation; but the Combine
that had shivered beneath his knife gave him all the honours of war. Gunsberg himself, full of condolences, came
to the steamer and filled the Chapins' suite of cabins with
overwhelming flower-works.

'Smilax,' said George Chapin when he saw them. 'Fitz
is right. I'm dead; only I don't see why he left out the
"In Memoriam" on the ribbons!'

'Nonsense!' his wife answered, and poured him his tinc-
ture. 'You'll be back before you can think.'

He looked at himself in the mirror, surprised that his
face had not been branded by the hells of the past three
months. The noise of the decks worried him, and he lay

down, his tongue only a little pressed against his palate.

An hour later he said: 'Sophie, I feel sorry about taking you away from everything like this. I—I suppose we're the two loneliest people on God's earth to-night.'

Said Sophie his wife, and kissed him: 'Isn't it something to you that we're going together?'

They drifted about Europe for months—sometimes alone, sometimes with chance-met gipsies of their own land. From the North Cape to the Blue Grotto at Capri they wandered, because the next steamer headed that way, or because some one had set them on the road. The doctors had warned Sophie that Chapin was not to take interest even in other men's interests; but a familiar sensation at the back of the neck after one hour's keen talk with a Nauheimed railway magnate saved her any trouble. He nearly wept.

'And I'm over thirty,' he cried. 'With all I meant to do!'

'Let's call it a honeymoon,' said Sophie. 'D'you know, in all the six years we've been married, you've never told me what you meant to do with your life?'

'With my life? What's the use? It's finished now.' Sophie looked up quickly from the Bay of Naples. 'As far as my business goes, I shall have to live on my rents like that architect at San Moritz.'

'You'll get better if you don't worry; and even if it takes time, there are worse things than—— How much have you?'

'Between four and five million. But it isn't the money. You know it isn't. It's the principle. How could you respect me? You never did, the first year after we married, till I went to work like the others. Our tradition and upbringing are against it. We can't accept *those* ideals.'

'Well, I suppose I married you for some sort of ideal,' she answered, and they returned to their forty-third hotel.

In England they missed the alien tongues of Continental streets that reminded them of their own polyglot cities. In England all men spoke one tongue, speciously like American to the ear, but on cross-examination unintelligible.

'Ah, but you have not seen England,' said a lady with iron-grey hair. They had met her in Vienna, Bayreuth, and Florence, and were grateful to find her again at Claridge's, for she commanded situations, and knew where prescriptions are most carefully made up. 'You ought to take an interest in the home of our ancestors—as I do.'

'I've tried for a week, Mrs. Shonts,' said Sophie, 'but I never get any further than tipping German waiters.'

'These are not the true type,' Mrs. Shonts went on. 'I know where you should go.'

Chapin pricked up his ears, anxious to run anywhere from the streets on which quick men something of his kidney did the business denied to him.

'We hear and we obey, Mrs. Shonts,' said Sophie, feeling his unrest as he drank the loathed British tea.

Mrs. Shonts smiled, and took them in hand. She wrote widely and telegraphed far on their behalf, till, armed with her letter of introduction, she drove them into that wilderness which is reached from an ash-barrel of a station called Charing Cross. They were to go to Rocketts—the farm of one Cloke, in the southern counties—where, she assured them, they would meet the genuine England of folklore and song.

Rocketts they found after some hours, four miles from a station, and, so far as they could judge in the bumpy darkness, twice as many from a road. Trees, kine, and the outlines of barns showed shadowy about them when they alighted, and Mr. and Mrs. Cloke, at the open door of a deep stone-floored kitchen, made them slowly welcome. They lay in an attic beneath a wavy, whitewashed ceiling, and because it rained, a wood fire was made in an iron basket on a brick hearth, and they fell asleep to the chirping of mice and the whimper of flames.

When they woke it was a fair day, full of the noises of birds, the smell of box, lavender, and fried bacon, mixed with an elemental smell they had never met before.

'This,' said Sophie, nearly pushing out the thin case-
ment in an attempt to see round the corner, 'is—what did
the hack——cabman say to the railway porter about my
trunk—"quite on the top"?'

'No; "a little bit of all right." I feel further away from
anywhere than I've ever felt in my life. We must find out
where the telegraph office is.'

'Who cares?' said Sophie, wandering about, hair-brush
in hand, to admire the illustrated weekly pictures pasted
on door and cupboard.

But there was no rest for the alien soul till he had made
sure of the telegraph office. He asked the Clokes' daughter,
laying breakfast, while Sophie plunged her face in the
lavender bush outside the low window.

'Go to the stile a-top o' the Barn field,' said Mary, 'and
look across Pardons to the next spire. It's directly under.
You can't miss it—not if you keep to the footpath. My
sister's the telegraphist there. But you're in the three-mile
radius, sir. The boy delivers telegrams directly to this door
from Pardons village.'

'One has to take a good deal on trust in this country,'
he murmured.

Sophie looked at the close turf, scarred only with last
night's wheels; at two ruts which wound round a rickyard;
and at the circle of still orchard about the half-timbered
house.

'What's the matter with it?' she said. 'Telegrams delivered to the Vale of Avalon, of course,' and she beck-
oned in an earnest-eyed hound of engaging manners and
no engagements, who answered, at times, to the name of
Rambler. He led them, after breakfast, to the rise behind
the house where the stile stood against the skyline, and, 'I
wonder what we shall find now,' said Sophie, frankly pranc-
ing with joy on the grass.

It was a slope of gap-hedged fields possessed to their
centres by clumps of brambles. Gates were not, and the
rabbit-mined, cattle-rubbed posts leaned out and in. A narrow path doubled among the bushes, scores of white tails

twinkled before the racing hound, and a hawk rose, whistling shrilly.

'No roads. No nothing!' said Sophie, her short skirt hooked by briers. 'I thought all England was a garden. There's your spire, George, across the valley. How curious!'

They walked toward it through an all-abandoned land. Here they found the ghost of a patch of lucerne that had refused to die; there a harsh fallow surrendered to yard-high thistles; and here a breadth of rampant kelk feigning to be lawful crop. In the ungrazed pastures swathes of dead stuff caught their feet, and the ground beneath glistened with sweat. At the bottom of the valley a little brook had undermined its footbridge, and frothed in the wreckage. But there stood great woods on the slopes beyond— old, tall, and brilliant, like unfaded tapestries against the walls of a ruined house.

'All this within a hundred miles of London,' he said. 'Looks as if it had had nervous prostration, too.' The footpath turned the shoulder of a slope, through a thicket of rank rhododendrons, and crossed what had once been a carriage-drive, which ended in the shadow of two gigantic holm-oaks.

'A house!' said Sophie, in a whisper. 'A colonial house!'

Behind the blue-green of the twin trees rose a dark-bluish brick Georgian pile, with a shell-shaped fan-light over its pillared door. The hound had gone off on his own foolish quests. Except for some stir in the branches and the flight of four startled magpies, there was neither life nor sound about the square house, but it looked out of its long windows most friendlily.

'Cha-armed to meet you, I'm sure,' said Sophie, and curtsied to the ground. 'George, this is history I can understand. *We* began here.' She curtsied again.

The June sunshine twinkled on all the lights. It was as though an old lady, wise in three generations' experience, but for the present sitting out, bent to listen to her flushed and eager grandchild.

'I *must* look!' Sophie tiptoed to a window, and shaded her eyes with her hand. 'Oh, this room's half-full of cotton-bales—wool, I suppose! But I can see a bit of the mantelpiece. George, do come! Isn't that some one?'

She fell back behind her husband. The front door opened slowly, to show the hound, his nose white with milk, in charge of an ancient of days clad in a blue linen ephod curiously gathered on breast and shoulders.

'Certainly,' said George, half aloud. 'Father Time himself. This is where he lives, Sophie.'

'We came—,' said Sophie weakly. 'Can we see the house? I'm afraid that's our dog.'

'No, 'tis Rambler,' said the old man. 'He've been at my swill-pail again. Staying at Rocketts, be ye? Come in. Ah! you runagate!'

The hound broke from him, and he tottered after him down the drive. They entered the hall—just such a high light hall as such a house should own. A slim-balustered staircase, wide and shallow and once creamy-white, climbed out of it under a long oval window. On either side delicately-moulded doors gave on to wool-lumbered rooms, whose sea-green mantelpieces were adorned with nymphs, scrolls, and Cupids in low relief.

'What's the firm that makes these things?' cried Sophie, enraptured. 'Oh, I forgot! These must be the originals. Adams, is it? I never dreamed of anything like that steel-cut fender. Does he mean us to go everywhere?'

'He's catching the dog,' said George, looking out. 'We don't count.'

They explored the first or ground floor, delighted as children playing burglars.

'This is like all England,' she said at last. 'Wonderful, but no explanation. You're expected to know it beforehand. Now let's try upstairs.'

The stairs never creaked beneath their feet. From the broad landing they entered a long, green-panelled room lighted by three full-length windows, which overlooked the forlorn wreck of a terraced garden, and wooded slopes beyond.

'The drawing-room, of course.' Sophie swam up and down it. 'That mantelpiece—Orpheus and Eurydice—is the best of them all. Isn't it marvellous? Why, the room seems furnished with nothing it it! How's that, George?'

'It's the proportions. I've noticed it.'

'I saw a Hepplewhite couch once'—Sophie laid her finger to her flushed cheek and considered. 'With two of them— one on each side—you wouldn't need anything else. Except —there must be one perfect mirror over that mantelpiece.'

'Look at that view. It's a framed Constable,' her husband cried.

'No; it's a Morland—a parody of a Morland. But about that couch, George. Don't you think Empire might be better than Hepplewhite? Dull gold against that pale green? It's a pity they don't make spinets nowadays.'

'I believe you can get them. Look at that oak wood behind the pines.'

' "While you sat and played toccatas stately at the clavichord," ' Sophie hummed, and, head on one side, nodded to where the perfect mirror should hang.

Then they found bedrooms with dressing-rooms and powdering-closets, and steps leading up and down—boxes of rooms, round, square, and octagonal, with enriched ceilings and chased door-locks.

'Now about servants. Oh!' She had darted up the last stairs to the chequered darkness of the top floor, where loose tiles lay among broken laths, and the walls were scrawled with names, sentiments, and hop-records. 'They've been keeping pigeons here,' she cried.

'And you could drive a buggy through the roof anywhere,' said George.

'That's what *I* say,' the old man cried below them on the stairs. 'Not a dry place for my pigeons at all.'

'But why was it allowed to get like this?' said Sophie.

' 'Tis with housen as teeth,' he replied. 'Let 'em go too far, and there's nothing *to* be done. Time was they was minded to sell her, but none would buy. She was too far-away-along from any place. Time was they'd ha' lived here theyselves, but they took and died.'

'Here?' Sophie moved beneath the light of a hole in the roof.

'Nah—none dies here excep' falling off ricks and such. In London they died.' He plucked a lock of wool from his blue smock. 'They was no staple—neither the Elphicks nor the Moones. Shart and brittle all of 'em. Dead they be seventeen year, for I've been here caretakin' twenty-five.'

'Who does all the wool belong to downstairs?' George asked.

'To the estate. I'll show you the back parts if ye like. You're from America, ain't ye? I've had a son there once myself.' They followed him down the main stairway. He paused at the turn and swept one hand towards the wall. 'Plenty room here for your coffin to come down. Seven foot and three men at each end wouldn't brish the paint. If I die in my bed they'll 'ave to up-end me like a milk-can. 'Tis all luck, d'ye see?'

He led them on and on, through a maze of back-kitchens, dairies, larders, and sculleries, that melted along covered ways into a farm-house, visibly older than the main building which, again, rambled out among barns, byres, pig-pens, stalls and stables to the dead fields behind.

'Somehow,' said Sophie, sitting exhausted on an ancient well-curb—'somehow one wouldn't insult these lovely old things by filling them with hay.'

George looked at long stone walls upholding reaches of silvery oak weather-boarding; buttresses of mixed flint and bricks; outside stairs, stone upon arched stone; curves of thatch where grass sprouted; roundels of house-leeked tiles, and a huge paved yard populated by two cows and the repentant Rambler. He had not thought of himself or of the telegraph office for two and a half hours.

'But why,' said Sophie, as they went back through the crater of stricken fields,—'why is one expected to know everything in England? Why do they never tell?'

'You mean about the Elphicks and the Moones?' he answered.

'Yes—and the lawyers and the estate. Who are they? I wonder whether those painted floors in the green room were real oak. Don't you like us exploring things together —better than Pompeii?'

George turned once more to look at the view. 'Eight hundred acres go with the house—the old man told me. Five farms altogether. Rocketts is one of 'em.'

'I like Mrs. Cloke. But what is the old house called?'

George laughed. 'That's one of the things you're expected to know. He never told me.'

The Clokes were more communicative. That evening and thereafter for a week they gave the Chapins the official history, as one gives it to lodgers, of Friars Pardon the house and its five farms. But Sophie asked so many questions, and George was so humanly interested, that, as confidence in the strangers grew, they launched, with observed and acquired detail, into the lives and deaths and doings of the Elphicks and the Moones and their collaterals, the Haylings and the Torrells. It was a tale told serially by Cloke in the barn, or his wife in the dairy, the last chapters reserved for the kitchen o' nights by the big fire, when the two had been half the day exploring about the house, where old Iggulden, of the blue smock, cackled and chuckled to see them. The motives that swayed the characters were beyond their comprehension; the fates that shifted them were gods they had never met; the sidelights Mrs. Cloke threw on act and incident were more amazing than anything in the record. Therefore the Chapins listened delightedly, and blessed Mrs. Shonts.

'But why—why—why—did So-and-so do so-and-so?' Sophie would demand from her seat by the pothook; and Mrs. Cloke would answer, smoothing her knees, 'For the sake of the place.'

'I give it up,' said George one night in their own room. 'People don't seem to matter in this country compared to the places they live in. The way *she* tells it, Friars Pardon was a sort of Moloch.'

'Poor old thing!' They had been walking round the farms as usual before tea. 'No wonder they loved it. Think of the sacrifices they made for it. Jane Elphick married the younger Torrell to keep it in the family. The octagonal room with the moulded ceiling next to the big bedroom was hers. Now what did *he* tell you while he was feeding the pigs?' said Sophie.

'About the Torrell cousins and the uncle who died in Java. They lived at Burnt House—behind High Pardons, where that brook is all blocked up.'

'No; Burnt House is under High Pardons Wood, *before* you come to Gale Anstey,' Sophie corrected.

'Well, old man Cloke said——'

Sophie threw open the door and called down into the kitchen, where the Clokes were covering the fire: 'Mrs. Cloke, isn't Burnt House under High Pardons?'

'Yes, my dear, of course,' the soft voice answered absently. A cough. 'I beg your pardon, madam. What was it you said?'

'Never mind. I prefer it the other way,' Sophie laughed, and George retold the missing chapter as she sat on the bed.

'Here to-day an' gone to-morrow,' said Cloke warningly. 'They've paid their first month, but we've only that Mrs. Shonts' letter for guarantee.'

'None she sent never cheated us yet. It slipped out before I thought. She's a most humane young lady. They'll be going away in a little. An' *you*'ve talked a lot too, Alfred.'

'Yes, but the Elphicks are all dead. No one can bring my loose talking home to me. But why do they stay on and stay on so?'

In due time George and Sophie asked each other that question, and put it aside. They argued that the climate— a pearly blend, unlike the hot and cold ferocities of their native land—suited them, as the thick stillness of the nights

certainly suited George. He was saved even the sight of a
metalled road, which, as presumably leading to business,
wakes desire in a man; and the telegraph office at the village of Friars Pardon, where they sold picture post-cards
and peg-tops, was two walking miles across the fields and
woods. For all that touched his past among his fellows, or
their remembrance of him, he might have been in another
planet; and Sophie, whose life had been very largely spent
among husbandless wives of lofty ideals, had no wish to
leave this present of God. The unhurried meals, the fore-
knowledge of deliciously empty hours to follow, the
breadths of soft sky under which they walked together and
reckoned time only by their hunger or thirst; the good grass
beneath their feet that cheated the miles; their discoveries,
always together, amid the farms—Griffons, Rocketts, Burnt
House, Gale Anstey, and the Home Farm, where Iggulden
of the blue smock-frock would waylay them, and they
would ransack the old house once more; the long wet afternoons when they tucked up their feet on the bedroom's
deep window-sill over against the apple-trees, and talked
together as never till then had they found time to talk—
these things contented her soul, and her body throve.

'Have you realised,' she asked one morning, 'that we've
been here absolutely alone for the last thirty-four days?'

'Have you counted them?' he asked.

'Did you like them?' she replied.

'I must have. I didn't think about them. Yes, I have. Six
months ago I should have fretted myself sick. Remember
at Cairo? I've only had two or three bad times. Am I getting better, or is it senile decay?'

'Climate, all climate.' Sophie swung her new-bought English boots, as she sat on the stile overlooking Friars Pardon,
behind the Clokes' barn.

'One must take hold of things, though,' he said, 'if it's
only to keep one's hand in.' His eyes did not flicker now as
they swept the empty fields. 'Mustn't one?'

'Lay out a Morristown links over Gale Anstey? I dare
say you could hire it.'

'No, I'm not as English as that—nor as Morristown. Cloke says all the farms here could be made to pay.'

'Well, I'm Anastasia in the *Treasure of Franchard*. I'm content to be alive and purr. There's no hurry.'

'No.' He smiled. 'All the same, I'm going to see after my mail.'

'You promised you wouldn't have any.'

'There's some business coming through that's amusing me. Honest. It doesn't get on my nerves at all.'

'Want a secretary?'

'No, thanks, old thing! Isn't that quite English?'

'Too English! Go away.' But none the less in broad daylight she returned the kiss. 'I'm off to Pardons. I haven't been to the house for nearly a week.'

'How've you decided to furnish Jane Elphick's bedroom?' he laughed, for it had come to be a permanent Castle in Spain between them.

'Black Chinese furniture and yellow silk brocade,' she answered, and ran downhill. She scattered a few cows at a gap with a flourish of a ground-ash that Iggulden had cut for her a week ago, and singing as she passed under the holm-oaks, sought the farm-house at the back of Friars Pardon. The old man was not to be found, and she knocked at his half-opened door, for she needed him to fill her idle forenoon. A blue-eyed sheepdog, a new friend, and Rambler's old enemy, crawled out and besought her to enter.

Iggulden sat in his chair by the fire, a thistlespud between his knees, his head drooped. Though she had never seen death before, her heart, that missed a beat, told her that he was dead. She did not speak or cry, but stood outside the door, and the dog licked her hand. When he threw up his nose, she heard herself saying: 'Don't howl! Please don't begin to howl, Scottie, or I shall run away!'

She held her ground while the shadows in the rickyard moved toward noon; sat after a while on the steps by the door, her arms round the dog's neck, waiting till some one should come. She watched the smokeless chimneys of

Friars Pardon slash its roofs with shadow, and the smoke of Iggulden's last lighted fire gradually thin and cease. Against her will she fell to wondering how many Moones, Elphicks, and Torrells had been swung round the turn of the broad hall stairs. Then she remembered the old man's talk of being 'up-ended like a milk-can,' and buried her face on Scottie's neck. At last a horse's feet clinked upon flags, rustled in the old grey straw of the rickyard, and she found herself facing the Vicar—a figure she had seen at church declaiming impossibilities (Sophie was a Unitarian) in an unnatural voice.

'He's dead,' she said, without preface.

'Old Iggulden? I was coming for a talk with him.' The Vicar passed in uncovered. 'Ah!' she heard him say. 'Heart-failure! How long have you been here?'

'Since a quarter to eleven.' She looked at her watch earnestly and saw that her hand did not shake.

'I'll sit with him now till the doctor comes. D'you think you could tell him, and—yes, Mrs. Betts in the cottage with the wistaria next the blacksmith's? I'm afraid this has been rather a shock to you.'

Sophie nodded, and fled toward the village. Her body failed her for a moment; she dropped beneath a hedge, and looked back at the great house. In some fashion its silence and stolidity steadied her for her errand.

Mrs. Betts, small, black-eyed and dark, was almost as unconcerned as Friars Pardon.

'Yiss, yiss, of course. Dear me! Well, Iggulden he had had his day in my father's time. Muriel, get me my little blue bag, please. Yiss, ma'am. They come down like ellum-branches in still weather. No warnin' *at* all. Muriel, my bicycle's be'ind the fowl-house. I'll tell Dr. Dallas, ma'am.'

She trundled off on her wheel like a brown bee, while Sophie—heaven above and earth beneath changed—walked stiffly home, to fall over George at his letters, in a muddle of laughter and tears.

'It's all quite natural for *them*,' she gasped. ' "They come down like ellum-branches in still weather. Yiss, ma'am."

No, there wasn't anything in the least horrible, only—only—
Oh, George, that poor shiny stick of his between his poor,
thin knees! I couldn't have borne it if Scottie had howled.
I didn't know the Vicar was so—so sensitive. He said he
was afraid it was ra-rather a shock. Mrs. Betts told me to
go home, and I wanted to collapse on her floor. But I didn't
disgrace myself. I—I couldn't have left him—could I?'

'You're sure you've took no 'arm?' cried Mrs. Cloke,
who had heard the news by farm-telegraphy, which is older
but swifter than Marconi's.

'No. I'm perfectly well,' Sophie protested.

'You lay down till tea-time.' Mrs. Cloke patted her shoulder. '*They*'ll be very pleased, though she 'as 'ad no proper
understandin' for twenty years.'

'They' came before twilight—a blackbearded man in
moleskins, and a little palsied old woman, who chirruped
like a wren.

'I'm his son,' said the man to Sophie, among the lavender
bushes. 'We 'ad a difference—twenty year back—and didn't
speak since. But I'm his son all the same, and we thank you
for the watching.'

'I'm only glad I happened to be there,' she answered, and
from the bottom of her heart she meant it.

'We heard he spoke a lot o' you—one time an' another
since you came. We thank you kindly,' the man added.

'Are you the son that was in America?' she asked.

'Yes, ma'am. On my uncle's farm, in Connecticut. He
was what they call road-master there.'

'Whereabouts in Connecticut?' asked George over her
shoulder.

'Veering Holler was the name. I was there six year with
my uncle.'

'How small the world is!' Sophie cried. 'Why, all my
mother's people come from Veering Hollow. There must
be some there still—the Lashmars. Did you ever hear of
them?'

'I remember hearing that name, seems to me,' he answered, but his face was blank as the back of a spade.

A little before dusk a woman in grey, striding like a foot-soldier, and bearing on her arm a long pole, crashed through the orchard calling for food. George, upon whom the unannounced English worked mysteriously, fled to the parlour; but Mrs. Cloke came forward beaming. Sophie could not escape.

'We've only just heard of it,' said the stranger, turning on her. 'I've been out with the otter-hounds all day. It was a splendidly sportin' thing——'

'Did you—er—kill?' said Sophie. She knew from books she could not go far wrong here.

'Yes, a dry bitch—seventeen pounds,' was the answer. 'A splendidly sportin' thing of you to do. Poor old Iggulden——'

'Oh—that!' said Sophie, enlightened.

'If there had been any people at Pardons it would never have happened. He'd have been looked after. But what can you expect from a parcel of London solicitors?'

Mrs. Cloke murmured something.

'No. I'm soaked from the knees down. If I hang about I shall get chilled. A cup of tea, Mrs. Cloke, and I can eat one of your sandwiches as I go.' She wiped her weather-worn face with a green-and-yellow silk handkerchief.

'Yes, my lady!' Mrs. Cloke ran and returned swiftly.

'Our land marches with Pardons for a mile on the south,' she explained, waving the full cup, 'but one has quite enough to do with one's own people without poachin'. Still, if I'd known, I'd have sent Dora, of course. Have you seen her this afternoon, Mrs. Cloke? No? I wonder whether that girl *did* sprain her ankle. Thank you.' It was a for-midable hunk of bread and bacon that Mrs. Cloke pre-sented. 'As I was sayin', Pardons is a scandal! Lettin' peo-ple die like dogs. There ought to be people there who do their duty. You've done yours, though there wasn't the faintest call upon you. Good night. Tell Dora, if she comes, I've gone on.'

She strode away, munching her crust, and Sophie reeled breathless into the parlour, to shake the shaking George.

'Why did you keep catching my eye behind the blind? Why didn't you come out and do your duty?'

'Because I should have burst. Did you see the mud on its cheek?' he said.

'Once. I daren't look again. Who is she?'

'God. A local deity then. Anyway, she's another of the things you're expected to know by instinct.'

Mrs. Cloke, shocked at their levity, told them that it was Lady Conant, wife of Sir Walter Conant, Baronet, a large landholder in the neighbourhood, and if not God, at least His visible Providence.

George made her talk of that family for an hour.

'Laughter,' said Sophie afterward in their own room, 'is the mark of the savage. Why couldn't you control your emotions? It's all real to *her*.'

'It's all real to *me*. That's my trouble,' he answered in an altered tone. 'Anyway, it's real enough to mark time with. Don't you think so?'

'What d'you mean?' she asked quickly, though she knew his voice.

'That I'm better. I'm well enough to kick.'

'What at?'

'This!' He waved his hand round the one room. 'I must have something to play with till I'm fit for work again.'

'Ah!' She sat on the bed and leaned forward, her hands clasped. 'I wonder if it's good for you.'

'We've been better here than anywhere,' he went on slowly. 'One could always sell it again.'

She nodded gravely, but her eyes sparkled.

'The only thing that worries me is what happened this morning. I want to know how you feel about it. If it's on your nerves in the least we can have the old farm at the back of the house pulled down, or perhaps it has spoiled the notion for you?'

'Pull it down?' she cried. 'You've no business faculty. Why, that's where we could live while we're putting the big house in order. It's almost under the same roof. No! What happened this morning seemed to be more of a—of a leading than anything else. There *ought* to be people at Pardons. Lady Conant's quite right.'

'I was thinking more of the woods and the roads. I could double the value of the place in six months.'

'What do they want for it?' She shook her head, and her loosened hair fell glowingly about her cheeks.

'Seventy-five thousand dollars. They'll take sixty-eight.'

'Less than half what we paid for our old yacht when we married. And we didn't have a good time in her. You were——'

'Well, I discovered I was too much of an American to be content to be a rich man's son. You aren't blaming me for that?'

'Oh no. Only it was a very businesslike honeymoon. How far are you along with the deal, George?'

'I can mail the deposit on the purchase money tomorrow morning, and we can have the thing completed in a fortnight or three weeks—if you say so.'

'Friars Pardon—Friars Pardon!' Sophie chanted rapturously, her dark-grey eyes big with delight. 'All the farms? Gale Anstey, Burnt House, Rocketts, the Home Farm, and Griffons? Sure you've got 'em all?'

'Sure.' He smiled.

'And the woods? High Pardons Wood, Lower Pardons, Suttons, Dutton's Shaw, Reuben's Ghyll, Maxey's Ghyll, and both the Oak Hangers? Sure you've got 'em all?'

'Every last stick. Why, you know them as well as I do.' He laughed. 'They say there's five thousand—a thousand pounds' worth of lumber—timber they call it—in the Hangers alone.'

'Mrs. Cloke's oven must be mended first thing, *and* the kitchen roof. I think I'll have all this whitewashed,' Sophie broke in, pointing to the ceiling. 'The whole place is a scandal. Lady Conant is quite right. George, when did you begin to fall in love with the house? In the green room— that first day? I did.'

'I'm not in love with it. One must do something to mark time till one's fit for work.'

'Or when we stood under the oaks, and the door opened? Oh! Ought I to go to poor Iggulden's funeral?' She sighed with utter happiness.

'Wouldn't they call it a liberty—*now?*' said he.

'But I liked him.'

'But you didn't own him at the date of his death.'

'That wouldn't keep me away. Only, they made such a fuss about the watching'—she caught her breath—'it might be ostentatious from that point of view, too. Oh, George,' —she reached for his hand—'we're two little orphans moving in worlds not realised, and we shall make some bad breaks. But we're going to have the time of our lives.'

'We'll run up to London to-morrow and see if we can hurry those English law— solicitors. I want to get to work.'

They went. They suffered many things ere they returned across the fields in a fly one Saturday night, nursing a two by two-and-a-half box of deeds and maps—lawful owners of Friars Pardon and the five decayed farms therewith.

'I do most sincerely 'ope and trust you'll be 'appy, madam,' Mrs. Cloke gasped, when she was told the news by the kitchen fire.

'Goodness! It isn't a marriage!' Sophie exclaimed, a little awed; for to them the joke, which to an American means work, was only just beginning.

'If it's took in a proper spirit'—Mrs. Cloke's eye turned toward her oven.

'Send and have that mended to-morrow,' Sophie whispered.

'We couldn't 'elp noticing,' said Cloke slowly, 'from the times you walked there, that you an' your lady was drawn to it, but—but I don't know as we ever precisely thought——' His wife's glance checked him.

'That we were that sort of people,' said George. 'We aren't sure of it ourselves yet.'

'Perhaps,' said Cloke, rubbing his knees, just for the sake of saying something, 'perhaps you'll park it?'

'What's that?' said George.

'Turn it all into a fine park like Violet Hill'—he jerked a thumb to westward—'that Mr. Sangres bought. It was four farms, and Mr. Sangres made a fine park of them, with a herd of faller deer.'

'Then it wouldn't be Friars Pardon,' said Sophie. 'Would it?'

'I don't know as I've ever heard Pardons was ever anything but wheat an' wool. Only some gentlemen say that parks are less trouble than tenants.' He laughed nervously. 'But the gentry, o' course, they keep on pretty much as they was used to.'

'I see,' said Sophie. 'How did Mr. Sangres make his money?'

'I never rightly heard. It was pepper an' spices, or it may ha' been gloves. No. Gloves was Sir Reginald Liss at Marley End. Spices was Mr. Sangres. He's a Brazilian gentleman—very sunburnt, like.'

'Be sure o' one thing. You won't 'ave any trouble,' said Mrs. Cloke, just before they went to bed.

Now the news of the purchase was told to Mr. and Mrs. Cloke alone at 8 P.M. of a Saturday. None left the farm till they set out for church next morning. Yet when they reached the church and were about to slip aside into their usual seats, a little beyond the font, where they could see the red-furred tails of the bell-ropes waggle and twist at ringing-time, they were swept forward irresistibly, a Cloke on either flank (and yet they had not walked with the Clokes), upon the ever-retiring bosom of a black-gowned verger, who ushered them into a room of a pew at the head of the left aisle, under the pulpit.

'This,' he sighed reproachfully, 'is the Pardons' Pew,' and shut them in.

They could see little more than the choir-boys in the chancel, but to the roots of the hair of their necks they felt the congregation behind mercilessly devouring them by look.

'*When the wicked man turneth away.*' The strong alien voice of the priest vibrated under the hammer-beam roof, and a loneliness unfelt before swamped their hearts, as they searched for places in the unfamiliar Church of England service. The Lord's Prayer—'Our Father, *which* art'— set the seal on that desolation. Sophie found herself thinking how in other lands their purchase would long ere this have been discussed from every point of view in a dozen prints, forgetting that George for months had not been allowed to glance at those black and bellowing head-lines. Here was nothing but silence—not even hostility! The game was up to them. The other players hid their cards and waited. Suspense, she felt, was in the air, and when her sight cleared, she saw indeed a mural tablet of a footless bird brooding upon the carven motto, 'Wayte awhyle—wayte awhyle.'

At the Litany George had trouble with an unstable hassock, and drew the slip of carpet under the pew-seat. Sophie pushed her end back also, and shut her eyes against a burning that felt like tears. When she opened them she was looking at her mother's maiden name, fairly carved on a blue flagstone on the pew floor:—

Ellen Lashmar. ob. 1796. aetat. 27.

She nudged George and pointed. Sheltered, as they kneeled, they looked for more knowledge, but the rest of the slab was blank.

'Ever hear of her?' he whispered.

'Never knew any of us came from here.'

'Coincidence?'

'Perhaps. But it makes me feel better,' and she smiled and winked away a tear on her lashes, and took his hand while they prayed for 'all women labouring of child'—not 'in the perils of childbirth'; and the sparrows who had found their way through the guards behind the stained-glass windows chirped above the faded gilt-and-alabaster family tree of the Conants.

The baronet's pew was on the right of the aisle. After service its inhabitants moved forth without haste, but so as to effectively block a dusky person with a large family who champed in their rear.

'Spices, I think,' said Sophie, deeply delighted as the Sangres closed up after the Conants. 'Let 'em get away, George.'

But when they came out many folk whose eyes were one still lingered by the lych-gate.

'I want to see if any more Lashmars are buried here,' said Sophie.

'Not now. This seems to be show day. Come home quickly,' he replied.

A group of families, the Clokes a little apart, opened to let them through. The men saluted with jerky nods, the women with remnants of a curtsey. Only Iggulden's son, his mother on his arm, lifted his hat as Sophie passed.

'Your people?' said the clear voice of Lady Conant in her ear.

'I suppose so,' said Sophie, blushing, for they were within two yards of her; but it was not a question.

'Then that child looks as if it were coming down with mumps. You ought to tell the mother she shouldn't have brought it to church.'

'I can't leave 'er be'ind, my lady,' the woman said. 'She'd set the 'ouse afire in a minute, she's that forward with the matches. Ain't you, Maudie dear?'

'Has Dr. Dallas seen her?'

'Not yet, my lady.'

'He must. You can't get away, of course. M—m! My idiotic maid is coming in for her teeth to-morrow at twelve. She shall pick her up—at Gale Anstey, isn't it?—at eleven.'

'Yes. Thank you very much, my lady.'

'I oughtn't to have done it,' said Lady Conant apologetically, 'but there has been no one at Pardons for so long that you'll forgive my poachin'. Now, can't you lunch with us? The Vicar usually comes too. I don't use the horses on a Sunday,'—she glanced at the Brazilian's silver-plated chariot. 'It's only a mile across the fields.'

'You—you're very kind,' said Sophie, hating herself because her lip trembled.

'My dear'—the compelling tone dropped to a soothing gurgle—'d'you suppose I don't know how it feels to come to a strange county—country, I should say—away from one's own people? When I first left the Shires—I'm Shropshire, you know—I cried for a day and a night. But fretting doesn't make loneliness any better. Oh, here's Dora. She *did* sprain her leg that day.'

'I'm as lame as a tree still,' said the tall maiden frankly. 'You ought to go out with the otter-hounds, Mrs. Chapin. I believe they're drawing your water next week.'

Sir Walter had already led off George, and the Vicar came up on the other side of Sophie. There was no escaping the swift procession or the leisurely lunch, where talk came and went in low-voiced eddies that had the village for their centre. Sophie heard the Vicar and Sir Walter address her husband lightly as Chapin! (She also remembered many women known in a previous life who habitually addressed their husbands as Mr. Such-an-one.) After lunch Lady Conant talked to her explicitly of maternity as that is achieved in cottages and farm-houses remote from aid, and of the duty thereto of the mistress of Pardons.

A gate in a beech hedge, reached across triple lawns, let them out before tea-time into the unkempt south side of their land.

'I want your hand, please,' said Sophie as soon as they were safe among the beech-boles and the lawless hollies. 'D'you remember the old maid in *Providence and the Guitar* who heard the Commissary swear, and hardly reckoned herself a maiden lady afterwards? Because I'm a relative of hers. Lady Conant is——'

'Did you find out anything about the Lashmars?' he interrupted.

'I didn't ask. I'm going to write to Aunt Sydney about it first. Oh, Lady Conant said something at lunch about their having bought some land from some Lashmars a few years ago. I found it was at the beginning of last century.'

'What did you say?'

'I said, "Really, how interesting!" Like that. I'm not going to push myself forward. I've been hearing about Mr. Sangres' efforts in that direction. And you? I couldn't see you behind the flowers. Was it very deep water, dear?'

George mopped a brow already browned by outdoor exposure.

'Oh no—dead easy,' he answered. 'I've bought Friars Pardon to prevent Sir Walter's birds straying.'

A cock pheasant scuttered through the dry leaves and exploded almost under their feet. Sophie jumped.

'That's one of 'em,' said George calmly.

'Well, your nerves are better, at any rate,' said she. 'Did you tell 'em you'd bought the thing to play with?'

'No. That was where my nerve broke down. I only made one bad break—I think. I said I couldn't see why hiring land to men to farm wasn't as much a business proposition as anything else.'

'And what did they say?'

'They smiled. I shall know what that smile means some day. They don't waste their smiles. D'you see that track by Gale Anstey?'

They looked down from the edge of the hanger over a cup-like hollow. People by twos and threes in their Sunday best filed slowly along the paths that connected farm to farm.

'I've never seen so many on our land before,' said Sophie. 'Why is it?'

'To show us we mustn't shut up their rights of way.'

'Those cow-tracks we've been using crosslots?' said Sophie forcibly.

'Yes. Any one of 'em would cost us two thousand pounds each in legal expenses to close.'

'But we don't want to,' she said.

'The whole community would fight if we did.'

'But it's our land. We can do what we like.'

'It's *not* our land. We've only paid for it. We belong to it, and it belongs to the people—our people, they call 'em. *I*'ve been to lunch with the English too.'

They passed slowly from one bracken-dotted field to the next—flushed with pride of ownership, plotting alterations and restorations at each turn; halting in their tracks to argue, spreading apart to embrace two views at once, or closing in to consider one. Couples moved out of their way, but smiling covertly.

'We shall make some bad breaks,' he said at last.

'Together, though. You won't let any one else in, will you?'

'Except the contractors. This syndicate handles this proposition by its little lone.'

'But you might feel the want of some one,' she insisted.

'I shall—but it will be you. It's business, Sophie, but it's going to be good fun.'

'Please God,' she answered, flushing, and cried to herself as they went back to tea. 'It's worth it. Oh, it's worth it.'

The repairing and moving into Friars Pardon was business of the most varied and searching, but all done English-fashion, without friction. Time and money alone were asked. The rest lay in the hands of beneficent advisers from London, or spirits, male and female, called up by Mr. and Mrs. Cloke from the wastes of the farms. In the centre stood George and Sophie, a little aghast, their interests reaching out on every side.

'I ain't sayin' anything against Londoners,' said Cloke, self-appointed Clerk of the outer works, consulting engineer, head of the immigration bureau, and superintendent of Woods and Forests; 'but your own people won't go about to make more than a fair profit out of you.'

'How is one to know?' said George.

'Five years from now, or so on, maybe, you'll be lookin' over your first year's accounts, and, knowin' what you'll know then, you'll say: "Well, Billy Beartup"—or Old Cloke as it might be—"did me proper when I was new." No man likes to have that sort of thing laid up against him.'

'I think I see,' said George. 'But five years is a long time to look ahead.'

'I doubt if that oak Billy Beartup throwed in Reuben's Ghyll will be fit for her drawin'-room floor in less than seven,' Cloke drawled.

'Yes, that's *my* work,' said Sophie. (Billy Beartup of Griffons, a woodman by training and birth, a tenant farmer by misfortune of marriage, had laid his broad axe at her feet a month before.) 'Sorry if I've committed you to another eternity.'

'And we shan't even know where we've gone wrong with *your* new carriage-drive before that time either,' said Cloke, ever anxious to keep the balance true—with an ounce or two in Sophie's favour. The past four months had taught George better than to reply. The carriage-road winding up the hill was his present keen interest. They set off to look at it, and the imported American scraper, which had blighted the none too sunny soul of 'Skim' Winsh, the carter. But young Iggulden was in charge now, and under his guidance Buller and Roberts, the great horses, moved mountains.

'You lif' her like that, an' you tip her like that,' he explained to the gang. 'My uncle he was road-master in Connecticut.'

'Are they roads yonder?' said Skim, sitting under the laurels.

'No better than accommodation-roads. Dirt, they call 'em. They'd suit you, Skim.'

'Why?' said the incautious Skim.

' 'Cause you'd take no hurt when you fall out of your cart drunk on a Saturday,' was the answer.

'I didn't last time neither,' Skim roared.

After the loud laugh, old Whybarne of Gale Anstey piped feebly, 'Well, dirt or no dirt, there's no denyin' Chapin knows a good job when he sees it. 'E don't build one day and dee-stroy the next, like that nigger Sangres.'

'*She's* the one that knows her own mind,' said Pinky, brother to Skim Winsh, and a Napoleon among carters who had helped to bring the grand piano across the fields in the autumn rains.

'She had ought to,' said Iggulden. 'Whoa, Buller! She's a Lashmar. They never was double-thinking.'

'Oh, you found that? Has the answer come from your uncle?' said Skim, doubtful whether so remote a land as America had posts.

The others looked at him scornfully. Skim was always a day behind the fair.

Iggulden rested from his labours. 'She's a Lashmar right enough. I started up to write to my uncle at once—the month after she said her folks came from Beerin' Holler.'

'Where there ain't any roads?' Skim interrupted, but none laughed.

'My uncle he married an American woman for his second, and she took it up like a—like the coroner. She's a Lashmar out of the old Lashmar place, 'fore they sold to Conants. She ain't no Toot Hill Lashmar, nor any o' the Crayford lot. Her folk come out of the ground here, neither Chalk nor Forest, but Wildishers. They sailed over to America—I've got it all writ down by my uncle's woman—in eighteen hundred an' nothing. My uncle says they're all slow begetters, like.'

'Would they be gentry yonder now?' Skim asked.

'Nah—there's no gentry in America, no matter how long you're there. It's against their law. There's only rich and poor allowed. They've been lawyers and such-like over yonder for a hundred years—but she's a Lashmar for all that.'

'Lord! What's a hundred years?' said Whybarne, who had seen seventy-eight of them.

'An' they write too, from yonder—my uncle's woman writes—that you can still tell 'em by headmark. Their hair's foxy-red still—an' they throw out when they walk. *He's* in-toed—treads like a gipsy; but you watch, an' you'll see 'er throw out—like a colt.'

'Your trace wants taking up.' Pinky's large ears had caught the sound of voices, and as the two broke through the laurels the men were hard at work, their eyes on Sophie's feet.

She had been less fortunate in her inquiries than Iggulden, for her Aunt Sydney of Meriden (a badged and certificated Daughter of the Revolution to boot) answered her inquiries with a two-paged discourse on patriotism, the leaflets of a Village Improvement Society, of which she was president, and a demand for an overdue subscription to a Factory Girls' Reading Circle. Sophie burned it all in the Orpheus and Eurydice grate, and kept her own counsel.

'What *I* want to know,' said George, when spring was coming, and the gardens needed thought, 'is who will ever pay me for my labour? I've put in at least half a million dollars' worth already.'

'Sure you're not taking too much out of yourself?' his wife asked.

'Oh no; I haven't been conscious of myself all winter.' He looked at his brown English gaiters and smiled. 'It's all behind me now. I believe I could sit down and think of all that—those months before we sailed.'

'Don't—ah, don't!' she cried.

'But I must go back one day. You don't want to keep me out of business always—or do you?' He ended with a nervous laugh.

Sophie sighed as she drew her own ground-ash (of old Iggulden's cutting) from the hall rack.

'Aren't you overdoing it too? You look a little tired,' he said.

'You make me tired. I'm going to Rocketts to see Mrs. Cloke about Mary.' (This was the sister of the telegraphist, promoted to be sewing-maid at Pardons.) 'Coming?'

'I'm due at Burnt House to see about the new well. By the way, there's a sore throat at Gale Anstey——'

'That's *my* province. Don't interfere. The Whybarne children always have sore throats. They do it for jujubes.'

'Keep away from Gale Anstey till I make sure, honey. Cloke ought to have told me.'

'These people don't tell. Haven't you learnt that yet? But I'll obey, me lord. See you later!'

She set off afoot, for within the three main roads that bounded the blunt triangle of the estate (even by night one could scarcely hear the carts on them), wheels were not used except for farm work. The footpaths served all other purposes. And though at first they had planned improvements, they had soon fallen in with the customs of their hidden kingdom, and moved about the soft-footed ways by woodland, hedgerow, and shaw as freely as the rabbits. Indeed, for the most part Sophie walked bareheaded beneath her helmet of chestnut hair; but she had been plagued of late by vague toothaches, which she explained to Mrs. Cloke, who asked some questions. How it came about Sophie never knew, but after a while behold Mrs. Cloke's arm was about her waist, and her head was on that deep bosom behind the shut kitchen door.

'My dear! my dear!' the elder woman almost sobbed. 'An' d'you mean to tell me you never suspicioned? Why— why—where *was* you ever taught anything at all? Of *course* it is. It's what we've been only waitin' for, all of us. Time and again I've said to Lady——' She checked herself. 'An' now we shall be as we should be.'

'But—but—but——' Sophie whimpered.

'An' to see you buildin' your nest so busy—pianos and books—an' never thinkin' of a nursery!'

'No more I did.' Sophie sat bolt upright, and began to laugh.

'Time enough yet.' The fingers tapped thoughtfully on the broad knee. 'But—they must be strange-minded folk over yonder with you! Have you thought to send for your mother? She dead? My dear, my dear! Never mind! She'll be happy where she knows. 'Tis God's work. An' we was only waitin' for it, for you've never failed in your duty yet. It ain't your way. *What* did you say about my Mary's doings?' Mrs. Cloke's face hardened as she pressed her chin on Sophie's forehead. 'If any of your girls thinks to be'ave arbitrary now, I'll—— But they won't, my dear. I'll see they do their duty too. Be sure you'll 'ave no trouble.'

When Sophie walked back across the fields, heaven and earth changed about her as on the days of old Iggulden's death. For an instant she thought of the wide turn of the staircase, and the new ivory-white paint that no coffin-corner could scar, but presently the shadow passed in a pure wonder and bewilderment that made her reel. She leaned against one of their new gates and looked over their lands for some other stay.

'Well,' she said resignedly, half aloud, 'we must try to make him feel that he isn't a third in our party,' and turned the corner that looked over Friars Pardon, giddy, sick, and faint.

Of a sudden the house they had bought for a whim stood up as she had never seen it before, low-fronted, broad-winged, ample, prepared by course of generations for all such things. As it had steadied her when it lay desolate, so now that it had meaning from their few months of life within, it soothed and promised good. She went alone and quickly into the hall, and kissed either door-post, whispering: 'Be good to me. *You* know! You've never failed in your duty yet.'

When the matter was explained to George, he would have sailed at once to their own land, but this Sophie forbade.

'I don't want science,' she said. 'I just want to be loved, and there isn't time for that at home. Besides,' she added, looking out of the window, 'it would be desertion.'

George was forced to soothe himself with linking Friars Pardon to the telegraph system of Great Britain by telephone—three-quarters of a mile of poles, put in by Whybarne and a few friends. One of these was a foreigner from the next parish. Said he when the line was being run: 'There's an old ellum right in our road. Shall us throw her?'

'Toot Hill parish folk, neither grace nor good luck, God help 'em.' Old Whybarne shouted the local proverb from three poles down the line. '*We* ain't goin' to lay any axe-iron to coffin-wood here—not till we know where we are yet awhile. Swing round 'er, swing round!'

To this day, then, that sudden kink in the straight line across the upper pasture remains a mystery to Sophie and George. Nor can they tell why Skim Winsh, who came to his cottage under Dutton Shaw most musically drunk at 10.45 P.M. of every Saturday night, as his father had done before him, sang no more at the bottom of the garden steps, where Sophie always feared he would break his neck. The path was undoubtedly an ancient right of way, and at 10.45 P.M. on Saturdays Skim remembered it was his duty to posterity to keep it open—till Mrs. Cloke spoke to him—once. She spoke likewise to her daughter Mary, sewing-maid at Pardons, and to Mary's best new friend, the five-foot-seven imported London house-maid, who taught Mary to trim hats, and found the country dullish.

But there was no noise,—at no time was there any noise, —and when Sophie walked abroad she met no one in her path unless she had signified a wish that way. Then they appeared to protest that all was well with them and their children, their chickens, their roofs, their water-supply, and their sons in the Police or the railway service.

'But don't you find it dull, dear?' said George, loyally doing his best not to worry as the months went by.

'I've been so busy putting my house in order I haven't had time to think,' said she. 'Do you?'

'No—no. If I could only be sure of *you*.'

She turned on the green drawing-room's couch (it was Empire, not Hepplewhite after all), and laid aside a list of linen and blankets.

'It has changed everything, hasn't it?' she whispered.

'Oh Lord, yes. But I still think if we went back to Baltimore——'

'And missed our first real summer together. No, thank you, me lord.'

'But we're absolutely alone.'

'Isn't that what I'm doing my best to remedy? Don't you worry. I like it—like it to the marrow of my little bones. You don't realise what her house means to a woman. We thought we were living in it last year, but we hadn't begun to. Don't you rejoice in your study, George?'

'I prefer being here with you.' He sat down on the floor by the couch and took her hand.

'Seven,' she said as the French clock struck. 'Year before last you'd just be coming back from business.'

He winced at the recollection, then laughed. 'Business! I've been at work ten solid hours to-day.'

'Where did you lunch? With the Conants?'

'No; at Dutton Shaw, sitting on a log, with my feet in a swamp. But we've found out where the old spring is, and we're going to pipe it down to Gale Anstey next year.'

'I'll come and see to-morrow. Oh, please open the door, dear. I want to look down the passage. Isn't that corner by the stair-head lovely where the sun strikes in?' She looked through half-closed eyes at the vista of ivory-white and pale green all steeped in liquid gold.

'There's a step out of Jane Elphick's bedroom,' she went on—'and *his* first step in the world ought to be up. I shouldn't wonder if those people hadn't put it there on purpose. George, will it make any odds to you if he's a girl?'

He answered, as he had many time before, that his interest was his wife, not the child.

'Then you're the only person who thinks so.' She laughed. 'Don't be silly, dear. It's expected. *I* know. It's my duty. I shan't be able to look our people in the face if I fail.'

'What concern is it of theirs, confound 'em!'

'You'll see. Luckily the tradition of the house is boys, Mrs. Cloke says, so I'm provided for. Shall you ever begin to understand these people? I shan't.'

'And we bought it for fun—for fun?' he groaned. 'And here we are held up for goodness knows how long!'

'Why? Were you thinking of selling it?' He did not answer. 'Do you remember the second Mrs. Chapin?' she demanded.

This was a bold, brazen little black-browed woman—a widow for choice—who on Sophie's death was guilefully to marry George for his wealth and ruin him in a year. George being busy, Sophie had invented her some two years after her marriage, and conceived she was alone among wives in so doing.

'You aren't going to bring *her* up again?' he asked anxiously.

'I only want to say that I should hate any one who bought Pardons ten times worse than I used to hate the second Mrs. Chapin. Think what we've put into it of our two selves.'

'At least a couple of million dollars. I know I could have made——' He broke off.

'The beasts!' she went on. 'They'd be sure to build a red-brick lodge at the gates, and cut the lawn up for bedding out. You must leave instructions in your will that *he's* never to do that, George, won't you?'

He laughed and took her hand again but said nothing till it was time to dress. Then he muttered: 'What the devil use is a man's country to him when he can't do business in it?'

Friars Pardon stood faithful to its tradition. At the appointed time was born, not that third in their party to whom Sophie meant to be so kind, but a godling; in beauty, it was manifest, excelling Eros, as in wisdom Confucius; an enhancer of delights, a renewer of companionships and an interpreter of Destiny. This last George did not realise till he met Lady Conant striding through Dutton Shaw a few days after the event.

'My dear fellow,' she cried, and slapped him heartily on the back, 'I can't tell you how glad we all are.—Oh, *she*'ll be all right. (There's never been any trouble over the birth of an heir at Pardons.) Now where the dooce is it?' She felt largely in her leather-bound skirt and drew out a small silver mug. 'I sent a note to your wife about it, but my silly ass of a groom forgot to take this. You can save me a tramp. Give her my love.' She marched off amid her guard of grave Airedales.

The mug was worn and dented: above the twined initials, G.L., was the crest of a footless bird and the motto: 'Wayte awhyle—wayte awhyle.'

'That's the other end of the riddle,' Sophie whispered, when he saw her that evening. 'Read her note. The English write beautiful notes.'

The warmest of welcomes to your little man. I hope he will appreciate his native land now he has come to it. Though you have said nothing we cannot, of course, look on him as a little stranger, and so I am sending him the old Lashmar christening mug. It has been with us since Gregory Lashmar, your great-grandmother's brother—

George stared at his wife.

'Go on,' she twinkled from the pillows.

—mother's brother, sold his place to Walter's family. We seem to have acquired some of your household gods at that time, but nothing survives except the mug and the old cradle, which I found in the potting-shed and am having put in order for you. I hope little George—Lashmar, he will be too, won't he?—will live to see his grandchildren cut their teeth on his mug.

Affectionately yours,

ALICE CONANT.

P.S.—How quiet you've kept about it all!

'Well, I'm——'

'Don't swear,' said Sophie. 'Bad for the infant mind.'

'But how in the world did she get at it? Have you ever said a word about the Lashmars?'

'You know the only time—to young Iggulden at Rocketts —when Iggulden died.'

'Your great-grandmother's brother! She's traced the whole connection. More than your Aunt Sydney could do. What does she mean about our keeping quiet?'

Sophie's eyes sparkled. 'I've thought that out too. We've got back at the English at last. Can't you see that *she* thought that *we* thought my mother's being a Lashmar was one of those things we'd expect the English to find out for themselves, and that's impressed her?' She turned the mug in her white hands, and sighed happily. ' "Wayte awhyle— wayte awhyle." That's not a bad motto, George. It's been worth it.'

'But still I don't quite see——'

'I shouldn't wonder if they don't think our coming here was part of a deep-laid scheme to be near our ancestors. *They*'d understand that. And look how they've accepted us, all of them.'

'Are we so undesirable in ourselves?' George grunted.

'Be just, me lord. That wretched Sangres man has twice our money. Can you see Marm Conant slapping him between the shoulders? Not by a jugful! The poor beast doesn't exist!'

'Do you think it's that then?' He looked toward the cot by the fire where the godling snorted.

'The minute I get well I shall find out from Mrs. Cloke what every Lashmar gives in doles (that's nicer than tips) every time a Lashmite is born. I've done my duty thus far, but there's much expected of me.'

Entered here Mrs. Cloke, and hung worshipping over the cot. They showed her the mug and her face shone. 'Oh, now Lady Conant's sent it, it'll be all proper, ma'am, won't it? "George" of course he'd have to be, but seein' what he is we was hopin'—all your people was hopin'—it 'ud be "Lashmar" too, and that 'ud just round it out. A very 'andsome mug—quite unique, I should imagine. "Wayte awhyle—wayte awhyle." That's true with the Lashmars, I've heard. Very slow to fill their houses, they are. Most like Master George won't open 'is nursery till he's thirty.'

'Poor lamb!' cried Sophie. 'But how did you know my folk were Lashmars?'

Mrs. Cloke thought deeply. 'I'm sure I can't quite say, ma'am, but I've a belief likely that it was something you may have let drop to young Iggulden when you was at Rocketts. That *may* have been what give us an inkling. An' so it came out, one thing in the way o' talk leading to another, and those American people at Veering Holler was very obligin' with news, I'm told, ma'am.'

'Great Scott!' said George, under his breath. 'And this is the simple peasant!'

'Yiss,' Mrs. Cloke went on. 'An' Cloke was only wonderin' this afternoon—your pillow's slipped, my dear, you mustn't lie that a-way—just for the sake o' sayin' something, whether you wouldn't think well now of getting the Lashmar farms back, sir. They don't rightly round off Sir Walter's estate. They come caterin' across us more. Cloke, 'e 'ud be glad to show you over any day.'

'But Sir Walter doesn't want to sell, does he?'

'We can find out from his bailiff, sir, but'—with cold contempt—'I think that trained nurse is just comin' up from her dinner, so I'm afraid we'll 'ave to ask you, sir . . . Now, Master George—Ai-ie! Wake a litty-minute, lammie!'

A few months later the three of them were down at the brook in the Gale Anstey woods to consider the rebuilding of a footbridge carried away by spring floods. George Lashmar wanted all the bluebells on God's earth that day to eat, and Sophie adored him in a voice like to the cooing of a dove; so business was delayed.

'Here's the place,' said his father at last among the water forget-me-nots. 'But where the deuce are the larch-poles, Cloke? I told you to have them down here ready.'

'We'll get 'em down *if* you say so,' Cloke answered, with a thrust of the underlip they both knew.

'But I *did* say so. What on earth have you brought that timber-tug here for? We aren't building a railway bridge.

Why, in America, half-a-dozen two-by-four bits would be ample.'

'I don't know nothin' about that,' said Cloke. 'An' I've nothin' to say against larch—*if* you want to make a temp'ry job of it. I ain't 'ere to tell you what isn't so, sir; an' you can't say I ever come creepin' up on you, or tryin' to lead you farther in than you set out——'

A year ago George would have danced with impatience. Now he scraped a little mud off his old gaiters with his spud, and waited.

'All I say is that you can put up larch and make a temp'ry job of it; and by the time the young master's married it'll have to be done again. Now, I've brought down a couple of as sweet six-by-eight oak timbers as we've ever drawed. You put 'em in an' it's off your mind for good an' all. T'other way—I don't say it ain't right, I'm only just sayin' what I think—but t'other way, he'll no sooner be married than we'll 'ave it *all* to do again. You've no call to regard my words, but you can't get out of *that*.'

'No,' said George after a pause; 'I've been realising that for some time. Make it oak then. We can't get out of it.'

'IN THE INTERESTS OF THE BRETHREN'

I was buying a canary in a birdshop when he first spoke to me and suggested that I should take a less highly coloured bird. 'The colour is in the feeding,' said he. 'Unless you know how to feed 'em, it goes. Canaries are one of our hobbies.'

He passed out before I could thank him. He was a middle-aged man with grey hair and a short, dark beard, rather like a Sealyham terrier in silver spectacles. For some reason his face and his voice stayed in my mind so distinctly that, months later, when I jostled against him on a platform crowded with an Angling Club going to the Thames, I recognised, turned, and nodded.

'I took your advice about the canary,' I said.

'Did you? Good!' he replied heartily over the rod-case on his shoulder, and was parted from me by the crowd.

. . . . .

A few years ago I turned into a tobacconist's to have a badly stopped pipe cleaned out.

'Well! Well! And how did the canary do?' said the man behind the counter. We shook hands, and 'What's your name?' we both asked together.

His name was Lewis Holroyd Burges, of 'Burges and Son,' as I might have seen above the door—but Son had been killed in Egypt. His hair was whiter than it had been, and the eyes were sunk a little.

'Well! Well! To think,' said he, 'of one man in all these millions turning up in this curious way, when there's so many who don't turn up at all—eh?' (It was then that he told me of Son Lewis's death and why the boy had been christened Lewis.) 'Yes. There's not much left for middle-aged people just at present. Even one's hobbies—— We used to fish together. And the same with canaries! We used to breed 'em for colour—deep orange was our speciality. That's why I spoke to you, if you remember; but I've sold all my birds. Well! Well! And now we must locate your trouble.'

He bent over my erring pipe and dealt with it skilfully as a surgeon. A soldier came in, spoke in an undertone, received a reply, and went out.

'Many of my clients are soldiers nowadays, and a number of 'em belong to the Craft,' said Mr. Burges. 'It breaks my heart to give them the tobaccos they ask for. On the other hand, not one man in five thousand has a tobacco-palate. Preference, yes. Palate, no. Here's your pipe, again. It deserves better treatment than it's had. There's a procedure, a ritual, in all things. Any time you're passing by again, I assure you, you will be welcome. I've one or two odds and ends that may interest you.'

I left the shop with the rarest of all feelings on me—the sensation which is only youth's right—that I might have made a friend. A little distance from the door I was accosted by a wounded man who asked for 'Burges's.' The place seemed to be known in the neighbourhood.

I found my way to it again, and often after that, but it was not till my third visit that I discovered Mr. Burges held a half interest in Ackerman and Pernit's, the great cigar-importers, which had come to him through an uncle whose children now lived almost in the Cromwell Road, and said that the uncle had been on the Stock Exchange.

'I'm a shopkeeper by instinct,' said Mr. Burges. 'I like the ritual of handling things. The shop has done me well. I like to do well by the shop.'

It had been established by his grandfather in 1827, but the fittings and appointments must have been at least half a century older. The brown and red tobacco- and snuff-jars, with Crowns, Garters, and names of forgotten mixtures in gold leaf; the polished 'Oronoque' tobacco-barrels on which favoured customers sat; the cherry-black mahogany counter, the delicately moulded shelves, the reeded cigar-cabinets, the German-silver-mounted scales, and the Dutch brass roll- and cake-cutter, were things to covet.

'They aren't so bad,' he admitted. 'That large Bristol jar hasn't any duplicate to my knowledge. Those eight snuff-jars on the third shelf—they're Dollin's ware; he used to work for Wimble in Seventeen-Forty—are absolutely unique. Is there any one in the trade now could tell you what "Romano's Hollande" was? Or "Scholten's"? Here's a snuff-mull of George the First's time; and here's a Louis Quinze—what am I talking of? Treize, Treize, of course—grater for making bran-snuff. They were regular tools of the shop in my grandfather's day. And who on earth to leave 'em to outside the British Museum now, *I* can't think!'

His pipes—I would this were a tale for virtuosi—his amazing collection of pipes was kept in the parlour, and this gave me the privilege of making his wife's acquaintance. One morning, as I was looking covetously at a jacaranda-wood 'cigarro'—*not* cigar—cabinet with silver lock-plates and drawer-knobs of Spanish work, a wounded Canadian came into the shop and disturbed our happy little committee.

'Say,' he began loudly, 'are you the right place?'

'Who sent you?' Mr. Burges demanded.

'A man from Messines. But *that* ain't the point! I've got no certificates, nor papers—nothin', you understand. I left my Lodge owin' 'em seventeen dollars back-dues. But this man at Messines told me it wouldn't make any odds with *you*.'

'It doesn't,' said Mr. Burges. 'We meet to-night at 7 P.M.'

The man's face fell a yard. 'Hell!' said he. 'But I'm in hospital—I can't get leaf.'

'*And* Tuesdays and Fridays at 3 P.M.,' Mr. Burges added promptly. 'You'll have to be proved, of course.'

'Guess I can get by *that* all right,' was the cheery reply. 'Toosday, then.' He limped off, beaming.

'Who might that be?' I asked.

'I don't know any more than you do—except he must be a Brother. London's full of Masons now. Well! Well! We must do what we can these days. If you'll come to tea this evening, I'll take you on to Lodge afterwards. It's a Lodge of Instruction.'

'Delighted. Which is your Lodge?' I said, for up till then he had not given me its name.

' "Faith and Works 5837"—the third Saturday of every month. Our Lodge of Instruction meets nominally every Thursday, but we sit oftener than that now because there are so many Visiting Brothers in town.' Here another customer entered, and I went away much interested in the range of Brother Burges's hobbies.

At tea-time he was dressed as for Church, and wore gold pince-nez in lieu of the silver spectacles. I blessed my stars that I had thought to change into decent clothes.

'Yes, we owe that much to the Craft,' he assented. 'All Ritual is fortifying. Ritual's a natural necessity for mankind. The more things are upset, the more they fly to it. I abhor slovenly Ritual anywhere. By the way, would you mind assisting at the examinations, if there are many Visiting Brothers to-night? You'll find some of 'em very rusty, but—it's the Spirit, not the Letter, that giveth life. The question of Visiting Brethren is an important one. There are so many of them in London now, you see; and so few places where they can meet.'

'You dear thing!' said Mrs. Burges, and handed him his locked and initialed apron-case.

'Our Lodge is only just round the corner,' he went on. 'You mustn't be too critical of our appurtenances. The place was a garage once.'

As far as I could make out in the humiliating darkness, we wandered up a mews and into a courtyard. Mr. Burges piloted me, murmuring apologies for everything in advance.

'You mustn't expect——' he was still saying when we stumbled up a porch and entered a carefully decorated ante-room hung round with Masonic prints. I noticed Peter Gilkes and Barton Wilson, fathers of 'Emulation' working, in the place of honour; Kneller's Christopher Wren; Dunkerley, with his own Fitz-George book-plate below and the bend sinister on the Royal Arms; Hogarth's caricature of Wilkes, also his disreputable 'Night'; and a beautifully framed set of Grand Masters, from Anthony Sayer down.

'Are these another hobby of yours?' I asked.

'Not this time,' Mr. Burges smiled. 'We have to thank Brother Lemming for them.' He introduced me to the senior partner of Lemming and Orton, whose little shop is hard to find, but whose words and cheques in the matter of prints are widely circulated.

'The frames are the best part of 'em,' said Brother Lemming after my compliments. 'There are some more in the Lodge Room. Come and look. We've got the big Desaguliers there that nearly went to Iowa.'

I had never seen a Lodge Room better fitted. From mosaicked floor to appropriate ceiling, from curtain to pillar, implements to seats, seats to lights, and little carved music-loft at one end, every detail was perfect in particular kind and general design. I said what I thought of them all, many times over.

'I told you I was a Ritualist,' said Mr. Burges. 'Look at those carved corn-sheaves and grapes on the back of these Wardens' chairs. That's the old tradition—before Masonic furnishers spoilt it. I picked up that pair in Stepney ten years ago—the same time I got the gavel.' It was of ancient, yellowed ivory, cut all in one piece out of some tremendous tusk. 'That came from the Gold Coast,' he said. 'It belonged to a Military Lodge there in 1794. You can see the inscription.'

'If it's a fair question,' I began, 'how much——'

'It stood us,' said Brother Lemming, his thumbs in his waistcoat pockets, 'an appreciable sum of money when we built it in 1906, even with what Brother Anstruther—he

was our contractor—cheated himself out of. By the way,
that ashlar there is pure Carrara, he tells me. I don't understand marbles myself. Since then I expect we've put in—
oh, quite another little sum. Now we'll go to the examina-
tion-room and take on the Brethren.'

He led me back, not to the ante-room, but a convenient
chamber flanked with what looked like confessional-boxes
(I found out later that that was what they had been, when
first picked up for a song near Oswestry). A few men in
uniform were waiting at the far end. 'That's only the head
of the procession. The rest are in the ante-room,' said an
officer of the Lodge.

Brother Burges assigned me my discreet box, saying:
'Don't be surprised. They come all shapes.'

'Shapes' was not a bad description, for my first penitent
was all head-bandages—escaped from an Officers' Hospital,
Pentonville way. He asked me in profane Scots how I expected a man with only six teeth and half a lower lip to
speak to any purpose, so we compromised on the signs.
The next—a New Zealander from Taranaki—reversed the
process, for he was one-armed, and that in a sling. I mis-
trusted an enormous Sergeant-Major of Heavy Artillery,
who struck me as much too glib, so I sent him on to Brother
Lemming in the next box, who discovered he was a Past
District Grand Officer. My last man nearly broke me down
altogether. Everything seemed to have gone from him.

'I don't blame yer,' he gulped at last. 'I wouldn't pass my
own self on my answers, but I give yer my word that so far
as I've had any religion, it's been all the religion I've had.
For God's sake, let me sit in Lodge again, Brother!'

When the examinations were ended, a Lodge Officer
came round with our aprons—no tinsel or silver-gilt confec-
tions, but heavily-corded silk with tassels and—where a
man could prove he was entitled to them—levels, of decent
plate. Some one in front of me tightened a belt on a
stiffly silent person in civil clothes with discharge-badge.
''Strewth! This is comfort again,' I heard him say. The
companion nodded. The man went on suddenly: 'Here!

What're you doing? Leave off! You promised not to! Chuck it!' and dabbed at his companion's streaming eyes.

'Let him leak,' said an Australian signaller. 'Can't you see how happy the beggar is?'

It appeared that the silent Brother was a 'shell-shocker' whom Brother Lemming had passed, on the guarantee of his friend and—what moved Lemming more—the threat that, were he refused, he would have fits from pure disappointment. So the 'shocker' went happily and silently among Brethren evidently accustomed to these displays.

We fell in, two by two, according to tradition, fifty of us at least, and were played into Lodge by what I thought was an harmonium, but which I discovered to be an organ of repute. It took time to settle us down, for ten or twelve were cripples and had to be helped into long or easy chairs. I sat between a one-footed R.A.M.C. Corporal and a Captain of Territorials, who, he told me, had 'had a brawl' with a bomb, which had bent him in two directions. 'But that's first-class Bach the organist is giving us now,' he said delightedly. 'I'd like to know him. *I* used to be a piano-thumper of sorts.'

'I'll introduce you after Lodge,' said one of the regular Brethren behind us—a plump, torpedo-bearded man, who turned out to be a doctor. 'After all, there's nobody to touch Bach, is there?' Those two plunged at once into musical talk, which to outsiders is as fascinating as trigonometry.

Now a Lodge of Instruction is mainly a parade-ground for Ritual. It cannot initiate or confer degrees, but is limited to rehearsals and lectures. Worshipful Brother Burges, resplendent in Solomon's Chair (I found out later where that, too, had been picked up), briefly told the Visiting Brethren how welcome they were and always would be, and asked them to vote what ceremony should be rendered for their instruction.

When the decision was announced he wanted to know whether any Visiting Brothers would take the duties of Lodge Officers. They protested bashfully that they were

too rusty. 'The very reason why,' said Brother Burges,
while the organ Bached softly. My musical Captain wriggled in his chair.

'One moment, Worshipful Sir.' The plump Doctor rose.
'We have here a musician for whom place and opportunity
are needed. Only,' he went on colloquially, 'those organ-
loft steps are a bit steep.'

'How much,' said Brother Burges with the solemnity of
an initiation, 'does our Brother weigh?'

'Very little over eight stone,' said the Brother. 'Weighed
this morning, Worshipful Sir.'

The Past District Grand Officer, who was also a Battery-
Sergeant-Major, waddled across, lifted the slight weight in
his arms and bore it to the loft, where, the regular organist
pumping, it played joyously as a soul caught up to Heaven
by surprise.

When the visitors had been coaxed to supply the necessary officers, a ceremony was rehearsed. Brother Burges
forbade the regular members to prompt. The visitors had to
work entirely by themselves, but, on the Battery-Sergeant-
Major taking a hand, he was ruled out as of too exalted
rank. They floundered badly after that support was withdrawn.

The one-footed R.A.M.C. on my right chuckled.

'D'you like it?' said the Doctor to him.

'*Do* I? It's Heaven to me, sittin' in Lodge again. It's all
comin' back now, watching their mistakes. I haven't much
religion, but all I had I learnt in Lodge.' Recognising me,
he flushed a little as one does when one says a thing twice
over in another's hearing. 'Yes, "veiled in all'gory and
illustrated in symbols"—the Fatherhood of God, an' the
Brotherhood of Man; an' what more in Hell *do* you
want? . . . Look at 'em!' He broke off giggling. 'See! See!
They've tied the whole thing into knots. *I* could ha' done it
better myself—my one foot in France. Yes, I should think
they *ought* to do it again!'

The new organist covered the little confusion that had
arisen with what sounded like the wings of angels.

When the amateurs, rather red and hot, had finished, they demanded an exhibition-working of their bungled ceremony by Regular Brethren of the Lodge. Then I realised for the first time what word-and-gesture-perfect Ritual can be brought to mean. We all applauded, the one-footed Corporal most of all.

'We *are* rather proud of our working, and this is an audience worth playing up to,' the Doctor said.

Next the Master delivered a little lecture on the meanings of some pictured symbols and diagrams. His theme was a well-worn one, but his deep holding voice made it fresh.

'Marvellous how these old copybook-headings persist,' the Doctor said.

'*That's* all right!' the one-footed man spoke cautiously out of the side of his mouth like a boy in form. 'But they're the kind o' copybook-headin's we shall find burnin' round our bunks in Hell. Believe me-ee! I've broke enough of 'em to know. Now, hsh!' He leaned forward, drinking it all in.

Presently Brother Burges touched on a point which had given rise to some diversity of Ritual. He asked for information. 'Well, in Jamaica, Worshipful Sir,' a Visiting Brother began, and explained how they worked that detail in his parts. Another and another joined in from different quarters of the Lodge (and the world), and when they were well warmed the Doctor sidled softly round the walls and, over our shoulders, passed us cigarettes.

'A shocking innovation,' he said, as he returned to the Captain-musician's vacant seat on my left. 'But men can't really talk without tobacco, and we're only a Lodge of Instruction.'

'An' I've learned more in one evenin' here than ten years.' The one-footed man turned round for an instant from a dark, sour-looking Yeoman in spurs who was laying down the law on Dutch Ritual. The blue haze and the talk increased, while the organ from the loft blessed us all.

'But this is delightful,' said I to the Doctor. 'How did it all happen?'

'Brother Burges started it. He used to talk to the men

who dropped into his shop when the war began. He told us sleepy old chaps in Lodge that what men wanted more than anything else was Lodges where they could sit—just sit and be happy like we are now. He was right too. We're learning things in the war. A man's Lodge means more to him than people imagine. As our friend on your right said just now, very often Masonry's the only practical creed we've ever listened to since we were children. Platitudes or no platitudes, it squares with what everybody knows ought to be done.' He sighed. 'And if this war hasn't brought home the Brotherhood of Man to us all, I'm—a Hun!'

'How did you get your visitors?' I went on.

'Oh, I told a few fellows in hospital near here, at Burges's suggestion, that we had a Lodge of Instruction and they'd be welcome. And they came. And they told their friends. And *they* came! That was two years ago—and now we've Lodge of Instruction two nights a week, and a matinée nearly every Tuesday and Friday for the men who can't get evening leave. Yes, it's all very curious. I'd no notion what the Craft meant—and means—till this war.'

'Nor I, till this evening,' I replied.

'Yet it's quite natural if you think. Here's London—all England—packed with the Craft from all over the world, and nowhere for them to go. Why, our weekly visiting attendance for the last four months averaged just under a hundred and forty. Divide by four—call it thirty-five Visiting Brethren a time. Our record's seventy-one, but we have packed in as many as eighty-four at Banquets. You can see for yourself what a potty little hole we are!'

'Banquets too!' I cried. 'It must cost like anything. May the Visiting Brethren——'

The Doctor—his name was Keede—laughed. 'No, a Visiting Brother may *not*.'

'But when a man has had an evening like this, he wants to——'

'That's what they all say. That makes our difficulty. They do exactly what you were going to suggest, and they're offended if we don't take it.'

'Don't you?' I asked.

'My dear man—what *does* it come to? They can't all stay to Banquet. Say one hundred suppers a week—fifteen quid —sixty a month—seven hundred and twenty a year. How much are Lemming and Orton worth? And Ellis and Mc-Knight—that long big man over yonder—the provision dealers? How much d'you suppose could Burges write a cheque for and not feel? 'Tisn't as if he had to save for any one now. I assure you we have no scruple in calling on the Visiting Brethren when we want anything. We couldn't do the work otherwise. Have you noticed how the Lodge is kept—brass-work, jewels, furniture, and so on?'

'I have indeed,' I said. 'It's like a ship. You could eat your dinner off the floor.'

'Well, come here on a bye-day and you'll often find half-a-dozen Brethren, with eight legs between 'em, polishing and ronuking and sweeping everything they can get at. I cured a shell-shocker this spring by giving him our jewels to look after. He pretty well polished the numbers off 'em, but—it kept him from fighting Huns in his sleep. And when we need Masters to take our duties—two matinées a week is rather a tax—we've the choice of P.M.'s from all over the world. The Dominions are much keener on Ritual than an average English Lodge. Besides that—— Oh, we're going to adjourn. Listen to the greetings. They'll be interesting.'

The crack of the great gavel brought us to our feet, after some surging and plunging among the cripples. Then the Battery-Sergeant-Major, in a trained voice, delivered hearty and fraternal greetings to 'Faith and Works' from his tropical District and Lodge. The others followed, without order, in every tone between a grunt and a squeak. I heard 'Hauraki,' 'Inyanga-Umbezi,' 'Aloha,' 'Southern Lights' (from somewhere Punta Arenas way), 'Lodge of Rough Ashlars' (and that Newfoundland Naval Brother looked it), two or three Stars of something or other, half-a-dozen cardinal virtues, variously arranged, hailing from Klondyke to Kalgoorlie, one Military Lodge on one of the fronts, thrown in with a severe Scots burr by my friend of the

head-bandages, and the rest as mixed as the Empire itself.
Just at the end there was a little stir. The silent Brother had
begun to make noises; his companion tried to soothe him.

'Let him be! Let him be!' the Doctor called profession-
ally. The man jerked and mouthed, and at last mumbled
something unintelligible even to his friend, but a small
dark P.M. pushed forward importantly.

'It iss all right,' he said. 'He wants to say——' he spat out
some yard-long Welsh name, adding, 'That means Pem-
broke Docks, Worshipful Sir. We haf good Masons in
Wales, too.' The silent man nodded approval.

'Yes,' said the Doctor, quite unmoved. 'It happens that
way sometimes. *Hespere panta fereis*, isn't it? The Star
brings 'em all home. I must get a note of that fellow's case
after Lodge. I saw you didn't care for music,' he went on,
'but I'm afraid you'll have to put up with a little more.
It's a paraphrase from Micah. Our organist arranged it.
We sing it antiphonally, as a sort of dismissal.'

Even I could appreciate what followed. The singing
seemed confined to half-a-dozen trained voices answering
each other till the last line, when the full Lodge came in. I
give it as I heard it:

> 'We have showèd thee, O Man,
>   What is good.
> What doth the Lord require of us?
> Or Conscience' self desire of us?
>   But to do justly—
>   But to love mercy,
> And to walk humbly with our God,
>   As every Mason should.'

Then we were played and sung out to the quaint tune of
the 'Entered Apprentices' Song.' I noticed that the regular
Brethren of the Lodge did not begin to take off their regalia
till the lines:

> 'Great Kings, Dukes, and Lords
> Have laid down their swords.'

They moved into the ante-room, now set for the Banquet, on the verse:

> 'Antiquity's pride
> We have on our side,
> Which maketh men just in their station.'

The Brother (a big-boned clergyman) that I found myself next to at table told me the custom was 'a fond thing vainly invented' on the strength of some old legend. He laid down that Masonry should be regarded as an 'intellectual abstraction.' An Officer of Engineers disagreed with him, and told us how in Flanders, a year before, some ten or twelve Brethren held Lodge in what was left of a Church. Save for the Emblems of Mortality and plenty of rough ashlars, there was no furniture.

'I warrant you weren't a bit the worse for that,' said the Clergyman. 'The idea should be enough without trappings.'

'But it wasn't,' said the other. 'We took a lot of trouble to make our regalia out of camouflage-stuff that we'd pinched, and we manufactured our jewels from old metal. I've got the set now. It kept us happy for weeks.'

'Ye were absolutely irregular an' unauthorised. Whaur was your Warrant?' said the Brother from the Military Lodge. 'Grand Lodge ought to take steps against——'

'If Grand Lodge had any sense,' a private three places up our table broke in, 'it 'ud warrant travelling Lodges at the front and attach first-class lecturers to 'em.'

'Wad ye confer degrees promiscuously?' said the scandalised Scot.

'Every time a man asked, of course. You'd have half the Army in.'

The speaker played with the idea for a little while, and proved that, on the lowest scale of fees, Grand Lodge would get huge revenues.

'I believe,' said the Engineer Officer thoughtfully, 'I could design a complete travelling Lodge outfit under forty pounds weight.'

'Ye're wrong. I'll prove it. We've tried ourselves,' said

the Military Lodge man; and they went at it together across the table, each with his own note-book.

The 'banquet' was simplicity itself. Many of us ate in haste so as to get back to barracks or hospitals, but now and again a Brother came in from the outer darkness to fill a chair and empty a plate. These were Brethren who had been there before and needed no examination.

One man lurched in—helmet, Flanders mud, accoutrements and all—fresh from the leave-train.

' 'Got two hours to wait for my train,' he explained. 'I remembered your night, though. My God, this *is* good!'

'What is your train and from what station?' said the Clergyman precisely. 'Very well. What will you have to eat?'

'Anything. Everything. I've thrown up a month's rations in the Channel.'

He stoked himself for ten minutes without a word. Then, without a word, his face fell forward. The Clergyman had him by one already limp arm and steered him to a couch, where he dropped and snored. No one took the trouble to turn round.

'Is that usual too?' I asked.

'Why not?' said the Clergyman. 'I'm on duty to-night to wake them for their trains. They do not respect the Cloth on those occasions.' He turned his broad back on me and continued his discussion with a Brother from Aberdeen by way of Mitylene where, in the intervals of mine-sweeping, he had evolved a complete theory of the Revelation of St. John the Divine in the Island of Patmos.

I fell into the hands of a Sergeant-Instructor of Machine Guns—by profession a designer of ladies' dresses. He told me that Englishwomen as a class 'lose on their corsets what they make on their clothes,' and that 'Satan himself can't save a woman who wears thirty-shilling corsets under a thirty-guinea costume.' Here, to my grief, he was button-holed by a zealous Lieutenant of his own branch, and became a Sergeant again all in one click.

I drifted back and forth, studying the prints on the walls

and the Masonic collection in the cases, while I listened to the inconceivable talk all round me. Little by little the company thinned, till at last there were only a dozen or so of us left. We gathered at the end of a table near the fire, the night-bird from Flanders trumpeting lustily into the hollow of his helmet, which some one had tipped over his face.

'And how did it go with you?' said the Doctor.

'It was like a new world,' I answered.

'That's what it *is* really.' Brother Burges returned the gold pince-nez to their case and reshipped his silver spectacles. 'Or that's what it might be made with a little trouble. When I think of the possibilities of the Craft at this juncture I wonder——' He stared into the fire.

'I wonder, too,' said the Sergeant-Major slowly, 'but—on the whole—I'm inclined to agree with you. We could do much with Masonry.'

'As an aid—as an aid—not as a substitute for Religion,' the Clergyman snapped.

'Oh, Lord! Can't we give Religion a rest for a bit?' the Doctor muttered. 'It hasn't done so—I beg your pardon all round.'

The Clergyman was bristling. 'Kamerad!' the wise Sergeant-Major went on, both hands up. 'Certainly not as a substitute for a creed, but as an average plan of life. What I've seen at the front makes me sure of it.'

Brother Burges came out of his muse. 'There ought to be a dozen—twenty—other Lodges in London every night; conferring degrees too, as well as instruction. Why shouldn't the young men join? They practise what we're always preaching. Well! Well! We must all do what we can. What's the use of old Masons if they can't give a little help along their own lines?'

'Exactly,' said the Sergeant-Major, turning on the Doctor. 'And what's the darn use of a Brother if he isn't allowed to help?'

'Have it your own way then,' said the Doctor testily. He had evidently been approached before. He took something the Sergeant-Major handed to him and pocketed it with a nod. 'I was wrong,' he said to me, 'when I boasted of our independence. They get round us sometimes. This,' he slapped his pocket, 'will give a banquet on Tuesday. We don't usually feed at matinées. It will be a surprise. By the way, try another sandwich. The ham are best.' He pushed me a plate.

'They are,' I said. 'I've only had five or six. I've been looking for them.'

''Glad you like them,' said Brother Lemming. 'Fed him myself, cured him myself—at my little place in Berkshire. His name was Charlemagne. By the way, Doc, am I to keep another one for next month?'

'Of course,' said the Doctor with his mouth full. 'A little fatter than this chap, please. And don't forget your promise about the pickled nasturtiums. They're appreciated.' Brother Lemming nodded above the pipe he had lit as we began a second supper. Suddenly the Clergyman, after a glance at the clock, scooped up half-a-dozen sandwiches from under my nose, put them into an oiled paper bag, and advanced cautiously towards the sleeper on the couch.

'They wake rough sometimes,' said the Doctor. 'Nerves, y'know.' The Clergyman tiptoed directly behind the man's head, and at arm's length rapped on the dome of the helmet. The man woke in one vivid streak, as the Clergyman stepped back, and grabbed for a rifle that was not there.

'You've barely half an hour to catch your train.' The Clergyman passed him the sandwiches. 'Come along.'

'You're uncommonly kind and I'm very grateful,' said the man, wriggling into his stiff straps. He followed his guide into the darkness after saluting.

'Who's that?' said Lemming.

''Can't say,' the Doctor returned indifferently. 'He's been here before. He's evidently a P.M. of sorts.'

'Well! Well!' said Brother Burges, whose eyelids were drooping. 'We must all do what we can. Isn't it almost time to lock up?'

'I wonder,' said I, as we helped each other into our coats, 'what would happen if Grand Lodge knew about all this.'

'About what?' Lemming turned on me quickly.

'A Lodge of Instruction open three nights and two afternoons a week—and running a lodging-house as well. It's all very nice, but it doesn't strike me somehow as regulation.'

'The point hasn't been raised yet,' said Lemming. 'We'll settle it after the war. Meantime we shall go on.'

'There ought to be scores of them,' Brother Burges repeated as we went out of the door. 'All London's full of the Craft, and no places for them to meet in. Think of the possibilities of it! Think what could have been done *by* Masonry *through* Masonry *for* all the world. I hope I'm not censorious, but it sometimes crosses my mind that Grand Lodge may have thrown away its chance in the war almost as much as the Church has.'

''Lucky for you the Padre is taking that chap to King's Cross,' said Brother Lemming, 'or he'd be down your throat. What really troubles him is our legal position under Masonic Law. I think he'll inform on us one of these days. Well, good night, all.' The Doctor and Lemming turned off together.

'Yes,' said Brother Burges, slipping his arm into mine. 'Almost as much as the Church has. But perhaps I'm too much of a Ritualist.'

I said nothing. I was speculating how soon I could steal a march on the Clergyman and inform against 'Faith and Works No. 5837 E.C.'

THE JANEITES

Jane lies in Winchester—blessed be her shade!
Praise the Lord for making her, and her for all
    she made!
And while the stones of Winchester, or Milsom
    Street, remain,
Glory, love, and honour unto England's Jane!

In the Lodge of Instruction attached to 'Faith and Works No. 5837 E.C.,' which has already been described, Saturday afternoon was appointed for the weekly clean-up, when all visiting Brethren were welcome to help under the direction of the Lodge Officer of the day: their reward was light refreshment and the meeting of companions.

This particular afternoon—in the autumn of '20—Brother Burges, P.M., was on duty and, finding a strong shift present, took advantage of it to strip and dust all hangings and curtains, to go over every inch of the Pavement—which was stone, not floorcloth—by hand; and to polish the Columns, Jewels, Working outfit and organ. I was given to clean some Officers' Jewels—beautiful bits of old Georgian silver-work humanised by generations of elbow-grease—and retired to the organ-loft; for the floor was like the quarter-deck of a battleship on the eve of a ball. Half-a-dozen brethren had already made the Pavement as glassy as the aisle of Greenwich Chapel; the brazen chapiters winked like pure gold at the flashing Marks on the Chairs; and a morose one-legged brother was attending to the Emblems of Mortality with, I think, rouge.

'They ought,' he volunteered to Brother Burges as we passed, 'to be betwixt the colour of ripe apricots an' a half-smoked meerschaum. That's how we kept 'em in my Mother-Lodge—a treat to look at.'

'I've never seen spit-and-polish to touch this,' I said.

'Wait till you see the organ,' Brother Burges replied. 'You could shave in it when they've done. Brother Anthony's in charge up there—the taxi-owner you met here last month. I don't think you've come across Brother Humberstall, have you?'

'I don't remember——' I began.

'You wouldn't have forgotten him if you had. He's a hairdresser now, somewhere at the back of Ebury Street. 'Was Garrison Artillery. 'Blown up twice.'

'Does he show it?' I asked at the foot of the organ-loft stairs.

'No-o. Not much more than Lazarus did, I expect.' Brother Burges fled off to set some one else to a job.

Brother Anthony, small, dark, and humpbacked, was hissing groom-fashion while he treated the rich acacia-wood panels of the Lodge organ with some sacred, secret composition of his own. Under his guidance Humberstall, an enormous, flat-faced man, carrying the shoulders, ribs, and loins of the old Mark '14 Royal Garrison Artillery, and the eyes of a bewildered retriever, rubbed the stuff in. I sat down to my task on the organ-bench, whose purple velvet cushion was being vacuum-cleaned on the floor below.

'Now,' said Anthony, after five minutes' vigorous work on the part of Humberstall. '*Now* we're gettin' somethin' worth lookin' at! Take it easy, an' go on with what you was tellin' me about that Macklin man.'

'I—I 'adn't anything against 'im,' said Humberstall, 'excep' he'd been a toff by birth; but that never showed till he was bosko absoluto. Mere bein' drunk on'y made a common 'ound of 'im. But when bosko, it all came out. Otherwise, he showed me my duties as mess-waiter very well on the 'ole.'

'Yes, yes. But what in 'ell made you go *back* to your Circus? The Board gave you down-an'-out fair enough, you said, after the dump went up at Eatables?'

'Board or no Board, *I* 'adn't the nerve to stay at 'ome—
not with Mother chuckin' 'erself round all three rooms like
a rabbit every time the Gothas tried to get Victoria; an'
sister writin' me aunts four pages about it next day. Not for
me, thank you! till the war was over. So I slid out with a
draft—they wasn't particular in '17, so long as the tally was
correct—and I joined up again with our Circus somewhere
at the back of Lar Pug Noy, I think it was.' Humberstall
paused for some seconds and his brow wrinkled. 'Then I—I
went sick, or somethin' or other, they told me; but I know
when I reported for duty, our Battery Sergeant-Major says
that I wasn't expected back, an'—an', one thing leadin' to
another—to cut a long story short—I went up before our
Major—Major—I shall forget my own name next—Major——'

'Never mind,' Anthony interrupted. 'Go on! It'll come
back in talk!'

''Alf a mo'. 'Twas on the tip o' my tongue then.'

Humberstall dropped the polishing-cloth and knitted his
brows again in most profound thought. Anthony turned to
me and suddenly launched into a sprightly tale of his taxi's
collision with a Marble Arch refuge on a greasy day after a
three-yard skid.

''Much damage?' I asked.

'Oh no! Ev'ry bolt an' screw an' nut on the chassis
strained; *but* nothing carried away, you understand me, an'
not a scratch on the body. You'd never 'ave guessed a thing
wrong till you took 'er in hand. It *was* a wop too: 'ead-on—
like this!' And he slapped his tactful little forehead to show
what a knock it had been.

'Did your Major dish you up much?' he went on over his
shoulder to Humberstall, who came out of his abstraction
with a slow heave.

'We-ell! He told me I wasn't expected back either; an' he
said 'e couldn't 'ang up the 'ole Circus till I'd rejoined; an'
he said that my ten-inch Skoda which I'd been Number
Three of, before the dump went up at Eatables, had 'er full
crowd. But, 'e said, as soon as a casualty occurred he'd re-

member me. "Meantime," says he, "I particularly want you
for actin' mess-waiter."

'"Beggin' your pardon, sir," I says perfectly respectful;
"but I didn't exactly come back for *that*, sir."

'"Beggin' *your* pardon, 'Umberstall," says 'e, "but I
'appen to command the Circus! Now, you're a sharp-witted
man," he says; "an' what we've suffered from fool-waiters
in Mess 'as been somethin' cruel. You'll take on, from now
—under instruction to Macklin 'ere." So this man, Macklin,
that I was tellin' you about, showed me my duties. . . .
'Ammick! I've got it! 'Ammick was our Major, an' Mosse
was Captain!' Humberstall celebrated his recapture of the
name by labouring at the organ-panel on his knee.

'Look out! You'll smash it,' Anthony protested.

'Sorry! Mother's often told me I didn't know my strength.
Now, here's a curious thing. This Major of ours—it's all
comin' back to me—was a high-up divorce-court lawyer; an'
Mosse, our Captain, was Number One o' Mosse's Private
Detective Agency. You've heard of it? 'Wives watched
while you wait, an' so on. Well, these two 'ad been regis-
terin' together, so to speak, in the Civil line for years on
end, but hadn't ever met till the War. Consequently, at Mess
their talk was mostly about famous cases they'd been mixed
up in. 'Ammick told the Law-courts' end o' the business,
an' all what had been left out of the pleadin's; an' Mosse
'ad the actual facts concernin' the errin' parties—in hotels
an' so on. I've heard better talk in our Mess than ever before or since. It comes o' the Gunners bein' a scientific
corps.'

'That be damned!' said Anthony. 'If anythin' 'appens to
'em they've got it all down in a book. There's no book
when your lorry dies on you in the 'Oly Land. *That's* brains.'

'Well, *then*,' Humberstall continued, 'come on this secret
society business that I started tellin' you about. When those
two—'Ammick an' Mosse—'ad finished about their matri-
monial relations—and, mind you, they weren't radishes—
they seldom or ever repeated—they'd begin, as often as not,
on this Secret Society woman I was tellin' you of—this Jane.

She was the only woman I ever 'eard 'em say a good word
for. 'Cordin' to them Jane was a none-such. *I* didn't know
then she was a Society. 'Fact is, I only 'ung out 'arf an ear
in their direction at first, on account of bein' under instruction for mess-duty to this Macklin man. What drew *my*
attention to her was a new Lieutenant joinin' up. We called
'im "Gander" on account of his profeel, which was the
identical bird. 'E'd been a nactuary—workin' out 'ow long
civilians 'ad to live. Neither 'Ammick nor Mosse wasted
words on 'im at Mess. They went on talking as usual, an' in
due time, *as* usual, they got back to Jane. Gander cocks one
of his big chilblainy ears an' cracks his cold finger-joints.
"By God! Jane?" says 'e. "Yes, Jane," says 'Ammick pretty
short an' senior. "Praise 'Eaven!" says Gander. "It was
'Bubbly' where I've come from down the line." (Some
damn revue or other, I expect.) Well, neither 'Ammick nor
Mosse was easy-mouthed, or for that matter mealy-
mouthed; but no sooner 'ad Gander passed that remark
than they both shook 'ands with the young squirt across the
table an' called for the port back again. It *was* a password,
all right! Then they went at it about Jane—all three, regard-
less of rank. That made me listen. Presently, I 'eard 'Ammick say——'

'Arf a mo',' Anthony cut in. 'But what was *you* doin' in
Mess?'

'Me an' Macklin was refixin' the sand-bag screens to the
dug-out passage in case o' gas. We never knew when we'd
cop it in the 'Eavies, don't you see? But we knew we 'ad
been looked for for some time, an' it might come any minute. But, as I was sayin', 'Ammick says what a pity 'twas
Jane 'ad died barren. "I deny that," says Mosse. "I maintain
she was fruitful in the 'ighest sense o' the word." An' Mosse
knew about such things, too. "I'm inclined to agree with
'Ammick," says young Gander. "Any'ow, she's left no direct an' lawful prog'ny." I remember every word they said,
on account o' what 'appened subsequently. I 'adn't noticed
Macklin much, or I'd ha' seen he was bosko absoluto. Then

'e cut in, leanin' over a packin'-case with a face on 'im like
a dead mackerel in the dark. "Pahardon me, gents," Macklin says, "but this *is* a matter on which I *do* 'appen to be
moderately well-informed. She *did* leave lawful issue in the
shape o' one son; an' 'is name was 'Enery James."

'"By what sire? Prove it," says Gander, before 'is senior
officers could get in a word.

'"I will," says Macklin, surgin' on 'is two thumbs. *An'*,
mark you, none of 'em spoke! I forget whom he said was
the sire of this 'Enery James-man; but 'e delivered 'em a
lecture on this Jane-woman for more than a quarter of an
hour. I know the exact time, because my old Skoda was on
duty at ten-minute intervals reachin' after some Jerry
formin'-up area; and her blast always put out the dug-out
candles. I relit 'em once, an' again at the end. In conclusion,
this Macklin fell flat forward on 'is face, which was how 'e
generally wound up 'is notion of a perfect day. Bosko
absoluto!

'"Take 'im away," says 'Ammick to me. "'E's sufferin'
from shell-shock."

'To cut a long story short, *that* was what first put the notion into my 'ead. Wouldn't it you? Even 'ad Macklin been
a 'igh-up Mason——'

'Wasn't 'e, then?' said Anthony, a little puzzled.

''E'd never gone beyond the Blue Degrees, 'e told me.
Any'ow, 'e'd lectured 'is superior officers up an' down; 'e'd
as good as called 'em fools most o' the time, in 'is toff's
voice. I 'eard 'im an' I saw 'im. An' all he got was—me told
off to put 'im to bed! And all on account o' Jane! Would
you have let a thing like that get past you? Nor me, either!
Next mornin', when his stummick was settled, I was at him
full-cry to find out 'ow it was worked. Toff or no toff, 'e
knew his end of a bargain. First, 'e wasn't takin' any. He
said I wasn't fit to be initiated into the Society of the
Janeites. That only meant five bob more—fifteen up to date.

'"Make it one Bradbury," 'e says. "It's dirt-cheap. You
saw me 'old the Circus in the 'ollow of me 'and?"

'No denyin' it. I '*ad*. So, for one pound, he communicated me the Password of the First Degree, which was *Tilniz an' trap-doors*.

' "I know what a trap-door is," I says to 'im, "but what in 'ell's *Tilniz?*"

' "You obey orders," 'e says, "an' next time I ask you what you're thinkin' about you'll answer, '*Tilniz an' trap-doors*,' in a smart and soldierly manner. I'll spring that question at me own time. All you've got to do is to be distinck."

'We settled all this while we was skinnin' spuds for dinner at the back o' the rear-truck under our camouflage-screens. Gawd, 'ow that glue-paint did stink! Otherwise, 'twasn't so bad, with the sun comin' through our panto-mime-leaves, an' the wind marcelling the grasses in the cutting. Well, one thing leading to another, nothin' further 'appened in this direction till the afternoon. We 'ad a high standard o' livin' in Mess—an' in the Group, for that matter. I was takin' away Mosse's lunch—dinner 'e would never call it—an' Mosse was fillin' 'is cigarette-case previous to the afternoon's duty. Macklin, in the passage, comin' in as if 'e didn't know Mosse was there, slings 'is question at me, an' I give the countersign in a low but quite distinck voice, makin' as if I 'adn't seen Mosse. Mosse looked at me through and through, with his cigarette-case in his 'and. Then 'e jerks out 'arf a dozen—best Turkish—on the table an' exits. I pinched 'em an' divvied with Macklin.

' "You see 'ow it works," says Macklin. "Could you 'ave invested a Bradbury to better advantage?"

' "So far, no," I says. "Otherwise, though, if they start provin' an' tryin' me, I'm a dead bird. There must be a lot more to this Janeite game."

' " 'Eaps an' 'eaps," he says. "But to show you the sort of 'eart I 'ave, I'll communicate you all the 'Igher Degrees among the Janeites, includin' the Charges, for another Brad-bury; but you'll 'ave to work, Dobbin." '

' 'Pretty free with your Bradburys, wasn't you?' Anthony grunted disapprovingly.

'What odds? *Ac*-tually, Gander told us, we couldn't expect to av'rage more than six weeks longer apiece, an',
any'ow, *I* never regretted it. But make no mistake—the
preparation was somethin' cruel. In the first place, I come
under Macklin for direct instruction *re* Jane.'

'Oh! Jane *was* real, then?' Anthony glanced for an instant at me as he put the question. 'I couldn't quite make
that out.'

'Real!' Humberstall's voice rose almost to a treble.
'Jane? Why, she was a little old maid 'oo'd written 'alf a
dozen books about a hundred years ago. 'Twasn't as if
there was anythin' *to* 'em, either. *I* know. I had to read
'em. They weren't adventurous, nor smutty, nor what you'd
call even interestin'—all about girls o' seventeen (they begun young then, I tell you), not certain 'oom they'd like
to marry; an' their dances an' card-parties an' picnics,
and their young blokes goin' off to London on 'orseback for
'air-cuts an' shaves. It took a full day in those days, if you
went to a proper barber. They wore wigs, too, when they
was chemists or clergymen. All that interested me on account o' me profession, an' cuttin' the men's 'air every
fortnight. Macklin used to chip me about bein' an 'air-
dresser. 'E *could* pass remarks, too!'

Humberstall recited with relish a fragment of what must
have been a superb commination-service, ending with,
'You lazy-minded, lousy-headed, long-trousered, perfumed
perookier.'

'An' you took it?' Anthony's quick eyes ran over the
man.

'Yes. I was after my money's worth; an' Macklin, havin'
put 'is 'and to the plough, wasn't one to withdraw it. Otherwise, if I'd pushed 'im, I'd ha' slew 'im. Our Battery Sergeant Major nearly did. For Macklin had a wonderful way
o' passing remarks on a man's civil life; an' he put it about
that our B.S.M. had run a dope an' dolly-shop with a
Chinese woman, the wrong end o' Southwark Bridge.
Nothin' you could lay 'old of, o' course; but——' Humberstall let us draw our own conclusions.

'That reminds me,' said Anthony, smacking his lips. 'I 'ad a bit of a fracas with a fare in the Fulham Road last month. He called me a parastit-ic Forder. I informed 'im I was owner-driver, an' 'e could see for 'imself the cab was quite clean. That didn't suit 'im. 'E said it was crawlin'.'

'What happened?' I asked.

'One o' them blue-bellied Bolshies of postwar Police (neglectin' point-duty, as usual) asked us to flirt a little quieter. My joker chucked some Arabic at 'im. That was when we signed the Armistice. 'E'd been a Yeoman—a perishin' Gloucestershire Yeoman—that I'd helped gather in the orange crop with at Jaffa, in the 'Oly Land!'

'And after that?' I continued.

'It 'ud be 'ard to say. I know 'e lived at Hendon or Cricklewood. I drove 'im there. We must 'ave talked Zionism or somethin', because at seven next mornin' him an' me was tryin' to get petrol out of a milkshop at St. Albans. They 'adn't any. In lots o' ways this war has been a public noosance, as one might say, but there's no denyin' it 'elps you slip through life easier. The dairyman's son 'ad done time on Jordan with camels. So he stood us rum an' milk.'

'Just like 'avin' the Password, eh?' was Humberstall's comment.

'That's right! Ours was *Imshee kelb*.[1] Not so 'ard to remember as your Jane stuff.'

'Jane wasn't so very 'ard—not the way Macklin used to put 'er,' Humberstall resumed. 'I 'ad only six books to remember. I learned the names by 'eart as Macklin placed 'em. There was one called *Persuasion*, first; an' the rest in a bunch, except another about some Abbey or other—last by three lengths. But, as I was sayin', what beat me was there was nothin' *to* 'em nor *in* 'em. Nothin' at all, believe me.'

'You seem good an' full of 'em, any'ow,' said Anthony.

'I mean that 'er characters was no *use*! They was only just like people you run across any day. One of 'em was a curate—the Reverend Collins—always on the make an' lookin' to marry money. Well, when I was a Boy Scout, 'im

[1] 'Get out, you dog.'

or 'is twin brother was our troop-leader. An' there was an
upstandin' 'ard-mouthed Duchess or a Baronet's wife that
didn't give a curse for any one 'oo wouldn't do what she
told 'em to; the Lady—Lady Catherine (I'll get it in a
minute) De Bugg. Before Ma bought the 'airdressin' business in London I used to know of an 'olesale grocer's wife
near Leicester (I'm Leicestershire myself) that might 'ave
been 'er duplicate. And—oh yes—there was a Miss Bates;
just an old maid runnin' about like a hen with 'er 'ead cut
off, an' her tongue loose at both ends. I've got an aunt like
'er. Good as gold—but, *you* know.'

'Lord, yes!' said Anthony, with feeling. 'An' did you find
out what *Tilniz* meant? I'm always huntin' after the meanin'
of things meself.'

'Yes, 'e was a swine of a Major-General, retired, and
on the make. They're all on the make, in a quiet way, in
Jane. 'E was so much of a gentleman by 'is own estima-
tion that 'e was always be'avin' like a hound. *You* know the
sort. 'Turned a girl out of 'is own 'ouse because she 'adn't
any money—*after*, mark you, encouragin' 'er to set 'er cap
at his son, because 'e thought she had.'

'But that 'appens all the time,' said Anthony. 'Why, me
own mother——'

'That's right. So would mine. But this Tilney was a man,
an' some'ow Jane put it down all so naked it made you
ashamed. I told Macklin that, an' he said I was shapin' to
be a good Janeite. 'Twasn't *his* fault if I wasn't. 'Nother
thing, too; 'avin' been at the Bath Mineral Waters 'Ospital
in 'Sixteen, with trench-feet, was a great advantage to me,
because I knew the names o' the streets where Jane 'ad
lived. There was one of 'em—Laura, I think, or some other
girl's name—which Macklin said was 'oly ground. "If you'd
been initiated *then*," he says, "you'd ha' felt your flat feet
tingle every time you walked over those sacred pavin'-
stones."

' "My feet tingled right enough," I said, "but not on account of Jane. Nothin' remarkable about that," I says.

' " 'Eaven lend me patience!" he says, combin' 'is 'air with 'is little 'ands. "Every dam' thing about Jane is remarkable to a pukka Janeite! It was there," he says, "that Miss What's-her-Name" (he had the name; I've forgotten it) "made up 'er engagement again, after nine years, with Captain T'other Bloke." An' he dished me out a page an' a half of one of the books to learn by 'eart—*Persuasion*, I think it was.'

' 'You quick at gettin' things off by 'eart?' Anthony demanded.

'Not as a rule. I was then, though, or else Macklin knew 'ow to deliver the Charges properly. 'E said 'e'd been some sort o' schoolmaster once, and 'e'd make my mind resume work or break 'imself. That was just before the Battery Sergeant-Major 'ad it in for 'im on account o' what 'e'd been sayin' about the Chinese wife an' the dolly-shop.'

'What did Macklin really say?' Anthony and I asked together. Humberstall gave us a fragment. It was hardly the stuff to let loose on a pious post-war world without revision.

'And what had your B.S.M. been in civil life?' I asked at the end.

' 'Ead-embalmer to an 'olesale undertaker in the Midlands,' said Humberstall; 'but, o' course, *when* he thought 'e saw his chance he naturally took it. He came along one mornin' lickin' 'is lips. "You don't get past me this time," 'e says to Macklin. "You're for it, Professor."

' " 'Ow so, me gallant Major," says Macklin; "an' what for?"

' "For writin' obese words on the breech o' the ten-inch," says the B.S.M. She was our old Skoda that I've been tellin' you about. We called 'er "Bloody Eliza." She 'ad a badly wore obturator an' blew through a fair treat. I knew by Macklin's face the B.S.M. 'ad dropped it somewhere, but all he vow'saifed was, "Very good, Major. We will consider it in Common Room." The B.S.M. couldn't ever stand Macklin's toff's way o' puttin' things; so he goes off rumblin' like 'ell's bells in an 'urricane, as the Marines say.

Macklin put it to me at once, what had I been doin'? Some'ow he could read me like a book.

'Well, all *I*'d done—an' I told 'im *he* was responsible for it—was to chalk the guns. 'Ammick never minded what the men wrote up on 'em. 'E said it gave 'em an interest in their job. You'd see all sorts of remarks chalked on the side-plates or the gear-casin's.'

'What sort of remarks?' said Anthony keenly.

'Oh! 'Ow Bloody Eliza, or Spittin' Jim—that was our old Mark Five Nine-point-two—felt that mornin', an' such things. But it 'ad come over me—more to please Macklin than anythin' else—that it was time we Janeites 'ad a look in. So, as I was tellin' you, I'd taken an' rechristened all three of 'em, on my own, early that mornin'. Spittin' Jim I 'ad chalked "The Reverend Collins"—that Curate I was tellin' you about; an' our cut-down Navy Twelve, "General Tilney," because it was worse wore in the groovin' than anything *I*'d ever seen. The Skoda (an' that was where *I* dropped it) I 'ad chalked up "The Lady Catherine De Bugg." I made a clean breast of it all to Macklin. He reached up an' patted me on the shoulder. "You done nobly," he says. "You're bringin' forth abundant fruit, like a good Janeite. But I'm afraid your spellin' has misled our worthy B.S.M. *That's* what it is," 'e says, slappin' 'is little leg. "'Ow might you 'ave spelt De Bourgh for example?"

'I told 'im. 'Twasn't right; an' 'e nips off to the Skoda to make it so. When 'e comes back, 'e says that the Gander 'ad been before 'im an' corrected the error. But we two come up before the Major, just the same, that afternoon after lunch; 'Ammick in the chair, so to speak, Mosse in another, an' the B.S.M. chargin' Macklin with writin' obese words on His Majesty's property, on active service. When it transpired that me an' not Macklin was the offendin' party, the B.S.M. turned 'is hand in and sulked like a baby. 'E as good as told 'Ammick 'e couldn't hope to preserve discipline unless examples was made—meanin', o' course, Macklin.'

'Yes, I've heard all that,' said Anthony, with a contemptuous grunt. 'The worst of it is, a lot of it's true.'

''Ammick took 'im up sharp about Military Law, which he said was even more fair than the civilian article.'

'My Gawd!' This came from Anthony's scornful midmost bosom.

' "Accordin' to the unwritten law of the 'Eavies," says 'Ammick, "there's no objection to the men chalkin' the guns, if decency is preserved. On the other 'and," says he, "we 'aven't yet settled the precise status of individuals entitled so to do. I 'old that the privilege is confined to combatants only."

' "With the permission of the Court," says Mosse, who was another born lawyer, "I'd like to be allowed to join issue on that point. Prisoner's position is very delicate an' doubtful, an' he has no legal representative."

' "Very good," says 'Ammick. "Macklin bein' acquitted——"

' "With submission, me lud," says Mosse. "I hope to prove 'e was accessory before the fact."

' "*As* you please," says 'Ammick. "But in that case, 'oo the 'ell's goin' to get the port I'm tryin' to stand the Court?"

' "I submit," says Mosse, "prisoner, bein' under direct observation o' the Court, could be temporarily enlarged for that duty."

'So Macklin went an' got it, an' the B.S.M. had 'is glass with the rest. Then they argued whether mess servants an' non-combatants was entitled to chalk the guns ('Ammick *versus* Mosse). After a bit, 'Ammick as C.O. give 'imself best, an' me an' Macklin was severely admonished for trespassin' on combatants' rights, an' the B.S.M. was warned that if we repeated the offence 'e could deal with us summ'rily. He 'ad some glasses o' port an' went out quite 'appy. Then my turn come, while Macklin was gettin' them their tea; an' one thing leadin' to another, 'Ammick put me through all the Janeite Degrees, you might say. 'Never 'ad such a doin' in my life.'

'Yes, but what did you tell 'em?' said Anthony. 'I can't ever *think* my lies quick enough when I'm for it.'

'No need to lie. I told 'em that the backside view o' the Skoda, when she was run up, put Lady De Bugg into my 'ead. They gave me right there, but they said I was wrong about General Tilney. 'Cordin' to them, our Navy twelve-inch ought to 'ave been christened Miss Bates. I said the same idea 'ad crossed my mind, till I'd seen the General's groovin'. Then I felt it had to be the General or nothin'. But they give me full marks for the Reverend Collins—our Nine-point-two.'

'An' you fed 'em *that* sort o' talk?' Anthony's fox-coloured eyebrows climbed almost into his hair.

'While I was assistin' Macklin to get tea—yes. Seein' it was an examination, I wanted to do 'im credit as a Janeite.'

'An'—an' what did they say?'

'They said it was 'ighly creditable to us both. I don't drink, so they give me about a hundred fags.'

'Gawd! What a Circus you must 'ave been,' was Anthony's gasping comment.

'It *was* a 'appy little Group. I wouldn't 'a changed with any other.'

Humberstall sighed heavily as he helped Anthony slide back the organ-panel. We all admired it in silence, while Anthony repocketed his secret polishing mixture, which lived in a tin tobacco-box. I had neglected my work for listening to Humberstall. Anthony reached out quietly and took over a Secretary's Jewel and a rag. Humberstall studied his reflection in the glossy wood.

'Almost,' he said critically, holding his head to one side.

'Not with an Army. You could with a Safety, though,' said Anthony. And, indeed, as Brother Burges had foretold, one might have shaved in it with comfort.

'Did you ever run across any of 'em afterwards, any time?' Anthony asked presently.

'Not so many of 'em left to run after, now. With the 'Eavies it's mostly neck or nothin'. We copped it. In the neck. In due time.'

'Well, *you* come out of it all right.' Anthony spoke both stoutly and soothingly; but Humberstall would not be comforted.

'That's right; but I almost wish I 'adn't,' he sighed. 'I was 'appier there than ever before or since. Jerry's March push in 'Eighteen did us in; an' yet, 'ow could we 'ave expected it? 'Ow *could* we 'ave expected it? We'd been sent back for rest an' runnin'-repairs, back pretty near our base; an' our old loco' that used to shift us about o' nights, she'd gone down the line for repairs. But for 'Ammick we wouldn't even 'ave 'ad our camouflage-screens up. He told our Brigadier that, whatever 'e might be in the Gunnery line, as a leadin' Divorce lawyer he never threw away a point in argument. So 'e 'ad us all screened in over in a cuttin' on a little spur-line near a wood; an' 'e saw to the screens 'imself. The leaves weren't more than comin' out then, an' the sun used to make our glue-paint stink. Just like actin' in a theatre, it was! But 'appy. *But* 'appy! I expect if we'd been caterpillars, like the new big six-inch hows, they'd ha' remembered us. But we was the old La Bassée '15 Mark o' Heavies that ran on rails—not much more good than scrap-iron that late in the war. An', believe me, gents—or Brethren, as I should say—we copped it cruel. Look 'ere! It was in the afternoon, an' I was watchin' Gander instructin' a class in new sights at Lady Catherine. All of a sudden I 'eard our screens rip overhead, an' a runner on a motor-bike come sailin', sailin' through the air—like that bloke that used to bicycle off Brighton Pier—and landed one awful wop almost atop o' the class. "'Old 'ard," says Gander. "That's no way to report. What's the fuss?" "Your screens 'ave broke my back, for one thing," says the bloke on the ground; "an' for another, the 'ole front's gone." "Nonsense," says Gander. 'E 'adn't more than passed the remark when the man was vi'lently sick an' conked out. 'E 'ad plenty papers on 'im from Brigadiers and C.O.'s reporting 'emselves cut off an' askin' for orders. 'E was right both ways—his back an' our front. The 'ole Somme front washed out as clean as kiss-me-'and!' His huge hand smashed down open on his knee.

'We 'eard about it at the time in the 'Oly Land. Was it reelly as quick as all that?' said Anthony.

'Quicker! Look 'ere! The motor-bike dropped in on us about four pip-emma. After that, we tried to get orders o' some kind or other, but nothin' came through excep' that all available transport was in use and not likely to be released. *That* didn't 'elp us any. About nine o'clock comes along a young Brass 'At in brown gloves. We was quite a surprise to 'im. 'E said they were evacuating the area and we'd better shift. "Where to?" says 'Ammick, rather short.

'"Oh, somewhere Amiens way," he says. "Not that I'd guarantee Amiens for any length o' time; but Amiens might do to begin with." I'm giving you the very words. Then 'e goes off swingin' 'is brown gloves, and 'Ammick sends for Gander and orders 'im to march the men through Amiens to Dieppe; book thence to New'aven, take up positions be'ind Seaford, an' carry on the war. Gander said 'e'd see 'im damned first. 'Ammick says 'e'd see 'im court-martialled after. Gander says what 'e meant to say was that the men 'ud see all an' sundry damned before they went into Amiens with their gunsights wrapped up in their puttees. 'Ammick says 'e 'adn't said a word about puttees, an' carryin' off the gunsights was purely optional. "Well, anyhow," says Gander, "puttees *or* drawers, they ain't goin' to shift a step unless you lead the procession."

'"Mutinous 'ounds," says 'Ammick. "But we live in a democratic age. D'you suppose they'd object to kindly diggin' 'emselves in a bit?" "Not at all," says Gander. "The B.S.M.'s kept 'em at it like terriers for the last three hours." "That bein' so," says 'Ammick, "Macklin'll now fetch us small glasses o' port." Then Mosse comes in—he could smell port a mile off—an' he submits we'd only add to the congestion in Amiens if we took our crowd there, whereas, if we lay doggo where we was, Jerry might miss us, though he didn't seem to be missin' much that evenin'.

'The 'ole country was pretty noisy, an' our dumps we'd lit ourselves flarin' heavens-high as far as you could see. Lyin' doggo was our best chance. I believe we might ha' pulled it off, if we'd been left alone, but along towards midnight—there was some small stuff swishin' about, but nothin' particular—a nice little bald-headed old gentleman in uniform pushes into the dug-out wipin' his glasses an' sayin' 'e was thinkin' o' formin' a defensive flank on our left with 'is battalion which 'ad just come up. 'Ammick says 'e wouldn't form much if 'e was 'im. "Oh, don't say *that*," says the old gentleman, very shocked. "One must support the Guns, mustn't one?" 'Ammick says we was refittin' an' about as effective, just then, as a public lav'tory. "Go into Amiens," he says, "an' defend 'em there." "Oh no," says the old gentleman, "me an' my laddies *must* make a defensive flank for you," an' he flips out of the dug-out like a performin' bullfinch, chirrupin' for his "laddies." Gawd in 'Eaven knows what sort o' push they was—little boys mostly—but they 'ung on to 'is coat-tails like a Sunday-school treat, an' we 'eard 'em muckin' about in the open for a bit. Then a pretty tight barrage was slapped down for ten minutes, an' 'Ammick thought the laddies had copped it already. "It'll be our turn next," says Mosse. "There's been a covey o' Gothas messin' about for the last 'alf-hour—lookin' for the Railway Shops, I expect. They're just as likely to take us." "Arisin' out o' that," says 'Ammick, "one of 'em sounds pretty low down now. We're for it, me learned colleagues!" "Jesus!" says Gander, "I believe you're right, sir." And that was the last word *I* 'eard on the matter.'

'Did they cop you then?' said Anthony.

'They did. I expect Mosse was right, an' they took us for the Railway Shops. When I come to, I was lyin' outside the cuttin', which was pretty well filled up. The Reverend Collins was all right; but Lady Catherine and the General was past prayin' for. I lay there, takin' it in, till I felt cold an' I looked at meself. Otherwise, I 'adn't much on excep' me boots. So I got up an' walked about to keep warm. Then I saw somethin' like a mushroom in the moonlight. It was the nice old gentleman's bald 'ead. I patted it. 'Im and 'is laddies 'ad copped it right enough. Some battalion run out in a 'urry from England, I suppose. They 'adn't even begun to dig in—pore little perishers! I dressed myself off 'em there, an' topped off with a British warm. Then I went back to the cuttin' an' some one says to me: "Dig, you ox, dig! Gander's under." So I 'elped shift things till I threw up blood an' bile mixed. Then I dropped, an' they brought Gander out—dead—an' laid 'im next me. 'Ammick 'ad gone too—fair tore in 'alf, the B.S.M. said; but the funny thing was he talked quite a lot before 'e died, an' nothin' to 'im below 'is stummick, they told me. Mosse we never found. 'E'd been standing by Lady Catherine. She'd up-ended an' gone back on 'em, with 'alf the cuttin' atop of 'er, by the look of things.'

'And what come to Macklin?' said Anthony.

'Dunno. . . . 'E was with 'Ammick. I expect I must ha' been blown clear of all by the first bomb; for I was the on'y Janeite left. We lost about half our crowd, either un- der, or after we'd got 'em out. The B.S.M. went off 'is rocker when mornin' came, an' he ran about from one to another sayin': "That was a good push! That was a great crowd! Did ye ever know any push to touch 'em?" An' then 'e'd cry. So what was left of us made off for ourselves, an' I came across a lorry, pretty full, but they took me in.'

'Ah!' said Anthony with pride. ' "They all take a taxi when it's rainin'." 'Ever 'eard that song?'

'They went a long way back. Then I walked a bit, an' there was a hospital-train fillin' up, an' one of the Sisters—a grey-headed one—ran at me wavin' 'er red 'ands an' sayin' there wasn't room for a louse in it. I was past carin'. But she went on talkin' an' talkin' about the war, an' her pa in Ladbroke Grove, an' 'ow strange for 'er at 'er time of life to be doin' this work with a lot o' men, an' next war, 'ow the nurses 'ud 'ave to wear khaki breeches on account o' the mud, like the Land Girls; an' that reminded 'er, she'd boil

me an egg if she could lay 'ands on one, for she'd run a
chicken-farm once. You never 'eard anythin' like it—outside o' Jane. It set me off laughin' again. Then a woman
with a nose an' teeth on 'er, marched up. "What's all this?"
she says. "What do you want?" "Nothing," I says, "only
make Miss Bates, there, stop talkin' or I'll die." "Miss
Bates?" she says. "What in 'Eaven's name makes you call
'er that?" "Because she is," I says. "D'you know what
you're sayin'?" she says, an' slings her bony arm round me
to get me off the ground. "'Course I do," I says, "an' if
you knew Jane you'd know too." "That's enough," says
she. "You're comin' on this train if I have to kill a Brigadier for you," an' she an' an ord'ly fair hove me into the
train, on to a stretcher close to the cookers. That beef-tea
went down well! Then she shook 'ands with me an' said I'd
hit off Sister Molyneux in one, an' then she pinched me an
extra blanket. It was 'er own 'ospital pretty much. I expect
she was the Lady Catherine de Bourgh of the area. Well,
an' so, to cut a long story short, nothing further transpired.'

"'Adn't you 'ad enough by then?' asked Anthony.

'I expect so. Otherwise, if the old Circus 'ad been carryin' on, I might 'ave 'ad another turn with 'em before
Armistice. Our B.S.M. was right. There never was a 'appier
push. 'Ammick an' Mosse an' Gander an' the B.S.M. an'
that pore little Macklin man makin' an' passin' an' raisin'
me an' gettin' me on to the 'ospital train after 'e was dead,
all for a couple of Bradburys. I lie awake nights still, reviewing matters. There never was a push to touch ours—
never!'

Anthony handed me back the Secretary's Jewel resplendent.

'Ah,' said he. 'No denyin' that Jane business was more
useful to you than the Roman Eagles or the Star an' Garter.
'Pity there wasn't any of you Janeites in the 'Oly Land. *I*
never come across 'em.'

'Well, as pore Macklin said, it's a very select Society, an'
you've got to be a Janeite in your 'eart, or you won't have

any success. An' yet he made *me* a Janeite! I read all her six books now for pleasure 'tween times in the shop; an' it brings it all back—down to the smell of the glue-paint on the screens. You take it from me, Brethren, there's no one to touch Jane when you're in a tight place. Gawd bless 'er, whoever she was.'

Worshipful Brother Burges, from the floor of the Lodge, called us all from Labour to Refreshment. Humberstall hove himself up—so very a cart-horse of a man one almost expected to hear the harness creak on his back—and descended the steps.

He said he could not stay for tea because he had promised his mother to come home for it, and she would most probably be waiting for him now at the Lodge door.

'One or other of 'em always comes for 'im. He's apt to miss 'is gears sometimes,' Anthony explained to me, as we followed.

'Goes on a bust, d'you mean?'

''Im! He's no more touched liquor than 'e 'as women since 'e was born. No, 'e's liable to a sort o' quiet fits, like. They came on after the dump blew up at Eatables. But for them, 'e'd ha' been Battery Sergeant-Major.'

'Oh!' I said. 'I couldn't make out why he took on as mess-waiter when he got back to his guns. That explains things a bit.'

' 'Is sister told me the dump goin' up knocked all 'is Gunnery instruction clean out of 'im. The only thing 'e stuck to was to get back to 'is old crowd. Gawd knows 'ow 'e worked it, but 'e did. He fair deserted out of England to 'em, she says; an' when they saw the state 'e was in, they 'adn't the 'eart to send 'im back or into 'ospital. They kep' 'im for a mascot, as you might say. That's *all* dead-true. 'Is sister told me so. But I can't guarantee that Janeite business, excep' 'e never told a lie since 'e was six. 'Is sister told me so. What do *you* think?'

'He isn't likely to have made it up out of his own head,' I replied.

'But people don't get so crazy-fond o' books as all that, do they? 'E's made 'is sister try to read 'em. She'd do anythin' to please him. But, as I keep tellin' 'er, so'd 'is mother. D'you 'appen to know anything about Jane?'

'I believe Jane was a bit of a match-maker in a quiet way when she was alive, and I know all her books are full of match-making,' I said. '*You'd* better look out.'

'Oh, *that's* as good as settled,' Anthony replied, blushing.

MARY POSTGATE

(1915)

Of Miss Mary Postgate, Lady McCausland wrote that she was 'thoroughly conscientious, tidy, companionable, and ladylike. I am very sorry to part with her, and shall always be interested in her welfare.'

Miss Fowler engaged her on this recommendation, and to her surprise, for she had had experience of companions, found that it was true. Miss Fowler was nearer sixty than fifty at the time, but though she needed care she did not exhaust her attendant's vitality. On the contrary, she gave out, stimulatingly and with reminiscences. Her father had been a minor Court official in the days when the Great Exhibition of 1851 had just set its seal on Civilisation made perfect. Some of Miss Fowler's tales, none the less, were not always for the young. Mary was not young, and though her speech was as colourless as her eyes or her hair, she was never shocked. She listened unflinchingly to every one; said at the end, 'How interesting!' or 'How shocking!' as the case might be, and never again referred to it, for she prided herself on a trained mind, which 'did not dwell on these things.' She was, too, a treasure at domestic accounts, for which the village tradesmen, with their weekly books, loved her not. Otherwise she had no enemies; provoked no jealousy even among the plainest; neither gossip nor slander had ever been traced to her; she supplied the odd place at the Rector's or the Doctor's table at half an hour's notice; she was a sort of public aunt to very many small children of the village street, whose parents, while accepting everything, would have been swift to resent what they called 'patronage'; she served on the Village Nursing Committee as Miss

Fowler's nominee when Miss Fowler was crippled by rheumatoid arthritis, and came out of six months' fortnightly meetings equally respected by all the cliques.

And when Fate threw Miss Fowler's nephew, an unlovely orphan of eleven, on Miss Fowler's hands, Mary Postgate stood to her share of the business of education as practised in private and public schools. She checked printed clothes-lists, and unitemised bills of extras; wrote to Head and House masters, matrons, nurses and doctors, and grieved or rejoiced over half-term reports. Young Wyndham Fowler repaid her in his holidays by calling her 'Gatepost,' 'Postey,' or 'Packthread,' by thumping her between her narrow shoulders, or by chasing her bleating, round the garden, her large mouth open, her large nose high in air, at a stiff-necked shamble very like a camel's. Later on he filled the house with clamour, argument, and harangues as to his personal needs, likes and dislikes, and the limitations of 'you women,' reducing Mary to tears of physical fatigue, or, when he chose to be humorous, of helpless laughter. At crises, which multiplied as he grew older, she was his ambassadress and his interpretress to Miss Fowler, who had no large sympathy with the young; a vote in his interest at the councils on his future; his sewing-woman, strictly accountable for mislaid boots and garments; always his butt and his slave.

And when he decided to become a solicitor, and had entered an office in London; when his greeting had changed from 'Hullo, Postey, you old beast,' to 'Mornin', Packthread,' there came a war which, unlike all wars that Mary could remember, did not stay decently outside England and in the newspapers, but intruded on the lives of people whom she knew. As she said to Miss Fowler, it was 'most vexatious.' It took the Rector's son who was going into business with his elder brother; it took the Colonel's nephew on the eve of fruit-farming in Canada; it took Mrs. Grant's son who, his mother said, was devoted to the ministry; and, very early indeed, it took Wynn Fowler, who announced on a postcard that he had joined the Flying Corps and wanted a cardigan waistcoat.

'He must go, and he must have the waistcoat,' said Miss Fowler. So Mary got the proper-sized needles and wool, while Miss Fowler told the men of her establishment—two gardeners and an odd man, aged sixty—that those who could join the Army had better do so. The gardeners left. Cheape, the odd man, stayed on, and was promoted to the gardener's cottage. The cook, scorning to be limited in luxuries, also left, after a spirited scene with Miss Fowler, and took the housemaid with her. Miss Fowler gazetted Nellie, Cheape's seventeen-year-old daughter, to the vacant post; Mrs. Cheape to the rank of cook, with occasional cleaning bouts; and the reduced establishment moved forward smoothly.

Wynn demanded an increase in his allowance. Miss Fowler, who always looked facts in the face, said, 'He must have it. The chances are he won't live long to draw it, and if three hundred makes him happy——'

Wynn was grateful, and came over, in his tight-buttoned uniform, to say so. His training centre was not thirty miles away, and his talk was so technical that it had to be explained by charts of the various types of machines. He gave Mary such a chart.

'And you'd better study it, Postey,' he said. 'You'll be seeing a lot of 'em soon.' So Mary studied the chart, but when Wynn next arrived to swell and exalt himself before his womenfolk, she failed badly in cross-examination, and he rated her as in the old days.

'You *look* more or less like a human being,' he said in his new Service voice. 'You *must* have had a brain at some time in your past. What have you done with it? Where d'you keep it? A sheep would know more than you do, Postey. You're lamentable. You are less use than an empty tin can, you dowey old cassowary.'

'I suppose that's how your superior officer talks to *you?*' said Miss Fowler from her chair.

'But Postey doesn't mind,' Wynn replied. 'Do you, Pack-thread?'

'Why? Was Wynn saying anything? I shall get this right next time you come,' she muttered, and knitted her pale brows again over the diagrams of Taubes, Farmans, and Zeppelins.

In a few weeks the mere land and sea battles which she read to Miss Fowler after breakfast passed her like idle breath. Her heart and her interest were high in the air with Wynn, who had finished 'rolling' (whatever that might be) and had gone on from a 'taxi' to a machine more or less his own. One morning it circled over their very chimneys, alighted on Vegg's Heath, almost outside the garden gate, and Wynn came in, blue with cold, shouting for food. He and she drew Miss Fowler's bath-chair, as they had often done, along the Heath foot-path to look at the biplane. Mary observed that 'it smelt very badly.'

'Postey, I believe you think with your nose,' said Wynn. 'I know you don't with your mind. Now, what type's that?'

'I'll go and get the chart,' said Mary.

'You're hopeless! You haven't the mental capacity of a white mouse,' he cried, and explained the dials and the sockets for bomb-dropping till it was time to mount and ride the wet clouds once more.

'Ah!' said Mary, as the stinking thing flared upward. 'Wait till our Flying Corps gets to work! Wynn says it's much safer than in the trenches.'

'I wonder,' said Miss Fowler. 'Tell Cheape to come and tow me home again.'

'It's all downhill. I can do it,' said Mary, 'if you put the brake on.' She laid her lean self against the pushing-bar and home they trundled.

'Now, be careful you aren't heated and catch a chill,' said overdressed Miss Fowler.

'Nothing makes me perspire,' said Mary. As she bumped the chair under the porch she straightened her long back. The exertion had given her a colour, and the wind had loosened a wisp of hair across her forehead. Miss Fowler glanced at her.

'What do you ever think of, Mary?' she demanded suddenly.

'Oh, Wynn says he wants another three pairs of stockings —as thick as we can make them.'

'Yes. But I mean the things that women think about. Here you are, more than forty——'

'Forty-four,' said truthful Mary.

'Well?'

'Well?' Mary offered Miss Fowler her shoulder as usual.

'And you've been with me ten years now.'

'Let's see,' said Mary. 'Wynn was eleven when he came. He's twenty now, and I came two years before that. It must be eleven.'

'Eleven! And you've never told me anything that matters in all that while. Looking back, it seems to me that *I've* done all the talking.'

'I'm afraid I'm not much of a conversationalist. As Wynn says, I haven't the mind. Let me take your hat.'

Miss Fowler, moving stiffly from the hip, stamped her rubber-tipped stick on the tiled hall floor. 'Mary, aren't you *anything* except a companion? Would you *ever* have been anything except a companion?'

Mary hung up the garden hat on its proper peg. 'No,' she said after consideration. 'I don't imagine I ever should. But I've no imagination, I'm afraid.'

She fetched Miss Fowler her eleven-o'clock glass of Contrexeville.

That was the wet December when it rained six inches to the month, and the women went abroad as little as might be. Wynn's flying chariot visited them several times, and for two mornings (he had warned her by postcard) Mary heard the thresh of his propellers at dawn. The second time she ran to the window, and stared at the whitening sky. A little blur passed overhead. She lifted her lean arms towards it.

That evening at six o'clock there came an announcement
in an official envelope that Second Lieutenant W. Fowler
had been killed during a trial flight. Death was instantaneous. She read it and carried it to Miss Fowler.

'I never expected anything else,' said Miss Fowler; 'but
I'm sorry it happened before he had done anything.'

The room was whirling round Mary Postgate, but she
found herself quite steady in the midst of it.

'Yes,' she said. 'It's a great pity he didn't die in action
after he had killed somebody.'

'He was killed instantly. That's one comfort,' Miss
Fowler went on.

'But Wynn says the shock of a fall kills a man at once—
whatever happens to the tanks,' quoted Mary.

The room was coming to rest now. She heard Miss
Fowler say impatiently, 'But why can't we cry, Mary?' and
herself replying, 'There's nothing to cry for. He has done
his duty as much as Mrs. Grant's son did.'

'And when he died, *she* came and cried all the morning,'
said Miss Fowler. 'This only makes me feel tired—terribly
tired. Will you help me to bed, please, Mary?—And I think
I'd like the hot-water bottle.'

So Mary helped her and sat beside, talking of Wynn in
his riotous youth.

'I believe,' said Miss Fowler suddenly, 'that old people
and young people slip from under a stroke like this. The
middle-aged feel it most.'

'I expect that's true,' said Mary, rising. 'I'm going to put
away the things in his room now. Shall we wear mourning?'

'Certainly not,' said Miss Fowler. 'Except, of course, at
the funeral. I can't go. You will. I want you to arrange
about his being buried here. What a blessing it didn't happen at Salisbury!'

Every one, from the Authorities of the Flying Corps to
the Rector, was most kind and sympathetic. Mary found
herself for the moment in a world where bodies were in
the habit of being despatched by all sorts of conveyances to
all sorts of places. And at the funeral two young men in

buttoned-up uniforms stood beside the grave and spoke to her afterwards.

'You're Miss Postgate, aren't you?' said one. 'Fowler told me about you. He was a good chap—a first-class fellow—a great loss.'

'Great loss!' growled his companion. 'We're all awfully sorry.'

'How high did he fall from?' Mary whispered.

'Pretty nearly four thousand feet, I should think, didn't he? You were up that day, Monkey?'

'All of that,' the other child replied. 'My bar made three thousand, and I wasn't as high as him by a lot.'

'Then *that's* all right,' said Mary. 'Thank you very much.'

They moved away as Mrs. Grant flung herself weeping on Mary's flat chest, under the lych-gate, and cried, '*I* know how it feels! *I* know how it feels!'

'But both his parents are dead,' Mary returned, as she fended her off. 'Perhaps they've all met by now,' she added vaguely as she escaped towards the coach.

'I've thought of that too,' wailed Mrs. Grant; 'but then he'll be practically a stranger to them. Quite embarrassing!'

Mary faithfully reported every detail of the ceremony to Miss Fowler, who, when she described Mrs. Grant's outburst, laughed aloud.

'Oh, how Wynn would have enjoyed it! He was always utterly unreliable at funerals. D'you remember——' And they talked of him again, each piecing out the other's gaps. 'And now,' said Miss Fowler, 'we'll pull up the blinds and we'll have a general tidy. That always does us good. Have you seen to Wynn's things?'

'Everything—since he first came,' said Mary. 'He was never destructive—even with his toys.'

They faced that neat room.

'It can't be natural not to cry,' Mary said at last. 'I'm *so* afraid you'll have a reaction.'

'As I told you, we old people slip from under the stroke. It's you I'm afraid for. Have you cried yet?'

'I can't. It only makes me angry with the Germans.'

'That's sheer waste of vitality,' said Miss Fowler. 'We must live till the war's finished.' She opened a full wardrobe. 'Now, I've been thinking things over. This is my plan. All his civilian clothes can be given away—Belgian refugees, and so on.'

Mary nodded. 'Boots, collars, and gloves?'

'Yes. We don't need to keep anything except his cap and belt.'

'They came back yesterday with his Flying Corps clothes' —Mary pointed to a roll on the little iron bed.

'Ah, but keep his Service things. Some one may be glad of them later. Do you remember his sizes?'

'Five feet eight and a half; thirty-six inches round the chest. But he told me he's just put on an inch and a half. I'll mark it on a label and tie it on his sleeping-bag.'

'So that disposes of *that*,' said Miss Fowler, tapping the palm of one hand with the ringed third finger of the other. 'What waste it all is! We'll get his old school trunk to-morrow and pack his civilian clothes.'

'And the rest?' said Mary. 'His books and pictures and the games and the toys—and—and the rest?'

'My plan is to burn every single thing,' said Miss Fowler. 'Then we shall know where they are and no one can handle them afterwards. What do you think?'

'I think that would be much the best,' said Mary. 'But there's such a lot of them.'

'We'll burn them in the destructor,' said Miss Fowler. This was an open-air furnace for the consumption of refuse; a little circular four-foot tower of pierced brick over an iron grating. Miss Fowler had noticed the design in a gardening journal years ago, and had had it built at the bottom of the garden. It suited her tidy soul, for it saved unsightly rubbish-heaps, and the ashes lightened the stiff clay soil.

Mary considered for a moment, saw her way clear, and nodded again. They spent the evening putting away well-remembered civilian suits, underclothes that Mary had marked, and the regiments of very gaudy socks and ties. A second trunk was needed, and, after that, a little packing-case, and it was late next day when Cheape and the local carrier lifted them to the cart. The Rector luckily knew of a friend's son, about five feet eight and a half inches high, to whom a complete Flying Corps outfit would be most acceptable, and sent his gardener's son down with a barrow to take delivery of it. The cap was hung up in Miss Fowler's bedroom, the belt in Miss Postgate's; for, as Miss Fowler said, they had no desire to make tea-party talk of them.

'That disposes of *that*,' said Miss Fowler. 'I'll leave the rest to you, Mary. I can't run up and down the garden. You'd better take the big clothes-basket and get Nellie to help you.'

'I shall take the wheelbarrow and do it myself,' said Mary, and for once in her life closed her mouth.

Miss Fowler, in moments of irritation, had called Mary deadly methodical. She put on her oldest waterproof and gardening-hat and her ever-slipping goloshes, for the weather was on the edge of more rain. She gathered fire-lighters from the kitchen, a half-scuttle of coals, and a faggot of brushwood. These she wheeled in the barrow down the mossed paths to the dank little laurel shrubbery where the destructor stood under the drip of three oaks. She climbed the wire fence into the Rector's glebe just behind, and from his tenant's rick pulled two large armfuls of good hay, which she spread neatly on the fire-bars. Next, journey by journey, passing Miss Fowler's white face at the morning-room window each time, she brought down in the towel-covered clothes-basket, on the wheelbarrow, thumbed and used Hentys, Marryats, Levers, Stevensons, Baroness Orczys, Garvices, schoolbooks, and atlases, unrelated piles of the *Motor Cyclist,* the *Light Car,* and catalogues of Olympia Exhibitions; the remnants of a fleet of sailing-ships from nine-penny cutters to a three-guinea yacht; a prep.-school dressing-gown; bats from three-and-sixpence to twenty-four shillings; cricket and tennis balls; disintegrated steam and clockwork locomotives with their twisted rails; a grey and red tin model of a submarine; a dumb gramophone and cracked records; golf-clubs that had to be broken across the knee, like his walking-sticks, and an assegai; photographs of private and public school cricket and football elevens, and his O.T.C. on the line of march; kodaks, and film-rolls; some pewters, and one real silver cup, for boxing competitions and Junior Hurdles; sheaves of school photographs; Miss Fowler's photograph; her own which he had borne off in fun and (good care she took not to ask!) had never returned; a playbox with a secret drawer; a load of flannels, belts, and jerseys, and a pair of spiked shoes unearthed in the attic; a packet of all the letters that Miss Fowler and she had ever written to him, kept for some absurd reason through all these years; a five-day attempt at a diary; framed pictures of racing motors in full Brooklands career, and load upon load of undistinguishable wreckage of tool-boxes, rabbit-hutches, electric batteries, tin soldiers, fret-saw outfits, and jig-saw puzzles.

Miss Fowler at the window watched her come and go, and said to herself, 'Mary's an old woman. I never realised it before.'

After lunch she recommended her to rest.

'I'm not in the least tired,' said Mary. 'I've got it all arranged. I'm going to the village at two o'clock for some paraffin. Nellie hasn't enough, and the walk will do me good.'

She made one last quest round the house before she started, and found that she had overlooked nothing. It began to mist as soon as she had skirted Vegg's Heath, where Wynn used to descend—it seemed to her that she could almost hear the beat of his propellers overhead, but there was nothing to see. She hoisted her umbrella and lunged into the blind wet till she had reached the shelter of the empty village. As she came out of Mr. Kidd's shop with a bottle full of paraffin in her string shopping-bag, she met Nurse Eden, the village nurse, and fell into talk with her, as usual, about the village children. They were just parting opposite the 'Royal Oak,' when a gun, they fancied, was fired immediately behind the house. It was followed by a child's shriek dying into a wail.

'Accident!' said Nurse Eden promptly, and dashed through the empty bar, followed by Mary. They found Mrs. Gerritt, the publican's wife, who could only gasp and point to the yard, where a little cart-lodge was sliding sideways amid a clatter of tiles. Nurse Eden snatched up a sheet drying before the fire, ran out, lifted something from the ground, and flung the sheet round it. The sheet turned scarlet and half her uniform too, as she bore the load into the kitchen. It was little Edna Gerritt, aged nine, whom Mary had known since her perambulator days.

'Am I hurted bad?' Edna asked, and died between Nurse Eden's dripping hands. The sheet fell aside and for an instant, before she could shut her eyes, Mary saw the ripped and shredded body.

'It's a wonder she spoke at all,' said Nurse Eden. 'What in God's name was it?'

'A bomb,' said Mary.

'One o' the Zeppelins?'

'No. An aeroplane. I thought I heard it on the Heath, but I fancied it was one of ours. It must have shut off its engines as it came down. That's why we didn't notice it.'

'The filthy pigs!' said Nurse Eden, all white and shaken. 'See the pickle I'm in! Go and tell Dr. Hennis, Miss Postgate.' Nurse looked at the mother, who had dropped face down on the floor. 'She's only in a fit. Turn her over.'

Mary heaved Mrs. Gerritt right side up, and hurried off for the doctor. When she told her tale, he asked her to sit down in the surgery till he got her something.

'But I don't need it, I assure you,' said she. 'I don't think it would be wise to tell Miss Fowler about it, do you? Her heart is so irritable in this weather.'

Dr. Hennis looked at her admiringly as he packed up his bag.

'No. Don't tell anybody till we're sure,' he said, and hastened to the 'Royal Oak,' while Mary went on with the paraffin. The village behind her was as quiet as usual, for the news had not yet spread. She frowned a little to herself, her large nostrils expanded uglily, and from time to time she muttered a phrase which Wynn, who never restrained himself before his womenfolk, had applied to the enemy. 'Bloody pagans! They *are* bloody pagans. But,' she continued, falling back on the teaching that had made her what she was, 'one mustn't let one's mind dwell on these things.'

Before she reached the house Dr. Hennis, who was also a special constable, overtook her in his car.

'Oh, Miss Postgate,' he said, 'I wanted to tell you that that accident at the "Royal Oak" was due to Gerritt's stable tumbling down. It's been dangerous for a long time. It ought to have been condemned.'

'I thought I heard an explosion too,' said Mary.

'You might have been misled by the beams snapping. I've been looking at 'em. They were dry-rotted through and through. Of course, as they broke, they would make a noise just like a gun.'

'Yes?' said Mary politely.

'Poor little Edna was playing underneath it,' he went on, still holding her with his eyes, 'and that and the tiles cut her to pieces, you see?'

'I saw it,' said Mary, shaking her head. 'I heard it too.'

'Well, we cannot be sure.' Dr. Hennis changed his tone completely. 'I know both you and Nurse Eden (I've been speaking to her) are perfectly trustworthy, and I can rely on you not to say anything—yet at least. It is no good to stir up people unless——'

'Oh, I never do—anyhow,' said Mary, and Dr. Hennis went on to the county town.

After all, she told herself, it might, just possibly, have been the collapse of the old stable that had done all those things to poor little Edna. She was sorry she had even hinted at other things, but Nurse Eden was discretion itself. By the time she reached home the affair seemed increasingly remote by its very monstrosity. As she came in, Miss Fowler told her that a couple of aeroplanes had passed half an hour ago.

'I thought I heard them,' she replied, 'I'm going down to the garden now. I've got the paraffin.'

'Yes, but—what *have* you got on your boots? They're soaking wet. Change them at once.'

Not only did Mary obey but she wrapped the boots in a newspaper, and put them into the string bag with the bottle. So, armed with the longest kitchen poker, she left.

'It's raining again,' was Miss Fowler's last word, 'but—I know you won't be happy till that's disposed of.'

'It won't take long. I've got everything down there, and I've put the lid on the destructor to keep the wet out.'

The shrubbery was filling with twilight by the time she had completed her arrangements and sprinkled the sacrificial oil. As she lit the match that would burn her heart to ashes, she heard a groan or a grunt behind the dense Portugal laurels.

'Cheape?' she called impatiently, but Cheape, with his ancient lumbago, in his comfortable cottage would be the last man to profane the sanctuary. 'Sheep,' she concluded, and threw in the fusee. The pyre went up in a roar, and the immediate flame hastened night around her.

'How Wynn would have loved this!' she thought, stepping back from the blaze.

By its light she saw, half hidden behind a laurel not five paces away, a bareheaded man sitting very stiffly at the foot of one of the oaks. A broken branch lay across his lap—one booted leg protruding from beneath it. His head moved ceaselessly from side to side, but his body was as still as the tree's trunk. He was dressed—she moved sideways to look more closely—in a uniform something like Wynn's, with a flap buttoned across the chest. For an instant, she had some idea that it might be one of the young flying men she had met at the funeral. But their heads were dark and glossy. This man's was as pale as a baby's, and so closely cropped that she could see the disgusting pinky skin beneath. His lips moved.

'What do you say?' Mary moved towards him and stooped.

'Laty! Laty! Laty!' he muttered, while his hands picked at the dead wet leaves. There was no doubt as to his nationality. It made her so angry that she strode back to the destructor, though it was still too hot to use the poker there. Wynn's books seemed to be catching well. She looked up at the oak behind the man; several of the light upper and two or three rotten lower branches had broken and scattered their rubbish on the shrubbery path. On the lowest fork a helmet with dependent strings, showed like a bird's-nest in the light of a long-tongued flame. Evidently this person had fallen through the tree. Wynn had told her that it was quite possible for people to fall out of aeroplanes. Wynn told her too, that trees were useful things to break an aviator's fall, but in this case the aviator must have been broken or he would have moved from his queer position. He seemed helpless except for his horrible rolling head. On the other hand, she could see a pistol case at his belt—and Mary loathed pistols. Months ago, after reading certain Belgian reports together, she and Miss Fowler had had dealings with one—a huge revolver with flat-nosed bullets, which latter, Wynn said, were forbidden by the rules of war to be used against civilised enemies. 'They're good enough for us,' Miss Fowler had replied. 'Show Mary how it works.' And Wynn, laughing at the mere possibility of any such need, had led the craven winking Mary into the Rector's disused quarry, and had shown her how to fire the terrible machine. It lay now in the top-left-hand drawer of her toilet-table—a memento not included in the burning. Wynn would be pleased to see how she was not afraid.

She slipped up to the house to get it. When she came through the rain, the eyes in the head were alive with expectation. The mouth even tried to smile. But at sight of the revolver its corners went down just like Edna Gerritt's. A tear trickled from one eye, and the head rolled from shoulder to shoulder as though trying to point out something.

'Cassée. Tout cassée,' it whimpered.

'What do you say?' said Mary disgustedly, keeping well to one side, though only the head moved.

'Cassée,' it repeated. 'Che me rends. Le médicin! Toctor!'

'Nein!' said she, bringing all her small German to bear with the big pistol. 'Ich haben der todt Kinder gesehn.'

The head was still. Mary's hand dropped. She had been careful to keep her finger off the trigger for fear of accidents. After a few moments' waiting, she returned to the destructor, where the flames were falling, and churned up Wynn's charring books with the poker. Again the head groaned for the doctor.

'Stop that!' said Mary, and stamped her foot. 'Stop that, you bloody pagan!'

The words came quite smoothly and naturally. They were Wynn's own words, and Wynn was a gentleman who for no consideration on earth would have torn little Edna into those vividly coloured strips and strings. But this thing hunched under the oak-tree had done that thing. It was no question of reading horrors out of newspapers to Miss Fowler. Mary had seen it with her own eyes on the 'Royal Oak' kitchen table. She must not allow her mind to dwell upon it. Now Wynn was dead, and everything connected with him was lumping and rustling and tinkling under her busy poker into red black dust and grey leaves of ash. The thing beneath the oak would die too. Mary had seen death more than once. She came of a family that had a knack of dying under, as she told Miss Fowler, 'most distressing circumstances.' She would stay where she was till she was entirely satisfied that It was dead—dead as dear papa in the late 'eighties; aunt Mary in 'eighty-nine; mamma in 'ninety-one; cousin Dick in 'ninety-five; Lady McCausland's housemaid in 'ninety-nine; Lady McCausland's sister in nineteen hundred and one; Wynn buried five days ago; and Edna Gerritt still waiting for decent earth to hide her. As she thought—her underlip caught up by one faded canine, brows knit and nostrils wide—she wielded the poker with lunges that jarred the grating at the bottom, and careful scrapes round the brickwork above. She looked at her

wrist-watch. It was getting on to half-past four, and the
rain was coming down in earnest. Tea would be at five. If
It did not die before that time, she would be soaked and
would have to change. Meantime, and this occupied her,
Wynn's things were burning well in spite of the hissing wet,
though now and again a book-back with a quite distinguish-
able title would be heaved up out of the mass. The exercise
of stoking had given her a glow which seemed to reach
to the marrow of her bones. She hummed—Mary never had
a voice—to herself. She had never believed in all those advanced views—though Miss Fowler herself leaned a little
that way—of woman's work in the world; but now she saw
there was much to be said for them. This, for instance, was
her work—work which no man, least of all Dr. Hennis,
would ever have done. A man, at such a crisis, would be
what Wynn called a 'sportsman'; would leave everything to
fetch help, and would certainly bring It into the house. Now
a woman's business was to make a happy home for—for a
husband and children. Failing these—it was not a thing one
should allow one's mind to dwell upon—but——

'Stop it!' Mary cried once more across the shadows.
'Nein, I tell you! Ich haben der todt Kinder gesehn.'

But it was a fact. A woman who had missed these things
could still be useful—more useful than a man in certain
respects. She thumped like a pavior through the settling
ashes at the secret thrill of it. The rain was damping the
fire, but she could feel—it was too dark to see—that her
work was done. There was a dull red glow at the bottom
of the destructor, not enough to char the wooden lid if she
slipped it half over against the driving wet. This arranged,
she leaned on the poker and waited, while an increasing
rapture laid hold on her. She ceased to think. She gave
herself up to feel. Her long pleasure was broken by a
sound that she had waited for in agony several times in her
life. She leaned forward and listened, smiling. There could
be no mistake. She closed her eyes and drank it in. Once it
ceased abruptly.

'Go on,' she murmured, half aloud. 'That isn't the end.'

Then the end came very distinctly in a lull between two rain-gusts. Mary Postgate drew her breath short between her teeth and shivered from head to foot. '*That's* all right,' said she contentedly, and went up to the house, where she scandalised the whole routine by taking a luxurious hot bath before tea, and came down looking, as Miss Fowler said when she saw her lying all relaxed on the other sofa, 'quite handsome!'

DAYSPRING MISHANDLED

> C'est moi, c'est moi, c'est moi!
> Je suis la Mandragore!
> La fille des beaux jours qui s'éveille à l'aurore—
> Et qui chante pour toi!
>
> C. NODIER.

In the days beyond compare and before the Judgments, a genius called Graydon foresaw that the advance of education and the standard of living would submerge all mind-marks in one mudrush of standardised reading-matter, and so created the Fictional Supply Syndicate to meet the demand.

Since a few days' work for him brought them more money than a week's elsewhere, he drew many young men —some now eminent—into his employ. He bade them keep their eyes on the Sixpenny Dream Book, the Army and Navy Stores Catalogue (this for backgrounds and furniture as they changed), and *The Hearthstone Friend,* a weekly publication which specialised unrivalledly in the domestic emotions. Yet, even so, youth would not be denied, and some of the collaborated love-talk in 'Passion Hath Peril,' and 'Ena's Lost Lovers,' and the account of the murder of the Earl in 'The Wickwire Tragedies'—to name but a few masterpieces now never mentioned for fear of blackmail —was as good as anything to which their authors signed their real names in more distinquished years.

Among the young ravens driven to roost awhile on Graydon's ark was James Andrew Manallace—a darkish, slow northerner of the type that does not ignite, but must be detonated. Given written or verbal outlines of a plot, he was useless; but, with a half-dozen pictures round which to write his tale, he could astonish.

And he adored that woman who afterwards became the mother of Vidal Benzaquen,[1] and who suffered and died because she loved one unworthy. There was, also, among the company a mannered, bellied person called Alured Castorley, who talked and wrote about 'Bohemia,' but was always afraid of being 'compromised' by the weekly suppers at Neminaka's Café in Hestern Square, where the Syndicate work was apportioned, and where everyone looked out for himself. He, too, for a time, had loved Vidal's mother, in his own way.

Now, one Saturday at Neminaka's, Graydon, who had given Manallace a sheaf of prints—torn from an extinct children's book called *Philippa's Queen*—on which to improvise, asked for results. Manallace went down into his ulster-pocket, hesitated a moment, and said the stuff had turned into poetry on his hands.

'Bosh!'

'That's what it isn't,' the boy retorted. 'It's rather good.'

'Then it's no use to us.' Graydon laughed. 'Have you brought back the cuts?'

Manallace handed them over. There was a castle in the series; a knight or so in armour; an old lady in a horned head-dress; a young ditto; a very obvious Hebrew; a clerk, with pen and inkhorn, checking wine-barrels on a wharf; and a Crusader. On the back of one of the prints was a note, 'If he doesn't want to go, why can't he be captured and held to ransom?' Graydon asked what it all meant.

'I don't know yet. A comic opera, perhaps,' said Manallace.

Graydon, who seldom wasted time, passed the cuts on to someone else, and advanced Manallace a couple of sovereigns to carry on with, as usual; at which Castorley was angry and would have said something unpleasant but was

[1] 'The Village that voted the Earth was Flat.' *A Diversity of Creatures.*

suppressed. Half-way through supper, Castorley told the company that a relative had died and left him an independence; and that he now withdrew from 'hackwork' to follow 'Literature.' Generally, the Syndicate rejoiced in a comrade's good fortune, but Castorley had gifts of waking dislike. So the news was received with a vote of thanks, and he went out before the end, and, it was said, proposed to 'Dal Benzaquen's mother, who refused him. He did not come back. Manallace, who had arrived a little exalted, got so drunk before midnight that a man had to stay and see him home. But liquor never touched him above the belt, and when he had slept awhile, he recited to the gas-chandelier the poetry he had made out of the pictures; said that, on second thoughts, he would convert it into comic opera; deplored the Upas-tree influence of Gilbert and Sullivan; sang somewhat to illustrate his point; and—after words, by the way, with a negress in yellow satin—was steered to his rooms.

In the course of a few years, Graydon's foresight and genius were rewarded. The public began to read and reason upon higher planes, and the Syndicate grew rich. Later still, people demanded of their printed matter what they expected in their clothing and furniture. So, precisely as the three guinea hand-bag is followed in three weeks by its thirteen and sevenpence ha'penny, indistinguishable sister, they enjoyed perfect synthetic substitutes for Plot, Sentiment, and Emotion. Graydon died before the Cinema-caption school came in, but he left his widow twenty-seven thousand pounds.

Manallace made a reputation, and, more important, money for Vidal's mother when her husband ran away and the first symptoms of her paralysis showed. His line was the jocundly-sentimental Wardour Street brand of adventure, told in a style that exactly met, but never exceeded, every expectation.

As he once said when urged to 'write a real book': 'I've got my label, and I'm not going to chew it off. If you save people thinking, you can do anything with 'em.' His output apart, he was genuinely a man of letters. He rented a small cottage in the country and economised on everything, except the care and charges of Vidal's mother.

Castorley flew higher. When his legacy freed him from 'hackwork,' he became first a critic—in which calling he loyally scalped all his old associates as they came up—and then looked for some speciality. Having found it (Chaucer was the prey), he consolidated his position before he occupied it, by his careful speech, his cultivated bearing, and the whispered words of his friends whom he, too, had saved the trouble of thinking. It followed that, when he published his first serious articles on Chaucer, all the world which is interested in Chaucer said: 'This is an authority.' But he was no impostor. He learned and knew his poet and his age; and in a month-long dog-fight in an austere literary weekly, met and mangled a recognised Chaucer expert of the day. He also, 'for old sake's sake,' as he wrote to a friend, went out of his way to review one of Manallace's books with an intimacy of unclean deduction (this was before the days of Freud) which long stood as a record. Some member of the extinct Syndicate took occasion to ask him if he would—for old sake's sake—help Vidal's mother to a new treatment. He answered that he had 'known the lady very slightly and the calls on his purse were so heavy that,' etc. The writer showed the letter to Manallace, who said he was glad Castorley hadn't interfered. Vidal's mother was then wholly paralysed. Only her eyes could move, and those always looked for the husband who had left her. She died thus in Manallace's arms in April of the first year of the War.

During the War he and Castorley worked as some sort of departmental dishwashers in the Office of Co-ordinated Supervisals. Here Manallace came to know Castorley again. Castorley, having a sweet tooth, cadged lumps of sugar for his tea from a typist, and when she took to giving them to a younger man, arranged that she should be reported for smoking in unauthorised apartments. Manallace possessed himself of every detail of the affair, as compensation for the review of his book. Then there came a night when, waiting for a big air-raid, the two men had talked humanly, and Manallace spoke of Vidal's mother. Castorley said something in reply, and from that hour—as was learned several years later—Manallace's real life-work and interests began.

The War over, Castorley set about to make himself Supreme Pontiff on Chaucer by methods not far removed from the employment of poison-gas. The English Pope was silent, through private griefs, and influenza had carried off the learned Hun who claimed continental allegiance. Thus Castorley crowed unchallenged from Upsala to Seville, while Manallace went back to his cottage with the photo of Vidal's mother over the mantelpiece. She seemed to have emptied out his life, and left him only fleeting interests in trifles. His private diversions were experiments of uncertain outcome, which, he said, rested him after a day's gadzooking and vitalstapping. I found him, for instance, one weekend, in his toolshed-scullery, boiling a brew of slimy barks which were, if mixed with oak-galls, vitriol and wine, to become an ink-powder. We boiled it till the Monday, and it turned into an adhesive stronger than birdlime, and entangled us both.

At other times, he would carry me off, once in a few weeks, to sit at Castorley's feet, and hear him talk about Chaucer. Castorley's voice, bad enough in youth, when it could be shouted down, had, with culture and tact, grown almost insupportable. His mannerisms, too, had multiplied and set. He minced and mouthed, postured and chewed his words throughout those terrible evenings; and poisoned not only Chaucer, but every shred of English literature which he used to embellish him. He was shameless, too, as regarded self-advertisement and 'recognition'—weaving elaborate intrigues; forming petty friendships and confederacies, to be dissolved next week in favour of more promising alliances; fawning, snubbing, lecturing, organising and lying as unrestingly as a politician, in chase of the Knighthood due not to him (he always called on his Maker to forbid such a thought) but as tribute to Chaucer. Yet, sometimes,

he could break from his obsession and prove how a man's
work will try to save the soul of him. He would tell us
charmingly of copyists of the fifteenth century in England
and the Low Countries, who had multiplied the Chaucer
MSS., of which there remained—he gave us the exact number—and how each scribe could by him (and, he implied,
by him alone) be distinguished from every other by some
peculiarity of letter-formation, spacing or like trick of pen-
work; and how he could fix the dates of their work within
five years. Sometimes he would give us an hour of really
interesting stuff and then return to his overdue 'recognition.'
The changes sickened me, but Manallace defended him, as
a master in his own line who had revealed Chaucer to at
least one grateful soul.

This, as far as I remembered, was the autumn when
Manallace holidayed in the Shetlands or the Faroes, and
came back with a stone 'quern'—a hand corn-grinder. He
said it interested him from the ethnological standpoint. His
whim lasted till next harvest, and was followed by a religious spasm which, naturally, translated itself into literature. He showed me a battered and mutilated Vulgate of
1485, patched up the back with bits of legal parchments,
which he had bought for thirty-five shillings. Some monk's
attempt to rubricate chapter-initials had caught, it seemed,
his forlorn fancy, and he dabbled in shells of gold and
silver paint for weeks.

That also faded out, and he went to the Continent to get
local colour for a love-story, about Alva and the Dutch,
and the next year I saw practically nothing of him. This
released me from seeing much of Castorley, but, at intervals, I would go there to dine with him, when his wife—an
unappetising, ash-coloured woman—made no secret that his
friends wearied her almost as much as he did. But at a
later meeting, not long after Manallace had finished his
Low Countries' novel, I found Castorley charged to burst-
ing-point with triumph and high information hardly with-
held. He confided to me that a time was at hand when great
matters would be made plain, and 'recognition' would be

inevitable. I assumed, naturally, that there was fresh scandal or heresy afoot in Chaucer circles, and kept my curiosity within bounds.

In time, New York cabled that a fragment of a hitherto unknown Canterbury Tale lay safe in the steel-walled vaults of the seven-million-dollar Sunnapia Collection. It was news on an international scale—the New World exultant—the Old deploring the 'burden of British taxation which drove such treasures, etc.,' and the lighter-minded journals disporting themselves according to their publics; for 'our Dan,' as one earnest Sunday editor observed, 'lies closer to the national heart than we wot of.' Common decency made me call on Castorley, who, to my surprise, had not yet descended into the arena. I found him, made young again by joy, deep in just-passed proofs.

Yes, he said, it was all true. He had, of course, been in it from the first. There had been found one hundred and seven new lines of Chaucer tacked on to an abridged end of *The Persone's Tale*, the whole the work of Abraham Mentzius, better known as Mentzel of Antwerp (1388–1438/9)—I might remember he had talked about him—whose distinguishing peculiarities were a certain Byzantine formation of his *g*'s, the use of a 'sickle-slanted' reed-pen, which cut into the vellum at certain letters; and, above all, a tendency to spell English words on Dutch lines, whereof the manuscript carried one convincing proof. For instance (he wrote it out for me), a girl praying against an undesired marriage, says:—

'Ah Jesu-Moder, pitie my oe peyne.
Daiespringe mishandeelt cometh nat agayne.'

Would I, please, note the spelling of 'mishandeelt'? Stark Dutch and Mentzel's besetting sin! But in *his* position one took nothing for granted. The page had been part of the stiffening of the side of an old Bible, bought in a parcel by Dredd, the big dealer, because it had some rubricated chapter-initials, and by Dredd shipped, with a consignment of similar odds and ends, to the Sunnapia Collection, where they were making a glass-cased exhibit of the whole history of illumination and did not care how many books they gutted for that purpose. There, someone who noticed a crack in the back of the volume had unearthed it. He went on: 'They didn't know what to make of the thing at first. But they knew about *me!* They kept quiet till I'd been consulted. You might have noticed I was out of England for three months.

'I was over there, of course. It was what is called a "spoil"—a page Mentzel had spoiled with his Dutch spelling —I expect he had had the English dictated to him—then had evidently used the vellum for trying out his reeds; and then, I suppose, had put it away. The "spoil" had been doubled, pasted together, and slipped in as stiffening to the old bookcover. I had it steamed open, and analysed the wash. It gave the flour-grains in the paste—coarse, because of the old millstone—and there were traces of the grit itself. What? Oh, possibly a handmill of Mentzel's own time. He may have doubled the spoilt page and used it for part of a pad to steady wood-cuts on. It may have knocked about his workshop for years. That, indeed, is practically certain because a beginner from the Low Countries has tried his reed on a few lines of some monkish hymn—not a bad lilt tho'—which must have been common form. Oh yes, the page may have been used in other books before it was used for the Vulgate. That doesn't matter, but *this* does. Listen! I took a wash, for analysis, from a blot in one corner—that would be after Mentzel had given up trying to make a possible page of it, and had grown careless—and I got the actual *ink* of the period! It's a practically eternal stuff compounded on—I've forgotten his name for the minute—the scribe at Bury St. Edmunds, of course—hawthorn bark and wine. Anyhow, on *his* formula. *That* wouldn't interest you either, but, taken with all the other testimony, it clinches the thing. (You'll see it all in my Statement to the Press on Monday.) Overwhelming, isn't it?'

'Overwhelming,' I said, with sincerity. 'Tell me what the tale was about, though. That's more in my line.'

'I know it; but *I* have to be equipped on all sides. The verses are relatively easy for one to pronounce on. The freshness, the fun, the humanity, the fragrance of it all, cries—no, shouts—itself as Dan's work. Why "Daiespringe mishandled" alone stamps it from Dan's mint. Plangent as doom, my dear boy—plangent as doom! It's all in my Statement. Well, substantially, the fragment deals with a girl whose parents wish her to marry an elderly suitor. The mother isn't so keen on it, but the father, an old Knight, is. The girl, of course, is in love with a younger and a poorer man. Common form? Granted. Then the father, who doesn't in the least want to, is ordered off to a Crusade and, by way of passing on the kick, as we used to say during the War, orders the girl to be kept in duresse till his return or her consent to the old suitor. Common form, again? Quite so. That's too much for her mother. She reminds the old Knight of his age and infirmities, and the discomforts of Crusading. Are you sure I'm not boring you?'

'Not at all,' I said, though time had begun to whirl backward through my brain to a red-velvet, pomatum-scented side-room at Neminaka's and Manallace's set face intoning to the gas.

'You'll read it all in my Statement next week. The sum is that the old lady tells him of a certain Knight-adventurer on the French coast, who, for a consideration, waylays Knights who don't relish crusading and holds them to impossible ransoms till the trooping-season is over, or they are returned sick. He keeps a ship in the Channel to pick 'em up and transfers his birds to his castle ashore, where he has a reputation for doing 'em well. As the old lady points out:

> "And if perchance thou fall into his honde
> By God how canstow ride to Holilonde?"

'You see? Modern in essence as Gilbert and Sullivan, but handled as only Dan could! And she reminds him that "Honour and olde bones" parted company long ago. He makes one splendid appeal for the spirit of chivalry:

> Lat all men change as Fortune may send,
> But Knighthood beareth service to the end,

and *then*, of course, he gives in:

> For what his woman willeth to be don
> Her manne must or wauken Hell anon.

'Then she hints that the daughter's young lover, who is in the Bordeaux wine-trade, could open negotiations for a kidnapping without compromising him. And *then* that careless brute Mentzel spoils his page and chucks it! But there's enough to show what's going to happen. You'll see it all in my Statement. Was there ever anything in literary finds to hold a candle to it? . . . And they give grocers Knighthoods for selling cheese!'

I went away before he could get into his stride on that course. I wanted to think, and to see Manallace. But I waited till Castorley's Statement came out. He had left himself no loophole. And when, a little later, his (nominally the Sunnapia people's) 'scientific' account of their analyses and tests appeared, criticism ceased, and some journals began to demand 'public recognition.' Manallace wrote me on this subject, and I went down to his cottage, where he at once asked me to sign a Memorial on Castorley's behalf. With luck, he said, we might get him a K.B.E. in the next Honours List. Had I read the Statement?

'I have,' I replied. 'But I want to ask you something first. Do you remember the night you got drunk at Neminaka's, and I stayed behind to look after you?'

'Oh, *that* time,' said he, pondering. 'Wait a minute! I remember Graydon advancing me two quid. He was a generous paymaster. And I remember—now, who the devil rolled me under the sofa—and what for?'

'We all did,' I replied. 'You wanted to read us what you'd written to those Chaucer cuts.'

'I don't remember that. No! I don't remember anything after the sofa-episode. . . . *You* always said that you took me home—didn't you?'

'I did, and you told Kentucky Kate outside the old Empire that you had been faithful, Cynara, in your fashion.'

'Did I?' said he. 'My God! Well, I suppose I have.' He stared into the fire. 'What else?'

'Before we left Neminaka's you recited me what you had made out of the cuts—the whole tale! So—you see?'

'Ye-es.' He nodded. 'What are you going to do about it?'

'What are *you*?'

'I'm going to help him get his Knighthood—first.'

'Why?'

'I'll tell you what he said about 'Dal's mother—the night there was that air-raid on the offices.'

He told it.

'That's why,' he said. 'Am I justified?'

He seemed to me entirely so.

'But after he gets his Knighthood?' I went on.

'That depends. There are several things I can think of. It interests me.'

'Good Heavens! I've always imagined you a man without interests.'

'So I was. I owe my interests to Castorley. He gave me every one of 'em except the tale itself.'

'How did *that* come?'

'Something in those ghastly cuts touched off something in me—a sort of possession, I suppose. I was in love too. No wonder I got drunk that night. I'd *been* Chaucer for a week! Then I thought the notion might make a comic opera. But Gilbert and Sullivan were too strong.'

'So I remember you told me at the time.'

'I kept it by me, and it made me interested in Chaucer—philologically and so on. I worked on it on those lines for years. There wasn't a flaw in the wording even in '14. I hardly had to touch it after that.'

'Did you ever tell it to anyone except me?'

'No, only 'Dal's mother—when she could listen to anything—to put her to sleep. But when Castorley said—what he did about her, I thought I might use it. 'Twasn't difficult.

He taught me. D'you remember my birdlime experiments, and the stuff on our hands? I'd been trying to get that ink for more than a year. Castorley told me where I'd find the formula. And your falling over the quern, too?'

'That accounted for the stone-dust under the microscope?'

'Yes. I grew the wheat in the garden here, and ground it myself. Castorley gave me Mentzel complete. He put me on to an MS. in the British Museum which he said was the finest sample of his work. I copied his "Byzantine *g*'s" for months.'

'And what's a "sickle-slanted" pen?' I asked.

'You nick one edge of your reed till it drags and scratches on the curves of the letters. Castorley told me about Mentzel's spacing and margining. I only had to get the hang of his script.'

'How long did that take you?'

'On and off—some years. I was too ambitious at first—I wanted to give the whole poem. That would have been risky. Then Castorley told me about spoiled pages and I took the hint. I spelt "Dayspring mishandeelt" Mentzel's way—to make sure of him. It's not a bad couplet in itself. Did you see how he admires the "plangency" of it?'

'Never mind him. Go on!' I said.

He did. Castorley had been his unfailing guide throughout, specifying in minutest detail every trap to be set later for his own feet. The actual vellum was an Antwerp find, and its introduction into the cover of the Vulgate was begun after a long course of amateur bookbinding. At last, he bedded it under pieces of an old deed, and a printed page (1686) of Horace's *Odes*, legitimately used for repairs by different owners in the seventeenth and eighteenth centuries; and at the last moment, to meet Castorley's theory that spoiled pages were used in workshops by beginners, he had written a few Latin words in fifteenth century script—the Statement gave the exact date—across an open part of the fragment. The thing ran: '*Illa alma Mater ecca, secum afferens me acceptum. Nicolaus Atrib.*' The disposal of the thing was easiest of all. He had merely hung about Dredd's dark bookshop of fifteen rooms, where he was well known, occasionally buying but generally browsing, till, one day, Dredd Senior showed him a case of cheap black-letter stuff, English and Continental—being packed for the Sunnapia people—into which Manallace tucked his contribution, taking care to wrench the back enough to give a lead to an earnest seeker.

'And then?' I demanded.

'After six months or so Castorley sent for me. Sunnapia had found it, and as Dredd had missed it, and there was no money-motive sticking out, they were half convinced it was genuine from the start. But they invited him over. He conferred with their experts, and suggested the scientific tests. *I* put that into his head, before he sailed. That's all. And now, will you sign our Memorial?'

I signed. Before we had finished hawking it round there was a host of influential names to help us, as well as the impetus of all the literary discussion which arose over every detail of the glorious trove. The upshot was a K.B.E.[1] for Castorley in the next Honours List; and Lady Castorley, her cards duly printed, called on friends that same afternoon.

Manallace invited me to come with him, a day or so later, to convey our pleasure and satisfaction to them both. We were rewarded by the sight of a man relaxed and ungirt—not to say wallowing naked—on the crest of Success. He assured us that 'The Title' should not make any difference to our future relations, seeing it was in no sense personal, but, as he had often said, a tribute to Chaucer; 'and, after all,' he pointed out, with a glance at the mirror over the mantelpiece, 'Chaucer was the prototype of the "veray parfit gentil Knight" of the British Empire so far as that then existed.'

On the way back, Manallace told me he was considering

[1] Officially it was on account of his good work in the Departmental of Co-ordinated Supervisals, but all true lovers of literature knew the real reason, and told the papers so.

either an unheralded revelation in the baser Press which should bring Castorley's reputation about his own ears some breakfast-time, or a private conversation, when he would make clear to Castorley that he must now back the forgery as long as he lived, under threat of Manallace's betraying it if he flinched.

He favoured the second plan. 'If I pull the string of the shower-bath in the papers,' he said, 'Castorley might go off his veray parfit gentil nut. I want to keep his intellect.'

'What about your own position? The forgery doesn't matter so much. But if you tell this you'll kill him,' I said.

'I intend that. Oh—my position? I've been dead since— April, Fourteen, it was. But there's no hurry. What was it *she* was saying to you just as we left?'

'She told me how much your sympathy and understanding had meant to him. She said she thought that even Sir Alured did not realise the full extent of his obligations to you.'

'She's right, but I don't like her putting it that way.'

'It's only common form—as Castorley's always saying.'

'Not with *her*. She can hear a man think.'

'She never struck me in that light.'

'*You* aren't playing against her.'

' 'Guilty conscience, Manallace?'

'H'm! I wonder. Mine or hers? I *wish* she hadn't said that. "More even than *he* realises it." I won't call again for awhile.'

He kept away till we read that Sir Alured, owing to slight indisposition, had been unable to attend a dinner given in his honour.

Inquiries brought word that it was but natural reaction, after strain, which, for the moment, took the form of nervous dyspepsia, and he would be glad to see Manallace at any time. Manallace reported him as rather pulled and drawn, but full of his new life and position, and proud that his efforts should have martyred him so much. He was going to collect, collate, and expand all his pronouncements and inferences into one authoritative volume.

'I must make an effort of my own,' said Manallace. 'I've collected nearly all his stuff about the Find that has appeared in the papers, and he's promised me everything that's missing. I'm going to help him. It will be a new interest.'

'How will you treat it?' I asked.

'I expect I shall quote his deductions on the evidence, and parallel 'em with my experiments—the ink and the paste and the rest of it. It ought to be rather interesting.'

'But even then there will only be your word. It's hard to catch up with an established lie,' I said. 'Especially when you've started it yourself.'

He laughed. 'I've arranged for *that*—in case anything happens to me. Do you remember the "Monkish Hymn"?'

'Oh yes! There's quite a literature about it already.'

'Well, you write those ten words above each other, and read down the first and second letters of 'em; and see what you get.'[1] My Bank has the formula.'

He wrapped himself lovingly and leisurely round his new task, and Castorley was as good as his word in giving him help. The two practically collaborated, for Manallace suggested that all Castorley's strictly scientific evidence should be in one place, with his deductions and dithyrambs as appendices. He assured him that the public would prefer this arrangement, and, after grave consideration, Castorley agreed.

'That's better,' said Manallace to me. 'Now I sha'n't have so many hiatuses in my extracts. Dots always give the reader the idea you aren't dealing fairly with your man.

[1] *Illa
alma
Mater
ecca
secum
afferens
me
acceptum
Nicolaus
Atrib.*

I shall merely quote him solid, and rip him up, proof for proof, and date for date, in parallel columns. His book's taking more out of him than I like, though. He's been doubled up twice with tummy attacks since I've worked with him. And he's just the sort of flatulent beast who may go down with appendicitis.'

We learned before long that the attacks were due to gall-stones, which would necessitate an operation. Castorley bore the blow very well. He had full confidence in his surgeon, an old friend of theirs; great faith in his own constitution; a strong conviction that nothing would happen to him till the book was finished, and, above all, the Will to Live.

He dwelt on these assets with a voice at times a little out of pitch and eyes brighter than usual beside a slightly-sharpening nose.

I had only met Gleeag, the surgeon, once or twice at Castorley's house, but had always heard him spoken of as a most capable man. He told Castorley that his trouble was the price exacted, in some shape or other, from all who had served their country; and that, measured in units of strain, Castorley had practically been at the front through those three years he had served in the Office of Co-ordinated Supervisals. However, the thing had been taken betimes, and in a few weeks he would worry no more about it.

'But suppose he dies?' I suggested to Manallace.

'He won't. I've been talking to Gleeag. He says he's all right.'

'Wouldn't Gleeag's talk be common form?'

'I *wish* you hadn't said that. But, surely, Gleeag wouldn't have the face to play with me—or her.'

'Why not? I expect it's been done before.'

But Manallace insisted that, in this case, it would be impossible.

The operation was a success and, some weeks later, Castorley began to recast the arrangement and most of the material of his book. 'Let me have my way,' he said, when

Manallace protested. 'They are making too much of a baby of me. I really don't need Gleeag looking in every day now.' But Lady Castorley told us that he required careful watching. His heart had felt the strain, and fret or disappointment of any kind must be avoided. 'Even,' she turned to Manallace, 'though you know ever so much better how his book should be arranged than he does himself.'

'But really,' Manallace began. 'I'm very careful not to fuss——'

She shook her finger at him playfully. 'You don't think you do; but, remember, he tells me everything that you tell him, just the same as he told me everything that he used to tell *you*. Oh, I don't mean the things that men talk about. I mean about his Chaucer.'

'I didn't realise that,' said Manallace, weakly.

'I thought you didn't. He never spares me anything; but *I* don't mind,' she replied with a laugh, and went off to Gleeag, who was paying his daily visit. Gleeag said he had no objection to Manallace working with Castorley on the book for a given time—say, twice a week—but supported Lady Castorley's demand that he should not be over-taxed in what she called 'the sacred hours.' The man grew more and more difficult to work with, and the little check he had heretofore set on his self-praise went altogether.

'He says there has never been anything in the History of Letters to compare with it,' Manallace groaned. 'He wants now to inscribe—he never dedicates, you know—inscribe it to me, as his "most valued assistant." The devil of it is that *she* backs him up in getting it out soon. Why? How much do you think she knows?'

'Why should she know anything at all?'

'You heard her say he had told her everything that he had told me about Chaucer? (I *wish* she hadn't said that!) If she puts two and two together, she can't help seeing that every one of his notions and theories has been played up to. But then—but then . . . Why is she trying to hurry publication? She talks about me fretting him. *She's* at him, all the time, to be quick.'

Castorley must have over-worked, for, after a couple of months, he complained of a stitch in his right side, which Gleeag said was a slight sequel, a little incident of the operation. It threw him back awhile, but he returned to his work undefeated.

The book was due in the autumn. Summer was passing, and his publisher urgent, and—he said to me, when after a longish interval I called—Manallace had chosen this time, of all, to take a holiday. He was not pleased with Manallace, once his indefatigable *aide,* but now dilatory, and full of time-wasting objections. Lady Castorley had noticed it, too.

Meantime, with Lady Castorley's help, he himself was doing the best he could to expedite the book; but Manallace had mislaid (did I think through jealousy?) some essential stuff which had been dictated to him. And Lady Castorley wrote Manallace, who had been delayed by a slight motor accident abroad, that the fret of waiting was prejudicial to her husband's health. Manallace, on his return from the Continent, showed me that letter.

'He has fretted a little, I believe,' I said.

Manallace shuddered. 'If I stay abroad, I'm helping to kill him. If I help him to hurry up the book, I'm expected to kill him. *She* knows,' he said.

'You're mad. You've got this thing on the brain.'

'I have not! Look here! You remember that Gleeag gave me from four to six, twice a week, to work with him. She called them the "sacred hours." You heard her? Well, they *are!* They are Gleeag's and hers. But she's so infernally plain, and I'm such a fool, it took me weeks to find it out.'

'That's their affair,' I answered. 'It doesn't prove she knows anything about the Chaucer.'

'She *does!* He told her everything that he had told me when I was pumping him, all those years. She put two and two together when the thing came out. She saw exactly how I had set my traps. I know it! She's been trying to make me admit it.'

'What did you do?'

'"Didn't understand what she was driving at, of course. And then she asked Gleeag, before me, if he didn't think the delay over the book was fretting Sir Alured. He didn't think so. He said getting it out might deprive him of an interest. He had that much decency. *She's* the devil!'

'What do you suppose is her game, then?'

'If Castorley knows he's been had, it'll kill him. She's at me all the time, indirectly, to let it out. I've told you she wants to make it a sort of joke between us. Gleeag's willing to wait. He knows Castorley's a dead man. It slips out when they talk. They say "He was," not "He is." Both of 'em know it. But *she* wants him finished sooner.'

'I don't believe it. What are you going to do?'

'What can I? I'm not going to have him killed, though.'

Manlike, he invented compromises whereby Castorley might be lured up by-paths of interest, to delay publication. This was not a success. As autumn advanced Castorley fretted more, and suffered from returns of his distressing colics. At last, Gleeag told him that he thought they might be due to an overlooked gallstone working down. A second comparatively trivial operation would eliminate the bother once and for all. If Castorley cared for another opinion, Gleeag named a surgeon of eminence. 'And then,' said he, cheerily, 'the two of us can talk you over.' Castorley did not want to be talked over. He was oppressed by pains in his side, which, at first, had yielded to the liver-tonics Gleeag prescribed; but now they stayed—like a toothache —behind everything. He felt most at ease in his bedroom-study, with his proofs round him. If he had more pain than he could stand, he would consider the second operation. Meantime Manallace—'the meticulous Manallace,' he called him—agreed with him in thinking that the Mentzel page-facsimile, done by the Sunnapia Library, was not quite good enough for the great book, and the Sunnapia people were, very decently, having it re-processed. This would hold things back till early spring, which had its advantages, for he could run a fresh eye over all in the interval.

One gathered these news in the course of stray visits as

the days shortened. He insisted on Manallace keeping to the 'sacred hours,' and Manallace insisted on my accompanying him when possible. On these occasions he and Castorley would confer apart for half an hour or so, while I listened to an unendurable clock in the drawing-room. Then I would join them and help wear out the rest of the time, while Castorley rambled. His speech, now, was often clouded and uncertain—the result of the 'liver-tonics'; and his face came to look like old vellum.

It was a few days after Christmas—the operation had been postponed till the following Friday—that we called together. She met us with word that Sir Alured had picked up an irritating little winter cough, due to a cold wave, but we were not, therefore, to abridge our visit. We found him in steam perfumed with Friar's Balsam. He waved the old Sunnapia facsimile at us. We agreed that it ought to have been more worthy. He took a dose of his mixture, lay back and asked us to lock the door. There was, he whispered, something wrong somewhere. He could not lay his finger on it, but it was in the air. He felt he was being played with. He did not like it. There was something wrong all round him. Had we noticed it? Manallace and I severally and slowly denied that we had noticed anything of the sort.

With no longer break than a light fit of coughing, he fell into the hideous, helpless panic of the sick—those worse than captives who lie at the judgment and mercy of the hale for every office and hope. He wanted to go away. Would we help him to pack his Gladstone? Or, if that would attract too much attention in certain quarters, help him to dress and go out? There was an urgent matter to be set right, and now that he had The Title and knew his own mind it would all end happily and he would be well again. *Please* would we let him go out, just to speak to—he named her; he named her by her 'little' name out of the old Neminaka days? Manallace quite agreed, and recommended a pull at the 'liver-tonic' to brace him after so long in the house. He took it, and Manallace suggested that it would be better if, after his walk, he came down to the

cottage for a week-end and brought the revise with him.
They could then re-touch the last chapter. He answered to
that drug and to some praise of his work, and presently
simpered drowsily. Yes, it *was* good—though he said it who
should not. He praised himself awhile till, with a puzzled
forehead and shut eyes, he told us that *she* had been saying
lately that it was too good—the whole thing, if we understood, was *too* good. He wished us to get the exact shade of
her meaning. She had suggested, or rather implied, this
doubt. She had said—he would let us draw our own inferences—that the Chaucer find had 'anticipated the wants
of humanity.' Johnson, of course. No need to tell *him* that.
But what the hell was her implication? Oh God! Life had
always been one long innuendo! *And* she had said that a
man could do anything with anyone if he saved him the
trouble of thinking. What did she mean by that? *He* had
never shirked thought. He had thought sustainedly all his
life. It *wasn't* too good, was it? Manallace didn't think it
was too good—did he? But this pick-pick-picking at a man's
brain and work was too bad, wasn't it? *What* did she mean?
Why did she always bring in Manallace, who was only a
friend—no scholar, but a lover of the game—Eh?—Manallace could confirm this if he were here, instead of loafing
on the Continent just when he was most needed.

'I've come back,' Manallace interrupted, unsteadily. 'I
can confirm every word you've said. You've nothing to
worry about. It's *your* find—*your* credit—*your* glory and—all
the rest of it.'

'Swear you'll tell her so then,' said Castorley. 'She
doesn't believe a word I say. She told me she never has
since before we were married. Promise!'

Manallace promised, and Castorley added that he had
named him his literary executor, the proceeds of the book
to go to his wife. 'All profits without deduction,' he gasped.
'Big sales if it's properly handled. *You* don't need money.
. . . Graydon'll trust *you* to any extent. It 'ud be a
long . . .'

He coughed, and, as he caught breath, his pain broke through all the drugs, and the outcry filled the room. Manallace rose to fetch Gleeag, when a full, high, affected voice, unheard for a generation, accompanied, as it seemed, the clamour of a beast in agony, saying: 'I wish to God someone would stop that old swine howling down there! *I* can't . . . I was going to tell you fellows that it would be a dam' long time before Graydon advanced *me* two quid.'

We escaped together, and found Gleeag waiting, with Lady Castorley, on the landing. He telephoned me, next morning, that Castorley had died of bronchitis, which his weak state made it impossible for him to throw off. 'Perhaps it's just as well,' he added, in reply to the condolences I asked him to convey to the widow. 'We might have come across something we couldn't have coped with.'

Distance from that house made me bold.

'You knew all along, I suppose? What was it, really?'

'Malignant kidney-trouble—generalised at the end. 'No use worrying him about it. We let him through as easily as possible. Yes! A happy release. . . . What? . . . Oh! Cremation. Friday, at eleven.'

There, then, Manallace and I met. He told me that she had asked him whether the book need now be published; and he had told her this was more than ever necessary, in her interests as well as Castorley's.

'She is going to be known as his widow—for a while, at any rate. Did I perjure myself much with him?'

'Not explicitly,' I answered.

'Well, I have now—with *her*—explicitly,' said he, and took out his black gloves. . . .

As, on the appointed words, the coffin crawled sideways through the noiselessly-closing door-flaps, I saw Lady Castorley's eyes turn towards Gleeag.

OTHER ANCHOR BOOKS OF INTEREST

OTHER DOLPHIN BOOKS

ESSAYS AND LETTERS

Turquoise